BLEEDING LIGHT

LIGHT

A NOVEL

ROB BENVIE

Invisible Publishing
Halifax & Prince Edward County

Library and Archives Canada Cataloguing in Publication

Title: Bleeding light / Rob Benvie.

Names: Benvie, Rob, 1975- author.

Identifiers: Canadiana (print) 20200410415
Canadiana (ebook) 20200410423 | ISBN 9781988784649 (softcover)
ISBN 9781988784731 (HTML)

Classification: LCC PS8603.E58 B54 2021 | DDC C813/.6—dc23

Edited by Leigh Nash
Cover and interior design by Megan Fildes | Typeset in Laurentian
With thanks to type designer Rod McDonald

Printed and bound in Canada

Invisible Publishing | Halifax & Prince Edward County
www.invisiblepublishing.com

Published with the generous assistance of the Canada Council for the Arts, the Ontario Arts Council, and the Government of Canada.

As we were standing there
You didn't speak a single word
But your eyes
Your eyes said you wanted me
Your touch said you needed me

Diana Ross & the Supremes,
"Forever Came Today"
(Holland-Dozier-Holland)

Why are you watching? Someone must
watch, it is said. Someone must be there.

Franz Kafka, "At Night"

THE MAN IN THE STORM

HE CAME OUT OF AN IMMEDIATELY FORGOTTEN NIGHTMARE to find the world awhirl. Gripping the arms of his seat, he fought to regain his whereabouts, aware of the stifling roar and a combined stink of perspiration, burned coffee, and some citrus-scented air-freshening agent. An intercom dinged, followed by a muffled voice warning of *a bit of brief activity, ladies and gentlemen.* Inventory of such elements reminded him: he was on a jittery Air Kenya DHC-6 Twin Otter, plowing through a patch of clear-air turbulence, which had launched his Beefeater and tonic into his lap.

Dabbing at his crotch with a paper napkin, he turned to the window. The corrugated contours of the Eastern Sahara lay below, desolate and infinite. It was morning; the previous night's transatlantic bolt was now behind him. Still fighting sleep's drag, he shut the shade.

Hey, bud. Keep that up.

Webb twisted in his seat. A man, white and shapeless in a mauve golf shirt, sized XL, sat in the row behind. Curled in his arm was a child sporting a plastic tiara adorned with glittered letters: CUTIE PIE.

My daughter wants to see, the man said.

Webb turned back around, unable in his present wooze to summon the requisite energy to tell the guy to fuck off. As the tiaraed child whined complaints, Webb retrieved his headphones from the seat pocket before him and slid them on. He pressed play on the Samsung hand-held digital recorder, returning to the drowsy murmurings of Dred Hausen.

For our birthdays our mother would prepare a viscid vanilla froth glazed with an icy boysenberry sauce. This sauce was so gum-numbingly sweet, it made those unaccustomed to its flavours gag on the first bite. It truly was something to behold—truly disgusting. Of course, my mother was herself a disgusting human being.

With the plane's conniptions subsiding, a sulky flight attendant came wheeling a cart down the aisle, offering packaged pretzels.

Webb paused the recording and requested a fresh drink, only to be told beverage service was unavailable during descent. Punctuating this point, another announcement came over the intercom: *Touching down in Nairobi in approximately twenty minutes.* The attendant moved on. Webb closed his eyes and compelled himself to not think about what lay ahead.

Jomo Kenyatta was an instant ordeal. At the gate's termination, a jerky escalator flowed passengers into passport control, where a mob of hundreds swarmed four booths. The collective mood was exhaustion: dour parents wrangling toddlers, overheated tourists laden with sacks of duty-free chocolate and cologne, soldiers in short sleeves manning every row, assault rifles at the ready—all equally debased in unconditioned air and the harsh inspection of fluorescent light.

Wobbling in the international visitors' queue, Webb found his shirt instantly saturated with sweat. On an adjacent wall, a sign was mounted bearing the Ministry of Tourism insignia and insistent red text: OVERSEAS VISITORS MUST PRESENT PROOF OF YELLOW FEVER VACCINE. He realized he'd left the proof-of-vaccination card provided by the travel clinic back in Los Angeles. As the line edged toward the security booth, Webb grew uneasy—a refusal would mean what? Forcible quarantine? But when his turn arrived and he handed his passport over, the yawning guard barely gave it a glimpse before stamping it and waving him through.

Agnes was there to meet him at the arrivals gate. Before he'd even introduced himself, she was ushering him through the throng, waving over a man in a Fila sweatshirt to haul his suitcase. They knifed in single file through the teeming terminal and to the exit, where they were blasted with the humid, even fouler air of outside. It was already evening. The parking lot was a scene of chaos, raging with honks and pleading voices, Mitsubishi matatu buses circling, men clustered in strenuous arguments. The hired man moved through the fray without hesitation, with Agnes close behind. Webb fought to keep up.

Only once in the refuge of the van cab did Agnes welcome him to Nairobi. As Dred Hausen's administrative assistant in Kenya, she'd been entrusted as Webb's chaperone throughout his stay and would be at his full disposal. Webb knew little about any of this; in the weeks up to the trip, his only correspondence with anyone at DHG had been a few cursory emails regarding his travel visa and flight itinerary.

Webb sank into his seat.

Let's get some AC, maybe?

In what Webb assumed to be Swahili, Agnes spoke to the driver, who muttered something back without diverting attention from the surrounding pandemonium.

The fans are working poorly, Agnes translated.

The driver pounded the horn as the van broke free of the lot's jam, peeling up an on-ramp and onto a road marked A104. Webb dug out his phone and checked for messages. There were none.

How was your flight? Agnes asked.

Transcendent.

I imagine you've visited far more interesting places than here.

Webb sniffed.

I guess.

Few of us in Kenya enjoy the opportunity to travel indiscriminately, as Americans do, she said.

I wouldn't say *indiscriminately*. I think you overestimate our access to leisure.

Agnes turned back, processing this.

Nairobi is awful, she said.

Webb had to agree: it was. The roundabouts writhed with sputtering motorbikes and minibuses, taxis crammed by three into single lanes, any order to traffic's flow amputated. The roadsides were a succession of skeletal plots and abandoned framework, ragged tarps cast in sooty utility light, everything seemingly half-built or half-demolished. As they pressed further through the nocturnal city, the floodlit shacks lining the highway surrendered to drab towers and asphalt plazas, billboards for Celtel and Nivea and 7 Up, slow floods of pedestrians on unlit sidewalks.

Webb again thumbed his phone, a message to his assistant Ellen: *just landed. resend dhg contract + terms. asap.*

North along Limuru Road, the scenery again shifted. Here long stretches of choppy woodlands alternated with shopping concourses and embassy estates, hotels framed in ornate shrubbery, gated subdivisions. They veered onto a twisting, unpaved private lane, passing imposing fences and walls of shadowed forest sundering away the city. The driver eased the van down the road to its termination at a metal security fence easily eight feet tall. A uniformed guard with a holster slung around his shoulders appeared from a booth; he gave them a nod, and a second later the gates parted. As they passed through, the guard locked eyes with Webb and saluted. Webb did the same in return.

It was almost nine o'clock by the time they rolled up to the Hausen compound. The house hid behind a wall of baobabs and hanging vines, no sign of lights in the windows of its vast stone face. Agnes hopped out without a word. Webb followed her lead. The driver withdrew his suitcase from the trunk, placed it on the ground, then climbed back in the van and pulled away.

Bag in hand, Webb followed Agnes down a short flight of stone steps and along a path to the backyard, where a small brick shed sat separate from the main house. Agnes worked the door's electronic security panel; then, once inside, she snapped a series of switches to reveal a low-ceilinged, carpeted single room. This, she explained, was the groundskeeper's residence, but since Samuel was off tending to his sick mother in Eldoret, Webb could stay here for the night before they headed to Lamu in the morning.

Webb considered the place before him. There was a pullout couch, a mini-fridge, a coffee-ringed table on which a portable television sat. A folding door opened to a compartment containing a toilet and sink. A fetid smell of cigars prevailed.

For fuck's sakes, he said.

I'll get Wangui to bring down some towels, Agnes said.

Dred's not around?

Not presently. But he knows you've arrived, and looks forward to your meeting.

Thank him for that. So much.

Agnes nodded, saying nothing.

I assume there are actual bedrooms in the house, Webb said.

Agnes again nodded.

But I'm stuck down here on this bullshit hide-a-bed. I suffer from a repetitive stress injury, you know. This will murder me.

I'm only following instructions.

Despite Agnes's dispassionate manner, there was a preoccupation there, behind her unfaltering eyes, her unfluctuating tone— concerns currently suppressed in the officiating of these tasks. Against the room's weak light, Webb found himself staring. She noticed, and he turned away.

Is there anything you need to settle in?

Webb scratched his face.

Settle in? Do I have the time zone right?

I could fetch you something from the kitchen upstairs.

Something sweet, like a Gewürztraminer, would be swell, he said. Actually, scratch that. Make it gin.

I can get you some bottled water.

Agnes. I've had a very long day. I barely know what continent I'm on. While I recognize that much of my agreement with Dred was left up in the air, several terms were not. And one thing I was told was I'd have everything needed to execute the job. Unless things lead me to understand otherwise, I'm going to accept that in a literal fashion. So, however it unduly imposes upon you...I need a drink. Drinks, plural.

Agnes folded her arms.

I'll call Samuel's brother. He helps with maintenance. Maybe he can fetch something from the grocer's.

Fantastic.

But after that, try to sleep well. Or as well as you can. Welcome to Kenya.

The grounds worker arrived soon after Agnes departed, handing over an unlabelled jug of almost-black wine before dashing off without a word. Despite downing two milligrams of alprazolam and draining the jug along with his daily Risperdal, Webb was up late watching Discovery World on the miniature TV, a show about the ecosystem of the East African Rift. One segment followed a half-dozen young antelope on a homeward trek as they became separated from the rest of their herd and then attempted to navigate around a barricading pride of lions. For days the antelope paced the arid terrain, the lions always in sight, the camera tracking them across the sweeping vista. A war of attrition unfolded between stalker and prey, an intimacy forged: the antelope seemed to recognize the inevitability of how, despite their most determined efforts, the scenario would play out. The program also took several asides to touch upon the geological activity of the region, showing in a side-split animation how the valley's tectonic plates were gradually separating into two distinct protoplates—the continent itself was fracturing. On the third morning, the antelope, seeing an opportunity while the lions lay lounging, collectively dashed for a break in the rocky reef facing them. It seemed they might manage to elude their predators. But as the lions finally roused and took up the chase, the antelopes' course became erratic with alarm. They tripped over themselves, losing sight of their goal, and soon the lions were upon them. From a distance, the only two antelope to successfully evade their hunters observed the bloodshed. Then they moved on, eager to rejoin the herd.

ON HIS TAX RETURN, AT LEAST, he still stated his vocation as a writer-slash-editorial-consultant. The mechanics of what this actually meant, however, had become increasingly remote with time. In actual practice it meant ghostwriting and contract hackwork—or, more often of late, deploying resources to fulfill those projects with as little of his own effort as possible. In this, he'd forged a livelihood. Or a viable version thereof, for a while at least.

There was little in his past to prefigure such a life. In the beginning, there was only his mother's voice, insistent as a pneumatic siren's wail, resonating through the floorboards of their Upper West Side townhouse and jostling all into capitulation—Webb, his sister Candace, any others who strayed into her range. She was incapable of moderating her volume, whether showering her children with praise, as she did often, or bewailing time's tragic toll on her skin's elasticity, which she did incessantly. His father was knowable only as an ethereal presence, rarely witnessed in full light. Reared in Iowa suburbs and educated at Dartmouth, he was always working, a wearer of ties and raincoats, a carrier of brief-cases. He eschewed Budweiser for Sprite; he followed the Packers. The image Webb retained of this man from those days was a figure bent in doorways, always arriving or leaving: a man as a fulcrum, bearing pressures. Above all, he was unfailing in the tireless task of making rich people richer. Deregulation had made his father's career, thus gilding the family's existence, so that any threat of crisis was only one of infinite possible futures.

Then came the savings and loans crisis. Wall Street went super-nova. Someone had to bear punishment for these crimes, and fault would be found in those who'd been most servile to their overlords. Webb's father and his colleagues avoided prosecution, though the extended deliberations thrust him into a state of suspended contrition, wringing him dry. When it concluded, he was a thinner, greyer version of his former self. The man became slight, even as the tensions increased. Late at night Webb heard him pacing the downstairs halls, huffing strings of unconnectable syllables to himself. A lamb, slaughtered.

So they'd forsaken Manhattan for Middlesex County. On the windswept shores of Old Saybrook, time endured material in the cobbled quaintness, the lighthouses and Georgian Revival taverns as remnants of dull glories. Despite their capacious beachfront colonial home, despite the gunkless sidewalks and taxi-free lanes, by all measures, this relocation was a downgrade—now their days were defined by public school and FoodWorks and Old Navy. It was understood implicitly, even if never discussed, how such changes were the ineluctable conditions of survival.

For Webb, these days were passed in languor and solitude. In winter he laced up his Klondikes to chart the roundhouse and turntable of the old Connecticut Valley Railroad and the remains of the Fort Saybrook signal tower buried decades beneath. From spring to autumn he roamed the beaches of the Long Island Sound, compiling driftwood and inventorying crab shells from the underbellies of creaking piers, such projects soundtracked by the shoosh of waves and Pat Metheny cassettes on his Walkman. History cascaded with his hours of school and sleep into one seamless flow. Against the ocean, all was rendered merely noise, painlessly tuned out. And in such emptiness, removed from everything, he found a type of tranquility.

After his father's third and ultimately permanent hospitalization, Webb went off to Cornell, where he read Romantic poetry until, revolted by dim-witted classmates and a world literature professor who struck him as particularly pusillanimous, he switched to an economics minor at the ILR School in his second semester. Like others in his cohort, he entertained thoughts of the LSE following graduation, but let deadlines slip. Instead, he moved to Greenpoint and worked in branded content for one of Condé Nast's less popular digital properties.

Office drudgery was a sentence, and the ceaseless anxiety of internal shakeups was enervating. He craved autonomy, self-propulsion. And, even more gnawingly: to not be like all the other glum-faced toilers on the M train.

Circumstances led to a lunch meeting at a cafeteria on Delancey with Shehryar, a former rival at Cornell, now a hothead junior literary agent out to prove himself valuable amid pending in-house shakeups. As Webb volleyed pitches, Shehryar wolfed down a Monte Cristo sandwich and pulsated with what seemed legitimate awe. Though none of these pitches moved ahead, the outcome was the ganging of Webb's name among the agency's highly regarded roster, shoving him into proximity of people of lustre and influence. Eventually he was contracted to work on the quasi-autobiography of a widely reviled television producer then in the news for a series of sex scandals. The man was a repugnant oaf, concerned mostly with settling scores with ex-wives, and the project proved a slog. It also required Webb's visiting Los Angeles thrice monthly, until—abandoning any sentimental notions of New York's past glories—he'd hastily purchased an extortionately priced bungalow in Atwater Village on a mortgage structure he couldn't conceive of upholding. It was a beautiful house, and a lifestyle he knew he deserved, even if he couldn't bankroll it. On his first night there he'd stood among heaps of unpacked boxes and looked out the window at the far-off Verdugo Mountains, trying to get his head around projected costs for plumbing and flooring work, when his phone had vibrated; it was his mother, yelling from Connecticut, informing him his father had died following a third heart attack while back in in-patient care, years of antipsychotic medications and Drum tobacco finally taking their toll.

The producer's book sold unexpectedly well upon publication, bringing Webb more work and allowing him to carve out something of a niche. The money was good, but the grind was dull. His stroke of genius was in realizing most of the tedious tasks could be outsourced for pittances to a select corps of debt-crippled graduate students and freelancers. With this came the blissful provision of less work for greater gains. Via a UCLA job board, he'd recruited Ellen in doing the actual assembly of manuscripts, the managing of files, and resolving of contractual muddles. Her complaints were few, even if her compensation was meagre—the job market was tough.

And so, for a while at least, he'd known some version of success. Shehryar lobbied fruitfully for Webb to ghostwrite, for Harper-Collins, the upcoming autobiography by an infamous adult film actress, a book intended more as an extended advertisement for her fragrance line and burgeoning personal brand as she attempted a mainstream crossover. Her name was Natalie, though she'd marketed herself professionally by more evocative names, and for weeks she and Webb met to tape long, meandering interviews at the Glendale townhouse she shared with her cousin. This was maybe the most intimate, sustained interaction he'd ever maintained with another human being, and he dreaded the impending deadline for delivery—not because he feared missing the targeted completion date, but because it would mean the end of their time together.

In the week before Christmas he found the book displayed in a bookstore in Los Feliz, his name misspelled in the acknowledgements' second-last paragraph. Due to poorly negotiated royalties, he'd pocketed little beyond his advance. But reviews were fondly unscathing, for the most part casting Natalie in the redemptive light she'd hoped to achieve. By then, of course, it was too late: Natalie herself was no more. Any sense of shared accomplishment they might have enjoyed together would never be.

He passed months in a void. Assignments trickled in and out, their volume gradually tapering. Hunkered in the sanctuary of his home office, he puzzled through problems he couldn't even identify, his mind detained in a type of idle catatonia, in nonsensical signals: thoughts of time, the problem of its flow, fear of things overlooked. This was not productive thought. Occasionally, he reviewed Ellen's drafts, rarely making remarks. He flipped through catalogues for custom Japanese bookcases that cost more than a small car. More often he drained entire mornings scrolling through online photos of old rivals from the Cornell writing guild to indulge in resuscitated resentments. His alcohol intake, unchecked since his undergraduate days, was increasingly paired with zolpidem or diazepam. His stomach began to creep over his belt. He perspired heavily, even when sedentary. Thoughts of writing anything at all evaporated. He was just a proxy, barely there. He was forty-one years old.

A voice spoke to him from another time, a forgotten place: *It grows and grows and eats you from inside out.*

In the spring, as Southern California lolled through another season of drought, Shehryar got in touch, reporting how the agency had recently inked a high-level, albeit eccentric client, a figure of serious means and repute, who was penning this sort of memoir-slash-business philosophy tome. It was kind of a kooky deal, Shehryar admitted. The individual had requested a collaborator, and it would involve international travel. The query initially did little to rouse Webb's interest; he didn't feel like going anywhere. But a follow-up email outlined the contract's unusual terms: the reclusive author would personally foot the bill for all editorial services, expenses included. The proposed fee, half on signing and half payable upon final delivery, was an amount Webb had never imagined he'd see next to his own name.

So he was flying again, nullifying miles. Mountains and savannah passed below. The tiny Cessna's sole attendant, who looked about fourteen years old, bid him good afternoon, offering a thimble of blazing chai and a shrink-wrapped mint. He declined both. When asked whether he'd require any special assistance upon arrival at Manda Island Airport, Webb looked across the aisle to Agnes, who was staring intently at her phone. He told the attendant yes, then no.

As the plane slammed against the runway, Webb felt his life's arc had met its terminus. But before he could finalize any self-eulogization, he and the dozen or so other passengers were unloading into vicious afternoon heat, filing from the plane to the bare-bones kiosk that served as an arrivals area, down a dusty path toward a floating dock. There, a pair of skiffs idled, manned by skinny operators beckoning to the dazed passengers. Agnes dropped a handful of coins into a boatman's palm, uttering a few words, then motioned for Webb to hand over his bags and hop aboard. He complied, taking a position on a bench near the stern.

Here, evidently, was the channel dimidiating the Lamu Archipelago, and farther out, the Indian Ocean. Fishing boats circled the calm waters; the air felt supernaturally clean. Lamu Island waited on the opposite side, a shambling shoreline of docks and thatched roofs and whitewashed stone buildings.

Dred's over on the island?

Agnes didn't answer. Besides the boatman, eight others were aboard, all white: a pair of older couples, cameras at the ready, speaking in what Webb took to be Swiss, along with three middle-aged British women in colour-coordinated kikois, and a twentyish backpacker in Ray-Bans and basketball shorts, a green bandana slung around his unshaven neck.

I neglected to tell you, Agnes said to Webb over the engine, there's a certain assumption of conduct.

Huh.

Lamu is a quiet Muslim fishing community. Very quaint. No disruption.

Wonderful.

That means no cars. No substances.

Sorry? That engine's a bit a-roar.

No drugs. Little alcohol. Restrictions of Islamic law.

But that has nothing to do with me. I'm an infidel.

Agnes looked away, facing ahead as they neared the shore.

They went aground among a mess of trawler lines. Shirtless boys swarmed the boat, guiding it onto the beach and swiftly knotting the lead to a sand-staked post. As the passengers disembarked into the algae-thick shallows, one of the Swiss men bleated in consternation as he dropped his Nikon into the water. A rangy guy in camouflage shorts scolded the boys for their slow tempo at manning the luggage; Webb noticed Agnes hastening ashore to meet him—this, presumably, was Jai, keeper of the inn where he'd be residing. Agnes made introductions, and they shook hands. Though Jai met him with a smile, Webb sensed his host's wary assessment.

They followed Jai and the attendants up the beach and into a crev-
iced passage leading uphill. They snaked through narrow arteries of
jagged slate, stone walls rising high around them, massive blobs of
donkey shit dotting the path. Huffing for breath, sweat puddling at
his beltline, Webb fought to keep up. Men peeked through mahogany doorways and weather-beaten arches as they passed. The town
seemed endless. Within its system, he was undoubtedly an invader.

Later, Webb sat alone in his room. Agnes had left him to get settled
and departed without further advisory. Apparently, a crew of Australians on a fishing excursion were expected in coming days, but for
now the inn, a multi-story structure of pigmented plaster cement
and coral, its walls open to air at all sides, sat disturbingly quiet. The
room he'd been assigned was sparingly furnished: a flimsy-looking
ceiling fan, polished cement floors with carpets still price-tagged, a
slatted north-facing window. A complicated mosquito net veiled
the single bed and box spring.

He was underslept and hungry, yet lacked the will to resolve
either deficit. He considered masturbating, but couldn't muster the
drive for even that. The eeriness of the place was overpowering. Everything squirmed: the anxious calls of terns over the beach, hoofs
echoing through the alleys, the ocean's oscillations.

He tore aside the net and dumped his bag's contents onto the
bed. Searching through, his heart sank: unimaginably, he'd left
the leather shaving kit containing his various pill bottles back at
the compound in Nairobi. This was not good. The cords of his
neck went taut, a familiar vexation welling. He paced the room,
looking for something to throttle, then gave up. Everything about
this situation was futile.

Among the things he'd remembered to pack was the file he'd
had Ellen compile on Dred Hausen. The records were skimpy,
reflecting the aura of secrecy surrounding the man. Dred's purported origins were in the Neuburg-Schrobenhausen district of
Bavaria, though the only affirmation of this was an offhand line

from a 2012 article in *Abendzeitung* about the ramifications of new appointments at Bundesbank. Like most of what was findable, this was purely unsubstantiated speculation. In the file, Ellen had included a few pages of corporate background, a half-page thing from a 1998 issue of *Fast Company*, a piece from the *Economist* about the Deutsch-Hausen Group, Dred's chief holdings company, and its sprawling interests throughout the Middle East and the Horn of Africa, as well as a section from a decade-old *New York Times* piece scrutinizing long-standing suggestions of bonhomie between Western shipping companies and certain parties within post-withdrawal Iraq—DHG was cited as one of the most stalwart and secretive of those mentioned. The most significant item in the file was a paper published in a Duke University Press journal about the CEN-SAD trade bloc, which included details of Hausen's forays in Northeast Africa over the last thirty years. But even these investigations relied heavily on conjecture and rumour. Here was a figure slathered in secrecy, a man spoken of in terms more like a rogue dictator than a CEO.

And then two days before his flight to Kenya, a FedEx envelope had arrived at Webb's bungalow containing a hand-held audio recorder and nothing else. On the recorder were dozens of tracks, some only a few seconds long, some upwards of a half-hour, all of the same droning voice. This, presumably, was Dred himself, dictating notes for this envisioned book. From TRACK 01 forward, most entries began mid-utterance, mid-idea, with no explanation or context given.

Thenceforth our family summered in Ueckermünde, a scenic yet terribly uninteresting locale. For my mother, this was bliss. She'd grown up in the Hochtaunuskreis, so to this day I have no idea of why she held such sentimental attachment to that place and its lagoons. My elder brother Landric and I were ferociously bored there.

The aged voice: steeped in a thick German accent that creaked like thermoformed plastic, often backgrounded with booming ambient noise, as if recorded in an airplane hangar. Yet the intonation was light, even melodious at times. So far, all the recordings had delivered were muttered reminiscences about a childhood in Bavaria, occasional musings on the Tao Te Ching, free-form anecdotes lacking context or frame. There seemed little point to continue plowing through. And yet Webb did.

One afternoon we found a unicycle discarded in a trash bin next to the farrier's. This provided a degree of amusement. It was a day of torrid heat, and in our spree we worked up a tremendous thirst, so we spent our last few pfennigs on a tankard of spring water. On the walk home we passed the water back and forth until I had a desperate need to urinate. Landric deemed me a waschlappen, and ordered me to wait until we got home. Which, of course, roused my insurrectionary spirit, and I refused to pass the water back. Not only would I drink all the water, but I would hold it inside me. Landric, enraged by my defiance, boxed me in the pelvis repeatedly, but I was determined to not loose the flood, no matter the pain. Once home, I relieved myself in the shed latrine, but the gesture had initiated something: a challenge to Landric's powers over me through a test of endurance. From that day forward he and I waged monumental water-drinking contests. We went from cottage to cottage stocking up from others' wells, amassing stacks of jars and carting them to our backyard. For hours we did nothing but drink water, as much as we could, fighting to see who could refrain the longest from urinating. Miraculous neither of us wound up stricken with hyponatremia. Most often I was the winner, for though Landric was physically stronger, I was mentally his superior, and my determination could not be swayed. Of course, at that time the region's water flowed cleanly and in abundance. The situation has since changed considerably. Today that water is undrinkable. Now it's all arsenic.

By night, the beach was different. A porthole moon beamed down. The tide had made its retreat, leaving the beach littered with crab exoskeletons, seaweed splotching the sand like liver spots. Webb walked south along the shore, his destination unsure. The beach led to a narrow stone embankment, with metered waves lapping below. From out of the dark came a small man dressed only in sandals and canvas shorts, tugging at a mule's rein. As they manoeu-vred past one another, Webb offered a weak hello. Neither man nor mule broke stride.

Rounding a bend, Webb was met by the sweaty smell of deep-frying. A patio restaurant appeared ahead, where a few patrons sat hunched over plates of clams. Lured by the oily odour, Webb took a seat near the window. A smiling waiter came, offering a plastic menu featuring watercolour illustrations of foodlike blobs. Webb asked for a beer.

No beer.

Of course not. Fucking hell.

Webb pointed at something on the menu resembling shrimp. The waiter thanked him, plucked the menu from his hands, and departed to the kitchen.

The wind was picking up. Bugs rattled in the light fixtures over-head. Next to the patio, a crew of stray cats sought refuge under a wooden cart, curling through the legs of the half-asleep donkey bridled to its hitch. These strays were smaller, scrappier, than house cats, yet bore no evident traces of mange. One slinked in Webb's direction, looking up with pleading eyes. He wadded up a serviette and biffed it, sending the cat ducking away.

Yo.

At an adjacent table sat a young dude, a book in his lap and an empty ketchup-streaked plate before him.

Be kind.

Looking closer, Webb recognized him as the backpacker with whom they'd shared the boat from Manda. American, maybe Latino by his aspect and accent. The book was a paperback of Gide's *La Porte Étroite*.

Don't tell me I'm not kind, Webb said.

This isn't your home. As outsiders, we have to show respect.

I do. I am.

The dude closed his book.

Doesn't seem so, bro. Seems you're getting a little carried away on your vacation.

I'm not on vacation. I'm working.

You're with the land commission or something?

I don't even know what that is. But no.

Well, either way, my man. Show respect. Move softly and you might hear something. Otherwise, you miss everything.

Webb went to counter this, but had no interest in indulging this irksome non-conversation. Though hungry, he left a plunk of shillings on the table, made his exit, and headed back to the inn with the acceptance of a day's defeat.

FOLLOWING AN INTERMINABLE NIGHT OF SHALLOW SLEEP, Webb woke with a headache and his stomach crawling. After battling his way free of the confounding mosquito net, he staggered to the bathroom and splashed lukewarm water on his face, swallowing back nauseous urges. He craved a steamy shower, but had been advised by the inn's attendants that hot running water would only be available between ten and twelve o'clock, and then only unreliably; it would be wise, was the suggestion, to lower his expectations in that regard.

Agnes was waiting for him on the inn's rooftop deck. She was already breakfasting, seated at a table with a white man Webb didn't recognize. The table was laid with teapots and carafes of yellowy juice, plates of soft-poached eggs and melon. After a perfunctory greeting, Webb drained a cup of herbaceous tea in two swallows, then began loading his plate.

You seem hungry, the white man said.

Do we have a waiter up here or something? From where I stand, eggs are never enjoyed properly without vodka.

Are you Russian?

What? Are you insane?

This is Anders Blakinger, Agnes said. He just got in from Stockholm.

Webb dipped a melon wedge in egg yolk.

You're with DHG, I'm going to assume.

We're gonna have some paperwork for you, Anders said, his voice carrying a distinct Texan inflection. Non-disclosure, et cetera.

Whatever you have, toss it at my assistant, Webb said. She'll take it from there.

Sounds like it's going to be really something else, Anders said. This book of Dred's.

Webb grunted and ate. Agnes rose from the table. Anders wiped his hands and followed her move.

Enjoy your breakfast, Agnes said to Webb. We'll meet our boat on the beach at noon.

We have a boat?

I have one booked to take us out for the afternoon. We'll head down south into the bay. You can do some fishing if you'd like, or just enjoy the ride. It should be lovely.

I'd rather not.

Agnes blinked.

Getting the feeling I have little say in the matter, he said. So we go fishing. Then we go see Dred?

Then...we'll see.

The essence of his profession was lives, and the repackaging of their incarnations: milking tropes and bending clichés, ratcheting downturns and redemptions, crafting mythologies out of the hum-drum. On some level, he'd believed that in editing Natalie's life, he might somehow help her. Not only was she an innately gifted performer—and not just with a penis, or penises, or in the quippy, communicative recounting of some gruesome on-set episode—but underneath the plasticized exterior she was, he'd discovered soon into their collaboration, a very likeable person, and painfully sincere in her hopes for a better life. In a parallel existence, she'd surely have found success in another non-pornographic field. But she'd been thwarted early on by the trebled curse of psychotic parents, an upbringing in the soulless, tan-lined nihility of the San Fernando Valley, and an injudiciously zealous adoration of money. Porn had paid well, but not nearly as well as she'd lived, leaving her with monstrous debts and, even with the book deal and endorse-ments lined up, dim career prospects. Longevity in her line of work wasn't really a thing, and the industry had crumbled over the previous decade, with video piracy decimating returns and pro-duction increasingly relocated to other territories: Eastern Europe, Brazil. As her own custodian of self-definition, with everything, always, evaluated only in terms of a day's earning and a night's spending, Natalie had set the stage for her own obsolescence. For this she couldn't exactly be admired.

And yet: she was the only one to remember his birthday, his fortieth, with vanilla cupcakes and prosecco. He wasn't sure how or when he'd disclosed the date to her, and was moved by the gesture, then infuriated by what he took to be an act of pity, then moved again; it was impossible to sustain any resentment toward Natalie, for she was incapable of insincerity. Every day they spent together, he fought to not act on the complex set of feelings he was developing toward her, sitting diffidently as she listed off in exacting detail how much she'd earned for each bukkake compilation, each triple penetration, each interminable girl-on-girl threesome despite her stated loathing of sex with women. She'd forwarded him an Excel spreadsheet documenting every scene and every performance agreement, each entry audited with fees invoiced, insisting it be included in the book. The publisher actually reproduced it as an appendix, and reviewers would praise this as an ironic statement on the adult industry's all-effacing commodification of the self. Natalie, of course, was oblivious to such nuance, and only sought recognition of her own shrewdness, the viability of her personal brand, and how tirelessly she'd strived for her true beloved: money. This was the only guiding principle that never lost its meaning in her disposable, lube-splattered world.

Regarding Webb's present circumstances, Natalie would have understood. A gig was a gig, rent must be paid, and each entry in the tally intrinsically added to one's value. Life itself was little more than a venture of gains and losses. As Natalie had once said, feet up on the balcony of her apartment overlooking the Ventura Freeway, a double dose of benzos weighting her eyelids: *I see the future and it looks just like the past, only more real.* Or not as real. Whatever. And so would come the inevitable point in those long afternoons when Natalie sank into morose broodiness; that was when Webb knew their day's work was done. He'd help her to the leather couch in the living room and leave her there, the radio tuned to KOST 103.5, *Feel Good for the Best Mix Of The '80s,*

'90s and Today, as she liked. Soon the drugs would overtake her system; her face would unclench and her anguished psyche would be temporarily at ease.

After breakfast, Webb wandered north toward Lamu Town. Tracing the shoreline, he passed thatched huts and M-Pesa outlets, wind-worn fences opening to sandy tracks snaking inland, a windowless building that bore a Tusker beer banner and a hand-painted sign: ADMINISTRATION POLICE CANTEEN. He passed men at work, fishermen dragging ropes, and a squad of construction workers gathered around a collapsed section of seawall, looking on as another worker attempted to rouse the ignition of a non-operational crane. Lamu: a coastline raised through slave trade and empire, in crateloads of rhino horn and mangrove, any veneer of its magic now usurped by the incursion of common infrastructural stratagem. So much of this was unfamiliar; so much was not.

The beachside path segued into the town's waterfront, a patchwork of frowning balconies and docks, locals slumped in every available sector of shade. Along the piers, boat operators courted attention with offers of sailboat hires and snorkelling excursions. Webb remained on alert, eyes to himself.

Sir.

A kid of about ten years old came bounding forth, blocking his way. Wearing plastic rainboots and shorts, his bony frame shirtless, he held a heart-shaped helium balloon bearing sparkly script lettering: HAPPY ANNIVERSARY.

You have some fun. Balloon.

No thanks, Webb said.

Small price.

Really, no.

Have fun.

Why the hell would I want a balloon?

The kid smiled.

Have some fun. Party.

Don't think so.

You smoke? Bob Marley cigarette?

The kid mimed a puff and exhale, a hammy show. Webb glanced around to see if anyone was observing this interaction, then let the kid lead him into a nearby doorway. The kid dug out a bundle of stalky joints bound in yellow cloth, pushing them insistently into Webb's hands. For four hundred shillings, a price Webb had no way of evaluating, he agreed to purchase three. The kid threw in a Bic lighter, saying, Good possibility, good possibility. Webb cupped the weed in his hands and took a whiff: it smelled like the sea. But everything here smelled like the sea.

He kept on, past the piers. The shoreline terminated at a tide-contused inlet where its detritus settled. Tissued reefs of algae lay heaped with garbage: shredded tires, rusted rotors, slime-caked sacks of waste once cast into the ocean, now returned to land. The stench was incredible. At the centre of this formation was a towering mound of water bottles, Aquafina and Dasani and Vittel, the plastic gleaming and warping in the sun.

At the inlet's opposite edge, Webb sat on a concrete bank and sparked one of the joints. As he smoked, he watched the garbage heap before him shifting with the motion of scavenging birds. A foursome of storks stepped gingerly through these layers of waste, pecking for any edible morsels. Their long, impossibly thin legs moved with twitchy precision, sharp against the mess, like vectored graphics on a screen. A westward wind pushed in off the ocean. The weed was already having a constricting effect. His head swam.

If reports were to be believed, Dred Hausen had staked his fortune in the blood of Afghan children. Though, as Ellen's file underscored, any account was subject to doubt. Like many far-reaching empires, Dred's drew its strength from its inscrutability.

One official corporate history stated the conglomerate's founding in 1978 as one of Munich's top commodities exporters, though its operations seemed to have really solidified in the early eighties, with the rush of deals following the Soviet deployment in Afghanistan. According to the Duke paper, Hausen was closely involved in Western capitalization of the conflict from the earliest days, establishing a system of customs registry claims and facilitating the movement of artillery and surveillance equipment out of Arlington warehouses and across the Atlantic, then by truckloads through Balochistan for conveyance to points beyond. As the operation expanded into an arms trade network of hydra-like insuperability, Deutsch-Hausen cargo serial numbers appeared stamped on the caches of forested militias and national armadas alike from the Congo to the Caspian Sea; for over a decade, every second bullet fired in Kabul was, directly or indirectly, DHG-commissioned. The arms shipped were known by those who crowbarred the crates and inspected the barrels to be shoddy, less durable versions of the Russian designs upon which they were based, and more accident-prone, but given the capacity at which they could be manufactured, this did little to deter their widespread adoption. In the late eighties, *Le Monde* published accounts of Afghan civilians—toddlers and grandmothers—grievously wounded in their own homes when clandestine stocks of grenades spontaneously blew during thunderstorms.

But no such calamity could hinder DHG's expansion, with tendrils reaching from Tripoli to Khartoum to Kashmir. Tracking such sprawling interests was like annotating the human genome. More cleanly documented was how, alongside these interests, DHG undertook numerous legitimate, or quasi-legitimate, ventures in the Central African natural resources and mining industries, as well as in consumer technology, most notably launching a hardware development branch in Milpitas just as notebook computing was penetrating the mainstream domestic market. The PCI card dockets and associated patents pioneered by the nascent firm's small team of engineers were accepted as industry standards almost by fluke, and circa millennium's turn the company—a majority share still held by Hausen alone, having taken over his brother Landric's interests following his passing—sold off 49.9 percent of the company to the Intel Corporation for a reported $2.2 billion. When Ellen reported this figure over the phone, Webb asked her if that number could be verified. As much as anything, she said.

With all this, Webb was naturally apprehensive about their impending meeting. There might have been moments when he questioned his involvement with other jobs, or as he'd often said, the wastes of pulp he helped unload—if he'd ever practised the necessary self-reflection. But the more he read about Dred, the more he understood: here was a figure who'd wreaked genuine havoc. Who'd purchased diamond mines in Côte d'Ivoire, then shut them down for hiring union-sympathetic foremen, and in doing so ablated entire economies. Who'd held a board position on Norwegian-backed petroleum projects in São Tomé and Príncipe, and whose contracted security personnel were credited with fuelling the republic's mercenary-led coup d'état in 2003. Who'd made enemies from Washington to Beijing, yet prospered undaunted. And now, here, Webb would polish the narrative of that life.

My mother was a marginal figure in her own life. I can still see her now, bent over the kitchen sink, swearing as she whisked eggs in a pot. Ceaselessly working, priming the home for some occasion that never transpired. Tremendous fingers, callused like concrete. If she'd been the last one at the pickle jar, good luck opening it yourself.

The voice on those recordings belonged to a person completely in control of himself, and of his world. This was something Webb rarely encountered, in the ordinary flow of his days: true, unabashed power.

He returned to the inn to find Agnes waiting for him at the entrance. He was very stoned, and had completely forgotten about their scheduled fishing trip. Despite his half-hearted protests, she led him back down to the beach, where crewmen were readying a dhow. Webb watched with laggy wonder as they raised a swinging lateen sail, its crescent and star whipping in the wind. Terms were negotiated, then the men gestured for Webb to climb aboard, and in seconds they were launching onto the water.

As they headed west and farther into the channel, Webb could feel his unsunscreened neck broiling. A choppy gust rose, sending the boat teetering and tormenting his guts, already uneasy from the potent weed and breakfast's eggs. He asked Agnes what the men were fishing for.

Marlin. But you never know when you might meet a shark.

If this was meant as a joke, Agnes didn't let on.

Jonathan, one of the boatmen, pointed to the beach ahead at Kizingoni, at the island's southwestern tip. Agnes relayed to Webb his suggestion that they anchor there to make lunch of the day's catch—the men already had a full net, with chapatis and utensils at the ready. Webb said that was fine, whatever they wanted. The other man, named Bonface, beckoned for his attention, pointing east.

Soon, Bonface said. The superhighway. Fibre optics.

I don't follow.

China.

Webb looked to Agnes.

He means the port projects, she said. Large-scale infrastructure efforts afoot. The transport corridor. Ports, pipelines. Very controversial.

Bonface frowned.

Kilovolts, he said.

Imagine Dred's got his fingers in that somehow, Webb said.

To this, Agnes said something in reply, but it was lost in the wind, the sail's thwap, the repeated whacks of the bow against coming waves. They came ashore and the men leaped out, tying lines and unloading packs with methodical efficiency up a slight incline and into a gazebo, surrounded by leleshwa shrubs. Webb wobbled onto the sand, his legs feeling like the crumpled sleeves of diner straws. Agnes offered her water canister, but he declined.

Bonface hauled a fat marlin from a net and slid his knife down its length, splitting its greyish flesh. As the loosed innards splatted on the sand, Webb swallowed back his stomach's acerbation, yet couldn't look away; there was something tauntingly obscene in such offhand butchery. The boatmen speedily assembled a fire, and the first fish was tossed upon the coals, then a second; the sizzling pyre swelled with smoke as the cords of tissue bubbled with heat. This was too much; Webb could hold it back no longer. He raced into the shrubs, making it just out of the others' sight before dropping to his knees and unleashing his insides upon the earth.

The Hausen complex at Matondoni was hidden behind a plot of mangrove-thick hills. Agnes had declined to hire a donkey at the dock, opting to climb the path through the forest by foot, despite the consuming heat. By the time they arrived, Webb's shirt was pasted to his flesh. Leading him inside, Agnes indicated an indoor well where he could wash up, near the front foyer. The well tapped into an underground spring, she said, dug out by Dred himself.

With his very own hands? Webb asked.

Agnes ignored this. The house was fashioned of bone-hued plaster cement, topped with long timber roofs reinforced by wattle and daub. Its design was disconcertingly bare; Webb saw only wicker stools for furniture, a sculpted hunk of shale and quartz that served as a shelving unit. The walls' only embellishment was a detailed map of the Lamu Archipelago and environs, mounted in a brass frame. Webb stared at this for a good half-minute before realizing what was so off about it: the map was inversed, with the land as rippling water, the ocean an encircling continent.

A servant materialized, addressed by Agnes as Timothy. He wordlessly motioned for them to follow him through sliding glass doors to the back veranda. Here was a dense garden of shoulder-height ferns and shrubbery, the angular topography disallowing any reliable ascertainment of its dimensions. At the garden's centre was a stone firepit and a cypress table with matching chairs. Agnes instructed Webb to take a seat, though she remained standing. She asked if he'd like a drink.

Definitely, he said. Something fizzy. Guts are still a bit raw.

Fizzy? Like champagne?

That would be lovely.

We don't have that.

Not for the first time, Webb felt he was being toyed with.

Please crush Mr. Gillespie some lime juice, Agnes said to Timothy. Add some seltzer. So it's *fizzy*.

Timothy accepted this with a bow, then dashed back into the house. Webb shifted in his chair as Agnes frowned at her phone.

I'll be back, she said, then hurried off.

Alone in the garden, Webb was again beset by a feeling of dread. Knowing what his contextual data suggested about Hausen, it was impossible to assess this scenario and not see sinister makings here in this kingdom of seclusion and impenetrability. But it wasn't *just* the circumstances, or some discomfiture of the exotic—or not just that anyway. The island itself felt implicated. Vines crawled, flies circled, shadows stretched. Time slowed.

Timothy re-emerged carrying a glass of something that looked like urine on ice. He served it to Webb; then, his duty fulfilled, disappeared. Webb set the glass aside untouched. Agnes returned a moment later, still eyeing her phone with a dissatisfied air.

No interview today, she said. Dred sends his apologies.

But we came all the way up here.

We did.

Well, where is he?

He'll be back soon.

So what do I do in the meantime?

I'm sure you know how to amuse yourself.

Webb didn't quite follow the insinuation in this, but whatever it was, he didn't appreciate it.

You have Dred's recorded notes, Agnes said. Those might present some stimulus for inspiration until you have an opportunity to work face to face.

Which will be when?

Your time will not go uncompensated.

He went to raise further objections, but there seemed little else to say. He drank the juice down, shuddering at the tartness. For now, he was at the kingdom's mercy.

IT WAS NEW YEAR'S EVE, 1987 into '88. Landric and I had holed up in a makeshift camp adapted from a sisal decortication plot on the western ridge of the Bié Plateau in Angola. After our planned deal with the MPLA went bungled on their end, we'd heard from our UNITA contacts of a rumoured foray by our foes into Cuito Cuanavale. Correct. I shouldn't say foes. Business rivals is perhaps more accurate. I have no foes.

Webb paused the recording to replay the last few seconds, making sure he'd heard this last line correctly—*I have no foes*—then let it play on.

Both by necessity and preference, I've strived to remain apolitical in my professional affairs, even in those early days of our expansion. But in such a place, with a melee of interests in constant collision, and every thug a factotum, things can go overlooked. Landric often failed to stay vigilant, and I was myself often too busy rooting out transgressions of the more corruptible elements in our operations to stay abreast of what faction was heading where and when. Let that be that. So when we took an order for an artillery shipment to some Cuban troops up north in Mavinga, we were unaware of the lines we'd crossed. Only when the lead convoy driver was found with his throat slashed behind a roadside filling station were we aware how negligent we'd been.

Webb paused the recorder. It was late in the day. The inn's roof looked down over the village Shela, a webwork of balconies strung with clotheslines, the poking minaret of the Riyadha Mosque like a rocket on its launch pad. He was, for now, alone up here. He leaned over the side of the cotton hammock to where a pail sat stuffed with ice and several bottles of White Cap lager, a commodity of great rarity here, only obtained after he'd repeatedly harassed the inn's staff. For meeting this request, he'd left the determined attendant a nine hundred shilling tip.

He uncapped another beer and slipped the headphones back on. These recordings leapfrogged years, abandoning any linear chronology. In this latest entry, Dred had moved on from the forests of Bavaria to his exploits running truckloads of arms around West Africa with his brother. Hurdling borders, contemning authorities—a life unyielding.

Within an hour of receiving this news we were hurrying west via the Benguela Railway, flashing falsified visas, with Uzis and small arms stashed in the trick compartments of our custom-built suitcases. Landric and I sat on the edges of our sleeper-car bunks, ready for whoever might come sliding down the aisles. But after hours of waiting with harried hearts and no sign of peril, we relaxed and opened one of several bottles of Stellenbosch wine we'd saved from the compound. By the time we'd crossed into Namibia early in the morning, we were both soused and ready for anything. By dawn I was driving a Jeep into the plateau with Landric passed out in the back. For the next week we hid out in the forests inland from the Skeleton Coast, hunting oryxes and tossing hand grenades for amusement. In this self-exile, we were free and unafraid, knowing that if our enemies came for us, we would surely go down with a joyful fight.

There was a break in the audio here, and a strange silence: an actual pause for reflection or a glitch in the recording, it was unclear. After a few beats, Dred began again.

One night, I left Landric to his slumbers and ventured off away from our camp, following some jackal tracks by flashlight. Those beaches are treacherous territory, strewn with the rusted husks of shipwrecks. Old pirates, just like us. Portuguese sailors used to call this coastline the Gates of the Bad Place. Not a place where one denies the existence of ghosts. On most nights, this tremendous fog rolls in off the Atlantic. I say it rolls, but it seems more to inflate. On that particular night I held my position there in the bitter cold with the wind high, amidst this desolation, this wreckage of human mishap, and faced the tyrant ocean.

And then I saw it, coming in. It came for me. An approaching wall of vapour, serous and condensed, like that meretricious dry ice they pump forth in concert arenas. It crept over the water's shore straight for me, as if magnetized by my attendance. As it landed, it enwreathed me in its gyrations, shifting from that leaden grey into a polychromatic radiance, finally coalescing into a formation of intemerate white light.

I have reflected on this incident endlessly in years since. I have no doubt about its authenticity and, more importantly, its implications. I have faced many cruel and dangerous men in my life, but any sense of awe I've known has been reserved for nature in all its pitiless manifestations. However, as I stared into that misty light, I saw something beyond the natural. Yes, I was malnourished and sleep-deprived. A state of mind that could generously be described as delicate. Yet none of that shakes my belief in what I beheld.

What that light offered, it was clear to me then, was access. Something previously withheld opened, delivering a direct and exclusive transmission of information. Meant for me alone. It was an invitation to another world, in which the trifles of man bear no consequence. A realm portending not only the possibility of transcendence, but the imperative of its undertaking. A place of true reckoning. A place, I understood then, past death. But a place only knowable to those permitted.

In that moment I wasn't prepared to accept its summoning embrace. Not then, not yet. I still had so much work to do, both in the immediate and in years then yet to come. And so, unresisting, trembling, I told those caressing forces: I will accept this invitation in the due course of things. And so, as the mists made their retreat back across the water, I bid my farewell with a promise of a future encounter.

In the days that followed, Landric and I made our way to Cape Town unmolested, then arranged for a flight back to Munich. We continued on. But from that encounter on the desert coast, my understanding of this world was irrevocably altered. This confirmation, this ordainment, has propelled me through the many rigours of my momentous life. It has made me fearless in certitude. And, buoyed by this inviolable hardihood, I have yet to fail.

Now then. The hour is late. As I record this, I am still on the Baltic with no access to AC power, and the batteries on this device are about to expire. So here is where I will conclude for—

There was the clunk and shuffle of Dred wrestling with the controls, then the recording stopped.

Webb removed his headphones and set them aside. He sat for a while, drinking, watching the sun sink into the horizon. From a distance came the evening call to prayer, the distorted voice of the muezzin squawking from struggling speakers, ringing over the village.

Returning to his room, he found a large cardboard box at the door. An envelope was taped to the box's side, stamped w. GILLESPIE. He pushed the box into the room and tore it open, finding six large bottles of Nolet's Reserve gin inside. The envelope contained a single typewritten card.

My regrets for delays. Work commences with the tides. DH.

As he reread the card, Agnes arrived in the doorway, holding a pair of pruning shears.

Time for my weekly trim already? he said.

These are for the parlour palms. I came to invite you to dinner.

Sounds dreamy. Just the two of us?

I've invited some visitors. Other guests. I expect them at eight, downstairs in the atrium. I hope you'll join us.

Honestly, rather not. Not feeling particularly sociable.

Some interesting people will be there. Interesting work. The chef has quite a remarkable spread planned.

Will Dred be there?

He's in transit. But he's expected soon. You really should come. I'm sure everyone would greatly enjoy hearing about your work.

There seemed no point in arguing. Webb presented his best attempt at a grin.

Well, I am a fascinating human being.

Once Agnes had departed, off again to who knew where, Webb extracted one of the bottles of gin from the box, opened it, and poured a generous splash into a mug. A small lizard skipped along the window ledge before him. He watched as it wove a nervous path down the wall to the floor, then absconded into a crack behind a corner tile—where it might go from there, he could only wonder.

The atmosphere in the atrium was heavy with charcoal and steam. A large dining table had been readied with fans of candles and woven placemats depicting cartoonish, elongated Maasai figures in zebra-stripe patterns. About a dozen guests settled in, most speaking English, as attendants brought dishes: coiling question marks of fat shrimp, plates of charred tilapia, a rhomboidal pewter tray of something stalky glistening in a beige sauce. Seated at one end of the table, overdressed in a Canali sport jacket, Webb found his forehead growing moist just looking at it all. He sought out one of several wine bottles on the table and topped up his glass.

Next to him were a married couple from Glasgow, both doctors, they explained, presently working in Burundi with Médecins Sans Frontières—she an obstetrician, he a biomedical analyst. Webb didn't catch their names, and didn't ask. Two weeks in Lamu, they said, provided a much-needed respite after the quagmires and tribulations of emergency medical fieldwork.

Mandatory stress leave, the man told Webb through a mouthful of fish. Two weeks every eight months. Gotta take it.

I must have done a hundred fistula operations this year alone, the woman said. It kind of dogs at you. But there's something to be said for living in a state of constant alarm.

Others at the table included three women in their twenties, all wearing sweatshirts with the logo of the children's charity they presumably worked for back in Toronto, along with an older bearded man introduced as working for the World Bank, something about digital entrepreneurship outreach that Webb didn't quite catch. To his other side was a woman from Amsterdam named Imma who'd come by way of Kampala, where she was conducting field research toward a master's thesis. As she described her work, Webb nodded along, pretending to listen, and almost didn't notice when she asked about his own reasons for visiting Kenya.

Um, writing, he said.

About?

To be determined.

De toekomst is een boek met zeven sloten, Imma said. A Dutch saying. The future is a book with seven locks.

Imma reached and refilled Webb's wineglass. He looked to the opposite end of the table, where Agnes sat among others in complaisant conversation. If there was any overarching purpose for this gathering she'd assembled, it remained unstated. In candlelight, with glassware twinkling, an air of uncomfortable density hung over the scene, insulating their fork scratches and unsettling the congenial chatter. The only move Webb saw was to keep drinking.

A main course of marlin shanks arrived, an agglomeration of blackened flesh on a wooden plank. The immolated fish's eyes peeped upward, seeking a possible sky now foreclosed. Someone at the table implored all to dig in. Webb was reluctant, still haunted by memories of the Kizingoni excursion, but at his turn dutifully portioned a wad of meat onto his plate, then passed the platter along to Imma. She seemed oddly fixated on him; as he nibbled sparingly at the fish, he felt the force of her attention.

What are your impressions of Lamu? the obstetrician asked him.

Webb picked at something in his teeth, a shard of cartilage from the broth.

I don't know, he said. It seems a little sure of itself.

To me it represents truth, she said. There's a purity and grace here unlike anywhere else. Purity and simplicity. It's in the people and their way of life. It's a place of magic.

Magic, Webb echoed.

Undoubtedly. There's so much here. We visited settlements on Siyu yesterday that date back to the thirteenth century. Hundreds of years of sheikdoms and conquests, but those walls are still standing. Coming here brings one closer to universal truth. I find myself in a constant state of wonder.

I'd say that says more about you and your expectations than anything about this place.

I fail to catch your implication.

You see what you're already looking for. If what you perceive is simplicity, it's probably you that's simple.

Oy! the woman's husband blurted.

A few months watching children die of malnutrition might alter your thinking, she said. In the face of that kind of tragedy, you inevitably gain a broader perspective on death. And a new respect for what it means.

Or you're just getting used to it, Webb said. One can get blasé about anything. Ask a death-row prison guard if he respects death. Or ask a coroner at four fifty-eight on a Friday. Why respect death? Death is lowly. It's *insectile*.

To this, she said nothing, clearly miffed. Webb sipped his wine. He felt sweat collecting in his crotch, his armpits, his socks. He was losing command of his train of thought, but kept going.

That kind of bromidic fluff is the worst kind of arrogance, he said. And, frankly, reveals a residual colonial mindset. What you call a state of wonder, I call delusion.

The man leaned in.

You've never had an experience that suggested the presence of something higher?

Uh, no. The word that comes to mind is *bunk*.

But what's *bunk* to you might be of intense personal significance to someone else. You need to see the world through a lens of acceptance.

Eh, Webb shrugged. I'd rather not. You can call an ungulate an ungulate, but it's still an ass.

You're sort of a shithead, aren't you? the woman said.

Webb ignored this.

What's of intense personal significance to me right now is a top-up.

He reached for the closest bottle but was stopped by a hand on his arm: Agnes.

You're speaking rather loudly and unpleasantly, she said.

I don't think I am.

He looked to the table.

Am I?

Silence met this entreaty. Imma stared back with that undeviating attention.

Everything's copacetic, Webb said, placing his own hand over Agnes's. Let's all just bask in the spirit of togetherness.

Agnes took her hand away.

Perhaps you should call it an early night.

He looked again to the others, to the expired eyes of the marlin. Everywhere, in all of this, all he saw was opposition.

Perhaps, he said.

Back in his room, he pried off his shoes and fell back on his bed with another mug of Nolet's and the stubbed remains of his second joint. He watched the smoke seep up through the fly net, carried away on an unfelt current. The dinner's debacle had exacerbated his nausea, his irritation, his feeling of dislocation. Even alone like this, stoned and soused, he was unable to shake away that unease. He longed for his pills.

The question had been posed: *You've never had an experience that suggested the presence of something higher?*

And the answer was clear: What these mists offered was access.

Dred Hausen, if he was to believed, had seen another world. A world unlike this one, in which the trifles of man bear no consequence—*not only the possibility of transcendence, but the imperative of its undertaking*. There was more than this lowliness, more than catering to the wills of whimpering subordinates. But only for those permitted to step into its light.

DAYS PASSED. Reports came of storms in the equatorial basin, with intimations of cyclonic activity approaching. Yet the island remained in stasis. Mornings brought echoes: the respiration of tides, the woody clonk of traps being loaded, the droning call from the mosque—in his half-slumber, clutching threadbare blankets, Webb mistook such sounds for traffic on the I-5, and rolled over, anticipating his king-size bed, his beautiful bungalow. But he wasn't there; he was still here, for reasons that were becoming less and less clear.

Agnes's calls would come as early as sunrise or as late as sundown. Each time, the message was the same: plans were delayed. Where was Dred? Mid-transit, somewhere over the Arabian Sea. Visiting manufacturers in Suzhou. Attending a geodiversity summit in Helsinki. Dred had promised *work commences with the tides*. But the tides rose and fell, and still Webb waited. The plan remained in place, Agnes asserted, and all would be reflected in the final invoicing. In the meantime, he was to stay put. Ruminate. Lap up the island serenity.

So he lost himself further in the recordings, abetted by gin, insulated by headphones.

Not exactly nightmares, precisely. I'll say disturbing concatenations. I think of that mirror room in Enter the Dragon, *the Bruce Lee film of 1973, a personal favourite. The vertigo, the multiplicity, the confusion. The enemy's all around you, images upon images, but which one is real? That scene rang many bells, echoing the inner tumult of early adolescence, the wrestling with the self. That particular fear, with shadings of a compulsive tendency, has mostly been overcome. It has been a long time since I experienced any such nightmare.*

Hausen's chronicle of his international enterprise continued, spanning continents and occupying many forms, with apparent internal contradictions. He spoke at length about his admiration for Hayek's *The Constitution of Liberty*, and expanded on his reliance on the Tao Te Ching for guidance. Webb fast-forwarded through much of this, hoping to come upon anything further regarding Dred's epiphany on the Skeleton Coast, that numinous presence and its teasing of other worlds.

Among many eminent figures in whom I locate historical kinship, I include Sri Ramakrishna, that venerable mystic, a figure of singular enormity. Like me, he was bestowed fatidic power through a vision. As a boy, while dawdling along a rice paddy in Kamarpukur, he saw a flock of white cranes rising against a backdrop of thunderclouds. The unexpected beauty of this formation sent him into an ecstatic trance. From this, his life's path was decided. To deny the vision would have been an insult to the universe. As teacher and cleric, Ramakrishna would be more than mankind could contain. Wisdom, he taught, came through introspection and individual rumination, and thus through detachment, rather than humdrum duty, priestly or bureaucratic or what have you. Some say humility through self-effacement, but that would be a gross misinterpretation. In answering the calling, there is an elevation of mind, and so of reach. This is something I've tried to impart to my own...son. But I see he lacks any capability of serious contemplation.

This was the first mention Dred had made of a son. He did so with apparent discomfort; even pronouncing the word itself, *son*, came with uncharacteristic hesitation. No more was made of it.

Like mine, Ramakrishna's purview was global and omnivorous. Yato mat, tato path: as many faiths, so many paths. And who, the yogi asks, is the truest devotee of the divine? The one who sees, free of shame or fear. Few will see. Those who do must act upon it, and with vigour. In the moment of illumination, only the hardiest of souls can face the light.

A team of fishermen were performing maintenance on an overturned barijah, hastening against the rising tide as it edged up the dock's algae-black posts. Another man stood to the side, giving directions while eating fried potatoes from a bunched wad of tinfoil. One of the men backed away from the boat, pumping a fist and crying out: *Ah!* It seemed they'd succeeded in their operations, and together the men tipped the boat aright, then lowered it over the dock's side. The other man crumpled his emptied tinfoil and tossed it into a bush before joining them. Soon, after a succession of hollers and heaves, the boat was launched and they all hopped aboard, raising the sail and gliding out onto the channel.

Webb watched this from the beach, seated just above the tide's hem, his toes planted in the cool sand, a few fingers left in his gin bottle. Witnessing this victory, he found himself envious. They'd moved with real objectives, with purpose.

He slid his shoes back on and considered his next move. To the south, the beach dissolved into the haze; to the west, ridges of scrubby brush led inland. And wardening it all: the spuming ocean, the wind swift across ataxic waves.

Little of this resembled the domesticated beaches of Old Saybrook. In those summer days a storm could change the voltage of the universe. Distended clouds would menace the coastline, stealing in like a contagion; their evacuation, when it finally came, was sudden and fierce. Amid such atmospheric bluster, all went loose: the puddled paths overrun with belching toads, the meadows reduced to living slime.

On one such weekend in August, Webb sat planted on the back deck of their house, observing as the downpour blitzed the beach. Beachgoers hurried to dismantle encampments; boaters tacked in for safety; neighbours on their riding mowers called quitting time. In the wake of this hubbub, he sighted a bright splotch of red on the vacated beach, stark against the water's glaucous wash. A man was running along the waterline; that red was the K-Way he wore over bright-blue bathing trunks. The man darted west to east until reaching the end of this immediate stretch, then he wheeled sharply and turned back, repeating this move once again at the beach's opposite end. He continued in this way, over and over, pausing intermittently mid-sprint to look out at the water, then resuming his laps with unabating intensity. Even as the lightning threatened closer, the intervals between each whack of thunder tightening, the man ran undeterred. Then, at no apparent prompt, he dropped and sat on the sand with legs folded, facing the water. Viewed from afar, he appeared framed in almost blueprinted symmetry: shoreline, banks to each side, and his erect posture, all aligned—and, mirroring the man's pose at his own distinct point along this arc, was Webb, watching from his sheltered distance. Neither of them moved for a while. The rain pounded. Then the man leaped to his feet and resumed racing back and forth with that same wild energy.

Webb's mother came out, chewing on a celery stalk, and joined him under the deck's awning. Webb asked if she knew what the man was doing. She told him to put trousers on for dinner, then headed back inside. But Webb couldn't turn away. In the distance, lightning lit the horizon and muffled thunder boomed across the water.

A lone figure now came into view down the shore, headed in his direction. Webb cringed, recognizing it as the backpacker: *Yo, be kind*. He hoped the dude might pass without any interaction, but he halted at a few strides' distance. For an extended moment, the dude simply stood there. When he finally spoke, it was loudly, over the waves' rush.

Just you and me out here.

Webb nodded.

Yep.

Just us and the ocean.

The dude inhaled deeply, placing his hands on his lower back and raising his chest in a long stretch. The green bandana had been shucked; sunglasses dangled from his neck on a leather strap, and he carried a netted sack slung over one shoulder. He opened the sack as he came closer.

Mango?

Webb took one: mottled green and red, ripe.

I met this man who keeps a plantation inland. Said some of his trees were over three hundred years old. Three hundred. That's just unreal to me. Unreal. Might need this.

He offered a knife. Wood handle, its serrated blade long and slender—like many Webb had seen displayed by the vendors in Shela market. Webb took it and picked at the mango's peel.

This coastline, the dude said, looking out. Eternal and untouched.

Actually, Webb said, I heard it's all being developed. This transport corridor, the hub for the pipelines.

No way. That'll never happen.

Pretty sure you don't have any say in it.

They can bulldoze whatever they want. But this ocean will be here long after you and I are gone.

Webb snorted and sipped the gin.

If you say so.

Webb's work on the mango had only rendered it a sticky, half-peeled mess, so he tossed it aside and handed back the knife. His repeated psychic commands for the backpacker to leave him alone were evidently having no effect.

The things revealed to us by nature, the eternal wisdom of it... Man, I've seen some shit you wouldn't believe. Shit I barely believe myself. But it detaches you from the obviousness of how most of us see things. So I take it as my personal obligation to assist the world in its survival. But it's also a blessing.

Neato.

The dude scowled.

You know, sarcasm is shitty.

I would say I'm sorry, but that'd just be me being sarcastic again.

So you feel no sense of duty to the world. No moral philosophy. No impetus to develop one. You feel entitled to just partake of its bounty without consequence.

The dude gawked at him, expecting something.

Well, Webb said, if I had to say anything to that, which I *don't*, I'd say a man isn't obliged to develop a moral anything. We live in mortgaged times. The asylum's in flames. The bad guys have won. Only an idiot would deny that.

Then I guess I'm an idiot. Because I disagree.

Webb took a solid look at him, this dude, now assuming a stance that was almost threatening.

Can I *do* something for you, man? Webb said. You need money or something? You're kind of overstaying your welcome.

To this, the dude gave his own version of a snort.

My welcome? Ain't your beach, bro.

Webb sighed.

No, it's cool, the dude said. I'll leave you. Thought we could have a civil conversation here. But I guess you're just a mean-spirited dick.

Even once left alone, Webb couldn't shake his irritation. Here before him again was that so-called *eternal wisdom*: the sun muscling through a bank of clouds, the tides moving in tired digestion, this bay heaving colossal reefs of human junk upon its shores. In the distance, a pair of cranes stood at the channel's northern reach, the booms extending high above the unfinished berth, all activity there presently stalled.

This world and its endings, its non-conclusions, its pollutions and abandonments—he knew it well.

...a recurring dream in which I am an Arctic fox, suggesting a symbolic kinship. Native to the Arctic tundra biome, it is by nature a solitary and determinedly adaptable creature. Short-muzzled and bushy-tailed, it possesses an understanding of its environment that stands unique among its co-inhabitants of the barren icy regions. Its chief predators are the wolf, the wolverine, and the golden eagle, as well as its dastardly cousin and arch-nemesis, the red fox. The red fox is an aggressively dominant species, though its testes are small compared with that of its Arctic rival. Where the Arctic fox is by nature opportunistic and scavenging, the red fox hunts ambitiously, even recklessly...

Jai came knocking at Webb's room early, warning that the upcoming weekend would find the inn overtaken by the Australian contingent. About a dozen men, mounting a deep-sea fishing excursion.

Hopefully they won't disturb your work, Jai said. And the power is out again. But don't worry. It will be restored.

Webb closed the door and latched it behind him. There were more tapes to go through.

Self-sequestration in his room had made him acutely aware of unpleasant sensations arising—symptoms, even. Along with trembling hands and cottony mouth, as well as a needling sensitivity to every blip of noise, an all-pervasive internal weakness had come upon him. His breath came short and his pulse felt faint. His bowels revolted frequently and unsatisfyingly. Perspiration gushed.

The question nagged: why was he here, really? It occurred to him this might all be some elaborate trial of his will, or his pliability. If so, it might be wise to forfeit. He could flee, enlist a boatman to take him back across to the airstrip on Manda, then hop the soonest flight to Nairobi and be over the Atlantic within hours. Why not? The consequences of any contractual breach could be argued later from the comforts of his office, among his bookshelves and central air and pristine oak flooring.

But each day's tide flowed into the next, and the more he mulled over such questions, the more he desired answers. He consulted Dred.

Not only is vulpes lagopus a nobly handsome species, but one fiercely resilient in the harshest of climates. Born into the world a deep brown, its fur whitens with age, and its paws' substantial padding allows it to safely tread on ice without fear of collapse. It is sullenly monogamous, and establishes intimate relationships with its brethren, keeping ties close. The Arctic fox rarely eats its young.

After enough time buried away like this, hours into days, he had to get out. Despite his rubbery legs and tremoring stomach, a failing sense of his own proportions, he needed to move, to shake off the excess sludge of gin and lassitude. And so: the beach, again. Headed north along a now-familiar route, he came across a group of shirtless boys engaged in a spirited soccer match. Two squads, three a side, kicked a half-deflated ball across a loosely delineated field of play. Any finesse was undermined by the complete absence of any of teamwork, each chasing the ball to execute his own routine once the opportunity could be seized. Any move to score a goal rapidly disintegrated into a sloppy pile-on.

One of the boys flubbed a pass, and the ball shuttled toward Webb, who was watching from the sideline. He trapped the ball with his heel and grinned back as the boys shouted at him. He pointed to one of the kids near the water, calling his readied shot like Babe Ruth in 1932. Before he could fire off the pass, however, another boy scurried up at his right, moving to steal back the ball. Caught off-guard, Webb made to dodge, and in doing so slipped and fell on his ass. The boys' high-pitched voices broke out in concern, or mockery. Webb lay back on the sand, facing the sky, or nothing. He let out a laugh, a single crazed blurt: *Fuck me*. The match resumed.

Agnes had mentioned hotels in Lamu Town that housed proper, actual bars. Webb found one place along the shore fronted by a shaded terrace, its hand-painted sign touting BLODY MARY's. He was the only patron, and as soon as he took a window table he felt a release of tension at its familiarity: here was a bar, a seat, a wine list. The bartender gave his name as Charles—*everyone on Lamu knows me!*—and suggested a house specialty of his own design: rum on ice with sweet vermouth and some syrupy strawberry liqueur. After confirming the cubes had been made with filtered water, Webb drank it down, cringing at the saccharine wallop. He then ordered another, cajoling Charles into doubling up on the Captain Morgan.

It was already almost dusk; the sun fell quickly here. Webb sat back and looked out on the water, the sailboats circling the channel in leisurely ambits. He imagined all this would soon be unrecognizable, if the proposed pipelines and deepwater ports continued as planned. The zest of industry was uncurtailable, even here.

He slipped on his headphones and pressed play on the Samsung recorder, TRACK 14.

A lifelong hedonist, my brother contracted AIDS in the early nineties. His was a torturesome decline. The last time I saw Landric was in Seattle in, I believe, 1996. After one of his degenerate consorts discovered him unconscious in his apartment, he was checked into Harborview under intensive care. Visiting him there, I found a cadaverous shadow of his former robust self. Treatment for the disease was then still embryonic and experimental, and no one was optimistic for his recovery. As I sat at his bedside, Landric and I reminisced together about our childhood in Ueckermünde, an indulgence of nostalgia uncharacteristic of our relationship. That alone suggested things would never again be as they once were.

The day after my return to Munich, I received a fax saying Landric had passed away from complications due to pneumocystis. Potentially remedied, I was later told, if he'd sought treatment earlier. But my brother, while anatomically stout, was psychologically a runt. Many times, I'd mapped out my intentions for the future we might enjoy together, both the adversity we would face and the spoils we could reap. Though Landric went along with my ambitions, he never understood their reach.

Oh, Landric. I miss you, and I pity you. I pity that you will never see all that I have seen. But you lacked the necessary mettle to reign. You were soft, and so you died a soft death. Do I myself possess such mettle? Of course I do. That's what has made my life such a treachery. Only the keenest, those who see through those beguiling veils of time and memory, emerge triumphant. At this point I should add that I consider that old saw of virtue being its own reward to be utter baloney. To a conquering soul, the only real point is victory.

Hello there.

Imma, the Dutch graduate student, leaned over his table, wearing a purple kikoi over basketball shorts, Maasai sandals exposing toenails painted bright green. Webb removed his headphones.

You're still here, she said.

I am.

Without an invitation, she took a seat. She had to be reminded of his name, though he knew hers, and also recalled her stated IDS program and research post in Uganda. This flattered her, and as he ordered another round of Charles's special for them both, her spirits were light. She began elucidating at length her field research, something involving, as she put it, emphasizing value chains and private sector infiltration in limited opportunity education. The work was fulfilling, she said, though it came with much frustration.

Take last month, she said. I visited this development site near Bwizibwera where OPEC had committed to implementing a trade school and library. But when I got there, there was nothing. I mean, nothing. Twenty-two months in and just a pile of lumber and trac- tor tracks. What do you think about that?

It's pretty appalling.

Damn right. It was disgraceful. It was *criminal*.

Imma sipped at her drink, looking pained.

This tastes terrible.

It really does.

And you're here writing about…what, exactly?

Webb was unsure of how to answer, or what he was even legally permitted to divulge. Ellen had delivered the non-disclosure agree- ment as requested, but he'd yet to sign anything. He made a mental note to get on it.

Fine points still pending, he said. Gathering research, refining material. My client presently has me in somewhat of a holding pattern.

And so how do you pass the time?

The usual divertissements. Distilled beverages. Pornography. Wordsworth.

Imma contorted her face in a sort of snicker, poking her tongue through her teeth. A somewhat ghastly move, and Webb had to look away.

You're a student of the sublime, she said. The *still sad music of humanity*. How posh.

Nothing like that. It's more…anthropological.

Imma seemed to accept this. As she looked around the bar, Webb saw how oversunning had seared her cheekbones and nose's bridge pink, though her forehead was pale. He recognized this pattern as the one created by the Dolce & Gabbana sunglasses Natalie had worn every day. There was a specific fervency in how she'd worn those sunglasses, propping them atop her head when ordering coffee, flipping them down when behind the wheel of her Integra. She'd kept, and flaunted, many such totems, such things-as-self, with the hope they'd become trademarkish components of her brand; a word she relished in repetition was *iconic*. Natalie's quasi-iconic eyes were hazel, but she wore green-tinted lenses, and her long tresses were a continuous work of ombré and splashlights and balayage. Everything had to be adjustable, customized, augmented—this would also become a not-too-subtle motif he worked in throughout the book. One night, emboldened by boxed rosé, Webb had speculated aloud regarding the pliancy of her expensive breasts, which had roused the impulses of umpteen thousand masturbators. Though only a few weeks out from another stint at Las Encinas, Natalie had gotten a bit giddy that night—with the wine, yes, but more so with the pleasure of expounding freely on her favourite subject, herself—and she'd obliged, hiking up her tank top to let him cop a feel. He'd expected the skin to feel strained and taut over the implants' imposition. But it was pleasingly soft, like well-nourished turf; she'd gotten her money's worth. Of course, any such success was attenuated in the context of how many loans she'd defaulted on, how many credit cards she'd racked. Her breasts hovered improbably, even as her credit score sank.

I appreciated what you said the other night at dinner, Imma said.

What's that now?

Shattering delusions. Upending assumptions. Challenging ideologies.

I said that?

Like your friend Wordsworth, I've had enough of tyranny. I seek a life free of oppression.

It's good to have aspirations, I suppose.

The neo-liberal monstrosity enslaves us through abstractions. Money and progress and all those constructs.

A lamentable thing.

It's time the cages got a rattling.

To this, Webb went to say something, but balked. Imma detected his reticence.

You don't think so?

Well.

Well what?

Well, we all live in cages, he said. Cages within cages. Interlocking cages. People are always proclaiming a desire to be free. But you open the gates, the animals don't make a run for it. They stay put.

So you say there's no emancipation. No outside.

I'm not saying anything in particular. I'm just…saying.

But there *are* those who exist outside. They work in the shadows, where they can't be touched.

Who? Grad students?

They go by many names. In some places, in some areas around here even, they're called witches.

Webb leaned back in his seat.

Witches. Like that TV show with, you know, *Who's the Boss?* and the sisters with the leather chokers?

Imma squared her eyes on him.

It's no joke.

Never said it was.

Witchcraft is very real. Witches operate through concealed forces, protecting arcane practices and staving off contamination. Manipulations at the most covert levels. Most of all, witches defy modernity. And with this comes risks. You hear about women and elders in the southwest villages being lynched or burned alive. The brokers of power want them erased, because they run counter to the seduction of foreign investment. Brokers need the confidence of measurable metrics. They need old knowledge wiped out, and the women sworn to protect it silenced. But the truth endures.

Huh.

I met a woman from Tsavo who escaped her district after a mob of Christians swarmed her family's home. She was a potter, and they claimed her clay pots contained spirits that possessed people when brought into their homes. They said the pots would levitate and yowl in the night, convincing women to castrate their husbands. Then the son of one businessman, a local big shot, drove a lorry off a cliff, and the blame landed on this one woman. Of course, the kid was zoinked up on khat and paint thinner. But no, they said it was the witch. A parish priest led the charge and the mob burned down her house. Fortunately, she escaped and fled to Gulu, which is where I met her, working a booth in the market. This woman was fifty-eight years old, but you'd swear she was twenty-five. Of course, she was also a lesbian, which made the scenario even more complicated.

Webb, again: Huh.

There's nothing the political elite fears more than that which falls outside orthodox frames of rationality. An autocratic state can manipulate an economically disaffected citizenry, sure. But they can't control a supernatural renegade.

With this, she sat back and took a long drink.

But this woman, Webb said, was she actually a *witch*?

Imma smacked her lips with displeasure.

I don't think I can drink this.

I have a case of good gin back at the inn. Or most of a case.

Let's go.

Webb paid their tab and they headed back down the beach. It was a relief of sorts to have a companion after several days solo, to have the silence filled, at least for a time, even if it was Imma: her unwavering eyes, her ceaseless perorating, that awful tongue.

At the inn, Imma used the toilet while Webb dug out a fresh bottle of Nolet's and poured drinks, then paced the room while checking his phone. There was only one message, Ellen telling him of an urgent call from the contractors presently repiping his kitchen, warning of complications that needed to be discussed immediately. Webb deleted it.

Something at the window caught his attention. On the ledge sat a pewter serving tray, loaded with what looked to be red snapper fillets, garnished with onions and leaves of romaine, sheening in the low light. The fish had gone grey, the lettuce flaccid; a smell of spoil came off it. He had no recollection of ordering this from the kitchen, though the slip tucked under a napkin bore his penned scrawl. As he came closer, the tray clicked with a rustle. He gave it a nudge and a large black beetle crept out from under a fold of fish, its mandibles seeking. It was followed by another, and another—the tray was a mass of antenna and thorax and ravaged lettuce, heaving with rot.

Webb stood motionless, uncertain if the wriggling horror he was seeing was actually there. What was seen was rarely the entire truth. He recalled those early mornings in the in-patient cafeteria at Connecticut Valley, benched opposite his father over cold toast and watery fruit salad, neither touching their plates, locked in silence. His father's bathrobe hung unsashed, exposing pyjamas swiped with ashes. When Webb finally pried open a packet of plastic cutlery to butter his toast, his father had jumped in his seat, practically convulsing: *You can't eat that.* Webb of course had asked why, even though he'd anticipated the answer coming, or something like it. *Because it grows and grows and eats you from inside out.*

Everything, everywhere, was a threat. The very mechanics shaping the quantifiable world—combustion, friction, decay, the surges and plummets of the markets—were those that would eradicate the self.

Webb instinctively looked for his shaving kit, then recalled its absence, cursing his idiocy once again for forgetting it. The Valium he could cope without. Risperdal withdrawal, however, was another thing altogether. His head pulsed. The roof of his mouth was corduroy.

The toilet whooshed, announcing Imma's return. Webb closed the window's shutters, hiding the tray, the beetles, and offered her a cup.

I'm having mine straight, he said. Not sure how you go.

She took a sip, her distaste clear.

I'm thinking pineapple, she said. Little maraschino and we could stir up some Harlems. That's what my mother always drank in the summers. We could find a market.

He'd hoped they could simply drink in ease, but this notion had taken a hold of her: she was determined to hunt down some pineapple.

Bringing the bottle, he followed her back downstairs to the maintenance office, finding two men from the kitchen staff smoking on the
tree-sheltered steps facing the back courtyard. Webb asked, not un-
sheepishly, if the kitchen had any pineapple on hand. Fresh, ideally.

I will find you a tin, one of the men said.

Bull*shit*, Imma declared. No way with that Del Monte poison.
We need real Kayunga pineapples.

The men looked at Imma as if she was insane. One suggested the
market in town, near the fort. But, he warned, it was likely closed
by this hour.

Imma started for the exit. The men gave Webb a look that was
impossible to read. Webb thanked them and followed Imma, swept
into her pull.

The streets behind Lamu Fort were emptying, the last marketeers
packing their wares in retreat ahead of foul weather looming. The
rumoured produce stall was nowhere to be found, and the locals
Imma interrogated offered no knowledge of pineapple or its avail-
ability. As they circled back toward the beach, Imma looked up at the
fort, its vaulted entrances and ramparts, a former Omani outpost and
then prison for the East Africa Protectorate, now remodelled into a
museum. She flapped her hands in a sort of condemning gesture.

This entire thing's a monument to atrocity, she said.

Her indictment ran wide: this island, the modern Kenyan state
and its parliament-mandated corporate collusion, centuries of sul-
tanates and sovereignties, the barbarity of antiquity. She was drawing some broad analogy that Webb couldn't quite follow, and when
she again fired her demand—*What do you think of that?*—he could
offer no response.

Again, there was that sense of inherent wrongness. A slippage
of sequence, location. Then it struck him: this must be part of his
trial. Imma, her solicitations and cues, her sweeping charges. Her
determination for real Kayunga pineapple. Yes, he was being tested.
But whether by Dred or by another entity—this was yet unknown.

They came onto the beach. Down the shoreline, a few boatmen were still at work. He had an idea, Webb told Imma, where they might rustle up some supplies. After making inquiries among the men through stilted dialogue and useless gestures, Webb located Bonface near where they'd docked on first arrival. Busy at work on his skiff, Bonface exhibited no recognition of Webb. And to the proposition put forth, he seemed highly dubious.

Just zip us around to Matondoni and back, Webb said. Name your price.

Bonface tossed aside the section of netting he'd been mending and, without a word, headed past Webb up the beach and slipped into a passage between two stone embankments. Imma came to Webb's side.

Is he coming back?

Webb wasn't sure. They sat together on the sand and passed the nearly empty bottle.

I feel melancholic and edgy, she said.

Do tell.

I'll be headed back to Kampala in the morning. And flying wrecks me. I get these vivid premonitions of disaster. The feeling comes upon me and just won't let go.

They have pharmaceutical remedies for that.

The sensation of plummeting as you sit there, belted in...before I'm even completely situated in my situation, it's as if it's already happening. Mentally, I'm already there. Even now.

Yes, you're pretty much a goner. But good news. Your last drink will have been with me.

Yeah.

She reached and took his hand. His reflex was to recoil, but she moved her fingers between his, pressing his palm. Her hands were rough and worked, nothing like his own fingers' fleshy, untoughened pads.

Do you ever see yourself as you'll be in the future? she asked.

Here was another question, another test. But he had an answer ready.

I see the future, he said, and it looks just like the past.

Only more real, Imma said.

She looked out at the ocean, the waves smooth and regulated.

I want to swim under the stars.

So go ahead, he said, drawing his hand away. Nothing's stopping you.

She snickered, that odious teeth-biting laugh, then leaped to her feet. She tore off her sandals, offered him a sort of curtsy, and then bounded for the water.

Webb remained seated on the sand. Blood came hot in his cheeks and temples. *I see the future and it looks just like the past*: he was speaking in Natalie's words, not his own. But then, Imma: *Only more real*. Echoing exactly how it had gone, or at least how he remembered it—much was now suspect. Somehow the departed spirit had been revivified. Certainly this was another part of his test.

Down at the waterline, Imma squealed as the waves lapped at her thighs. She called for Webb to join her. He rose from the sand, but didn't advance. Imma was a cipher. An enemy of money and of colonial appetence, a champion of shadow dwellers. A necromancer speaking in a porn star's voice.

Yes: Imma herself was the test, or its administer. She was a witch.

Bonface returned, dragging another coil of net, shaking his head.

Not going, he told Webb.

What do you mean, not going?

Called Agnes.

And?

She says no.

Webb considered trying to persuade him, but he'd lost any enthusiasm for the caper. Crashing Dred's complex for provisions, whether for pineapples or Uzis or any act of insurrection against the absent overlord, was undoubtedly a foolhardy move. Powerful forces were at play here—*manipulations*, as Imma said, *at the most covert levels*—and any errant moves would only tempt their ire. If there were indeed a mist-shrouded world beyond this one, he'd have to prove himself worthy of access. Who would be permitted? Sultans who laughed at typhoons. Weapons smugglers who flouted international law. Dazed actresses blowing kisses into digital lenses. *Those who see through those beguiling veils of time and memory.*

He found himself hurrying from the beach and inland, back to the enclosed alleys—how one could become disoriented so quickly on so small an island was truly dumbfounding. He heard Imma calling after him, but he continued his flight, feeling his way along the rough cement walls until, rounding a turn, he was engulfed in something wet and clinging. Tearing at his face and hands, he slipped on the loose ground and went down. A belt of pain telegraphed from his ankle. He looked up, finding broad panels hovering across the path, splayed like heraldic banners. Here was another barrier, another denial of access.

Something previously withheld opened, delivering a direct and exclusive transmission of information. It was an invitation, meant for me alone, to another world, in which the trifles of man bear no consequence.

As he fought his way back to his feet, his vision adjusted. The obstruction refusing him was simply a row of dangling sheets of laundry, linen swaths strung across the alley on a clothesline. Against his howling ankle, he tore aside the damp sheets and hobbled ahead into the dark, making his escape.

THE STORM FINALLY LANDED IN THE NIGHT. Fractals of lightning strobed the sky, the inn's sills shaking with each clap of thunder. By morning, the rain's intensity had ebbed, but remained sporadic.

Webb lay on the bed, the net retracted, headphones on. Above him a sliver of cobweb clung to the window's slats, fluttering in a suggestion of breeze.

What cannot be seen is called evanescent. What cannot be heard is called rarefied. What cannot be touched is called minute. These three cannot be fathomed.

And so they are confused and looked upon as one.

A pause, a rustle. Slow nasal breath. Dred was delivering another extended riff on the Tao Te Ching. The track gave off a blank mechanical rumble: Dred was again airborne, between phases.

I understand this to suggest that what we deem to be mystical experience is more often simply the ordinary confusion of unfocused desire. The mind disappoints in its flocculence.

Of evanescence, Webb thought of Natalie. Natalie, again and always: scratching at her cuticles, yelling at her phone, peeking out through aluminum blinds at the parking lot below. As a symbol, as a thing for interpretation, she was that purest of devices, ready to assume any trappings launched upon her, at any level. A figure of arousal, but only in the most disposable of modes. A player, juggling masks atop masks. One day, a cackling dominatrix in latex; the next, but one body among many, silent and spread in a poolside orgy. But with a fragrance line, aloft the aromatic zephyrs rustling the sunset palms of Miami Beach, comes permanence: the *mainstream*.

As the publisher's deadline for delivery neared, Webb had arranged to meet Natalie there, in Miami, where she was shooting a two-episode stint on a crime procedural drama for Starz, a potential coup for what she optimistically termed her crossover career. The show was shot alternately between a former Lockheed plant in San Clarita and on location throughout southern Florida, and for her scenes she'd been holed up in Key Biscayne. Only later did Webb ascertain that the acting job had actually fallen through, and while in Miami Natalie had instead been working lucrative private dates for off-season Dolphins. Work on the book fell by the wayside, leaving him days to loiter in beachside bars alone, any melancholy curtailed by quality cocaine; once expenses were tallied versus advances and earnings, he'd most likely gone into the red across the life of the project. But he'd enjoyed those indolent beachside days, marvelling at the gloss masking scuzz, the oiled torsos and the grinding of speedboat engines. Miami was a place of flexible truth, and numbing repetition only made it truer. Natalie understood this; like Webb, she was empty, and always had been. She'd seen the future and it looked just like the past, only more real. *Or not as real*. Whatever.

Webb fast-forwarded. Dred continued.

What do the keepers of wisdom say? This is the shape that has no shape, the image without substance. Indistinct and shadowy. Go up to it and you will not see its head. Follow behind it and you will not see its rear.

Webb recognized at least one aspect of the fear he'd seen in Natalie's worst moments: the clawing expectation of disappointment, and the hope for a release. He'd seen it in his father, a man as a refuse heap. But nothing changed, and nothing improved.

Some men of means collect fine art, or cars, or wives. I collect damnations. Such is the encumbrance of my chosen path, a life of proximity to violence. And in this, many have deemed me an evildoer. A murderer. Rest assured I feel no onus to defend my reputation or my methods to any lily-livered consultants or advisors, those puny men. This world is a barnyard of low appetites and dalliances—uncivilized territory, waiting for the swiftness of a machete. I've been shown what the truth demands. It's a sacrifice of blood, nothing more and nothing less. I was chosen by the mists to see beyond all such considerations. I've been given licence to leave behind such piddling quarrels. To a sculptor of vision, everything is but plaster.

I accept my damnations. And so, death surrenders its monopoly. Death powers me, steering me through the night's brume toward that other realm. It waits for me, like a lover. Or like a whore. Yes, like a whore.

Each day's tide flowed into the next.

The Australians had arrived. Their brays rang throughout the stairwells, across the balconies: *Tobias, get in here so we can have this fuckin' lunch. The ocean awaits.* Emerging from his room, Webb found they'd overtaken the common area. The table was set with heaping platters and pots of tea, and the men—six buzzed heads atop hillocks of shoulder—were plowing through the food with unswaying determination. As Webb availed himself of a carafe of water, no one acknowledged his arrival. Here were ignoble men, unhindered and crude; in another context, he'd have scoffed openly at their ilk. But here, everything was subject to doubt. To them, to all terrestrial souls, he was now invisible. He'd shifted to another plane, relegated to provisional status by the forces governing this island. *Indistinct and shadowy*. He drank his water and returned to his room.

During his earliest days, the stakes presented to him were clear. Here is a system of conditions and expectations. Here is the Middlesex County district school bus that will discharge and return you through the order of your days. Here is your psychiatrist, in whom your innermost terrors must be confided and in whose prescriptions you must trust. Here are your joyless custodians, the kratocracy of your peers. Through appeasement of these accomplices, through staunch compliance and dutiful social participation, you can achieve a comfortable mediocrity.

But with his mother and father's energies vitiated by their own preoccupations, he was free to rove. In his wanderings, he began to suspect the foundations on which he relied might be less than firm. Trudging through the town in solitude, particularly in its slushy off-season catalepsy, hidden truths wormed forth. The people of Old Saybrook placed unwavering faith in two pillars: tradition and a seasonal economy. But a freak hailstorm could wreck a propitious July weekend, and faith in any imagined common cause would only lead to betrayal—just as his father's faith in the imagined freedoms of the Monetary Control Act had been his undoing.

No, even then there was something beneath the surface, calling to him. An element, a substance, a pattern. He needed to keep scratching at the loose edges until he could peel back the shell to draw out the true thing, the ugly thing, inside.

The distinctive howl of the Arctic fox alternates between a cry that carries warnings to imperilled whelps over great distances, even through raging tundra storms, and a high-pitched undulating whine employed to daunt enemies in territorial skirmishes. Travelling in stealthy packs, trailing marauding polar bears over icy plateaus to pick at any scavengeable remains, the Arctic fox finds strength in the conservation of energy, with time its solemn ally. Oh, if only more creatures roaming this earth could do so with such valour.

In the afternoon he loped back north toward the hotel bar, thirsting for Charles's house special. He'd drained the last of the gin early that morning, and was not feeling good for it. The storms had chastened the town, leaving mkungu trunks flattened and sodden debris scattered across the road, drawing bands of roving cats. The untroubled demeanour of the fishermen, again at work drying out sails and scraping barnacles from the hulls of their dhows, suggested this was a regular phenomenon—conditions Lamu had come to know, and work within.

Webb wiped his sand-glopped feet at the bar's front mat and started inside. But Charles headed him off, raising his hands and looking distraught.

Closed today, he said. Trouble with pipes.

Pipes?

Floor. Under.

Charles made a gesture to demonstrate: *whoosh*. Overnight rainfall had devastated the plumbing. The hotel was in crisis mode, overwhelmed with emergency repairs.

Tragic, Webb said. So let's enjoy a cocktail and bury our worries. Let's talk. Let's get into what's going on with *you*. I want to know. I want to hear.

Sir. No. Closed.

Don't dick me around, Charles.

Sir.

Webb scratched his face, considering the situation. The room was rank with mildew and sewage.

I see with clear eyes, he said. Believe me.

Charles looked at him, blank. Webb leaned in close.

This is a test, right?

Still Charles stared. Webb pushed past and headed behind the bar. The shelves were thinly stocked, but a sealed fifth of J&B offered itself to him. Webb snatched it, dumped a wad of hundred-shilling notes on the counter, then departed without registering Charles's reaction.

Back on the beach, he encountered a now-familiar scene: the scrawny boys, vying in battle for their half-deflated soccer ball, hustling and tackling with that same clumsy, inexhaustible drive. The foul weather hadn't curtailed them; rather, the clouds' threat seemed to only drive them to wilder forays. Webb found a seat on a rusted section of rail to watch from a distance, cradling the bottle. They took no notice of him there, in his ephemeral state. His evanescence.

Letting his buzzed gaze trail farther down the shoreline, he sighted a familiar figure approaching: Agnes. He waved, but she didn't return the gesture. When had he last seen her? Even from afar she projected expeditiousness, something self-restricting and moderated. She seemed unsurprised to discover him there.

Another day, he said.

Yes.

She sat next to him on the rail, maintaining that stiffness. He corrected his own slouch and offered the bottle, but she declined.

You're enjoying yourself? she asked.

Always. Or never.

They watched the boys scurrying and stumbling. Another downpour seemed imminent.

I admire you, Agnes, he said.

You admire me.

This air of...composure you radiate.

It's part of my job.

What are the other parts?

To this, she only shook her head.

And you have a long history with DHG?

Long? I was hired out of university. That was seven years ago. Almost eight years ago. I was fortunate to be given the opportunity. So I work to meet the obligation.

You're the gatekeeper. The steady hand at the wheel. Mission control.

I don't know what that means.

You have responsibilities. You work directly for Hausen.

By this point, you should understand the path these things follow is rarely direct.

The shape that has no shape. Go up to it and you will not see its head.

But you know him. You speak with him. You pass information back and forth.

I do. We do.

Has he ever spoken to you about his...beliefs?

The Hausens are reformist Lutherans. His parents are buried in an evangelical cemetery in Tutzing.

I don't mean denominationally. I mean, in a sense of...further. Beyond.

Beyond what?

Before Webb formulated his next words, he was distracted by something ahead. The Australians had descended on the beach and were now interacting with the soccer kids in a way that didn't seem entirely playful. One had intercepted a pass and was juggling the ball tauntingly on his meaty white thighs, daring the soccer kids to steal it back from him: *Come on, you*. His cronies looked on, snickering.

One of the kids came lunging for the ball, but the man blocked this advance with the barest tilt of his hips. The kid persisted, but proved useless against the large man's barricading. Finally, the boy stomped his entire weight on the man's sandalled foot, pinning it and forcing the Australian to lose balance and fall to the sand. The kid deftly stole the ball back and raced away. His friends cheered in triumph.

The man rose to his knees, spitting, his Carlsberg T-shirt smeared with wet sand. He went for the first thing in reach, a fistful of worn stones, and fired them at the boys. A few connected, prompting a flurry of cries.

Fucking *brats*, the man growled.

Webb set the bottle in the sand and started over. Agnes said something, but he didn't hear her—he was shifting again between dimensions, regaining materiality, returning.

Hey, chuckles.

Back on his feet, the first man squinted, sizing him up.

What?

You gentlemen need to dial it down, Webb said.

The others lumbered over, rallying.

And who the fuck're you?

Webb grinned.

I'm the mayor of Lamu.

What? Piss off.

What's your name? another of the men demanded.

Landric Hausen.

What?

This isn't your home, Webb said. We have to show respect. Move softly and you might hear something.

These men: built like racks of ham, the sort who gleefully fire off headbutts outside taverns in the early afternoon. One of them poked Webb in the shoulder.

Fuck this poof.

Fuck this cunt back to his playpen.

Yeah, Webb said. I'm not even here, am I?

The obfuscation seemed to only further wind them up. The first man motioned at Webb with his chest out.

You're here, all right. Feel me?

He delivered Webb a solid shove that set him off balance. Somehow Webb kept his footing.

Apologize to those kids.

Fucking hell I will.

This is their beach.

Yeah. And not yours, poof.

This man, repugnant as he was, was correct. *Ain't your beach, bro.* Webb had no more claim on this place than did these swinish men. He had no status.

So get the fuck on then, one of the other men said.

The men were now very close.

Apologize, Webb said.

A blow came, open-handed, cracking him across the face. Webb didn't see who delivered it. But when the palm's meat connected with his cheekbone, its force resonated through his entire skeletal system, twisting his neck in a way it wasn't meant to twist. His eyes welled; his throat went thick.

Agnes came and took Webb by the arm. He allowed himself to be drawn away; there was nothing for him to do here. As she led him away, he smiled at the boys as they looked on. None smiled back.

As they headed back along the shore, Webb felt his digestion lurch and he faltered, swallowing back a paroxysm of gastric acid. Agnes noticed.

You look bad, she said. When was the last time you had anything to eat?

He wasn't sure. A while. He muttered something about rotten snapper, then lost his train of thought.

I received a call from Samuel, back at the house in Nairobi, Agnes said. They found a bag in the groundskeeper's residence. It contained a number of pill bottles.

Webb raised a hand to silence her.

Tell me about the mists, he said.

Samuel described the bag's contents. It was somewhat alarming.

The mists, the light that came to him. Do you know.

One was a powerful antipsychotic medication. If there are prescriptions you're supposed to be taking…

Agnes paused, her attention diverted by something across the water. Webb followed her sightline: a helicopter came flying low across the channel, blunt against the overcast sky, its metred chug climbing in pitch.

There he is, Webb said.

As the helicopter swung south, Webb hurried to the shoreline's edge to hail it. Swooping lower, the copter seemed to face him, wobble mid-air, its blades nearly invisible with velocity, its passengers concealed behind tinted glass. Webb sensed its appraisal and gave himself up to it with arms spread wide.

It came for me.

The copter pitched away from the shore and resumed its trajectory. Already winded, he moved to follow, but his bum ankle buckled and he went down. The copter kept on.

Agnes came to his side.

That's not Dred. It's just the fishing charter, picking up those men.

Watching the copter vanish around the island's northern point, he felt bludgeoned with disappointment: both in the indignity of kneeling there, wretched and impotent, and at being left behind.

He'd listened. He'd tried. Yet here he was: just another fool, yoked to the earth.

Agnes led him back through the village, saying little as they moved through the winding alleys. He was powerless to resist.

They arrived at a narrow wooden door. Agnes unlocked it and they ducked inside. Since arriving on Lamu, Webb hadn't thought to consider where Agnes herself resided, assuming she'd taken a rented room like his own. But this apartment, dim with drawn curtains, was apparently hers. It was tiny, with barely space to stand upright; entering, he whacked his head on the ceiling-mounted smoke alarm.

Agnes began rifling through the cupboards above a two-burner gas stove. Webb found a seat on the only couch, clearing a space among a pile of blankets, file folders, a Lenovo laptop. He pushed these things aside and leaned back against the thin foam cushions, breathing methodically.

I'm meant for it, he said.

Agnes returned.

Pardon me?

It's supposed to happen. I'm supposed to be here.

People often arrive here with specific expectations, she said, standing over him. And they're often disappointed. Here.

She presented him with a cloth dripping cold water.

For your face. You look swollen.

He took it.

The stove is on low, she said. We'll eat soon. I need a shower and a short nap. Make yourself comfortable. Hopefully the electricity remains on.

She withdrew down the hall. He pressed the cloth to his face, listening: from the bathroom came the mechanical thunk of piping, then the lap of unsteady water pressure. The stove hissed.

Outside, thunder came in filtered, complicated echoes. Webb thought of Imma and her premonitions. She was likely somewhere over northern Tanzania right now, the airliner in flames and plummeting through a lightning-crazed sky as she poked her tongue through her teeth.

He felt in his pockets. All he had was his room key, a few shillings, and, as always, Dred's recorder. There were only a few minutes of audio remaining. Dabbing his face with the cloth, he turned the recorder over in his hands.

In the technology sector, there is forever a race for the new. These self-styled pioneers are in actuality mere hirelings, endlessly fretting over who is trimming production costs where, who is shipping on what deadline, who can boast what feat of infinitesimal innovation. These are measly accomplishments by unimpressive men. Overweight, sexually incapable milksops. No true sight is possible when all you read are lines of code. You see no history, with all its misdirection, and so you see nothing. Just last month I visited the Herzog August Bibliothek in Wolfenbüttel to view the Gospels of Henry the Lion. I know old Welf to be my predecessor, spiritually and likely genetically, and through his artifacts I see proof of my dynastic birthright. I know his frustrations and vindication in the conquering of Bardowick. That kind of knowledge is something you can't experience in a laboratory conducting embedded systems testing. Interjection here, a note to incorporate my extensive notes from January regarding the abolishment of museums. And then, now.

A pause, a clunk, then the track ended. And with that, he'd come to the end of the recordings.

The water in the bathroom stopped. A door opened, followed by the creak of floorboards. Webb stood, leaving the recorder and wet cloth on the couch, and went to the kitchen. Here were chipped tiles, a sink streaked with rust. A large potted palm stood in the corner. On the stove, a stewpot issued fishy vapours. A small pile of books was stacked next to the fridge: a Good News Bible, an LSAT study guide, a Jon Krakauer paperback. And, to his dismay, among them: Natalie's book, with several pages marked by sticky notes. He opened to one: *A lot of people say Los Angeles is a place where dreams go to die. Maybe it is. But, you know, dreams can die anywhere. For a certain kind of dream, there's only one place where it can survive. And maybe even come true.*

The evidence would suggest he'd written these words, or at least typed them. But the sentiment here was incomprehensible to him now. Worse: contemptible, shameful. Here was an abhorrent text, and he'd been its obedient scribe. He placed the book in the sink and ran the faucet on high, letting the water flow over and into its pages. It had to be done. Let the cut-rate paper stock moulder. Let this execrable testament be banished from existence. Let the words die.

He placed his hands in the faucet's stream and watched them tremble. But he held fast, commanding his hyper-reflexive muscles to loosen. After a while, they did.

The bedroom down the hall had no door, only a curtain of woven beads. A single-panel window, glazed with rain, was shut tight. The room bore a smell of human warmth. On a mattress and box spring, Agnes lay facing the wall, a blanket around her shoulders. Webb stood in the entrance, the curtain's beads clinking down his shoulders like a braided mane. A digital clock sat on a shelf; he watched an entire minute process and redisplay before moving.

He lowered himself onto the mattress, aware of the springs' wince. His damp clothes chafed; his eyes itched. Agnes remained unstirred. Above them, the clock's readout tracked minutes. Webb slowly curled over onto his side and swallowed, conscious of his throat's click. His eyes fell shut—he was tired, very tired, but knew rest wouldn't come.

When he opened his eyes, he found Agnes now lying on her back, staring at the ceiling, her lips pursed tight. The expression on her face was one of absolute fury.

He leaped from the bed and fled the room.

YES, BY PROFESSION HE'D CONSIDERED HIMSELF A WRITER, though obliged to his trade only as a deforestation labourer feels beholden to the acres he razes: work to be surmounted, invoices to clear. He was no visionary, like Wordsworth, whose ambition was to sing a human song, rejoicing in *the presence of truth as our visible friend and hourly companion*, or like Natalie, who hoped her story, sung in its own graphic, gossipy refrains, might *inspire young women everywhere to believe in themselves, in their bodies (no matter what size or shape!), and in their ability to achieve great things despite the odds*— or so read the marketing copy. Webb had never made any claims of sagacity; his aperture was always, intentionally or not, dialled to minimum. But even at his most befogged, he felt the certainty of things inevitable, a carnivorous and brutish future. Of course Natalie would meet her end, her lungs surrendering and her body, so delicate yet so resilient to manipulation, subdued by a combination of benzodiazepines and cocaine during a sudden relapse, spurred by a bad weekend surrounded by bad people—it was simply meant to be, just as Webb's father was meant to die alone and afraid in the emergency ward, a bedsheet pulled to his throat as his heart arrested. Certainty, or the idea of certainty generated in rewrites and fact-checking, stabilizes such endings and gives them weight. This was Webb's job: he was no visionary, merely a clerk committed to balancing others' accounts.

In the rain, with night falling, navigating the village's pathways proved even trickier. The island had become a frustrating purgatory of interplaying forces without meaning: *the shape that has no shape*. By now he understood to let instinct be his guide, and pushed on. After several twists and dead ends, he emerged at the village's outskirts, back facing the beach. The wind hit him like a haymaker.

The afternoon storms rolling in off the Long Island Sound often lasted well into the evening. Webb had watched for what seemed like hours as the man in the K-Way ran lengths of the beach in the pounding rain, stopping occasionally to park himself on the sand and stare out at the water, then resuming. Here was a figure depleted, as insubstantial as a wisp of light.

The man in the storm was, of course, Webb's father. His spells had begun well before Connecticut, and presumably long before Webb, young and self-immersed, began to notice. As these episodes increased in frequency and depth, any trace of his father's former self wavered in and out of accessibility. Leaving the city had been a necessary act of preservation, but nothing had been solved. In the placid town, near the seashore, in hours of CNBC broadcasts, Webb watched his father search desperately for something. But whatever he expected to find simply wasn't there.

When his father finally came plodding back up to the house that day after his run, sopping and shivering, he'd fallen into his seat at the kitchen table with the unmistakable look of one beaten. He sipped a glass of water and accepted a plate without comment. Webb and his sister poked at their overgrilled hamburgers and now-cold potatoes, waiting for some cue, some explanation. His mother too had remained unusually quiet—more than anyone, she saw where things were soon headed.

Now Webb was the man in the storm, baffled by his situation and reeling against latitudes, looking out to the horizon for clues to his own mysteries. Surely there were CIA drones or targeting satellites on patrol in those clouds, tracking all breaches with time-stamped surveillance: this was, after all, still the modern world, woven with its networks—no one was truly *alone* anymore. But he also felt he'd strayed outside any such jurisdiction; now was the time to overcome all regulation. Out in the farthest reaches, there were still shipwrecks and escapes. Dred Hausen, gun-running profiteer and administrator of death, had been deemed deserving to stroll the exclusive corridors of a hidden world. He'd found something that other, lesser men could not. Now Webb stood ready to claim that light for himself. To offer whatever sacrifice. He whispered it aloud: *I'm here*.

Shuffling along the water's edge, he passed a hillside of spiny acacias, the blanched walls of old fortifications at the crest. Another uncertain measure of time passed before he realized he wasn't alone. A figure was trailing him along the shore, about fifty yards back. At first he took it to be one of the Aussie lunks, still hungry to assert supremacy. He continued, arriving at a point where the sand ahead sank into an untraversable trench, widening with rushing water and clogs of black seaweed. Here he paused, watching the foamy tendrils flow in, then drain back out. He braced himself, then turned to face his pursuer.

His sensors had been wrong; it was the American dude, the back-packer. He wore a rain jacket loose over a Phoenix Suns jersey. The green bandana was back.

Afraid to ask what you're doing out here, the dude shouted over the wind, pulling back his hood.

Me? I'm looking.

Yeah? For what?

For you. You're all I have right now.

The dude cocked his head, a touch of amusement.

Well, *mortgaged times*. Right?

Webb didn't answer. The dude reached into his jacket's pocket and produced one of those undersized mangoes.

Got one of those for me? Webb said.

The dude reached into his pocket for another mango and tossed it over.

And that, Webb said.

Meaning the knife. The dude hesitated, then flipped it around to offer it handle-first. Webb held it firm, feeling its weight.

I'll be out of here soon, the dude said. Headed to the Gulf of Aden this week, if everything pans out. Makes me sad to leave.

He looked up at the sky, taking an evaluative breath.

This rain feels good.

Webb's intended move was for the knife to squarely enter the dude's throat. But the manoeuvre wasn't clean, nor delivered with confidence, and he flinched away before the blade landed. Its edge met his left cheek, loosing an instant slash of red. Yet the dude raised no defence, no fingers to the wound; his expression displayed only shock. The next strike was more decisive. The blade entered the base of his neck, just above his collarbone. It found a softness there, and went deep. Webb threw his weight behind the knife, pushing deeper, but in doing so lost his foothold. The dude grabbed at Webb's sleeve and they both slipped, tumbling down into the rushing trench.

Thigh-deep in water, Webb sloshed through the waves, limping against his ankle, and climbed on top of the dude, planting a knee on his chest and pressing down. Dark clouds seeped into the lapping foam. The dude flailed against this pressure, clawing at the sand, at the knife embedded in his neck, but still made no audible cry. Clutching the jacket's collar, Webb dug his fingers into the wet earth, scooping up wads of muck and twists of seaweed and smeared it onto the dude's half-submerged face. The gasping mouth, the astonished eyes—all was erased. The dude thrashed with his arms, but there was no strength behind his movement, and eventually it abated. The jacket's fanned plastic bobbed in the water, the knife's blade poking upward like a mast.

Webb looked out at the water. He was aware of lightning, somewhere, possibly. As he caught his wind, he took the mango from his pocket and attempted a bite, but the unpeeled skin resisted his teeth. He pitched the fruit aside.

And then I saw it, coming in. It came for me.

More time passed. He waited, watching the waves. Nothing happened.

Again, he said it: *I'm here.* And again, his announcement went unanswered.

Tromping through the water, he was able to manoeuvre the dude to the trench's edge. He tore off the rain jacket and allowed the water to carry it away, then wrenched the knife free and let it sink, begone to the mire. With great effort, he hauled the body by its ankles back onto dry sand. There Webb fell to his knees, panting. Something whopped in the vicinity of his sternum. But he continued.

He took the dude under his arms and dragged him up the abutting slope. It was a tough climb, requiring a multi-staged sequence of attempts with pauses to regain his breath. Finally, he reached the ridge's summit, panting and dripping. Squinting against the dark, he discerned a shallow depression farther uphill among the shrubs and brush. He pulled the dude by his feet and positioned him there, fashioning a cover with palmfuls of sand topped by a layer of gangly branches. In the dark, it was impossible to gauge any whether any of this was effective.

Bent over, cradling his head in his arms, he fought to slow his body's systems, compelling his rib cage to not erupt. He suppressed an urge to sob.

Then: something crackled in the nearby trees. He spun to look, but saw nothing. He remained still, wild-eyed, reluctant to breathe. After a few seconds, he again heard the distinct crunch of feet on branches. This wasn't the wind's respiration, or the settling of rainfall. He had a witness.

Webb rose to his feet, and yes: a figure was there, shrinking back into the trees, then scurrying downhill. Webb launched in pursuit. An indistinct path zagged down the ridge's other side, flanked by reservoirs of rainwater. He placed his faith in this path. But hurrying down, he missed a drop, and his aggrieved ankle gave way. He slipped ass-first down the slope, slamming his coccyx into a knuckle of roots. An efflux of pain threatened to steal his consciousness.

He remained there, deactivated. The sky shrank. Coarse twigs pecked at his ears. The heat in his chest went nuclear. Rain cried down his cheeks, though his mouth was parched; he wished he hadn't tossed away the mango. No further sign appeared of his observer, or anyone else.

Now, he thought, would be a good time to give up. Here was the furthest reach of his powers. He closed his eyes, again bracing for any signal, any jolt. He breathed in the salty air, waiting to see what would happen. Nothing did.

EVEN BEFORE HE'D SET DOWN HIS BAGS, it was clear something had gone wrong. The ripe stench of backed-up water hung throughout the house. In the kitchen, he found the new flooring, still several installments from being paid off, in ruins. Last seen as immaculate butterscotch oak, it now lay coated in a gummous brownish film and steeping in semi-dry feculence.

There were calls he would have to make, complaints to wage, accountability to be demanded. But he couldn't take that on, not yet. He toed off his wet shoes and left them in the hallway.

In the bathroom, he ran the tub. Steam rose. He peeled off his clothes, then cleared a streak on the mirror. His face was puffy, redder than ever, cragged with furrows. The equatorial sun had not been kind.

He'd woken late in the morning, back in his room. He sat up, his hands shaky and his vision cloudy, fighting to parse the state of his present situation. The dishevelment was distressing: the floor a mess of his grimy clothes and soiled towels, sills lined with bottles, the infernal mosquito net hopelessly tangled.

It grows and grows and eats you from inside out.

And when the knock came at his door, he felt no sense of alarm; all was surely transpiring as it was meant to. It was Agnes, her canvas tote bag over her shoulder packed with papers and folders. Webb invited her in, but she remained in the doorway.

We've had a change of plans. There's a reservation for you on KLM for this evening.

Today? Tonight?

We'll have you back home as soon as possible.

I don't understand.

She reached into the bag and produced an envelope, handing it to him. It bore the DHG corporate logo, no other markings.

I don't understand, he said again, and it sounded even more use-less a second time.

The ferry departs in an hour. Jai will have someone come up shortly and help you with your bags. We'll be in touch with next steps.

Agnes extended a hand. Good luck, Webber.

There seemed nothing else to say. He shook her hand. You too.

Back in Nairobi, he'd been assigned a Mitsubishi Pajero with a driver already advised of his airport destination. But Webb sur-prised even himself by requesting he instead be dropped off at the Hilton on Mama Ngina Street, the tiled pillar he'd seen rising from downtown's drab business district. The driver, citing his instruc-tions, was resistant to alter plans, and Webb had to insist repeatedly until he relented and swung the car north.

The hotel reintroduced Webb to a world he understood: auto-mated, climate-controlled, fluffy. Prying off his musty clothes, he folded gelatinous into the king-size bed with his phone at his ear, barely aware of his own navigation of the KLM service line, absorb-ing the fee for the reservation change as readily as he absorbed two fingers of Crown Royal from the mini-bar. Provided these comforts, he found his tremors subsiding. Later, he elevatored to the outdoor pool, where he sat mummified in towels, watching two blond boys play in the shallow end. Their mother observed from a deck chair, and when she looked his way he offered one of the two Heinekens he'd brought down with him. They drank together, conversing in the easy shorthand of travellers temporarily isolated from the outside world. She was from London, and like Webb was headed home—the kids' father, an American, was a design consultant on President Kenyatta's industrialization initiatives, specializing in outsourcing implementation, and his firm was orchestrating the transformation of five thousand acres of land south of Nairobi into a technology hub. When asked, Webb said he was a travel writer re-viewing restaurants for the U.K. edition of *Esquire*. She seemed im-pressed, saying it sounded like a fun job. He said: sure, sometimes.

The woman confessed that she detested Kenya, as did her chil-dren, and her marriage was suffering as a result. She'd begged her husband to return to England, or even back to the States. But her husband took great pride in his international existence, having worked hard to escape his upbringing in a stifling suburb of Cleveland. Funny, Webb said, that's where my father grew up. Really, the woman said, and is he still with us? Nope, Webb said. He is no longer with us.

Back in his room, Webb stripped naked and ordered a Liam Neeson movie on pay-per-view, but conked out even before the opening credits had rolled. At some point in the night the bedside phone rang, but he ignored it, and nothing came of it.

The next morning the driver was waiting in the lobby to cart him to Jomo Kenyatta. Through the airport rituals, every security check and passport scan, he braced for sirens and batons. None came. A wave of metal detector, two glasses of white wine in the departure lounge, then he was buckling in for takeoff, struggling to sit still. As the sweep of miles faded into an unclocked slipstream, he dug out the envelope Agnes had given him, which he'd almost forgotten about. Inside was a note, a single letter-sized page on DHG letterhead.

Unforeseen developments necessitate logistical changes. Evidence has revealed your unsuitability for the task that lies ahead. Presumably your time has not been squandered. Take comfort as you will. Keep in mind that continuity is a shackling, and history is only one premise among many. But as the Honourable Dick Cheney once quipped, we go where the business is. Do well. DH.

At home he spent an entire day in bed, feverish and depleted, his stereo pumping an algorithmic playlist titled *Infinite Ambient Vibes* on repeat, well into the evening. The following morning brought several rounds of increasingly hostile phone calls with the contractors over the bungalow's destruction, with ambiguity as to what would happen next. He went about his day: an uncomfortable meeting with his accountant, a haircut in Koreatown, waiting in line at CVS to renew his prescriptions. Gradually, he began to feel better—or at least more like himself, which wasn't necessarily an improvement. Every time his phone jolted with an incoming message, he braced for the worst: authorities, evidence, interrogations. But no such call came. Each day's tide flowed into the next.

Finally, he opened a bottle of Nebbiolo, downed two alprazolam, and forced himself to sort through his neglected messages. Among the usual junk and minor work concerns, two emails stood out. The first was from Ellen, of considerable length and clearly composed with some circumspection, inventorying her many frustrations with her work—chiefly her paltry pay, but also in her view the unreasonable, even at times insulting, expectations Webb had placed on her over these last few years. An itemized list of her grievances was included in bullet points; he skimmed past this to her concluding paragraph.

In some other conceivable scenario, perhaps I might be able to continue on as your assistant in some reconfigured capacity. But my scenario, unlike yours, is one that exists squarely in reality. With this in mind, I hereby withdraw my services, immediately as of this writing. A final invoice is attached, the full amount of which I have already transferred to myself from your chequing account.

The second email was from Agnes. There was no text, but two files were attached. One was a memorandum closing his contract, tacking on a ten percent bonus to his initial fee and a revision to their non-disclosure agreement, requiring his signature. The other was an image titled *kizingoni-monday.jpeg*, a photograph from their fishing expedition, one he didn't remember being taken: Agnes and Webb on the beach, against a backdrop of that almost-monochrome junction of blue ocean and blue sky, standing next to Jonathan, dangling a gigantic marlin on a hook. Agnes looked agonized at being photographed, while Webb simpered like a buffoon, his sunglasses sliding down his sweaty nose. The marlin's mouth was spread wide, as if in surprise.

He stared at this picture for a while, then deleted the message. He went to the balcony, drenched in sunlight as always at this time of day. He listened to the dull palpitation of traffic, his neighbours' voices echoing down the twisting road below. The view of the mountains was clear, the air quality index moderate. From this sheltered roost he'd on occasion been tempted to scream, to project imbecilic rage out at the city. Today, he felt no such urge.

Somewhere foxes were observing the shifting atmosphere, muzzles raised as the skulk huddles, waiting out storms, their lamentation only for the rising and falling of suns. There would be recognition of a rightful order to things, dignified resistance when necessary, refuge sought when faced with dispiriting odds. Such grace was unachievable by the civilized, networked soul—it was something he could never access. The evidence had shown him unworthy. Any conclusion remained out of reach.

It was the first day of summer.

THE DEVIL IN THE MIRROR

IT MIGHT BE A DREAM, BUT IT FEELS LIKE A MEMORY. A teenage girl breaststrokes through rushing water. A starless sky stretches above. The shoreline behind her lit only with the staccato flickers of flashlights. Voices ring, calling after her. She swims away, treading through water where water shouldn't be. The current takes her. She's afraid of where she's headed. The lights gradually diminish. She is alone.

Early on Monday morning, Jovena Hoedemaeker stepped out the front door of her house on Mitchell Street to find a man on fire staggering across her lawn. She watched as the man moved through the overgrown grass and across the concrete walkway, then stumbled into the empty recycling bin at the driveway's foot. The flames lapped his clothes and his hair crackled like a barbecue pit, but the man himself issued no sound. On the street a car, a late-nineties Buick, surged with noxious smoke. From across the street three children watched, perched on BMX bikes. Jovena heard someone shout Get the phone! and a neighbour, a hefty ex-Marine, rushed forward with a wool blanket, tackling the flaming man with a smothering hug, yelling for everyone to stand clear. Jovena remained on her doorstep, holding her sweatshirt's hood tight at her throat. Sirens echoed from down the block as an ambulance and PFD trucks stormed the scene. Medics rushed to ease the man onto a stretcher while firefighters doused the Buick with foam. Soon the flames were tamed, leaving little more than a blackened chassis. Jovena checked the mailbox, took a last look at the street, then turned back inside.

She'd hoped today's mail might include something from Miguel, but there were only grocery store flyers, a plea from the Valley of the Sun United Way, and a Verizon bill addressed to her mother.

The last piece of mail, or any message at all, she'd received from her brother now sat on the kitchen counter. It wasn't actually a proper postcard, but a photograph he'd printed and stamped. It showed a taxi van on a crowded city street in what the postmark suggested to be Nairobi; emblazoned above the van's windshield, fierce yellow text read *We Be Jammin'*. The message Miguel had inscribed on the card's opposite side was brief, reporting that he'd recently returned to Kenya, was healthy and safe, was not in need of a money transfer, and pending visa details would hopefully soon be journeying to Mullaitivu, in Sri Lanka's north, or possibly the Arabian Peninsula. *Hit you back when I know what's what*, he wrote.

Jovena stood at the counter once again reading this message, drinking a mug of tap water. Weeks had passed since the card's arrival. Typically, her brother emailed or texted at every possibility— even a quick *yo*, just to establish contact. Where Miguel actually, really, was at this moment was impossible to know. Jovena opened a drawer and dug out a Nexium tablet for her esophagitis, swallowed it with the rest of the water, and headed back to her bedroom. Outside the sirens began again.

Riding the 7th Street bus south to Mother Teresa High School to begin the first day at her new job, Jovena was nervous. She'd been informed by Alison, the administrative supervisor, that the workday began promptly at eight o'clock, so she'd given herself ample time to arrive early. Staring out the window from the bus, she felt queasy: ordinary first-day jitters, but also an unshakable sensation of being on display. It was a feeling of disconsonance, of accusation, as if while she sat there among the other commuters, something marked her as an aberration. At several points during the ride, she feared she might have to exit early to vomit. But, to her relief, the bus soon arrived at her stop and she was released.

The school itself was an unremarkable building of anemic blue and beige, sided by a fenced-in basketball court and soccer field with portable bleachers. An undeveloped lot lay to the west, a range of patchy woods beyond. On her way to the main entrance, Jovena sighted coloured blotches out there, among the trees: students clustering before the morning bell.

After passing through the metal detectors, Jovena did as Alison had instructed, informing the security guard on duty who she was and the specifics of her appointment. The guard let her through without question. She moved through the empty halls, following signs for the main office. MTHS's interior was much like any other public high school's, at once austere and motley, the floor plan's irregular rectilinear angles making sightlines confusing, walls still decked with the handmade banners and trimmings of previous semesters.

The office had yet to open, so she waited in the hallway. Taking a seat in a moulded plastic chair, she felt her nausea returning, and with it all sorts of creeping fears. She commanded herself to concentrate on the actual task now facing her: to make positive first impressions, to not wilt under scrutiny, to not let things go the way they so often did.

Alison finally came charging down the hallway, jangling a bulky ring of dozens of keys. She ushered Jovena into the office, where they ran through the HR paperwork and a refresher on the job's varied priorities and duties.

Nothing you'll find too demanding, Alison said. Plus, summertime, everything's *slooooow*.

Alison introduced her to Billie Yu at the front desk, with whom she'd be working most closely. Billie, evidently a veteran in her role, seemed like someone it would be wise to make an ally. Alison left Billie to show Jovena to her desk, a corner station outfitted with nothing but a computer and a laminated staff directory pinned to the wall. She was free to decorate as she chose, Billie said, pics of boyfriends or internet memes or whatever, to make it as homey as possible. The only limitation was the school had been designated a scent-free zone, so any air fresheners or perfumed doohickeys would be nixed. Jovena said that wouldn't be a problem.

I set up a temporary password for your email login, Billie said. It's werewolf. Double-you ee are ee double-you oh ell eff.

Werewolf, Jovena repeated back as she keyed this in. Why that?
Billie smiled.
I guess I kind of wanted to freak you out a bit.

Walking back from the bus stop, Jovena found Mitchell Street by late afternoon in its usual summer drowse. Rock radio played from down the block; somewhere, a motorcycle engine hacked and revved. The Buick was now gone, leaving a smear of black ash on the asphalt. A scab of charred grass traced the flaming man's crossing across the lawn.

It was almost five years ago that this house had become theirs—five years since their lives' irrevocable alteration. From as early as Jovena could remember, she and Miguel and their mother had vaulted from state to state, maundering in debts and denials, settling wherever they could until circumstances inevitably tore them back into unrest: another Greyhound, another storage unit, another motel. The demons haunting their mother could be fled, but never escaped. Many a night she wept apologies to her children, sorry she'd led them into this life.

Bad decisions, she moaned. *Bad decisions* and bad people can cost you your life.

Following yet another season of turmoil, they'd been renting a triplex unit in Riverside, Jovena and Miguel sharing the one bed, their mother on a pullout in the living room. Among the slew of bills and overdraft fees came a thick envelope from a legal firm in Tempe; sifting through the pile, Jovena had almost tossed it, dismissing it as another collections notice, gussied up in legalese and a fancy logo. It wasn't.

The house in Coronado had belonged to a great-aunt Jovena and Miguel had never met, of whom their mother had never spoken, though upon receiving this notice she exalted the woman gushingly in memoriam. With this bestowal, their mother saw an overdue destiny fulfilled. Built almost a century ago, the small two-bedroom bungalow had received little in the way of upkeep, and now stood out as a neglected misfit among its better-maintained neighbours. Their mother nonetheless saw it as a palatial miracle, marvelling at the picture windows spilling forth morning light, the honeysuckle and weeping dalea sprouting in the backyard, praising it all as the realization of something that, tearful and quaking, she lacked the vocabulary to properly express. For her, the house sanctioned the possibility of something greater—to be a homeowner was to be a participant in the actual functioning world, a true American. They'd occupied so many places, temporary way stations up and down the coast, across states. This house, though, could be a *home*, with all the intimacy and pride such a sentiment implied. And so their mother's joy, even if brought on by desperation, was genuine.

But in the fugue of her agonizing final weeks, as she lay medicated to near paralysis, her vision of the house had changed. The ecstasies that had levitated her disappeared, surrendering to her old fits of paranoia. The evidence of decrepitude she'd previously overlooked, or had been unwilling to see—the wonky furnace, the mildewed siding, the caving foundations—she bemoaned as impossible hurdles cast against her, her many bedevilments returning with renewed hunger.

This distress was more than mere gloominess. Threats abounded. In every mirror or shadow she glimpsed sneaking, conspiratorial apparitions.

We don't belong here, she would shriek, staring teary-eyed into empty corners. *We aren't supposed to be here*.

It was impossible not to see all this structural ruin as exteriorizing the degeneration to which their mother eventually succumbed. And now the house was Jovena's, left in intestacy to be shared between her and Miguel. Their mother hadn't left a will; her personal worth stood at four hundred dollars in a checking account against a maxed-out Aspire Visa. But settlement of the estate proved only a minor headache, and applications filed through AHCCCS curtailed a crisis on outstanding medical bills. Throughout all this, selling the house was never suggested.

Owning it, and regulating all its troubles, was to manage a lease on something greater than just property. It was the only thing their family had ever really owned.

That evening Jovena was sitting on the couch, eating microwave risotto while watching *Shrek the Third* on TBS, when her phone buzzed. The caller came up as unknown. She hesitated, then set aside her plate to answer. At first she heard only breathing. She repeated: hello. More huffs and throaty sounds. She went to hang up, but then the person on the line spoke. I know all about you, it said in a deep, calm voice. *You're a pig.* Jovena asked who it was. The voice said: *You're a pig and there's evil in your soul.* Jovena thought she recognized the voice, but no name or face came to mind. The voice said: *and even when you think the door behind you is closed, another one opens.* Then, silence. Jovena sat still, the phone pressed against her ear. After a few seconds, she rang back the incoming number, but received only a recording: *Your call could not be completed as dialled.*

THE BOMB SCARES HAD BEGUN just after the Christmas break. The first message had been left on the main office voice mail, so no one at Mother Teresa had spoken directly to the caller; described as young, or young-sounding, and male, he'd relayed in detail the nature and quantity of explosives planted in the school, but not their exact location. Nothing actually came of it, but as school board policy was to treat every possible emergency with utmost seriousness, security procedures were subsequently taken that to some seemed unnecessarily rigorous: evacuation drills, procedural checklists, tightened traffic monitoring, upgrades of existing facilities. Similar threats followed in subsequent weeks, but as any traceable evidence failed to emerge, each successive round of cautionary procedures seemed less justifiable.

Toward winter's end, eleventh-grader Wesley Drimmer was reported missing by his parents. This incident was disclosed to the students in morning announcements, a carefully worded missive framed as an appeal for information—there was a worry that, with Wesley being one of those kids of an insubordinate bent, publicizing his disappearance in any overtly dramatic fashion might lead others to withhold any details. It was optimistically assumed that Wesley had simply run away and would soon return, as young people did, though no evidence supported this possibility. The case remained open.

Early one morning in late March, a sophomore reported entering the school's basement drama studio to find the hacked remains of departmental instructor Jean-Michel Lavoir. Police immediately shut the school down, and by the day's end Lavoir's common-law girlfriend had been taken into custody, though no confession was reported. The studio remained closed for the remainder of the semester, with any students' incomplete credits to be made up over the summer or, optionally, the following fall. The memorial service was attended by hundreds; the MTHS senior choir sang an excerpt from the fourth movement of Brahms's *Requiem*.

A grim mood befell the school. The sight of uniformed officers on school grounds had become common, and any prolonged student gatherings after official hours were discouraged. Occasionally, morale spiked: a divisional win in girls' volleyball, two tenth-graders earning honours at a city-wide science exhibition sponsored by Intel. But such rises were short-lived, and any jubilation felt strained. Everyone was frazzled and anxious, and the general feeling was that all these problems would cease with semester's end.

The final weeks of classes brought the usual angst of exams, capped off with an afternoon graduation ceremony held on the east field, featuring a rousing speech from valedictorian Brittany Wothousin. The theme of her well-received address was *What does America of the future look like to you?*

MTHS served as the district's base for the summer session. With an unusually high number of students picking up credits following the previous semester's disruptions, along with the usual flunkers or stragglers bussed in from proximal zones, the provisional staff of part-timers faced a busy June. Among those who'd opted to take on this term, the collective spirit was of mild umbrage, of malaise, of just getting it over with. Even more than in past years, these weeks felt like little more than epilogue.

By the end of her first week, Jovena was already swamped. There were months of spreadsheets to be cross-checked and reams of left-over filings for the PUHSD office, mundane clerical work that Billie referred to as *the real gruel*. The possibility of Jovena being brought on full-time come fall was touched upon in her first interview, but had not been mentioned since. For now, she dug in on the tasks at hand. Days ticked by.

As she moused through endless entries, hour by hour, a narcosis crept over her, and she found her face drawn closer and closer to her monitor's screen.

She was roused by Billie, at her station, swivelling to face her.

You okay? The system's making sense? Network and everything?

So far.

You're already disgruntled as hell.

I'm not. Really.

The kids, they're awful, aren't they?

This was more of a statement than a question. Jovena didn't know how to respond.

Has he come by to harass you yet?

Billie thumbed in the direction of the door opposite Jovena's corner. This led to the office of principal Rick Ortigosa, who she'd yet to encounter. Budget talks were underway at the district board, necessitating his being downtown all week. In the meantime, his door had remained shut.

Not yet, she said.

He'll come over and try to intimidate you. He does that. He's a smug prick.

Oh.

Billie drummed restive fingers on her knees. She checked her computer, then swivelled back to face Jovena.

Can I fetch you an iced capp? I'm going. On me.

I'm not really a coffee person.

Billie scowled.

What? That's just demented. But I do see that certain glow in your cheeks. High on life.

In her purse, Jovena's phone buzzed. She made no move to answer.

You answering that? Billie said.

Sorry?

Your phone's ringing.

Oh. I'm sorry.

Jovena reached and silenced the phone's ringer without looking at it, then went back to concentrating on her spreadsheets. Billie scrutinized her for a moment, then decisively swivelled back around.

For the first few days, Jovena had brought her lunch from home. But this was a chore that required advance planning and effort, so she began taking her breaks at a taqueria a few blocks from the school, an unassuming, three-table place along a bleak stretch of retail strips and auto shops, where she could enjoy a reprieve of temporary invisibility. A window booth became her regular station, looking out on a sleepy intersection below a Coors Light billboard.

She sat there, eating a carne asada taco and half-reading a discarded newspaper, a headline screaming DOZENS PERISH IN KHANH HOA LANDSLIDE. A bell rang at the door as a man in a grey track suit entered. White-haired and fidgety, he stood by the door, taking in the room and its few occupants. Jovena averted her eyes, turning back to her paper, but it was too late. The man started over.

I can tell, he said, standing over her.

I'm sorry?

By your face, that smile.

Jovena looked up. She wasn't smiling.

You have a secret. But if you let it out, it gets swallowed by language. The evildoers feed on the silence. They'll cut out your spine. That's how they baptize you.

Jovena looked around, but the restaurant's only other patron, a man in a work coverall hunched over a plate of chilaquiles, paid no notice.

My father sacrificed me to the hog breeders. He had the snout of a wolf and legs made of clay. My father was a holy man. And an evildoer. He thought he could escape this world with a wish. But his legs trapped him to the ground. That was his curse.

Oh.

The man's eyes darted around the restaurant. The old Mexican woman behind the counter looked on, but kept quiet.

We shouldn't even be in here, the man said. The air conditioning. It blisters.

He leaned in further. His clothes, something on him, gave off an odour like burnt chocolate.

Vanity keeps the townspeople from lighting fires. You see?

I don't, Jovena said.

It's the sea and the storm. The way the light bleeds. It knows your malediction.

Please, Jovena said, just…leave me alone.

The man's expression shifted. His eyes widened. He backed away, waving a damning finger at her.

Oh, he growled. You do see. You *do*.

Jovena watched as the man left. The door's bell dinged. She took a sip of water from her paper cup, then coughed it back up. Water spilled onto the table, into her food, down her blouse. She hurriedly mopped up the mess she'd made with her sleeve, hoping no one had witnessed this embarrassment. No one had.

She returned from lunch to find a student leaning against Billie's vacant desk. The girl had taken a framed photograph of Denise, Billie's daughter, from the desk and was turning it over in her hands.

Please don't touch that, Jovena said.

The girl looked at her, then returned the photo to its place.

I need a blue slip.

Jovena moved to her own desk and moused her computer back to life, keeping an eye on the girl: backpacked, dark-haired, wearing thick-framed glasses, she floated incautiously through the office, her ease here obvious.

Are you replacing Akua? the girl asked. Because Akua was pretty incompetent. Not surprised she got the shitcan.

I have no idea where Billie keeps the blue slips, Jovena said. Maybe you should come back later.

Without hesitation, the girl snatched a pad from a shelf and presented it to Jovena. Here, evidently, were the blue slips.

Alejandra Ortigosa. I can spell it for you?

Jovena peeled a slip from the pad and began to fill it out, repeating: *Ortigosa*. As in, it was presumably meant to be understood, Rick Ortigosa.

I need a reason for excusal, Jovena said.

Before the girl responded, Billie charged in, laden with Office-Max bags. She threw the bags on her desk, clearly upset. Seeing Alejandra there, she drooped.

Allie honey. Holy hell.

The halls rang with a clamour: classrooms emptying, questioning voices. Jovena watched as Alejandra thumbed her phone, scowling at what she saw there. Then the alarms sounded.

Let's all just relax, Billie shouted.

Following drill procedure, the evacuating students assembled in the parking lot, corralled into designated zones by signalling teachers, who themselves seemed unclear about the process. The feeling was less of fear than of exasperation; these scares were now habitual, and the students seemed to almost savour the conflicted expectations of these exercises.

This is a thousand percent traumatizing. Oh my god.

So sick of this.

I will seriously fight the guy that did this one. I'm a serious guy ready to fight.

Where's the *media*?

I will seriously fight the media.

Jovena and Alejandra followed Billie to a position near the bleachers.

Another one called in, Billie said, checking her phone.

This is a bomb threat? Jovena asked.

Or some idiot wanted to get out of their biology quiz. Who knows. But believe me, one day one of these half-toasted Pop-Tarts whips out an AK-47. And then, yikes.

Jovena looked to Alejandra, who rolled her eyes.

The alarms ceased. A few kids whooped. A tall man in a tan suit approached the bleachers, a security guard tailing him.

Do we know the story? Billie asked them.

Someone reported a kid on the third floor waving a pistol, the guard said. Turns out it's just a Maglite. But some folks are, like, hello.

The man removed his jacket and slung it over his shoulder, then went to Alejandra, wrapping a custodial arm around her. This, Jovena surmised, was Rick Ortigosa, principal and father.

Are we all out? he said.

Think so, Jovena said, though in truth she had no idea.

Ortigosa craned his neck to survey the lot and the students milling about: a gesture connoting either how he took this situation personally, or was intent on presenting appearances that he did.

Words escape me. Where are we headed, with all this *chaos*?

It was unclear if this question demanded an answer; no one volunteered one. Across the lot, a student was shouting *human rights human rights*.

Let's cut our losses and get all these kids home, Ortigosa said.

He turned to Billie.

Mind getting Allie back to her mother's place?

Billie puckered her lips.

Actually left my car at home today.

Then take my Tahoe. I'll call a cab. I need to stick around here for a bit.

Billie grimaced.

There's some issues, she said. With my licence.

A pause. Rick regarded her with the sort of disdain that bespoke a history between them.

Christ, Billie. You rack another suspension and we'll need to take this conversation elsewhere.

Dad, Alejandra groaned, I'll just take the bus.

Rick looked displeased. He eyed each of them in turn, landing on Jovena.

You.

Steering the hulking SUV through the lot, then onto the boulevard, was like saddling an ornery bronco. Jovena had barely driven in recent years, aside from chauffeuring her mother to church in their fatigued old Golf until it met its humble demise. This was not like that.

If someone wanted to really shake things up, Alejandra said, they'd kidnap the governor or something. This is just *weak*.

Just thank god it was a false alarm, Jovena said, eyes glued ahead.

One day it won't be.

Jovena braked hard at a crosswalk. Students streamed past, enlivened by an unexpected afternoon of freedom. One boy, sighting Alejandra, made a gesture Jovena didn't understand, but by Alejandra's unamused expression, she took it to be something offensive and sexual.

Some of these kids are real sociopaths, Alejandra said.

You know, you're one yourself.

I'm not a sociopath.

I mean a kid. You're a kid too.

Hm.

As they resumed motion, merging into traffic, Alejandra abruptly reached over and put a hand on Jovena's arm.

Turn right.

Your father said you're up north, near 36th?

Just take a right. Please. I'll show you where.

Jovena did as ordered, turning south. Alejandra eased back in her seat, rubbing her elbow.

Thank you.

Jovena's attentions toggled between the dashboard's perplexing graphical menus and Alejandra at her side: checking her phone, running fingers through her hair. They continued down the boulevard, headed for the freeway and into a smeary afternoon sun, their new destination still left unstated. Alejandra put her phone away, sighing.

There's so much that nobody even sees.

Sees?

Past all of this. Inside of it. Everyone blocks it off. But it's there, blasting us, all the time. Screaming at us. They just don't want to hear what it's saying. They'll hear it soon, though.

I'm not sure I...

Oh, nothing. Forget it.

They'd gone many blocks south, toward an area of the city Jovena didn't know. Crossing an overpass, the dry bed of the Salt

River lay to both sides, busy with rebuking safety signage, its winding contours patched with brush.

Slow down, Alejandra said. Here.

There was nothing there, only a chain-link fence, the river's ditch, a set of derelict utility buildings about a hundred yards in.

But your father said home.

Yeah, right here...

Jovena signalled and pulled over to the road's shoulder. Alejandra turned, cupping her hands in an exaggerated bow.

Thank you thank you *thank you*. Don't tell Dad. Really. He's got high blood pressure. Please.

Her eyes pleaded. Jovena understood.

I won't.

Alejandra smiled, then sprang from the car. She went to a specific point in the fence, found a break in the chains and peeled it back, then ducked to pass through, continuing down the riverbank before vanishing from sight. Jovena watched after her for a moment, then drove away.

THERE IS A RARE BREED OF BELLFLOWER that grows only in the southern areas of Chile, primarily in the hilly forests along Chapo Lake, near the Calbuco volcano. Considered the most striking of its genus *Lapageria*, its petals are a pale pink, almost translucent, and it bears no scent, produces no fruit, and flourishes only in extreme humidity. Old stories said this bellflower had magical properties, bringing fortune to those able to keep it healthy and nourished; conversely, those who were not vigilant enough to tend it through its delicate lifespan would likewise decline during their own earthly tenure. Jovena's mother had shared memories of hunting the flower near her home in Quillaipe, of long afternoons shaking away the rain while pawing the trees of roadside forests, looking for those singular lip-like petals. A hunt could last hours, whole days, with little success. And even if one found a perfect specimen of the flower, the fickle bellflower defied harvesting, as its seeds or cuttings often refused to germinate in soil it hadn't chosen for itself. In this, the bellflower's rarity carried more meaning than the flower itself.

One night, Jovena, then barely a teenager, was trying to sleep when her mother came and knelt at her bedside. Their one-bedroom apartment in Poway had no light fixtures in the ceilings, so they relied on cheap floor lamps from Walmart, and in the dimness, her mother's face was sunken and raw-boned. Miguel was passed out on his mattress on the floor, but Jovena didn't bother pretending to be asleep; her mother could tell. She told Jovena that even though things were tough right then, one day she'd look back on these times as happy. To this, Jovena said nothing. Her mother asked if Jovena was angry with her. Jovena said no, of course not.

Her mother asked if she remembered the stories she'd been told of the bellflower. Jovena said she did. Jovena's mother warned her to not dismiss the stories as mere superstition. The stories were important, and Jovena should believe in them.

When I was pregnant, just before I left home, I planted a flower for you on the volcano, her mother said. I collected clippings from six other flowers and laid them all in the soil. They say you can't just plant it wherever you want. Bad stuff might happen. They say if you got lost up in those mountains, you could get eaten by a demon. But I knew I was blessed. *You* are my blessing. I tucked the flower into the wettest patch of ground I could find, high up there, where things grow free. And I bet it's still there.

Jovena said she really didn't think that was possible.

Well, her mother said, rising from the floor, who cares what you think.

Jovena knocked at Rick Ortigosa's office. Receiving no answer, she entered. Other than a window overlooking the athletics field, a large desk, and a phalanx of metal file cabinets, the office's most significant feature was a colourful backdrop for a previous Thanksgiving fundraiser, set against one wall: an oversized, googly-eyed, cardboard turkey, collapsed into sections.

Of course she'd returned Ortigosa's SUV to his reserved space, terrified of scuffing the bumper against the curb as she backed in, then pulled out and back in several times, ensuring as perfect a perpendicular alignment as she could manage. In her relief at the task's completion, she'd hurried to the bus stop and straight home. Only during this morning's commute did she find the Tahoe's keys still in her sweatshirt pocket.

This forgetfulness was worrying. It was happening more and more of late. This was her mother's type of trouble, such lapses in time, lapses in location. Even before her illness, she'd dwelled in a thick fog of seething. Each parking lot was a battleground, every sidewalk passerby another agent of malice. Time's passage meant nothing, and no wisdom was ever gained: her mind's countless battles raged simultaneously, and old grudges from years before could return unpredictably, often with great venom. The hope had been that their relocation to Phoenix, to claim the house and all it represented, would bring peace.

For Jovena, the life they'd made would always be someone else's. Phoenix was a beige wasteland of hostility, rampant with squinting neighbours and white ogres in pickup trucks. It was too flat, too open, too raked in sun. And the house, despite the name on the deed, still carried traces of its previous occupants and would never really be theirs. Through a placement agency, she found an administrative job in the San Diego school system that was open immediately. Against her mother's pleas, Jovena headed back west down Interstate 10.

In San Diego, things went badly.

In the heat of Jovena's ensuing legal throes came her mother's muttered early-morning phone calls, complaints of light-headedness and shortness of breath, then discouraging ultrasound results and a dismal prognosis of hepatic encephalopathy. Her health insurance was a labyrinthine, decades-deep mess of conditions and unmet deadlines—Arizona was maybe the worst place in America to be poor and sick. By then, Miguel was already somewhere in the Serengeti, another universe, return date unfixed. There was no way around it: Jovena was needed.

So she'd returned to Phoenix, leaving behind three months of postdated cheques and a month of meetings, *investigative proceedings*, scheduled with district management. The slow season that followed brought unbending schedules of tending to her mother's agonies between hospital stays: administering medicinal doses at specific intervals, frustrating calls to the HMO, constantly pureeing vegetables and making laundromat trips, working to sustain a weakened body that had long overextended its tenure. For months she dabbed apple juice from her asterixis-plagued mother's chin as they watched television from late afternoon to midnight. Invoices from the clinic arrived, and every week their tally ballooned, even as the patient herself shrank.

There's so much that nobody even sees.

Jovena now looked for a place to deposit the fob of keys. Ortigosa's desk bore neat piles of mail and papers, an unopened pack of Winstons, nail clippers, a stapled Best Buy receipt. Photos in frames:

Ortigosa himself, younger, arms locked with two other men, all in mud-spattered rugby shirts. Another showed Alejandra in a swim cap and bathing suit, an ornate medal around her neck. Here was the blue effulgence of a competition pool, nose plugs dangling by a strap, a crinkled smile that suggested unabashed pride, a security of self. This world knew nothing of fleeing apartments in the dead of night, of curling up against one's unconscious mother in a dark stairwell, of pernicious demons. There was, in this image, evidence of what might be called *bliss*.

Someone arrived at the door. *Definitely not ten thousand. It's like eight thousand and change. Don't try and preach morality to me, María.*

Jovena braced herself as Ortigosa entered, phone at ear. He moved past her to the desk, seemingly unperturbed at finding her in his office.

Get off your high horse, he told the phone. I will hang up. I'm seriously considering hanging up right now.

He sat, extending an open palm to Jovena. She was unsure what this meant. He mouthed the word: *keys*. Whispering a hurried apology, she handed them over.

Goddammit, he said to the phone. I have no interest sitting here eating crap while you...

He gripped the phone as if trying to squeeze it of some inner juice, then placed it face down on the desk. From his breast pocket he produced a pack of nicotine gum and jammed a piece in his mouth. His eyes remained on the desk as he chewed.

Ever try this stuff? Pretty raunchy.

I don't smoke, Jovena said.

I gnaw and gnaw and wait for the effects to kick in. But, nada. I'm a little keyed up these days. Stress levels are high.

There was a pause. Jovena wondered if this was her cue. But then he spoke.

You drove her right home.

Yes. I am so so sorry. I only realized this morning. I hope you weren't...

You two didn't stop anywhere.

Stop?

You went straight home? No detours?

Honestly, I'm not much of a driver. The traffic, you know. It gets hectic.

So you're saying no.

Jovena nodded. Ortigosa looked at her, chewing.

Hoedemaeker, he said. That your husband's name?

My father's.

And your people are from where.

I was born in Fullerton.

Okay. I'm really not supposed to ask this, but you don't have anything I'm going to want to know, do you? In terms of being undocumented or anything. I know how it is, I have cousins in Guerrero, and these days, they're... Actually, scratch that. I don't want to know. I *can't* know.

As Jovena sought a response to this, her phone vibrated in her pocket. She tried to ignore it, but Ortigosa gave a prompting look.

Sorry, she said.

Ortigosa waved dismissal as she answered. Once again, the caller came up as unknown.

You think you're free. A pig like you. Walking around in your pig stink.

Jovena felt her face instantly flash with heat, her neck's nape breaking into sweat.

You actually think you're getting away with something. But that door's gonna come flying open. Just a matter of time.

I think you have the wrong number, Jovena said, disconnecting and hiding the phone away.

Problem? Ortigosa asked.

Jovena forced a smile, squelching her stomach's revolt, ruing not taking her anti-reflux medication this morning.

Not feeling a hundred percent today, she said.

Well, if all works out, come fall we'll all be enjoying the benefits of the revised insurance coverage structure. If these pricks at the board

don't negotiate us back into the eighties. As is, it's pretty comprehensive. Best thing about teaching in this district.

Jovena's phone buzzed again in her pocket. She tried to ignore it,
but it persisted.

I'm not a teacher, she said.

Here were directories, inventories: pivot tables, sums and means,
formulae in urgent red, headers bolded in green—with each key-
stroke another entry, tabbed through in sequence, alphabetized
cells scrolling without end. The scale widened and contracted, the
tallies constantly adjusted. In these late-afternoon hours, with only
the fewest of stragglers prowling the halls, the ducts shooshing
and Billie's desk radio seeping 92.9 Jack FM, such numbness led
Jovena's thoughts to treacherous places.

I just want something to be devoted to. Completely. The lime
popsicles melted quickly in the afternoon sun, the sticky runoff
trickling down her hands. They occupied adjacent swings, their
feet buried in gritty sand. A playground, a place for children; a
popsicle, a thing for a child to eat.

Here was that long spring, and here was Tess, never bashful,
never even aware of any need for bashfulness as she lapped green
drippings from her wrists. Then, slurping down the final glob, she
pitched its straw into the bushes and began to swing. Clutching
the steel chain, she pumped her feet to gain velocity, her hair fan-
ning winglike around her head. When Jovena tried to mimic these
moves herself, her stomach flopped with the motion, forcing her
to abandon her attempts.

Tess: ageless, her attentions fleeting, her exuberance so easily
inflated. Such surety disguised the secret ache she surely must have
held inside: *just pure devotion and nothing else.*

Jovena heard someone saying her name. It took a second for her
to identify the origin: at the front desk, Billie was answering the
main line, telling the caller to hold. Cupping the phone, she looked
over, a question. Jovena felt her pulse jump—another call, another

threat. But she had no choice but to comply, and gestured for Billie to put the call through.

Am I speaking with... Is it *Jovena*? Last name Ho— I'm having a problem with this name.

The voice was an older woman's, brusque, a hint of a snarl.

Hoedemaeker. You are. Yes. That's me.

This is the office of Overseas Citizens Services at the U.S. State Department Bureau of Consular Affairs. Following up on a report you filed regarding a missing individual.

Oh.

You filed this report?

I... Yes. My brother.

Right. This is *Miguel*? Em eye gee you ee ell. Same last name.

Yes.

Now, your brother is currently where?

I don't know. He's missing.

I mean the region or territory.

Last I heard from him, he was in Nairobi. In Kenya. But that was, I mean, that was a while ago.

The OCS generally recommends waiting two to three weeks before reporting family members as missing.

Oh. I'd say it's been about that.

Two weeks? Or three?

I'd say three. No... Yes, it's been three. More than three.

I'm going to need you to hang on for a minute, the woman said.

Jovena heard a keyboard clacking, then silence. She pictured the woman at a desk like hers, a cubicle probably, similarly staring at a screen for hours on end.

Whether or not Miguel was truly missing, she couldn't know. Close to a year ago he'd had an experience that led him to undergo, by his own account, a seismic shift in worldview. Off from UCI for the summer, he'd been clocking hours at a Barnes & Noble in Redlands, and Jovena was then still employed in San Diego with the Unified School District, but both still managed to make it back to Phoenix for occasional visits. He usually made his way by bus or a hitched ride, but one weekend he'd pulled into the driveway atop a motorcycle, a growling Shadow VT1100C3, much to their mother's delight and Jovena's bemusement.

Later, he and Jovena sat over takeout burgers in the backyard while their mother took her nightly bath. There, Miguel had made his declaration: weeks before, he'd had a profound transformative experience, he said, a kind of awakening that triggered a spiritual survival instinct. And since then, he told her, he was done with living life as a semi-active participant. Done with conformity, done with pointlessness, done living with his mind shuttered. He'd received a message.

A message?

Yes, he said. Unquestionably, a message.

He described how earlier that month he'd taken the Honda out for an open-ended ride, end point undetermined, starting from his place in San Bernardino and extending farther southeast over a couple of days, led only by a desire for motion, until he reached the remote ends of the Texan Chihuahuan Desert. There he'd gone off the US-385 and headed miles into the unruly terrain, parking the bike in the shelter of a rock formation and continuing on foot into an unnamed canyon. There was no purpose to this, he'd told her, but he'd felt a palpable force summoning him—pulling me, he said. And instead of resisting his instincts, as he'd done for so long, he heeded this call, allowing it to draw him forward.

He'd arrived at the canyon's basin late in the afternoon. He found a spot on the arid soil and rested there, surrounded by yucca and creosote bushes, and sank into a dreamless sleep. When he woke, night had fallen and the temperature had plummeted. But the canyon was bright, the moon full in an unfiltered sky of stars. As Miguel described it, he sat up to find a break, or a kind of fracture, parting in the very air before him, as if a panel was sliding open in the night's reality. And again came that call: non-verbal, soundless, but insistent.

I felt something there, Miguel said. Unmistakable, an actual thing. And then he appeared.

Jovena asked who.

A man, wearing a long trench coat with big metal buttons, bare feet. He came toward me, then he turned and crouched in the dust over a pool of water, which hadn't been there before. He dipped his hands in the water and splashed it on his face. He looked right at me, and as the water dripped from his beard, I could see the drops hanging mid-air, as if time were slowing, or stopping. And I felt this huge relief, like this pressure being lifted. I could see that the pressure was time itself, and it came from my own limited perception of the universe. If I got past that limitation, I could free myself of it and be one with a universal reality. A universal truth.

As soon as I became self-conscious about what was happening, time started up again. The drops of water hit the pool's surface, and the pool began to overflow and spread, like oil burbling over the earth. The pool expanded until it became this shadow filling the entire canyon, or as much of it I could see. That's when I realized the man was gone.

I rode back home that night in a total daze, stopping only for a couple hours' shut-eye at a motel near Tucson. Only later on, after doing some research, did I really understand what had happened. It was a manifestation of this thing called *kashf*. A Sufi concept of revelation. *Mukashafa*, the unveiling, they say. The seeker comes into the presence of God. *Mushahadha*, bearing witness. And when that happens, the inner and outer senses unite. Our perception's all based on time, right? And time is nothing, really. Everything in our minds is just a re-enactment of the eternal. So human beings, all we really are is just a conduit for God's power. All that binds us together is this transference of energy. That's all we have. In *kashafa*, the mind glimpses proof of God's objective truth, which exists past time itself. It's serious stuff.

How did you learn this? Jovena asked.

I looked it up. You know.

So what was the message?

It was, he admitted, not so clear. But what was clear was there was a galaxy of experience out there, wonders to be beheld, and he'd never find wonder stacking bookshelves. The motorcycle was only one component of this awakening. Above all else, he needed to be mobile, unchained. A traveller on a quest for the truth. *Mukashafa*.

Jovena had no counter to any of this. Their family were non-practising Catholics; all these references were lost on her. She wasn't even certain was a Sufi was.

Most people go their entire lives without encountering any kind of truth, Miguel said, crunching his burger wrapper in his fist. Me, I'm not like that anymore. I have an *obligation*.

At the time, Jovena had said she understood what he meant. But she hadn't, and still didn't. Reaching for the impossible, harbouring lofty fantasies—this could only lead to resentment toward the lot one was given. Their family was unlucky and poor, as a lot of families just are. This was their state of being. She'd barely known her father; a lifelong addict and petty criminal, pathologically selfish and by all suggestions impenitent in his ways, he was now serving four years at La Tuna for involvement in robbing a Mobil station in Yucaipa. Since adolescence Miguel had lived in fear he might also be fated to a similar path; prone to fractious fits of brash resistance, his own eschewal of authority was a defining thing. Nothing riled him more than the prospect of accepting his own inconsequentiality.

And now he was gone, off seeking something greater and wilder. His absence clawed at her. He alone demanded nothing of her.

The woman from the State Department came back on the line.

Sorry for the holdup. So, question. Did you attempt to contact the American embassy over there?

I didn't know the right thing to do. I read a travel advisory on the—

That's fine, the women said, cutting her off. Those advisories don't necessarily reflect reality. It's always like, Al-Shabaab this and that. Sometimes there's updates just for updates. It's a thing. Right now all I need to know is what's in which file where. Where we have systemic discrepancies, that's where you're gonna get friction. We have the info you provided in your statement. Right now I'm going to send you back a confirmation and tracking number, with a way to upload a recent picture of your husband.

My brother.

Right. Hang on.

More clacking. The woman was an astonishingly fast typist.

I would tell you to try your best to not worry. Things almost always work themselves out. He's probably just…doing something.

Jovena almost said: of course he's *doing something*, he's on a spiritual journey. But she refrained, answering the woman's few remaining questions as best she could, taking her suggestion to note the direct extension to call when she checked back in later next week, and providing her own in return.

We hear this same story all the time, the woman said, and believe me, you've got nothing to get all wacko about. People go off the radar. It happens. But these days, no one really gets lost anymore.

After hanging up, Jovena sat back in her chair and drank from her Nalgene bottle, wondering if searching Al-Shabaab would trigger an alert on the network's content filter.

Things cool over here?

Billie came over, her purse slung over her shoulder.

I'm done up to April, Jovena said, indicating the complex colour-coded spreadsheet occupying her screen.

Billie didn't look. Yeah. So I'm busting out to meet my sister at that diarrhea palace on Jefferson for a liquid lunch. The one with the sign. You could tag along.

I'm fine, Jovena said. I'll get something down the street.

I realize this is sort of a cunty thing to say, but you're looking a little bedraggled.

Just tired, I guess. It's been so hot the last few nights.

I know you're still in, like, a preliminary phase, Billie said, but you really don't need to pretend to give so much of a shit. No one's peeking over your shoulder. Especially not this time of year.

I don't mind.

Billie looked at her wrist, as if checking the time. She didn't wear a watch.

Well. In my humble opinion, it's shiraz o'clock. Later.

Under untempered midday sun, the boys' B squad softball team executed drills on the west field, snatching grounders and receiving pop flies, their graceless moves governed by two junior coaches both wearing valiant but premature attempts at goatees. A hubbub rose from the infield: near third base, two bodies in bright blue uniforms scuffled in the dirt. A cry went out, and all flocked to cheer on the violence.

Jovena stood back near the enclosing fence, looking past the scene to the field's opposite periphery. There Alejandra and a girl Jovena didn't recognize sat on a bench, facing one another in some exchange of mutual engagement, though their attention was diverted by the melee now unfolding. The coaches blew whistles to defuse the skirmish, and the boys were torn from one another. This tussling realm of scrappy socialized competition, such playground carnage, the dirt-smeared faces, was all familiar to Jovena. Every school she'd known had been a place of nightmarish cruelty; that she now, as an adult, found employment in the education system was a strange irony not lost on her. *Better than cleaning houses*: this was the criterion by which her mother gauged any job. Anything, anything was better than menial labour.

Across the field, Alejandra and the other girl rose and started back along the sideline. Jovena mirrored their trajectory with the aim of intersecting with them at the far corner. The field stirred anew with resumed play.

Her phone buzzed. She hoped to ignore it, but the possibility existed of some emergency back at the deserted office. She was, technically, still on work hours.

That same voice: close and clear. *A lovely day. Bright and beautiful. And I know how much you appreciate beauty.*

Jovena stopped and turned away from the field. Her gastrointestinal tract burned and contorted.

But you, when you see something beautiful, you just want to ruin it. You can't stand to see it survive. That's your way. You destroy and destroy. That's all you do.

No, she tried.

Oh. The little pigeon starts to peck. Where're you laying your nest lately, baby bird? Doesn't matter. I know where to find you when the time comes. Might be sooner than you think. I do love sucking down that desert air.

The phone went silent. Jovena waited, unsure whether the connection had been lost. Across the field, Alejandra and the other girl had already passed through the parking lot to the street, and were now disappearing around the corner and out of sight.

At her usual table at the taqueria, Jovena stared into her lemonade and wondered how worried she should be about Miguel. Something had gone wrong—she felt it, no matter how irrationally, even if the directives issued by the State Department were right, even if *no one really gets lost anymore*. People did get lost, or lose themselves, all the time.

At the counter, two PhxPD officers in uniform, replete with armoured vests, were regaling the woman behind the counter and her teenage son with an animated re-enactment of an on-job incident.

And the guy is just, like, shaking. He's got his dinky little piece out, like this...

The policeman unholstered his pistol to demonstrate, holding it backward, the barrel pointed at himself.

...and he's all like, *Don't move!*

Laughter.

And we're like, hey, go ahead, buddy. Fire at will.

God help us, it's true, his partner said, wiping his eyes. Crackheads.

But seriously, the first officer said, mock-serious, in the end we were able to neutralize and apprehend the perp. Just whipped 'em out and...

Again, the backward-gun routine.

...*Stop or I'll shoot!*

More laughter.

As the woman at the counter handed the policemen a bag of tacos and two enormous sodas, the front door's bell dinged. The man Jovena had encountered here before entered, dressed in the same grey track suit. He cast a glazy look around the shop.

That's him, the woman said, pointing at the man. That guy threw the rock at Gloria.

The officers sipped their straws and watched with interest as the man tramped unsteadily down the row of tables. He had something tucked tightly under his arm and looked to be targeting Jovena. His former manic energy now seemed withdrawn.

I found this, the man whispered, his voice hoarse. Or should I say, it came into my possession. But it's not for me.

He placed the bundle on the table before her.

And it's not for you.

The man backed away, headed for the door. Only then did the policemen advance on him, grilling him about the rock he'd allegedly thrown. While they conducted their interrogation, Jovena examined the bundle placed before her: a small package, wrapped in a Best Buy flyer and bound in twine. Held in the twine's knot was a key of dull metal, what looked to be brass.

One of the policemen took the track-suited man by an arm.

Hold up, big papa. Let's just get you back to the puzzle factory and let these fine folks here get back to their jobs.

The man sagged into the officer's hold without resistance, allowing himself to be whisked out the door. The other officer came to Jovena's table, rubbing his palms together in a motion that gave the impression of much practice.

Hope that old coot doesn't have you spooked, the officer said. Lot of yo-yos on patrol around here lately. Must be something in the wind. I mean, you got to have empathy. But still, it's like, come on.

Back on school grounds, Jovena found a recessed area by the south entrance and took a seat on the concrete steps. Turning the bundled package over in her hands, she felt a familiar pull, the feeling of time slackening.

Miguel: *Everything in our minds is just a re-enactment of the eternal.*

As she removed the key at the knot's centre, the twine unravelled. The newspaper fell away, revealing its contents.

Wrapped inside was a sparrow, dead, crusted with blood.

It's not for you.

Jovena leaped to her feet and let the gory wad of paper and twine slip to the asphalt. She hurried inside the school, leaving the package behind.

Only later, back at her desk, did she realize she was still holding the key.

SO MANY NIGHTS: THE THREE OF THEM, crammed together on an overnight bus or in her mother's ailing grey Chevette, always sneaking off with bills unpaid or speeding to meet some unclear deadline, a new place beckoning in Oxnard or Huntington Beach or Boyle Heights, some convergence of fortune that could only happen if they arrived in time. The next thing, Jovena's mother promised, will surely be better than the last thing—whatever succedent disaster in their ongoing sequence of disasters. Through the night her mother talked non-stop, clasping Miguel's hand, Jovena's head resting in her lap, tote bags and knapsacks stuffed around them like fortifications, her chatter a defence against the latent forces of evil that she believed hid everywhere.

The big shots out there running things don't think demons are real. But people who live close to the ground know what's really going on. That's why you can't trust anything you can't see, because it has no body. A ghost is always out to trick you, and a demon wants to eat you. The most important things in life are your money and your eyeballs. But you'll never have enough money, and they use that to play tricks on your brain. You can trick a dog into walking into a puddle with a Milk-Bone, because he doesn't see anything else. That's money. So you have to keep your eyes open. Even when you're sleeping, you have to keep seeing. A ghost will write you a cheque, but you better see him sign it, and you better cash it next business day. Hold that money tight. Even with your pockets full, you never know when a demon's going to jump you. It'll eat you and spit you out like *nothing*.

These were some of Jovena's happiest memories, staring out at the highway by night, the billboards and eighteen-wheelers hurtling by, the glow of sleeping neighbourhoods beyond exit ramps, her imagination wild with the scope and complexity of the hugeness of it all, listening closely as her mother spoke, stroking her hair and squeezing her earlobes.

Demons are everywhere, her mother said. *Traucos* and *wekufes* and *cucuys* and all those creeps. They know what's really in your soul. The only way to keep demons from crawling in our windows is to keep looking out for each other. We stick together. Demons hate families. That's why you never see one hanging around a cookout or at the movies. You only see demons when you're all alone.

The school was cold early in the mornings, even with temperatures soaring throughout the valley. Constructed in the early sixties, the building seemed exhausted by its own existence, and renovations in recent years toward energy efficiency and better air ventilation had accomplished little: fans toiled, radiators clunked, mould thrived. Rumours were the city was fielding bids on the associated land parcel, factoring in the costs of treatment and disposal of hazardous materials. Speculation suggested the next school year could be MTHS's last.

This morning Jovena had come in early to get a head start on tackling some glitches. Gaps had arisen in the closing ledgers, some budget line items not squaring and student records out of date. Jovena had delayed doing anything about it, hoping the matters would just go away on their own. They didn't, and when she finally pulled the openings up on her screen, Billie had looked over her shoulder and sniffed knowingly. They'd need to take a peek at previous summaries, she said. One of them would have to head downstairs to B-5 to do some archaeology. The implication was she wouldn't be doing the digging.

The hallways clanged with vacancy, a state of suspension in the pre-classes calm. The north wing was a zone Jovena had so far left unexplored, but it was identical to the others: rows of lockers, chipping paint in primary colours, scuffed industrial vinyl flooring. She followed the hallway to its furthest reach, finding a stairwell leading down to the sub-level drama studio, placarded B-5. The door was unlocked, but she paused before entering. She recalled what she'd been told about the events of last spring: the discovery of the drama instructor Lavoir's body, the expeditious moves to protect the student populace from trauma, unanswered questions regarding internal security and motives. But that was another time.

She entered, snapping light switches. The room was divided into halves, one side carpeted and stuffed with coat racks and prop trunks and wall-mounted wipe boards, the other a rehearsal area of faux-hardwood flooring, a small platform serving as a stage. To her surprise, Jovena discovered she wasn't alone. At a digital piano set to the stage's right, someone sat at the bench, slumped face first over the keyboard, long hair falling over folded arms.

Roused by the lights, Alejandra looked up.

What.

Jovena found herself explaining her search for the required files. Blinking, unhurried, Alejandra said she knew where to look. She'd been doing drama since tenth grade and knew the studio well. She led Jovena to the back shelves of the supply closet where Lavoir had kept pertinent papers. The records were filed sequentially and the folders Jovena sought were easily located.

I appreciate the help, Jovena said.

Alejandra pulled her bag onto her shoulder.

All good.

You're allowed down here?

No one comes down here. It's quiet.

She looked at the floor. Jovena followed her gaze to the tiles, their chevron pattern in alternating tan and orange.

This is where they found him, Alejandra said. Right there, in front of the stage.

Did you know him?

I did.

Alejandra added nothing further. Jovena pinched the file folder in her fingers, pressing the pages' edge to her chin.

It's good to have respect for the dead, she said.

They started back upstairs together, Jovena following Alejandra. She took the stairs slowly, still without hurry. Back at the ground floor, they continued down the main hallway.

What are you taking this summer? Jovena asked.

Geology.

And how's that?

A bit rocky.

Jovena took a second.

Oh. That's funny.

Alejandra paused at a water fountain, leaning over on one leg to drink while extending and pointing the other behind her, a move like a sloppy arabesque.

You know, I didn't tell him anything, Jovena said. Though I probably should have.

Alejandra returned her stance to upright and backed from the fountain, wiping her mouth, processing this.

Oh. My father. Okay, good. You're a blessing.

A blessing. The casual way Alejandra said this, it sounded like something she likely said often. They resumed walking.

But where I let you out, Jovena said, by the river. What's there?

There? A place.

You and your friends go down there.

We go there, we go lots of other places. We're everywhere. We're like microbes in the dirt.

So it's not some special place.

No, it is. Special. Sure, you could say that.

You know, you could hurt yourself down there.

How?

Jovena had no answer to this. They arrived at the hallway's end. The way to the office lay to their left, the main doors to the right, the sun's wash infiltrating rows of residue-streaked Plexiglas. Jovena watched as Alejandra ran fingers through her hair, sieving away non-existent dust.

In geology they say everything happens in long waves, Alejandra said. Until a massive event happens and the flow's interrupted. That's catastrophism. As opposed to uniformitarianism. It's about how the world is shaped by sudden blasts.

I see.

And that's the thing in society too. The history of America is really all about disruptions. Same with the history of the whole world. Most of everything just happens the way it does because it's just the established order. Not everything's straightforward. There are forces, other forces, manipulating things. Those are the powers that are really doing things. And most people don't know, or they just don't care.

No, they don't. You're right.

But when things really happen, and when it comes together, they're going to see.

In this, Jovena heard Miguel.

A transference of energy, she said.

Alejandra stopped and faced her.

What did you just say?

Jovena was, of course, only quoting her brother. But there was no way Alejandra would know that.

It's nothing. Something I heard.

You heard something? You got a message? Tell me what it said.

I don't know what you're... I don't understand.

Alejandra frowned, reading her. Other students were arriving now, dead-eyed in the morning trudge. Alejandra rubbed her nose, started away, then turned back.

All right. This is you and me here. Just us. Private. Don't talk to anyone else about any of this.

I'm not even sure what we're saying.

Promise me.

I promise.

Alejandra rubbed her nose again, then headed off, presumably to class. Jovena watched her go. As she stood there, unmoving, all felt slow and draggy; her gastritis flared. When the morning buzzer came over the PA, commencing first period, she recoiled as if slapped in the face.

The key sat on her desk, next to her water bottle and the ever-present stack of manila folders, an anachronistic artifact with its tarnished metal ring and nubby teeth. On its own, a key was nothing, a piece of metal, meaningless until its cuts found their cylinder. Like a cell formatted in a spreadsheet, any value the single unit might carry was only realized in its result, its output tainted by common human error. Plugging in data, the flow of figures and requisition numbers, Jovena fought to work with an attentive eye, knowing any mistake could corrupt the final summation, necessitating a second or third pass. Unless each figure was entered accurately, the cumulative whole would be a hash—a collection of old keys rattling around in a junk drawer, the locks they opened lost to time.

The job was to achieve a complete and accurate record, from which reports could then be generated in response to queries. Inter-trustee budgetary squabbles, Billie had told her, repeatedly came down to minute comparisons between particular targets. A comprehensive database—impartial, inarguable—was required. But her work was continually derailed by her own questions, her own unresolved sums. Everything churned in dread. She suppressed anxious yawns; her stomach burned.

And when the email arrived in her inbox flagged URGENT, the sender Rick Ortigosa with a meeting request for later that morning, she already knew what was coming. It was inevitable: she'd be presented with facts demanding corroboration or denial, requiring her to account for her ways. Over the next two hours she made repeated trips to the bathroom, where she locked herself away in a stall, bent over on the toilet with her head on her knees, making vague prayers for amnesty from what awaited.

But there was no escaping it. Contrition was due, even if the specifics defied all reason. As they recounted history to her, these men citing sources both official and anecdotal, there was little she could confirm, and less she could deny.

Theresa, Ortigosa said, reading from his computer screen. Or, Tess. That was her name.

This statement was its own question. Jovena, rigid in her seat, fought to maintain composure. According to Ortigosa, they'd done a partial check of her references during the interview phase—she'd been truthful but sparing in the application information—but with the term closing, the offices in San Diego had only gotten back to them now. So now she was here in his office, the interrogation attended by a man from the district board introduced only as Glenn, who sat angled on the ledge by the window, propped there like a TV homicide detective.

The history they gave us from down at San Diego Unified was, um, exhaustive, Ortigosa said, eyes still on his screen. Not all of this is anything we need to get into right now. But let me tell you the story as it came to me.

Jovena nodded. She wondered who exactly in San Diego they'd spoken to about her, but it didn't matter. She'd left no sympathies there.

The first complaint was filed in the winter. You'd been there since the fall. So, three, four months?

She nodded again.

Alleged code of conduct violations. Meeting this student after hours. Inappropriate conversation brought to the attention of administration, and apparently taken seriously? Before this is investigated in full, there's this second complaint. This time not by the student directly, but on her behalf by her brother, also a student. Unnamed here.

The memory fumed: the outraged kids tearing away across a busy intersection, Jovena driving her own sidewalk-scraped knuckles into her temples. *Pure devotion and nothing else.*

Says a meeting took place at the Office of the Deputy Superintendent, Ortigosa went on. Results stated as satisfactory. No disciplinary measures taken or loss of pay, though it says something about external counselling?

They'd met in the afternoons, thrice as dictated, at the clinic on 4th Street. The therapist tapped a page on a clipboard with her burgundy acrylic nails as she read off functional analysis prompts. *What would you say are the areas of distortion causing you to return to those recognizable patterns?* Jovena, lulled into a near-hypnotic state by those talons and their percussive taps, was unconscious of any answers she'd given. At each session's end, she was assigned a folder of worksheets to complete in the interval before the next session.

These had sat untouched on her refrigerator under a box of Trader Joe's tea bags, until there hadn't been any more sessions. All she recalled now were those clicking nails.

The next entry is in the new year, Ortigosa continued, scrolling. Now the parents are involved. We have this slew of text messages, and there's this statement by a security guard at a Culver's or something? The mother kept things. Timelines, screenshots. It's almost forensic.

That woman's voice, the sputtering motor of her sobs: *You stay away or I or I or I...*

This girl, Tess...there's something with the student government association? That's why the private meetings?

She was the treasurer, Jovena said. I helped her organize a fundraiser.

Ortigosa looked from the screen.

She was in twelfth grade? She was graduating?

This was true. Her future looked bright. And when she'd received her notice of acceptance from the Cronkite School, Jovena was the first person Tess had called. Not her sister, not her mother. The integrity of their trust was true, and real, though Jovena knew none of that would be derivable from the docket now presented. All they saw was what they'd already deemed wrong.

Ortigosa leaned back in his seat and looked to Glenn.

Dismissal in one state doesn't necessarily have bearing on what happens here, Glenn said in a voice so low Jovena had to strain to hear. Technically, fault is tough to determine. And the timing of the whole thing is pretty sucky. We're going to have to take this back downtown and mull it over.

Ortigosa shrank in his seat.

This is kind of on us.

That said, Glenn said, you might want to consider having legal counsel on standby.

Glenn looked over Ortigosa's shoulder at the screen in a way that indicated he was already familiar with the information it displayed.

A question, he said, about chronology. Before the restraining order was issued, you'd already left San Diego?

Jovena nodded. But Glenn wanted more.

My mother was sick, she said.

They used to make fun of me, her mother said, reclining on the living room sofa, the parted curtains striping her throat and sternum in sunlight. All the time, when I was young. I was amazing then, you know. My head floated in the mountains. I'd tell all my friends: there's a thirsty demon up there! You go fetch your little sister and, next thing you know, you get kissed by a hellhound. The other kids told me I was stupid. But I was always one step ahead of everyone. I was a dreamer, but I knew things about the way things were. Chile in the seventies wasn't like it is now. But I guess the same goes for California. And everywhere.

The ravage could not be slowed, but the painkillers kept her dim, less harried. She reminisced aloud in disassociated leaps, and she seemed to have some purpose in this remembering, though the effort wore her out and she often dozed all afternoon. Jovena remained by her side through her sweats and thirsts, from laughing jags to caterwauls of pain.

They mocked me because I said the clouds were giants, her mother said.

Maybe they *were* giants, Jovena said, stroking her mother's overlong, dust-coloured hair. You were probably just smarter than them.

Than who?

Than whoever you were talking about, Mom. You were floating. The clouds were giants.

But that's what I'm saying! The clouds were just full of piss. Piss piss piss.

In the final days, her mother's swirling mind kept her perpetually, inconsolably frightened. Her gastroenterologist at St. Joseph's said it was the creep of her condition, the irreversible hepatitic ruin. If a diagnosis had been reached earlier, more effective steps might have been taken. But she'd downplayed her symptoms, keeping her torments to herself. By the time she'd sought testing, even the best treatment could only do so much. The situation had to be accepted. Jovena held her hand and listened to her complaints: the television was too quiet, the house too stuffy, even with windows wide and rotary fans growling in every room.

One night, her mother collapsed and didn't wake. As brutish, tattooed EMTs who looked and behaved like nightclub bouncers sieged the house, Jovena stood in the corner, incapacitated with embarrassment for herself, for her mother, for this entire pitiful scene. At the hospital, her hands trembled as she signed the identification record, and she could barely count out the two dollars in quarters needed for the bus ride back home.

The urn was buried at Holy Redeemer in the desert earth, with no ceremonial rites or attempted elegy—with no idea what her mother would have wanted for herself, Jovena had planned nothing. Not that it really mattered. Her mother's life had been one of constant crisis, and its conclusion provided little reprieve. This desperate life, in all its pinings and gropes, came to its end plainly, almost indetectably.

Piss piss piss.

Jovena walked south along 19th Avenue, into the reclining sun. Transport trucks roared past, blowing dust in their wake. The sidewalk here was barely a sliver of fissured concrete, skirted by a nothingness of wildflowers and patchy palms to one side, to the other a Cemex lot populated by ranks of mixers. No other pedestrians met her here.

Nearing the river, she found the fence and followed it until locating the break she'd seen Alejandra pass through. The opening was clean, by appearances pared out with bolt cutters. She ducked through and headed down the slope. The riverbed below was dry, as she'd always known it to be. The spillways of the Roosevelt Dam upriver had given way to flash floods on occasion over the years, but that was before her time in the city. Now there was just its usual shallow basin of rubble and cracked soil. The track she followed wound southwest, terminating at the opposite bank among the vestiges of a long-collapsed concrete embankment, slashed with spray paint. Here was evidence of occupation, human debris: Corona bottles and Chick-fil-A bags, heaps of cigarette butts and condom wrappers, strips of hacked tires.

Light-headed from the heat, she searched her purse and dug out a nearly empty Dasani bottle. She downed what remained, then tossed it against the embankment: *donk*.

Litterbug.

Jovena almost shrieked. She turned to find a teenage boy, walking with a slight limp. He seemed to have come from the east, from upriver.

That shit doesn't just disintegrate, he said. Think about it.

He stretched his arms, as if having just risen from a nap. Jovena placed him now, from the police photographs.

Wesley?

Heyo.

He came closer, circling her. Wesley Drimmer, officially missing since April, was only a teenager, a thing still blooming. Yet here, now, he was something greater, something elemental. With his appearance, everything else receded: river and sun, the rattling freeway, the city's edacious sprawl.

Everyone's looking for you, Jovena said. Where have you *been*?

That sick heat continued to rise, threatening her balance. Her cheeks and forehead burned. She longed for more water.

I've been looking for something, Wesley said. This *key*. You haven't seen one lying around, maybe?

Jovena hesitated.

No.

Rats. Looks like I kind of blew things. Everything made sense at first. There was a message, and we figured it out. That's where the covenant came from. But we got it all wrong. Now I'm thinking I need to find that darn key. Something's gotta get unlocked. Or maybe something's gotta get locked back up. It's all pretty confusing, to be honest.

Each word was emphasized in a light, almost singsong cadence.

You should go home, she said. Call your parents.

Wesley spat on the ground.

Call my parents what?

If you've done something...

Yeah, I did something. I did something pretty bad. But we all pull some wacky shit now and then. Haven't you?

She had indeed pulled some wacky shit. Her mother's sorrowful voice had warned: *Bad decisions and bad people can cost you your life.* Badness was all her mother had known, and this had held true for Jovena. She'd fantasized about leaving everything that had happened behind, but true escape was only that: a fantasy. In San Diego she'd made minimum wage and received not-so-gentle reprimands for wearing the same nineteen-dollar Target pants every day. In that miserable office she'd devolved into an insect: deferential, squishable. Once, she'd overheard her supervisor on the phone referring to her as *that aloof chica cooze.* Her only method of resistance was to suffer silently. Yes, everything Ortigosa accused her of was true. But those crimes were only entries in a database without end or beginning. Bad decisions came with costs, and bad people could ruin you—and she was bad herself, maybe the worst of all.

The dizziness rose, overwhelming her. Everything defocused. She braced herself against the embankment's corroded concrete.

Heard we're getting another dry-ass summer, Wesley said, looking downriver. But you can't trust the Weather Channel. Know what I mean.

The arroyo was fluxing. The river, bone-dry, was overflowing.

She was thirteen years old, unfed and unwashed and barely clothed. She was a child of six, grinding her knuckles into her eyes' crooks and yearning for sleep. She was an old woman, withered, yellowed, failing. The only connection she held to anything was discomfort, just aching shoulders and greasy skin, sore gums, nausea, lethargy—her life's sum a pile of irritated flesh and tissue, leaching with rash and emanating a stench that was specifically, loathsomely, hers.

Jovena wiped tears from her eyes. The sun was slipping behind the distant peaks of the Sierra Estrella. Wesley Drimmer was nowhere to be seen.

The lawn's grass, untended for weeks and wild with weeds, now came up to her shins. Clusters of flies suffused the growth like a gas. It was up to her to tame this mess, but she had no idea how to even begin. In a driveway across the street, a pair of women consoled a sobbing girl in a bike helmet. Jovena didn't know this child or her attendants. She knew her neighbours only to nod and wave, the young families sliding in among Coronado's deeply embedded long-time residents. Phoenix's housing market had been rocky lately, and forecasts saw gaps further widening, prices climbing, demographics shifting. But there would always be some struggle. People persisted, or made their best attempts at persisting. The girl in the helmet cried *the thing is too fast why is it too fast*. Jovena batted flies from her hair.

A man had died here, on this lawn, incinerated into a husk, and she hadn't even thought to learn his name.

Weariness tugged on her. She headed inside. But as she wiped her feet on the doormat, she halted. Something was wrong. There was a strange scent, sugary and rough. In the living room, she scanned the sofa, the television, the shelves still containing her mother's photo boxes and tchotchkes, finding no sign of molestation. She cleared her throat as an announcement to any trespasser, a ridiculous action. There was nothing—but there was something.

Keeping the lights off, she found her purse lying open on the coffee table. She dug out her phone. No messages showed. Deeper within the purse's mess of crumpled tissues and nasal spray and bus tokens, she found the brass key. She turned it idly in her hands.

Something's gotta get unlocked.

Then, from down the hall: the sharp interruption of smashing glass.

Even before Jovena entered the kitchen, she felt the creature's presence. The shelf above the counter had been torn from its hinges. Shattered bottles of soy sauce and balsamic vinegar lay puddling on the floor's tiles. The room was choked with the vinegar's acridity, intermingling with the scorched scent of diesel exhaust.

The demon hunched behind the refrigerator door, grunting in rapid heaves. Jovena couldn't bring herself to look at it. But she felt its breath everywhere: on her flesh, in her stomach's inflammation.

Facing the wall, she edged around the counter, moving slowly across the room. It had not only ransacked the shelves but had burrowed through the array of tins and the shoebox of papers atop the refrigerator; receipts and unopened bank notices fanned the floor, saturated with spilled oil. None of this mattered. There was nothing here but the creature, holding dominion. Jovena continued around the room's perimeter, as much drawn by the monster as repulsed by it. Even as it remained concealed behind the door, she sensed its every contour: its pincer claws, the pulsing cords of its hulking neck, the curtains of gore dribbling from its lips.

Even though this was not something to be believed, she knew it to be true.

I know about you, it growled. *There's evil in your soul.*

Reaching the back door, Jovena slowly released its lock, fighting to dampen the click. She waited, listening to the fridge's lower compartments slide open behind her, the creature panting as it hunted fresh plunders. She eased the door open and slid out into the backyard, closing the door behind her.

With night's falling, the wind had picked up, foretelling bad weather. The backyards of the houses down the block were a kaleidoscope of swinging clotheslines. Overhead, a jet in descent bisected the yellow desert moon.

LAST WINTER, ALEJANDRA ORTIGOSA TRAVELLED TO MEXICO CITY. The trip was planned under the auspices of visiting her grandmother Ximena, a writer and poet of high regard not just in her home country but internationally, now enduring the late stages of pancreatic cancer and by all reports not long for this world. Privately, however, the true motive behind Alejandra's trip was the hope of losing her virginity—finally, she'd just get it over with. She was the last remaining virgin among her friends, and while she hadn't really suffered any censure or mockery for this status, she'd mostly just grown tired of thinking about it. There had been enjoyable flings with some boys, any of whom might have proven a practicable candidate for her first time, but she was always unable to rouse enough enthusiasm to take the negotiations any further, and those basement gropings invariably resulted only in nervous giggles and her own abrupt escape. To her, the total irretrievability of the act meant it could only occur in anonymity, elsewhere—another latitude, another phase of the moon. So, when she received notification from her cousin Armando of a planned gathering at Ximena's deathbed, an opportunity seemed to present itself. Alejandra texted her father asking for a loan on the airfare and, as expected, Rick promptly issued her a business-class ticket on Mexicana with no expectation of reimbursement.

The southbound flight brought the first quivers of excitement she'd felt since who knew when. Endless fields of puff and blue rolled below; she wore her new grey blazer from Saks; the flight attendants called her *madame* and offered her cocktails and warm towels. Such ecstasies drove her to down three gin and tonics, a drink she'd never tasted, and by the time her cousin Renata met her at Aeropuerto Internacional she had a ripping headache and was having trouble staying upright. The first day of her mission was thus squandered on Renata's sofa, soothed by takeout pozole and seltzer.

Bloated and wiped, she fell asleep staring at her phone, reading texts from Gwendolyn and Julia, who were both starting retail jobs at the Metrocenter that week and were both thrilled at the prospect. *Employee discount hell yeah*, Gwendolyn wrote.

On the second day, Alejandra hired a taxi and headed to her grandmother's apartment in Colonia Roma. There she joined her cousins as they gathered quietly around her abuelita, now a jaundiced hint of a woman, swaddled in musty blankets. With curtains drawn and windows sealed, the room was like a humidor—purposed for the storage, Alejandra thought grimly, of death. Prayers were said, but in Spanish, and Alejandra couldn't follow. Later, over coffee in the kitchenette, Armando explained how, as with many well-regarded Latin American poets, a wide disproportion existed between Ximena's critical appreciation and her actual earnings. He stirred his cup and rued how, in his mind, Ximena's body of work had been grossly misinterpreted; in a short piece in the *London Review of Books* earlier that year, she'd been described as, he quoted, *Mexico's most cherished archivist of dismay*. What, he wondered aloud, did that even mean? He was concerned whether the words that would sanctify her memory, any eulogies or memorials to come, would effectively convey what he saw as the principal themes of her many published volumes: beauty and transcendence. Alejandra had on a few occasions attempted to delve into her grandmother's poetry, but much of it was composed in a very deliberate hybrid of archaic Spanish and Nahuatl that didn't lend itself to accessibility, even in translation. The phenomenon besieging the old woman's wilting body, Armando said, was like an insult to such investment in beauty. How, then, to appropriately honour her artistic ambitions?

Armando wondered aloud if there was anything tougher than coffee around. Raiding the shelves, he located a half-bottle of Johnnie Walker. Pouring two glasses, Armando said Ximena had been in chronic pain for years, with stabbing aches in her abdomen and kidneys, but she'd kept smoking cigarillos and drinking Bud Light like water, spending most days watching soccer on satellite television, despite her worsening cataracts. Alejandra couldn't imagine anything crueller; her own body still seemed an undrainable battery of fledgling energy. Someday it too would fail, this she of course knew, but the concept was totally abstract, and not yet anything of real concern.

Before leaving the apartment, she returned to the bedroom, this time unaccompanied. Ximena was of course still lying there as before, as she surely would until her passing. There was no way of knowing whether she was aware of Alejandra's presence. Alejandra placed her palm on the old woman's forehead and closed her eyes. However briefly, she felt a connection. A transference, some alchemy at work. Ximena was diminishing, molecule by molecule, even as Alejandra herself bloomed.

On the third day Alejandra woke early with a vow to shake the numbing melancholy, to refocus on her trip's purpose and the hope of finding something actually good in it. She straightened her hair, charged her phone, and donned the leather boots she'd bought in San Diego last fall: slightly too slutty for school, they'd sat unworn in her closet since, but here they seemed perfect. At a cantina near Renata's apartment, she devoured two steamed cactus tacos and, consulting online reviews, found four nightclubs that seemed cool, marking the addresses for later. On the recommendation of the woman at the cantina, she spent the morning skimming the rooms at the Museo Nacional de Antropología. Pausing before the Olmec colossal heads from Tabasco and Veracruz, she tried to derive some significance from the stone, but could not. The idea of mingling meaningfully with the souls of past generations felt insincere.

At a Starbucks in the Centro Histórico, Alejandra tried to work her way back into her paperback of *Song of Solomon* as prep for her upcoming American Lit paper. Though the book was clearly something to admire, she kept spacing out with every line. At the next table, a guy wearing bronze-framed aviators spoke into his phone in loud, lispy English: *It's an imperfect system, but I tell you the money is there.* He caught her glance, and soon he was leaning across the table, removing his shades, introducing himself as Andreas. With stringy curls framing a taut, pock-cheeked jawline, he clearly he saw her as a tourist, a naive foreigner. Alejandra didn't bother to correct him, since this assessment was at least partially true. He described with pride how he'd travelled widely: reared in business at UMI in Culiacán, he said he'd then completed an MBA at Columbia where, in his words, he *destroyed it*. She asked where in New York he'd lived. Manhattan, he said. But where? Downtown, he said. But downtown where? He only flicked away a strand of hair and requested her phone number. This overconfidence struck her as shady; he was clearly somewhat of a ghoul. But they exchanged numbers and arranged to meet later at a bar, the location of which she pretended to recognize. Andreas then slipped back out into the city.

The next few hours passed like awaiting a medical screening. Alejandra wandered the streets, watching butchers in bloodstained aprons boarding up their windows and teary-eyed strikers bullhorning in the Zócalo. Entering a dimly lit courtyard, she found a crowd swarming a corner bar where a large screen played a soccer match. Groups of women in sweatshirts and capris sat outside smoking and talking. Alejandra timidly asked in English if she could take their picture, indicating her phone. The women offered little reaction, so Alejandra aimed her phone and snapped a picture anyway. The flash froze the entire courtyard in light, drawing stares. Alejandra moved on, feeling like an idiot.

By nine o'clock she was tired of wandering and ready to head back to Renata's, but she ordered herself to uphold her meeting with Andreas: it was the only opportunity she had. Arriving at the address he'd given, instead of the sleazy, overheated nightclub she'd expected, she found another undistinguished corner bar, mostly unoccupied, with a pool table in the rear and Alice in Chains playing on a digital jukebox. Andreas was nowhere to be seen. She suspected she'd been duped.

She was about to take flight when the bartender caught her eye and gestured for her to take a stool. Sporting the same overlogoed T-shirt and hideous biker jeans as every second guy she'd seen since arriving, he was handsome in his own way. Come, he said, I'll make you my signature drink. After a whirlwind of splashes and clanked strainers, he laid out two pairs of shot glasses, each containing a dark brown liquid. It was something he called *el diablo en el espejo*: the devil in the mirror. We drink the first one fast, he instructed, then we sip the second one slowly. Combined, he said very seriously, it generates a specific psychological effect. You'll see. Alejandra bit her lip. They downed the first round, which slid through her throat with a weird incendiary pleasure. The emptied glasses vanished. These second ones, the bartender advised, should be taken with a degree of care, with control. We are multiplying vortices, he said. She didn't know what this meant, but with one sip it became clearer: the leisureliness of the second drink brought sensations, tastes, beyond the first. Something was definitely happening.

A group of men in suits entered the bar, post-office types, soliciting the bartender's attention. As he went to serve them, Alejandra stared into her glass. Her thoughts turned to the recent past. Last winter, unbeknownst to anyone, she'd tried to kill herself. A three-day vacation had been planned with her stepmother's family at their chalet time-share near Sandia Peak. Her father was elated at the prospect of slopes doused in fresh powder, but Alejandra, with an overdue Global Issues makeup paper to finish and no fondness for skiing, had stayed behind with microwaveable meals and an emergency envelope of twenties. The first night, Alejandra sat for hours over her laptop at the dining room table, trying to write an introductory paragraph about the M23 rebellion in the DRC based on the instructional handout's designated essay points. Nothing came, and she soon gave up, instead loafing on the couch watching *Dateline NBC* over a cardboard tray of lasagna. Later, in her parents' bedroom, she brushed her hair with her stepmother's brush, almost laughing at how her own black hairs threaded between Sharon's blond sheddings. The glass of the window above the dresser offered two overlapping views: Alejandra's reflection and the lawn beyond, its uniform sheet of neatly trimmed grass. A possibility that had been faintly lurking took shape. In a lower bathroom drawer, she found a vial of estazolam; she took a bottle of Smirnoff down from the top kitchen shelf. With these supplies, she sat in the dining room and began. The pills went down hard, the vodka stinging with each swallow. The clock on the wall counted away a stretch of time. From there forward, the night mostly went black; the next thing she recalled was pounding her fists on the front door of Schexnayder's' down the street, wearing only her bra and jeans, a mix of tomato sauce and something bloody streaking from her chin to her sternum. Her pleas there went unanswered, and another cavity of time swallowed her. Then she was in her parents' bathtub, unclothed and shivering, trying to remember where she'd left the vodka bottle. The whirring bathroom light seemed like a constant yell, berating her, and moving from bathtub to bed seemed an impossible task. But the impossible was made possible, and though she slept for a long time, she did not die. All of her messes could be shampooed away. Her father and stepmother returned late on Sunday afternoon, and for the half-assed essay she submitted later that week, Alejandra received a C. The missing pills were never mentioned.

That night now felt so distant, it almost seemed to not have happened. Or maybe another entire reality had spun out of it during the blackouts, but she was too stupid to remember. There seemed to her to be many possible worlds, worlds spinning within worlds, deaths between lives, so unreal and yet so obvious. Devils in mirrors, beauty seen through cataract-clouded eyes.

Alejandra raised her attention from the glass to find the bar filling with loud young men congregating around jugs of beer. Her armpits were incredibly sweaty. Andreas was now almost an hour late, and her phone showed no messages. She admitted surrender. On the costly taxi ride back to Renata's, Alejandra was searching her wallet for pesos when she discovered a blot of blood on her mouth, self-inflicted from involuntarily biting her lower lip. The ferric taste was weirdly evocative of another time; it was the type of wound suffered by a child. And for every way in which she'd grown, there were many more ways in which she'd remained childlike. Foolishly, idiotically so.

She'd planned to visit Ximena again the next morning before leaving, but she slept too late and there simply wasn't time, so she hastily packed her things, hugged Renata goodbye, and taxied to the airport. The plane was underbooked, and she was relieved to have an entire row to herself. Rain sloshed the wings on takeoff and she slept the entire ride, roused only briefly by rollicking turbulence over the Sierra Tarahumara. But this passed, and soon they were touching down at Sky Harbor. Once through customs, she checked her phone to find a message from Armando: her grandmother had passed away just hours before. There was speculation about who'd been the last to hear her speak, and someone had suggested the final witness had been Alejandra. Any dying words Ximena might have offered would be of great interest, he said, perhaps illumining some aspect of her work as a final testament to this legacy. Alejandra listened to this message twice, then deleted it.

Returning to her father's house, she tossed her suitcase on her bed and sat on the floor, dabbing her face with a smelly T-shirt from her laundry basket. When Gwendolyn called later, saying there was a thing that night at Calvin's, Alejandra was powerless to resist. An hour later, she was spilling red wine on her grey blazer; the stain would prove unerasable. Later still, she was being undressed by Bartek in an upstairs bedroom. As he slid off her underwear, Alejandra ordered him to leave the lights on. A full-length mirror was propped beside the bed, and she stared into it, watching closely as everything occurred. Nothing would be left unrevealed.

THE LIFTING OF THE VEIL DANCE was typically held at semester's end, preceding the swell of anticipation surrounding graduation but still within the plod of classes' wrap-up, when the fatigue and dread of finals were at their apex and the school day as a unit of time, of thralldom, was felt at its most punishing. The origins of this event were indefinite: one notice on the school's website attributed its genesis to Aztec rites from a symbolic march to Mictlan, while an article in the *MTHS Bugle* from the late nineties claimed it began as a mock ceremony performed by the Tohono O'odham along the Santa Cruz River, parodizing the Jesuit missionaries of the Sonoran Desert. Whatever its beginnings, its customs had remained intact, decades of yearbooks showing gawky teenagers fixed in camera flashes, framed in lacy swirls of chenille adorning the school's entrance.

As always, the students' anticipation for the Lifting was high, even amid, or even despite, the resonances of recent trauma. But these hopes were quashed when, after an extended lull, another bomb threat came just a week before the dance's scheduled date in late May. After hasty deliberation, the event was cancelled, for the first time in anyone's recollection. This was met with great outcry, and with the summer session's atypically high numbers—a result of both the interrupted classes and a generally poor academic showing —a push had followed to revive a midsummer version. Valedictorian Brittany Wothousin had introduced the prospect in her convocation address, invoking reverence for tradition as a buttress against fear. These efforts galvanized the students' collective will, and so the announcement came of an unprecedented late-June Lifting, with all students invited, graduates as well as those returning. The horrors of past months had since, it was hoped, been overcome.

Alejandra stood at the base of the first-floor stairs, reading a poster on the wall announcing, in glittered, glue-sticked letters, the rei-magined Lifting of the Veil. She'd yet to discuss this development with the others, and how it might alter their intended plans. Maybe it didn't matter.

She was late for English, already in session. Dolen had warned her a second non-attendance would mean a call home, and a third would mean expulsion from the term, meaning an entire year re-peated. Another year in captivity. But Julia had called this morning with an urgent plea, asking Alejandra to meet her. She and Julia were, after all, still self-designated *best friends*, and even though their bond had weakened steadily since middle school, it still car-ried a sense of obligation. And so, when Julia came trudging down the hallway in a state of obvious distress, Alejandra dutifully opened her arms and let Julia's head fall on her shoulder. Julia sustained the embrace for maybe a bit too long. She said she needed a Jamba Juice, so they headed out, taking the south doors to avoid detection.

Up until the spring semester, Julia had boasted a sparkling record, a transcript of conquering grades in all honours courses plus an impressive list of extracurriculars. With eyes on metabolomics at Scripps in La Jolla, she'd gone into application season feeling good. But around winter's end, things had gone off track. As she described it, a powerful fatigue had overtaken her, a complete physical and mental zonkage that made it impossible to meet the demands of as-sistant captaining A Squad Volleyball, let alone keeping her grades tight. Her nights were haunted by gruesome recurring dreams. She dreamed she was being led through a dark cavern or subterranean passage-type thing by unseen stewards, beings she could feel and hear—their deep voices reprimanding her, scolding as if she was a disobedient dog—but she couldn't see, for as part of whatever ter-rible process she was undergoing, there was a kind of screen blind-ing her. All she could make out were jerky hints of motion in the shadows. She knew she was headed toward something important, toward some culminating destination at the end of the passage, but in her blindness she was helpless to do anything about it.

Alejandra said she understood what Julia was talking about. There's a lot going on, she said. But we just need to stick with the plan and everything will be fine. Remember the covenant.

Julia didn't seem convinced. Her dreams never ended with her waking in pulse-pounding fright, as nightmares typically did. They just kept on and on until her alarm clock buzzed. Even more worrying, though, were the spells she was now having throughout the day, random snatches of confusion and disassociation. It was, she was realizing, her dreams infiltrating her waking hours. Some days she just sat in the school hallways for hours, staring at nothing, listening to the critical voices and allowing herself to be led into something unknown. Her doctor had put her on Paxil and recommended she up her iron intake, while her mother was convinced she was pregnant—no way that was possible, Julia laughed. Almost three months had passed with her languishing this way. Now she'd blown the entire semester. Hence: summer school. The weeks ahead would be torturous. And still, sleeplessness.

As they left the shop with twenty-four-ounce Watermelon Breezes in hand, Julia said she understood the importance of the covenant. But right now things were so wonky, practically speaking, and she had a lot on her mind. I'm with you, Julia said to Alejandra. I'm with you, and I'm with the others. Gwendolyn and Calvin, even Bartek. I am. But I keep asking myself what's really important. And what's really *there*. You know?

Alejandra only slurped her straw. She'd been listening to Julia's complaints for years, and her sympathies extended only so far. If Julia was so concerned about college acceptances and appeasing her meddlesome parents, then she didn't understand what was at stake. Julia expected Alejandra to offer reassurances, to tell her it was cool to bail on the whole thing and focus on her own concerns. But it wasn't cool. In breaking her oath, Julia would be drawing an irrevocable line. So there was little for Alejandra to say. Plans would continue with or without Julia.

They followed the sidewalk back toward Mother Teresa. Everything about these overfamiliar scenes filled Alejandra with loathing:

the grimy boulevard of city buses, the beat-down storefronts and sagging palms, signs for CHEQUES CASHED and CHINESE FOOD "EAT HERE OR TO-GO" and BARBER: FADES TAPERS REGULARS. The midday heat only intensified the bleakness. What used to be wide-ranging disgust with her city had advanced into something fiercer—a feeling of things being overdue, past-prime. Her father would lecture: *The most direct way to achieve positive results is to practise assertive influence on one's environment.* But this environment was long run dry, sucked of joy, withered beyond any powers of *influence* she might have.

Seeing the man in the grey track suit approaching, Julia and Alejandra both tensed. He moved with syncopated jerkiness, the telltale gait of a messed-up person. As their paths converged, his eyes lit up.

Pardon me. Do you speak the language?

Alejandra moved to sidestep him, but Julia had already stopped.

Hablas español?

The man frowned.

I mean the secret language. The path of the river and the ordure of Mastema. The cursed symbols.

Look, Alejandra said, I don't know what you're on, but you can't be hanging around near school grounds. Cops will be called.

At this, the man laughed, a titter of delight. Alejandra yanked at Julia's sleeve, but Julia didn't budge.

It goes to the water, the man said, but it doesn't end there. It's farther down, in the future. Follow it to the outside. Don't listen to the hog breeders and deceivers. They're just as mixed up as you and me.

Then that's pretty mixed up, Alejandra said. Come on, Jules.

But Julia didn't move. Alejandra took her by the arm and forced her past the man. Without looking back, they hurried down the block, then cut through a parking lot to the south side of the MTHS soccer field. At the bleachers, Julia stopped. Her hands trembled as she drank down her juice, her lips clenched around her straw.

Do you know that ding-dong back there? Alejandra asked.

Julia looked at Alejandra. Her terror was plain.

I just really want to wake up, she said. Can I wake up now?

This year was supposed to be the year Alejandra learned to drive. Two weekends of driving school and she could have her Class G licence, with a solid commitment from her father to pick up the lease on an old hatchback or something. Enough, finally, of her bus pass and reliance on others' chauffeuring. No longer these grue-some trudges in the heat and interminable rides on the Central Avenue bus back to Pomelo Park. And with such emancipation, her options as far as summer jobs, and thereby a radical reconfiguration of her financial situation, would broaden exponentially. Through Gwendolyn, she had an in at the Forever 21 in Chandler. Further beyond that lay infinite possibilities. She could split mid-semester with a full tank and blast off to the coast, follow the I-5 north to San Francisco, to Alaska, wherever. She could be transported. With mobility, she could achieve mastery.

But such plans were doomed from the start. She could fantasize about getting past all the drudgery and shit, but her true future would be a middling program at ASU, another timetable and an-other empty allegiance. There would be valuation and protocol, debt, cellulite, some asshole guy with a barbecue belly next to her in bed. There would be expectations and disappointments, quick-flash interruptions between long sloughs of tedium. This was the shape most lives took, and this was the path they followed. To resist would be to end up like one of those miserable, half-alive slumps you saw collected down on 3rd Avenue; to comply was to be like her father, less a man and more a sentient knot of stress.

All routes led nowhere. Unless, of course, the promises of the message actually came true.

The first call had come on a Wednesday, one of those chilly March nights with wind swooping the street, sending the wind chimes on the back patio into a tinkling frenzy. She was sitting on her bedroom floor, listening to music, picking dead skin from her scabby toes, or doing nothing at all—this memory from mere months ago was already fading. All she remembered now was her phone announcing an incoming call, then the voice on the line: a man's, deep, insistent but cool.

I ask you to use your powers of imagination. To try and see past the frame of this world. For past these corporeal plains, things await unlike anything of this despoiled earth—portals to places untraceable. Gateways to realms unfathomable.

As she listened, a sensation of weightlessness overtook her—as if she were being cast into a dark sea. The message, however perplexing, felt crucial. She needed to understand. Any failure to do so, to misread the information imparted, would be to reveal her own foolishness.

The child looks across the divide, bereft for the expiation he has yet to plot. For too long this child has stood at the gates. The temptation is fierce, the desire to transcend this foul sphere. The credit of mercy is weighed in the perspiration of the condemned, the fervour of the misled, the impatience of the venom-blooded. In such bewilderment is power generated. And this power, once generated, can be transferred. This is your future. The child is you.

Some phrases were repeated as refrains; much of it was inscrutable. But the voice never wavered in its imperative. There was no questioning its authority. As further messages arrived over subsequent nights, she both understood less and understood more.

With cunning, in enmity and conviction, all this can be just a distant hum. No more obstructions. Look for the moment when the clouds gather. The moment of catastrophe, when the driest river overflows with stormwater. When it arrives, let nothing hinder your progress. You mustn't avert your eyes. Tear ahead and claim your rightful spoils. A spiteless world will be yours.

But first, the blade must be swung. Sacrifices will be required. Then you can shed these lower ways and join us in the mists.

When, in the days that followed, she discovered others had received similar entreaties, her heart broke, ever so slightly. The messages came with the intimacy of trusted confidence, and it stung to know she wasn't the only one to be so trusted. The group met at the river and exchanged what they knew. Interpretations varied as to what it all might mean. It was Gwendolyn who'd first voiced what they all seemed to be thinking: they had been selected for a purpose. Something was going to happen, and they needed to prepare themselves. If there were to be sacrifices, it was better to be doing the sacrificing than to be the ones sacrificed.

And so a special pact was forged between them—a covenant. They all agreed, and any misgivings Alejandra may have had, she kept to herself. If, when, the gateway opened as promised, she'd be there to receive what was to come: her *rightful spoils*. If there actually was some greater world as he described, Alejandra would see for herself.

She'd waffled on phoning the driving school to set up registration and payment for lessons until the very last minute—no good reason for this, purely procrastination—only to find she was too late, and the classes were booked full for the remainder of the session. Once again, she'd fucked herself. Her fantasies of cruising west were dashed, but to her own surprise, she wasn't all that disappointed. Another calling had replaced her other desires. Her liberation now rested in the covenant. All she could do was stay sharp and be ready.

This is your future. The child is you.

The automatic utility lamps switched on, remaking the shopping plaza and parking lot as even more ragged and foreboding. The nail salon and dry cleaners were closed and the old Payless was long boarded up; only the corner liquor store and the Korean takeout still had lights on. Other than intermittent blips of traffic on the thoroughfare to the south, no human presence was detectable here.

Crossing the lot, Alejandra was nervous about what awaited her here. Why this place, why tonight. The text she'd received had relayed the specific location and time, followed by a command: *be there. come alone.* Caller unknown, but she knew who, and what, it was. Reaching out so directly was unprecedented. Clearly, this was important. The next phase was surely imminent. And it appeared no one else had been summoned, only her. And so, with her nerves: a certain thrill.

She rounded the northeast corner, into the service lane that stretched alongside the plaza. A rank of garbage bins lined the brick wall, stinky and swarmed with flies. She could discern how past the row the wall jutted in, into a loading bay's unlit recess. As far as she could tell, the location pinpointed in the message was just ahead, in the loading bay.

Facing the darkness, she was struck by something she'd heard her grandmother, the poet, once say. Since Ximena's death earlier that year, Alejandra had compiled the few videos and interviews she could find online related to her. In one BBC interview from the mid-nineties, the old woman had sat on a panel among other writers nominated for some award and been questioned as to how she defined her understanding of beauty, the subject she'd undertaken in various forms throughout the entirety of her work. For her, Ximena said, beauty wasn't found in decay—the ungainly vacancy of the industrialized world, the debasement of the spirit, all those postmodern fixations—nor was it found in the gleam of the soul's animation, death's hinged chambers, as in the lusty effusiveness of the Romantics. For her, beauty resided in *claimless forms of the ineffable*. More specifically, it was found in the release achieved by encounters with unknowability, futility: *the unburdening*, she called it. Her interviewer asked: *So how does this relate, as it seems to in your writing, to sex?* Ximena, shot in a tight close-up, had batted her eyebrows and taken a slow drag of her cigarette. *Whatever do you mean? A lady never discusses such things.* Followed by coughing laughter.

Alejandra moved past the garbage bins, grimacing at the smell of rot. The next partition was marked with signage: NO UNAUTHORIZED PARKING NO DUMPING. She again checked her phone: no new calls or messages, and the battery was almost drained. She kept going.

This so-called unburdening, Ximena asserted later in that same interview, might allow access to zones beyond the quotidian. It was difficult to ascertain through her deadpan delivery how literally she meant this to be taken—she spoke of spirit dimensions, zones populated not by vengeful phantoms or winged cherubs but by energies through which one could probe and interrogate the inner self. All modes of knowledge were only facets of our interaction with such realms, even if the ordinary self, the mind in all its discontent, received only coded glimpses. These things, she suggested, might harmonize with the *infinite resignation* that Kierkegaard saw as a requisite of faith. The universe of the poet-as-visionary could, in a sense, be like that of theoretical physics: both sought explanations through models of the infinite. Possibilities, never impossibilities. We were condemned to cosmic silence, true, but that unfulfilled expectation could infuse in us a certain power.

It's a frustrating way of getting through the day, Ximena laughed to her interviewer, tooting smoke through puckered lips. But it's what we do.

Alejandra reached the loading bay's waist-high ledge and peered into its cavity. Something skittered inside—a rustle of leaves or a nest of rats, impossible to tell. Her pulse quickened, urged as much by irritation as fear. With a wavering voice, sounding more wracked than she'd hoped, she called out: I'm here.

Ahead down the lane, headlights ignited.

Alejandra backed away from the ledge. The car rolled toward her. She tucked her phone into her pocket and started back the way she'd come. She chanced a look back, but the headlights, beams on high, obscured the car and its driver. It was a thing of pure light, widening in its approach, accelerating.

Go away, she whispered.

The car pulled up, almost upon her. Alejandra pinned her back against the brick wall. The headlights prismed.

Again: *Go away*.

When Alejandra tried to imagine what form her own unburdening might take, she could only think of some sort of release of pressure, like a valve loosened. As a geologist observes: layers of rock erode away to free underlying igneous formations of their stresses, to expand and unload, fracturing and releasing. The thing imprisoned, relieved of its weight, is exhumed. And in surfacing, it becomes something wholly new.

The car braked and the driver's-side door opened.

And what do we have here, Bartek sang.

Alejandra charged over and swung at his face with her elbow: a kung fu move, praying mantis–style, retained from YMCA self-defence classes a thousand years ago. Bartek ducked out of range, but his goofy grin disappeared—the intention behind the move was communicated.

That was you? she said. You could've said so.

I'm keeping coms tight. I picked up this burner phone.

He waved a cheap flip phone, the kind they sold at the counter at Circle K.

Everything's traceable. The feds are always listening. They have bots and shit to pick up suspicious activity over the networks. Serious. You gotta get a burner phone.

And first thing you do with it is text me. Way to outfox 'em, genius.

Alejandra looked back over her shoulder. The realization sank in, just how wrongly she'd read this situation.

Why am I here? What's going on?

I can't believe you're even asking that. You know what's going on, Ortigosa. The moment of catastrophe, it's almost here. I feel it, you feel it. We all yap and yap, but nothing's *happening*. Someone's got to bring down the fucking hammer.

Sure.

Think I'm kidding? I'll show you all. I'll mash all you fucks into mashed potatoes.

Bartek looked at her then, his face half-caught in the headlights, and his expression told her: he was just as deep in this as she was. Deeper, possibly. Or was he pulling something here? He wasn't one to advertise his impulses so baldly.

And you dragged me down here, to this grossness, just to tell me that.

Maybe if you had a burner phone, we could've coordinated…

Will you please stop saying *burner phone*?

Bartek took a step back. He hopped up onto the ledge and into the bay.

Just come in here with me. I'll show you exactly what I have going on.

He moved into the bay, into the darkness. She didn't follow. He called to her again, something about the stockpile. Then: a metallic clatter from the shadows. Alejandra turned away. As she hastened back toward the parking lot, she tuned out Bartek's calls after her. She was already far from his displays and pleas, far from the grime of this lifeless place. Soon enough, a true message would come, infusing her with its power. Until then, she would wait.

They came together at the river later, under cover of night, as always.

It's insincerity, Calvin was saying.

It's *not*, Julia said. It's about saying something exists that doesn't exist. I'm just trying to do the right thing with his feelings and everything.

Calvin paced, in constant motion as always.

You're ignoring the actual reality. You're so manipulative.

It's just mercy. It's being basically merciful. Honestly, I don't see what's wrong about that.

But you know, Gwendolyn chimed in, that guy is kind of a puss. He cries a lot.

So I'm being insensitive? Julia said. I'm not sensitive?

Calvin, leery, squeezed his crotch.

I'll show you bitches what's sensitive.

They all laughed. Close to the push of outbound city traffic but bulwarked by gravel banks, nothing but a dead auto yard to the south and the barren riverbed to the west, this place offered a certain unmapped sanctuary. No one came down here—there was no reason anyone would want to. So they could gather unhindered by any external forces.

Alejandra, sitting on an open case of Bud Light, slowly drinking her second can, heeded her friends' conversation with only the barest of interest. Their goofy chatter, whatever they were talking about, was only to displace the subject on all their minds.

Gwendolyn came over and kicked the case. Alejandra reached between her legs and fished out a beer.

I told you I got another call? Gwendolyn said, cracking the can.

Alejandra was surprised to hear this, but offered nothing back.

It wasn't all that long. It was just more of a quick, here's the situation. But the timing's still kind of interesting.

I got another call too, Calvin said.

What? Alejandra said. When?

Calvin smirked.

Okay. I didn't.

Julia and Gwendolyn laughed. Alejandra didn't. She again resolved to purge herself of all toxic substances, repeating an inner pledge she'd made following her recent flunk-outs. The chemicals, the distractions, the troubled sleep—it was all destabilizing her neurotransmitters, clouding her mind, her processes of recall losing their oomph.

The day she'd known for certain the semester was truly sunk was also the last time she'd seen Wesley, during mid-terms for Global Issues. Until that day, her failure had only been a likely but still-unrealized outcome. All that school year she'd been a phantom, catching up to her future, fucking-up self, culminating in that miserable morning: cramming past midnight, chugging Dunkin Donuts coffee on the bus, loping into Mr. Darnelle's classroom, pencil case tucked in her armpit, penning her name at each page's top right corner in advance. All was preordained; she was merely executing necessary motions. As the second hand snapped to the hour, they turned their papers over and began. The dates and sequences pounded into her memory from the course notes were a garble. Brundtland Commission 1987. Rio de Janeiro Summit 1992. Declaration on the Rights of Indigenous People 2007. For the final essay section, she'd chosen Topic C: *What is an example of how a government policy decision has had a direct effect on a specific community in an area of global concern? Explain in your own words, but provide specific examples, both recent and historical.* After the usual introductory bullshit, she'd blanked. Key names and terms came in recall, hasty bullet points from her terribly taken notes: *scarcity displacement refugee crisis structural adjustment sovereign immunity.* But none of it connected into anything like an actual idea. The utensils of her salvation slipped from her clammy grasp.

When the first hour was up, marking the minimum allotted time, she waited with head bowed, not wanting to be the first to hand in the test and in so doing publicly announce how badly she'd blown it. Time crawled; she sat stunned with dismay. This was interrupted by Wesley's rising and marching to the front, where he slapped his own test down on Darnelle's desk and bolted. After what seemed an appropriate wait, Alejandra did the same.

She found Wesley on a bench by the baseball diamond, watching ninth-graders run wind sprints. Of Global Issues, nothing was said. Wesley told her he'd received another call, just the night before. When she asked what it had said, he hawked pointedly onto the bench beside him. He'd heard something he hadn't heard before, he said. The covenant still stood, and had to be respected. But how he saw the pieces fitting together, and how he fit into it—this had changed.

There has to be a sacrifice, Wesley had said. A blood sacrifice.

At the time, Alejandra had raised no objections, demanded no further details.

The runners on the field wrapped up their drills to a whistle's call. Wesley pointed out a kid who'd tucked his gym shirt into his tighty-whities, and they laughed. When Alejandra went to leave, Wesley offered a hand, and they fumbled a semi-high-five, semi-handshake. She told him to let her know how things went, and wished him luck.

Wesley smiled.

Luck schmuck, he said.

Three days later, Phoenix PD issued the missing persons bulletin.

Seriously, Calvin was now saying, *I'm* the one who should be running the program. Not you wimps. Definitely not Wesley. Like a fruitso like him could hack the tough stuff.

We're kind of all getting away from the whole concept, Gwendolyn said.

If there even is a concept, Julia said.

Of course there is, Gwendolyn said. That's pretty crystal clear. We do the thing, keep it sub rosa, then the other thing comes to us all. Everything falls into place. This isn't hard to get your brain around.

But it's been months, Julia said. What do we even know? It's all just this hypothetical blah.

No, it isn't, Gwendolyn said. The thing's just waiting for us. You just have to be not so whiny about it.

I'm not whining. I'm just thinking. And there's more to the situation than just what we want.

Sure, Gwendolyn said. Think what you think. Think think think. But for me, a covenant's stronger than any law. That's what *I* think. And for sure what Wesley thinks.

Wesley went one hundred percent psychopathic.

Gwendolyn pointed at Julia, prodding with an aggressive index, a thing she did when she expected to be taken seriously.

Wesley held up his end, she said, just like he was supposed to. Maybe you need to ask yourself some questions, Jules. As far as where you are with everything.

Julia looked away, down the river.

All I know, Calvin said, is when things come together, all of you are going to bow the fuck down.

Hold up, Gwendolyn laughed, who's bowing down to who?

All of you. Bow down.

Gwendolyn bonked Calvin on the head with her empty beer can, initiating a half-hearted scuffle. As they crawled over one another, Alejandra remained seated, watching Gwendolyn closely. The claims she made were plainly lies. She hadn't received a message, no way. Why Gwendolyn would say such a thing, and what she thought she might gain from it, wasn't clear. But if whatever it was undermined the conditions of the covenant, then Alejandra would have no choice but to regard this, and her, as a threat. She hadn't told the others about her meeting with Bartek, and had decided to leave it unmentioned. There too was a potential threat.

Yes, she had to stay sharp. Unclouded. There were *gateways to realms unfathomable*, unlike this one—of this she was certain. The real question was who would be sanctioned to pass through. Who among them would be granted access.

Everyone's dedication would soon be tested. *There has to be a sacrifice.*

Returning to her father's house, Alejandra found her stepmother still up. Sharon sat on the living room floor surrounded by boxes and envelopes, stacks of negatives, leather-bound albums: consolidating and digitizing years of photographs had been her much-discussed and long-delayed project, and it seemed she'd finally dug in. When Alejandra entered the room, Sharon started, looking bleary. She invited Alejandra to sit with her—there were things she wanted her to see. Here was the compiled evidence of a life. A photograph: corralled around a barroom table spilling with ashtrays and Corona bottles, half a dozen young women, all sun-seared, hairsprayed, skimpily attired. Cancun 1995, Sharon explained, pointing herself out. Alejandra squinted against the picture's groggy focus. This young babe—bangs crimped, wearing a purple bikini top under a baggy Ron Jon Surf Shop T-shirt—was a stranger.

When you're young, God's on your side, Sharon said. But then you wake up and it's just you. I wish I hadn't been so damn *happy*.

Sharon flipped through more photos, frolics in snorkel gear and morning hotel sloppiness, more nightclubs and drink-laden tables. Toward the bottom of this set she came to another picture of her younger, blonder self, found here on a dance floor in the embrace of a stocky guy with bleached, chin-length hair, her mouth against his. The camera's flash illumined a wet peek of tongue. At this, Sharon fell mute. Alejandra left her and headed upstairs.

This selfish sentimentality made her sick. Nostalgia was just a noose. Right now, she was young, and someday she would be old, but these were no longer considerations of any importance. *I will never be like you*, she silently swore to her stepmother. This tiresome world, festering in all-inclusive vacations and academic transcripts and premenstrual acne, its people mollified by temporary glimmers, would soon dissolve, dropping like a curtain to reveal the thing, the true thing, behind.

THE FIRST NIGHT SLEEPING IN THE DRAMA STUDIO HAD BEEN AGONY. The makeshift bunk she'd fashioned in the back of the supply closet out of fabric heaps and sofa cushions was workable, though the unventilated closet was stuffy with the sick tang of carpenter's glue, and the cushions' coarse material left her cheeks itchy and red. The building's every tic and shudder kept her on edge, fearful of an alarm's triggering or some night custodian barging in; she kept the lights off and held her bladder. Eventually, in her dreary grotto of wigs and AC extensions and bristol board, Jovena found fitful, dreamless sleep. Come morning, she hastily showered in the girls' lockers and was at her desk well before Billie's arrival. As subsequent nights passed without detection or incident, she grew accustomed to being down there, hidden away in the dark. This lightless, airless realm had unexpectedly analgesic properties—as if a filter kicked in, dimming low-simmering panic into sedative white noise. But this refuge came with inbuilt time limits—even if, following Ortigosa's rendering of judgment, she somehow clung to her job, the school would soon be closed until the fall semester.

Decisions would soon have to be made. Returning to the house was no longer possible. It belonged to the demon now. Maybe it always had.

I look around and all I see is this shithole of blown possibilities. This was Miguel, staring into a half-drained moonshine margarita, his chin wet with molten mozzarella. For his birthday last year, he and Jovena had hit a beer garden on 4th Avenue to demolish a platter of chili nachos. The night was pleasantly cool, with desert winds skimming the city. But Miguel was in a funk. He was ready to leave it all, disgusted not just with California but the entirety of his milieu, everything. Increasingly, he spoke in axioms and absolutes, scorning the smog and drought management, the deep-seated inequity and anti-intellectual paranoia that had come to permeate America's collective identity, the friends he'd forsaken for their small-mindedness. UCI, he said, had become a corporate mill mass-producing mediocrity, and he'd left with much coursework unsubmitted, consequences be damned.

Here, he said, in all this... I can't hear anything through all the noise.

Still, he refused to cave to cynicism, and yearned to rekindle his own inner fire. That was the night he'd first informed her of his plans abroad. The school-building initiative in Bukedea, in Uganda, would last seven weeks; after that, he'd be equipped with a six-month visa carrying him to year's end. After that, who knew. He had notions of an ESCWA internship in Yemen, but there were paperwork considerations still to deal with.

The effects of his eye-opening *kashf*, Miguel claimed, had been significant. This encounter had brought him a clearer understanding of universal order, and consequently a truer sense of purpose. *Even if we don't understand the plan, we gotta remain open to how it unfolds.* Only way we approach God's truth is through brief encounters with his grace. To Jovena, such attestations made little sense. Unlike Miguel, always restless, or their mother, warring against her own self-foreclosing mind, Jovena had never waged resistance against anything. Her thirty-one years had passed in a shudder. Even Miguel seemed only half-aware of her presence as she listened dutifully to his tirades while poking at blobs of molten pepper jack left on the tray.

We can't dwell on old days, he'd said. *Life is transformation. So we have to allow ourselves to be transformed. Otherwise we're pretty much already dead.*

All this was true. But the future held its own horrors too. He'd left, and now she was truly alone—alone in the shithole.

When the State Department number showed on her phone's display, she took the call knowing any satisfaction coming out of it was unlikely. A different woman was on the line this time, gruffer in tone. She began by restating the details of the initial query, which Jovena confirmed. The woman said there had been an alteration to the file status, but she needed to check on something first, and would Jovena please hold.

As she waited, Jovena's eyes were drawn to the potted cactus on her desk next to her monitor. A gift from Billie, a single fuzzy stub in a ceramic pot—super low maintenance, Billie had said. Who knew what comfort such a thing was meant to provide. As Jovena stared at its prickled hide, another image came, of other flora twisting against human domination, of bellflowers planted on hilltops, free and untrampled by rotten people. If only such a place existed, where all thrived on pure devotion and nothing else. But fragile things always fell. Cries for mercy and gentleness were forever muffled by industry. No one heard; no one cared. She sipped her water bottle and rubbed her eyes.

When the woman came back on the line, the results she gave were inconclusive, as expected. It seemed a reply had been received from the embassy in Nairobi, but little could be confirmed. An alert was filed with local authorities, but rarely did anything come of these. Other routes would involve proceeding at a heightened level, which was a whole other thing.

Chances are, the woman said, your brother was just out having an adventure and got carried away. What was best, she advised, was to get the word around online and whatnot, and just hold tight. To this, Jovena could only agree—there was nothing to do but wait.

But that night, a beckoning came.

It was almost ten o'clock. By the light of a single desk lamp, Jovena sat trying to read lines from *Tartuffe* in the *Anthology of Living Theatre* she'd found among the closet shelves. Instead, she found her eyes continually drawn to the drama studio floor. The tiles' pattern created a rotational optical effect, drawing her focus to an approximate central nucleus: the spot, according to Alejandra, where Lavoir had been found. By accounts, the man had been cleaved into sections, with the remains strewn here. It was an unthinkable thing, a desecration.

What it would feel like, to be torn apart so completely?

When the sound came, it took a moment for her to make it out. She held her breath and listened. And there it was, resonating from some origin outside the room, beyond the basement—whether the yawn of the building's innards or some security mechanism's hearkening, it could not be ignored. This call was for her.

Oooooooo.

Emerging from the subterranean studio, she climbed the stairs to the north hallway, listening for the creak of wringer wheels, though the custodian on duty had long wrapped his route. The darkness was concentrated, syrupy; dimensions expanded and contracted. The weak light of an exit sign pointed the way past trophy cases, adornments and banners, MTHS's official crest vowing AD MAIOREM DEI GLORIAM, all scaled down to teenager-apposite dimensions. This was a school, and like all schools a type of factory, churning out adolescent worry, even if its output in this regard was presently low.

She came to the cafeteria's double doors and pushed through. Watchful for any movement, she moved down the centre aisle, past the grid of tables, the corralling steel barriers and windows with security shades drawn. At the room's opposite end was a potential source of the summoning sound: a Pepsi machine, its blue light transmuting the proximity into a subaquatic abyss, its fan or some mechanism venting a displeased tone. Jovena knuckled one of the machine's glowing plastic buttons, as if a can of 7 Up might magically be ejected. Nothing happened.

She returned unsatisfied to the hallway. To one direction lay the route from which she'd come, and a return to the basement; to the other was the central concourse and the front stairwell. There was a decision to be made, but there really wasn't. All impulse was subordinate to the forces compelling her.

And when the sound again came, louder now—*oooooooo*—she had no choice but to chase it. She hesitated at the stairwell's base, listening. The second floor went mostly unused during the summer, the classrooms locked and bathrooms receiving only superficial maintenance. Staring up through the stair's slats, she was dimly aware of her phone vibrating with an incoming call.

The voice hissed with unconcealed delight.

You know what's waiting for you, don't you?

From somewhere behind her came a rustling, a scurry of motion in staccato clacks. Claws on tiles.

You, who infested our world. You, who sat there in the sun for hours, staring at the garage door. Trying to steal what wasn't yours. Whose fingers pressed until bruises broke. Who cried and cried.

The caller's voice sounded burdened with a resignation that hadn't been there in previous calls. The voice had changed, as if performing a reluctant impersonation of itself.

She moved away from the stairs, drawn by the clacking sound. Another corridor, another twisting path into darkness. She tried to work her way forward using the sonar of her boot heels on the linoleum, but almost immediately she lost her way. The decrepit school was a creature twisting inside an ever-disjointing endoskeleton, growing around her, its limbs lengthening, reaching.

More scurrying came from ahead. Then the low, heaving respiration of her attendant fiends.

Remember. Tess called you an evil psychotic fuck. A crazy dyke. She knew. She saw through you. She knew you were a monster.

This sounded familiar. But the actual circumstances, what had really occurred—Jovena simply couldn't recount anymore.

Your gluttony pollutes the world. Now all that awaits you is the pain you deserve.

This was now another voice entirely, one unconnected to San Diego, or any place or time at all.

This history of foulness. A family of low-born bitches. Stupid and poor, like cockroaches in the sewers. Cursed.

Fear had kept her under rule, shuttering her away even as she tempted exposure to the world's afflictions. Yes, like a cockroach.

Something sliced through the gloom ahead, a shard of light down an adjacent hallway. She chased it, losing any feeling of the floor beneath, forgetting the pangs in her stomach. She recalled Miguel's desert revelation, how his vision of night's reality went skewed, how the unveiling that had granted him the affirmation he sought. But this was nothing like that. The demons sniffing after her dwelled past barriers of time and geography. They fed on the past.

Why did they hunger for her so?

That light intensified as she drew nearer. She now saw: the light was a doorway. The school was just an antechamber. The way through lay farther ahead, waiting for her.

Eventually you'll find yourself where you belong. At the farthest reach, where the scum collects. When you get there, you'll understand. There's nothing there. No portion of any glory for you. No peace and no conclusion. The curse can't be lifted.

She went for her phone, hoping to use its light. Her phone wasn't there. It hadn't been there.

And then she was outside, floating across the southeast parking lot, to the basketball court, through the chain-link fencing to the soccer field, headed for the woods. A dog sprinted the field's length chasing a tennis ball, followed by a figure in neon-yellow shorts and smoking a cigarette, but these were denizens of another plane, now behind her. The sky throbbed with rising force, its rage mounting.

Things, finally, were about to change. She now understood what Alejandra Ortigosa had meant: *Everything happens in long waves, until a massive event happens and the world is shaped by sudden blasts.*

As Jovena left the field, her feet lost contact with the coarse grass beneath. The earth became steam.

Things were becoming so much clearer. No longer would she be punished for her yearning. She could be transient again, as in those infinite nights on the highway, laying her head in her mother's lap, letting her hair be stroked, as quiet as a corpse. She could be lost, another item deleted from the record in order to stabilize projections, to keep things straight.

Even as one door behind you closes, the voice told her, *another one opens.*

They came to her as she entered the woods. All around her, her fellow demons circling in formation, *the traucos and wekufes and cucuys and all those creeps*. Infernal chisellers, the soulless creatures of tendon and fat. The destroyers and dreamers. From all sides she heard the subsonic rumble of their growls, their panting, as they welcomed her.

THEIR DOMINION WAS TAKEN AWAY, *yet their lives were prolonged for a season and a time* read the purple-and-gold-tasseled banner governing the buffet table. Though hung with care and pride, the old banner had become ratty with years, a disappointment furthered by the lacklustre spread it highlighted: a few bags of Ruffles, a tray of cauliflower florets sided with a suspect ranch dip, a punch bowl of something reddish and filmy. The traditions of the Lifting of the Veil were entrenched in MTHS's history, and the ad hoc planning committee had made a valiant effort to remake the gymnasium in ceremonial trappings: that time-worn banner, floor-length gossamer drapes hiding the cement walls, imposing papier-mâché columns coated in a patina of blended latex paints arranged along the sidelines. The stage's proscenium curtains, usually furled for concerns of safety, had been deployed. And hovering over centre court: an actual chandelier, donated back in the nineties by some student's antique-dealer parents, hung by a chain and twinkling in its stainless-steel frame despite the smudges and cracks of its blown glass candle fittings. The planning committee was even rumoured to have tried to negotiate, as a nod to tradition, the arrangement of an indoor spit and an actual goat for slaughter from a ranch in San Tan Valley—but such plans, if true, had evidently not come to pass.

The night was sticky with atmospheric tension. Heavy rainfall via a storm front from the southeast was causing reported power outages in Chandler and areas of Tempe, with closures along Interstate 10. The storm had so far held off from hitting central Phoenix, but warnings of flash floods were circulating.

Despite such portents, they came. Attendance was sparse, given the rescheduling, but a commemorative air still pervaded. The Lifting was meant to represent the year's zenith: a brightness post-doldrums and the scrapping of responsibilities, fused with the melancholy of a chapter's conclusion. As was customary, the occasion began in solemnity. The students filed in through the gym entrance, now festooned as a garlanded archway; dressed almost entirely in white, also as per tradition, together they formed a colligated, washed-out blur of non-identity. The introductory music over the PA was low-key, a quasi-nostalgic signifier of olden days: Glenn Miller, Louis Armstrong, Sinatra. Kids, solo and in twos, crowded the refreshments table and staked out vantages against walls and on bleachers. A few boys broke into spurts of goofish, self-conscious dancing in the gym's open centre before retreating back to the periphery.

As a Santo and Johnny number faded up, a sextet of girls, tenth-graders in a coordinated set of lavish vintage gowns, recognized this as a cue and moved to the floor's centre. There they arranged themselves into a grid and, with a shared look, began to sway side to side in choreographed time, continuing into a simple, unshowy sequence of half and full spins, gowns flowing, feet pivoting. Onlookers pointed phones to catch pictures. Someone pointed one of the stage spotlights their way, casting the girls in a lunar radiance. The dancers basked in the attention, twirling and shuffle-stepping, their faces serene.

Alejandra stood by herself at the sidelines, watching this unfold. It was something to see, this exultation, such reassurance found in togetherness. She envied these girls.

Her attention, however, stayed on Bartek. Audacious in a white tuxedo jacket with coordinating trousers and rhinestoned cowboy boots, he and a few other guys had taken a spot at the far corner along the gym's east wall, atop the retracted bleachers, a vantage point from where to overlook the room. She'd texted him repeatedly in the preceding days, demanding to know what exactly he had in the works for tonight. Bartek was usually snappy with replies, pervy jokes. But lately, he'd been weirdly evasive. Tonight, as she'd waited at home for Julia and the others to pick her up, his reply had finally come to her queries: *all good. see ya at river later.*

He was obviously fucking with her. Whatever he had planned, it ventured outside the terms of the covenant, and those terms were already dicey enough. Alejandra understood that the covenant, and any possibility of its achieving anything, rested on him just as much as it did on her. But how it would play out—they all had different ideas in that department. Bartek's thirst for chaos had been announced loudly and repeatedly: *Someone's got to bring down the fucking hammer.*

Now, watching him, she felt her sense of general worry morphing into something more like real alarm. While his allies brazenly swilled liquor from a passed pocket flask, Bartek seemed sober, or soberish. Leaning in his supremely preposterous getup, he gazed upward, transfixed by the crappy chandelier. Or something else, some focal point exclusive to him alone.

Sweat trickled down the small of her back. She adjusted her dress, which was nothing special, a basic thing from her closet.

The canned music faded and a clonk from the PA announced a turn in the program. A Korean girl Alejandra recognized but didn't really know came onstage and checked a microphone: *Test test.* To her right, a guy plugged an electric guitar into a small amp, the patch cord's noisy crackle turning heads and quieting chatter. There was no introduction heralding their performance; they simply began. The boy strummed a sequence of minor chords, and though the guitar hung unwieldy on his lanky frame, he seemed to know what he was doing. He let a suspended chord hang as the girl licked her lips, staring past her onlookers. When her voice came, it was little more than a whisper, yet cut cleanly through the gymnasium's cavernous acoustics.

Such a soft song, night above the river floats. Factory gleams in a faraway light. Somewhere a train is riding in spots of fire.

Alejandra felt her palms go cold, her stomach struck with a demanding pain. Her balance careened. She backed against the wall, crumpling, clutching her midsection while pressing her head against the cold concrete.

Her vision fractured; she lost hold of her surroundings. Something was happening.

Somewhere under the rowan tree, boys are waiting for me.

Vance Dolen, reviled English teacher and one of the luckless staffers saddled tonight with chaperone duty, stood leaning against a nearby pommel horse ornamented with tissue paper roses. Seeing Alejandra on the floor, he came over and jostled her by the shoulder, asking over the music if she needed him to fetch an Advil or something. Alejandra, breathing in gasps, could only shake her head in refusal.

As the girl's song glided into another verse, there was a disruption at the front of the room. A figure wildly stalked the gap between stage and audience, flailing arms and yelling, as if daring any bystander to approach. The singer continued unfazed, though the audience was effectively rattled. In her agony, Alejandra looked and recognized the inciter: Calvin. Such behaviour, such flagrant aggression, was not out of character; he was an incorrigible shit-disturber. What was unusual was for him to be acting alone, unbacked by any of his crew. They tended to travel in a pack. Calvin, still bounding about in furious motion, reached into his pocket to produce a fistful of bottle caps and began firing them at the chandelier above. The *tink* of metal on glass rang out. Voices came in objection, yet still no one made moves to subdue him.

As Calvin's gesticulations increased in their mania, Alejandra looked back across the gym to see Bartek in motion, scrambling over the bleachers in the opposite direction of the stage. At the far end he hopped down onto the floor, checked back over his shoulder, then made for the exit doors.

Alejandra alone saw what was happening: a distraction was being created.

When Calvin seized the closest bystander, a pipsqueak ninth-grader in a seersucker suit and coordinated fedora, and began swinging him violently by his lapels, Vance Dolen finally moved to intervene. The crowd pressed forward. Photo flashes went off.

Alejandra attempted to stand, but her legs buckled. The weakness was total and overwhelming—some essential inner power was being drained out of her. There was something familiar in this feeling. She'd felt like this months ago, hovering at Ximena's bedside in Mexico. With the old woman packed under fusty blankets, her disembodied head of dry lips and ashen skin the only suggestions of life still sustained, Alejandra had felt something occur between them, a sort of transference. And with it, the possibility that even though the body's shell might falter, some reserve of energy it held might yet endure. But if such convection had really occurred, feeding her Ximena's fuel, it stood to reason it could just as easily drain back out.

Oh, curly rowan tree, flowers so white, why are you grieving now?

A girl in a yellow chiffon evening gown came to her side, offering an arm for support. Alejandra took it and managed to rise, allowing herself to be led through the crowd. The girl spoke to her several times, but Alejandra, still impaired, missed what she said. Only when they'd reached the exit doors did Alejandra even realize the girl was Julia. Her brunette locks had been combed into tight waves and her eyelids fluttered under the weight of silk lashes—she looked a bit like Lillian Gish. To Julia's concerned inquiries, Alejandra only nodded, dazzled by the sight of Julia's resplendence. It couldn't be denied: her friend of years had been remade into something else completely.

The main entrance's bright light came like a slap. Traffic in and out of the gym and throughout all accessible zones was supervised by two private security guards in embroidered jackets. Leaving Julia in the gym, Alejandra made it past and into the hallway without attracting attention. She paused at a water fountain and drank, fighting this disequilibrium, readying for a dash around the corner. But before she made her move, a guard appeared, blocking her path.

Bathroom, she said.

Back there, the guard said, pointing.

But the machine that works is in the one down there. Tampons.

An old ploy—as always, it worked.

Make it snappy, the guard said, standing aside. Don't want kids lining up down here to go sniff Javex or whatever it is you do.

As she hurried down the hall, her stomach surged again. This wasn't the pulse of bad digestion, or the clang of common cramps. Her body was turning itself inside out. She pushed on.

Bartek wasn't at his locker. But then she heard the echo of something clanking farther down the hallway. In an alcove beneath the foot of the south wing stairs, crouched over a large Bauer hockey bag, was Bartek. He looked up as she approached.

Oh, he said. Having fun tonight?

Are you?

He withdrew a long leather case from the bag.

Yeah. I love to party. That's all I do. Party party party.

Me too.

Feeling all right? You look like ass. No offence.

She watched as he unzipped the case to produce a rifle, tucking its stock under his armpit.

Don't do this, she said. I'm serious.

You know I have to. Blood sacrifice.

I don't know anything. Neither do you.

He rummaged further in the bag to produce a magazine. The way he jammed it into the rifle's body with one confident move indicated he'd done this before.

I know what I know, he said. My eyes are peeled. And now's the moment. If I need to shoot someone in the face to move things forward, he said, then that's what's happening. The blade must be swinged. You know. You agreed.

I didn't agree to this stupid shit.

Don't call me stupid.

I'm not calling you stupid. I'm saying this is stupid. And it's swung.

Swing swang swung. Fuck it.

He stood, holding the rifle by its grip.

Where'd you get that thing? she said. And how'd you get it past the metal detectors?

Do you know what a lacrosse-stick case looks like?

No.

Well, neither does that drip-dick who watches the door here in the mornings. See, I plan ahead. I'm smart. There's three Mylar canisters of demolition C4 in this building with charges set to go. I made that happen.

What?

I tried to show you. But you had your head too far up your vagina to see.

Bartek came closer. She felt his wolfish glare working her over, but her eyes remained drawn to the rifle.

You say I don't know anything. But here's what I know. You can kick the crap out of your dog every day and it won't run off. Maybe it'll be afraid to look you in the eyes. But maybe one night that dog'll come in while you're sleeping and bite your face off.

Alejandra didn't follow what he was talking about, or what it had to do with anything. Things were slipping in a direction she wasn't prepared for. She was having difficulty concentrating on anything but the rifle. Sleek and solid, incontestable—it had a gravitational pull.

You never thought there'd be a cost to getting what you want? That's what a sacrifice *is*.

Alejandra kept silent.

All right, Bartek said.

With the rifle held tight under his arm, he kicked the hockey bag into the corner and made to leave. Alejandra met his move, an attempt to block his path.

Please, she said. You'll go to jail. Or worse.

Ha. They're not putting me anywhere.

Please.

Bartek sneered in disgust.

Get out of here, Ortigosa. Honestly, I have no problem clocking a chick.

He moved, and she again tried to impede him, pressing against him with what feeble strength she had, a desperate manoeuvre that became more of an awkward semi-hug. It wasn't enough. With his free arm, he peeled her off and shoved her aside.

Marching toward the stairs, weapon in hand, Bartek grew in stature. His slumpy body inflated, gaining in magnitude. The doofus she'd known, had bickered with, had fucked, was now transforming into a beastly thing of righteousness. Maybe this was the inevitable resolution of their covenant, a thing as abstract as a dream, now becoming real. An old permutation was surrendering to the new.

The moment of catastrophe. When it arrives, let nothing hinder your progress.

As Bartek stomped upstairs, Alejandra looked around, searching her vicinity. A fire alarm pull station was mounted on the opposite wall. With this, a choice fell upon her: between the known and the unknowable, the ordinary way of things or the possibility of all that was promised. She knew which was the right choice. She chose the other.

Wind whipped the parking lot as they streamed from the school, sending dresses flapping and hairdos into disarray. The alarm pounded. Confusion reigned. Abandoning tested fire drill procedures and ignoring their chaperones' pleas to form orderly lines, the exiting crowd's progress stalled in a glut at the front doors, then pushed through. The collective disposition was past irritation—this violation, this sabotage, was yet another affront to sacred tradition.

Who's the motherfucker this time.

This is major bullshit.

Such bullshit.

Alejandra followed the crowd, by all signs one of the last to exit the school. The security guard who'd interrogated her earlier stopped her, asking if there was anyone still inside. She said no.

Sirens soon rose down the street, broadcasting the arrival of fire engines. In the blaze of emergency light, all was recast in lurid red. Cheers broke out; phones documented the pandemonium. Alejandra pushed her way through the parking lot in a daze, looking for her friends. She checked her phone, finding nothing. What had just happened, what was really happening, was already eluding her.

Allie?

Brittany Wothousin, the junior class's horselike overachiever, hurried over. Her eyes were wide with fear.

What do we do?

The flow of events that followed would forever be scrambled in Alejandra's memory. A series of actions and subsequent effects rippled out from an epicentre to ambiguous end points. If, as the textbook contended, geological history was only understandable as long troughs of inchoate time interrupted by cataclysmic jolts, of a transference of power, then what occurred—a spray of blood, a decisive thump—should have persisted in her recall as vivid and firm. But when, in days and years to come, she tried to piece things together, all she recalled was the pure horror of incomprehension. The gunshot's crack echoed across the grounds and perimeter, its origin unlocatable. In an instant everyone scattered in a chorale of screams. Then, a second shot. Alejandra took cover with others behind the hood of a parked car. Even amid the insanity, it was to be understood: this moment, however traumatic and awful, represented only the latest stage in a longer, complicated sequence that had been unfolding for months, possibly much longer. What was occurring was horrible, but it wasn't *wrong*. Wothousin was a negligible loss, one among many. And this was, on some level at least, precisely what they'd anticipated. There were underlying forces at play. There was a destination.

Someone shouted: *No no no*.

AS ALWAYS, THEY ENDED UP AT THE RIVER. They left Calvin's Jetta by the road, ducking through the break in the fence and easing down the slippery bank. Calvin and Gwendolyn took the lead, arm in arm, drinking tall cans of Tecate and bantering in bad Spanish—*¿Quién es el demonio más bonito de la ciudad?*—with Alejandra and Julia following. Mosquitoes and robber flies whorled. The wind had eased as the storm moved on.

They were taken aback by what they discovered below. The bed of the Salt River almost always sat dry along this stretch, but the flooding upriver had led to an overflow at the diversion dam. The radio had said any hazardous areas had been contained, and the ADEQ was reporting uncontaminated waters, though with cautions for safety. Yet despite this, the section of river where they usually gathered now flowed with dirty water.

Never seen it run so high, Gwendolyn said.

Bust out the Jet Skis, Calvin said.

They followed the river's curve as it extended downstream. Where the shoreline sank under the water's reach, they climbed a concrete wall bordering the bank and continued in single file along its narrow ledge. The river's motion played tricks with distance: the wall could have been a hundred feet high, the water's surface hiding untold fathoms or ankle-deep currents.

At the lead, Calvin took another of the beers dangling from his belt loop, raised it to the sky, and cracked it. Foam flew.

To Bartek! And Wesley!

Gwendolyn whooped her assent. Julia laughed, but said nothing. Alejandra inhaled the warm and mulchy air; though the sickness assailing her had mostly passed, the accompanying dread was unremitting. Tonight was meant to have brought the culmination of these nervous seasons: semesters conquered, covenants fulfilled, veils lifted. But instead, everything was falling into disarray.

They continued along the crumbling wall until they reached another section of dry bank. Here they lingered, orbiting one another nervously. The flood had perturbed the riverbed; trash drudged up in the overspill covered the ground. Gwendolyn cried out in disgust, scraping off a used condom plastered to her shoe.

What are we doing now, exactly? Julia said.

Sort of thought we'd know when we got here, Calvin said. Think maybe we pooched it.

I don't think so, Alejandra said.

Alejandra found Julia looking at her, a question in her eyes. It was obvious that, for Julia, no longer having to wait for the covenant's resolution would be a relief, regardless of the outcome. This detour into contingency, into some non-future, didn't jibe with her prospects of endowments and internships, all the esteem to come. Alejandra turned away from her—as far as she was concerned, Julia was no longer a factor in the covenant's realization.

Where *is* Bartek? Gwendolyn asked.

Police pinched him, Calvin said.

He burst into a ball of flame, Gwendolyn said, and flew away into the clouds.

Really?

I don't know, Gwendolyn said. For sure he got away. He'll be here.

She checked her phone. They each did; they found nothing.

Calvin, again: Think we pooched it.

And the fire? Gwendolyn said. The hell. Must've started in the bathroom.

There wasn't any fire, Alejandra said. I pulled the alarm.

The others glared.

Why? Julia said.

Why? Bartek was heading into the gym with an assault rifle. And he had a bomb. Or some kind of... bomb.

The AR-15 isn't an assault rifle, Calvin said. It's a semi-automatic.

Gwendolyn aimed a finger at Alejandra.

So you screwed us.

I did not.

You wrecked the plan. Or maybe you don't even understand the plan.

Oh, I understand. Do you?

There was no bomb, Calvin said. That's just stupid Bartek playing with you.

Playing? Were you even *there*?

Bartek was doing exactly what we all knew had to be done, Gwendolyn said. Blood sacrifice.

Bartek doesn't know shit about shit. He misinterpreted.

You're just feeling personally disrespected, Julia cut in, because of what went on between you and him. You need to take a look at yourself first before you start—

Shut up, Alejandra said. You don't know anything, you fucking baby.

Gwendolyn drained her beer.

This is so dumb. I'm going home.

As she said this, headlights appeared over the ridge above them, accompanied by the crunch of slow tires on gravel. They all froze. A pair of police cruisers crawled into sight, the one in the lead pointing a searchlight down the bank.

No signal was necessary; they scattered. Gwendolyn and Julia fled back via the embankment wall and the way they'd come. Calvin dashed up the slope, maybe hoping to cut back behind the cops and reach his car on the road.

Alejandra found herself unable, or unwilling, to run. For a moment, she remained unmoving. Then she slid over the wall and into the damp crevice behind it. She crouched there, her back against the concrete, listening. A car door slammed, then another. A voice, a man's, shouted, but she couldn't make out what was said.

Exhaustion overcame her. Some kind of insect whined close to her ear. She closed her eyes.

The error she'd made was becoming clear. In her contempt for this place and all within it, she'd only been chasing some validation of her own worthiness. This was her vanity at work. Her arrogance. The messages, babbling to her across dimensions, had teased this possibility. What might come following the covenant's fulfillment had never been a consideration. Bartek, a dope in so many ways, had seen through her. *You never thought there'd be a cost to getting what you want?* In this, if only this, he was right. She'd wanted what she wanted, to strike a wound without bloodying her own fingers, and never considered the possibility of collateral damage. All that mattered was not being here anymore. Imagining this destined ascent to glory had shielded her from the truth: she yearned to become more, to be proven as more, because she herself was nothing. Just another lazy, short-sighted fool. She was undeserving. She'd pooched it.

The temptation is fierce, the desire to transcend this foul sphere, the message had said.

The truth widened to her now: these transmissions were from the future. They'd spoken of things yet to be—not judgments, but warnings. Possibilities abounded, multiplied, rife with dangers. Worlds spinning within worlds.

Again came memories of Ximena's deathbed, and the faint energy she'd felt seeping from the old woman's waning body into her own. The possibility that anything might live on past expiry to become more than it was—this was a terrible idea. Better for all things, all covenants and longings, to simply come to an end, as they were meant to. The dilemma was in knowing the real ending, and what just appeared to be one.

Wesley learned this, and he was the first to go. He wouldn't be coming back. For the rest of them, the summer would unfold in the madness of a gunshot's echo, then, eventually, secede to autumn and another semester. The order of things would continue, following an established design. More classes, more timetables. More sleepy mornings and sweat-crusted nights. More bomb threats, more panic pulls.

The future stretched out, its promises unfulfilled.

The future: a woman drags a rusty rake across a patch of back lawn. Sounds: the wheeze of a garbage collection truck, a leaf blower's hum, the crack of joints. She shakes her hair from its elastic and redoes her ponytail. Later, she drives through traffic, alone, the steering wheel pressed between her knees. The streets of a city's outskirts flow past. She walks the aisles of an enormous grocery store, astounding in its plenitude and brightness, among heaps of limes and avocados, lustrous flanks of fish on beds of ice, a mountain of beer cases. In the early evening she returns to the backyard and smokes a joint. The faint etches of a meteor shower cross the northeast sky. The entire day passes without her once speaking.

There was a path, and Alejandra, willingly or not, was already on it. And yet so many things remained unsettled.

An indeterminate measure of time slipped by. Alejandra was roused from her reverie—by what, precisely, she wasn't certain. Slinking out from behind the wall, she searched the riverbank and the ridge above, finding no one there. The police cruisers appeared to have moved on. The floodwater moved unhurried.

From upstream, a strange mass was rolling in. Her first thought was it was smoke, spewing from a forest fire off South Mountain maybe. But this gassy lump came slithering across the river's surface, unlike the languor of the post-thunderstorm fog that on rare occasions deluged the city. It moved with intent. And as it inched closer up the bank, she discerned shafts of luminescence inside it, spectra of shifting colour: a soft pinkish hue into violet, vivid blue into a deep auroral green, all pulsing together into pure white.

The light opened, washing over her. She raised her hands. Its form carried no odour, only reassuring warmth. Here, perhaps, was the lenity she'd been hoping for—the unburdening. Despite her many fuck-ups and missteps, what had been promised was coming true. The barriers were dropping.

Alejandra.

The voice came from somewhere else, behind her. The name it called meant nothing. Even the act of its suggestion was laughable. Only the light mattered. Through its iridescent wash, she made out angles, uncertain planes of distance: a city skyline, cranes towering over an excavated tract, an unbuilt tower's steel skeleton, a place unrecognizable. She took a step forward, but felt no link between impulse and muscle.

The call came again. *Alejandra.*

She turned from the light to discover a figure stumbling over the bumpy terrain toward her. Where this person had come from, why they were here—what she was seeing made no sense.

You have to be careful. Some of these kids are real sociopaths.

Jovena came forward, smiling. Her sweatshirt and jeans were soaked through; veins of wet hair clung to her cheeks. Alejandra backed away, feeling the pain in her abdomen seethe anew. Already the light was receding, its mists withdrawing back to the river. Gone was what awaited her. What had been offered was rescinded.

I have something for you, Jovena said.

Before Alejandra could react, Jovena grabbed her wrist, forcing something into her palm and closing her fingers around it. Cold and firm: a key.

What?

I thought it was for me, Jovena said, but it's not. It's for you. You were right. There are powers out there, doing things. And people just don't care. But I do, I really do. And I know you do too. We're the same. I'm you, you're me. No difference. It's just energy, passed back and forth. Everything comes together. We don't have to suffer. You see it.

Why the school secretary was down here, what she was saying— it was as nonsensical as a dream.

You see it.

And something was there, just behind Jovena, clinging to her: spiky and bestial, a nimbus snarling with impatience, baring fangs.

El diablo en el espejo: the devil in the mirror.

Alejandra moved to take back her hand. But Jovena held her firm, exercising greater strength than her gangly frame suggested.

Let go, Alejandra said.

Listen. Everything's quiet. You understand.

Let me go.

Tell me you understand. I know you do.

Alejandra saw: she would not be dissuaded.

I understand. Yes.

To this, Jovena's eyes welled with emotion, something like relief. She threw herself around Alejandra, who went limp in the wet embrace.

No one can see us, Jovena whispered, burying her face in her hair. We're completely invisible.

This was too much. Alejandra tried to tear away, but Jovena held her tight. In desperation, Alejandra threw a wild elbow and connected, sending Jovena recoiling back, coughing, cupping her nose.

From the road above, a siren blooped. Police cruiser lights again peeked over the ridge.

Alejandra knew she had to go. That key was still in her hand, but she rejected any thought of tossing it away and instead tucked it into her dress. She looked to Jovena, bent, wilting—whatever beast had powered her, it had fled.

A radio crackled; figures wielding flashlights came charging down the bank. The only available move was to the water. Hurrying to the river's edge, she cast a glance upstream, from where the light had come. It too was gone.

She treaded forward into the shallows. The silt's suction clamped her feet and grassy strands slimed her forearms. Here was water where water shouldn't be. The current moved quicker than it appeared, enveloping her, incontrovertible. It would take her now, dragging her downstream and away from the city, pulling her southwest down to the Gila River, her body as river scum, riding contours warped into formation by late Cenozoic catastrophes and carved by the industrial passions of generations, the force swallowing her into its enormity, until all that remained of her flowed freely from the Colorado Delta to the Gulf of California, finally swept out to diffuse on the great ocean's tides.

Voices called to her from the shore, but she ignored them. The way was closing behind her. She was alone.

THE UTILITY SHROUD

SHE CAME OUT OF THE MISTY LIGHT into a dark meadow rustling with soft winds. No moon or stars were visible above, no beacon ahead. The only light came from the luminescence wafting around her, languid like a cigarillo's smoke on a warm afternoon.

Forest hugged the meadow's perimeter, walls of pines to all sides. She chose a static point among the trees and aimed for it, walking uphill through tall grasses, barely feeling their touch. Though it seemed she was alone here, she kept vigilant; any threats would likely be unfamiliar ones, and she might not recognize them as such before it was too late.

A filtered whine rose from unseen origins. As its amplitude increased, the source became clear: an airplane approaching, strobes winking. She watched as it passed overhead then sank past the forest ahead, its roar dwindling with a Doppler wane.

She resumed walking. The glow was already receding.

Reaching the threshold between meadow and forest, she hesitated. The way facing her was only pillars of tree trunks and an unbroken ceiling of branches. But her reluctance was really only preparatory, for there was no actual choice.

The forest came in waves, a puzzle of roots and uneven terrain, and the going was slow. Twigs raked her face and arms. With every step she kept alert for any howl or hiss. But here too, it seemed, she was alone.

Her recollection of circumstances before arriving here was dim: late morning rain collecting under leaky bedroom windows; a headache's urgency; a web of cracks above a door frame; the astringent taste of pills' enteric coating. There were voices, coming from people who should be familiar to her, but none she could reconcile. She was old, then young again. Here was no dream, nor death. Here was neither more nor less real than her habitual existence, as immaterial as the beer and *mota*-inspired laze in which she'd done her best work. Questioning this situation would take her nowhere. The best thing was to keep moving.

Just as her frustration with the gruelling forest was leading into the stirrings of panic, a clearing opened. A kind of reservoir lay ahead, about a quarter-mile wide and enveloped by forest at all sides. And on the opposite shore, past the range of trees, was a suggestion of light. As far as she could tell, this was the same bearing the airplane had followed.

Continuing along the shore, she sighted an elongated, curved shape ahead: a wooden rowboat, two oars tucked inside like an invitation. Still, she wavered. Theft in unfamiliar territory was a risk of doubtful reward. But the path laid before her could not be denied.

Sliding the boat to the water was tough work, and even out on smooth water, paddling it pushed the limits of her meagre upper-body strength. She executed her best version of an even stroke, the paddle angled as a rudder, but keeping a steady course proved difficult, and it took her longer than expected to reach what seemed the halfway point. Pausing to regather her strength, she set the dripping oars on her knees. All was still, the only sound the lap of water against the hull.

She almost didn't notice the shape bobbing on the surface, a few strokes away. At first it appeared to be driftwood, or some refuse risen from the deep. But as she stared it moved, revealing a humanoid form. She paddled in that direction. Easing forward, she saw this shape was in fact a young man, bare-torsoed, clinging to what looked like some sort of plastic panel. His face barely broke the water's surface.

The bow swung to the right as she fought to pull closer without colliding with him. She extended one oar, careful not to strike him in the face, and told him to grab a hold. He made no move. She repeated this direction, again to no avail. As she began to sense her attempts would be in vain, the man made weak motions, transferring his hold from the plastic panel to the outstretched oar. With this, she carefully drew him in. Once he was in reach, however, she saw how hard it would be to actually get him into the boat. She reached for his forearms, her stomach pressed painfully against the gunwale. With great effort, she hauled him closer, but lacked the strength or leverage to lift his limp weight.

Can you...

But he couldn't. He was young, even a teenager. Barely conscious, his eyes shut.

She leaned back to consider this conundrum. The rowboat was outfitted with metal mounts for locking the oars into place. She slid one in, leaving the young man hanging on its blade, and paddled with the other. It was difficult, maintaining motion while ensuring he kept his hold. But they moved.

The opposite shore lay ahead. She told him: Just hang on.

When they reached the other side, she hopped out to ground the boat. Crouching in the shallows, she hoisted the young man by his underarms and eased him onto the shore. There she sat beside him and caught her breath, feeling her biceps pulse. Wearing only striped boxer shorts, the young man was white, blond, baby-faced. His breath was faint but there. Only then did she see: his flesh was hacked with deep, vicious cuts, his chest and back a tatter of blood and mangled flesh.

He coughed, gagging, then in a burst of motion sprang to his feet, staking himself unsteadily there, spitting. Her impulse was to back away. But she reached to him, offering assistance.

Nuh, he grunted.

He looked around, evaluating the scene: the shore, the reservoir, his rescuer—striving for focus, like a sleepwalker tracing his path upon waking.

Corporal punishment, he said, then dashed into the trees.

She saw no reason to give chase. She'd done her part, fishing him out. But he was ailing, in need of help, possibly afraid. So she followed after him. Back in the confusion of trunks and branches, she was again disoriented. She discerned an indistinct glow ahead, and took this as her indicator of direction. There was no sign or sound of the boy. She called out: Hello. This voice, her voice, rang feeble.

There was a peculiar comfort in the woods. The crisp night air conjured memories of atmospheres she'd known in childhood, in Nauhcampatépetl's shadow. The quiet was a relief; her every footfall resonated cleanly.

Eventually she arrived at a narrow, unpaved road, where she found the glow's source: a street light posted on the shoulder. No traffic, no sign of the young man or anyone else. The direction of the plane's path, as far as she could tell, aligned roughly with the road's curve to her right. With no other option apparent, she headed that way.

AT A JUNCTION MARKED BY ANOTHER STREET LAMP, the road soon joined another, wider road of unspoiled asphalt. The dense trees ceded to rolling fields. To her left, the incline climbed to a hilly range, at the crest of which stood a small building. All there was dark. To her right, a parcel of clear land unfurled, inscribed by a series of emergency-orange posts repeating into the distance. A driveway broke off from the road and cut through this field, leading to a broad, one-storey structure of glass and concrete. Lights were visible inside.

Nearing the building, she took it to be some type of hangar. A pickup truck was parked outside. Above a large hydraulic door, now closed, a sign pronounced this to be TERMINAL 1. Through its glass revolving door she saw what appeared to be a waiting area, with plastic chairs in rows, a baggage carousel, vending machines. Two men were seated and engaged in conversation, one in cover-alls and the other in a raincoat with a duffle bag at his feet. When she entered, both men started.

Oh, the raincoated man said.

The man in coveralls stood, looking alarmed.

Looking for someone? he asked in English.

No, I...

She was more tired than she'd realized. She forced herself to con-centrate, to summon the words.

...There was a young man. *Lesionado*. Injured. He might be in danger...

Even as she said this, she understood how ridiculous it sounded. The men stared back, offering nothing.

...I don't know. I guess you could say I'm a bit lost.

Lost? the man in coveralls said. How'd you get here?

She remembered: a wave of prismatic light, then the meadow.

I came across that lake, the reservoir. Out of the woods and followed the road.

Well, yes. That's one way.

Are you flying out tonight? the raincoated man said.

The man in coveralls sniffed.

She's not on this flight.

This young man, he'd been attacked, she said. He didn't even have clothes.

The man in coveralls curled a lip.

If he's stumbling around out there in the altogether, the sheriff and his boys'll pick him up. What do you expect us to do about it?

I'm not...expecting anything, she said. I wouldn't mind just resting for a few minutes, if that's all right.

The men exchanged glances.

Usually this area's reserved for ticketed passengers, the man in coveralls said, but hey. Knock yourself out.

She took a seat in the front row. The man in coveralls continued to observe her with blatant distaste.

I'm the terminal line technician, he said. If anything happens here, it's on me. Don't make me regret not kicking your ass out.

With this, he headed off, exiting through a door past the dormant baggage carousel. The raincoated man extended a hand to be shaken.

Don.

Ximena.

Fiftyish and white-haired, he wore glasses with photochromic lenses currently at mid-shade. Decorum seemed to suggest she should make conversation, but her present weariness was overpowering, sapping any desire to do so.

I'm a little anxious, Don said. Feels like I've been waiting forever. Hopefully I can chill out and catch some Zs on the plane.

Where are you going?

He smiled.

I guess you are lost.

How's that?

You know there's only one route, yeah?

This confirmed her deduction that this was the airport, and the adjacent field its landing strip. It was all very peculiar, and begged decipherment, but she didn't know where to begin.

The town's just a mile or so down the road, Don said. Straight shot. This used to be the middle of nowhere, but there's a real development effort. Infrastructure and stuff. Everything's changing.

You're from here? she asked.

Me? Heck no. Nevada boy, born and bred. You?

Mexico City.

Ah. Explains the accent. I was down over the border there once, way back. Did a night in Juarez with some buds. Hoo boy, now there was a scene. Guess we can't go waltzing back and forth across like that anymore these days, huh. Can I ask you a question?

But before he could ask, the line technician came charging back into the room, wielding a hand-held electronic device.

It's happening, he announced.

A distant roar was audible, from outside. Don stood and threw his bag over his shoulder.

Finally.

Patience is a virtue, Ximena said.

Don looked at her in a way that suggested he'd never heard this idiom.

Wow. What a nice thing to say.

Ximena remained seated as Don hustled to the hangar doors. He handed a paper ticket to the line technician, who gave it a cursory look before handing it back, then ran his scanner over Don's arms and legs, down his back and up his crotch. Satisfied with whatever results he'd gathered, he hit a switch on the wall. Motors whirred. The hangar doors slid up and open.

From this angle, Ximena could see how the posts dotting the field demarcated a runway. And, aligned with this path, an airplane now emerged out of the sky's murk, its engine bellowing. Whether the same plane as before or another of similar make, she had no way of knowing.

Right on time, the line technician remarked.

As the plane drew closer she saw it was small, a twin turboprop airliner, like the forty-seat Dash 8 she'd once taken to visit her cousins in Culiacán. As it came into its final stages of descent, she felt a twinge of worry—its downward pitch seemed too steep, the velocity too hurried—but as its wheels touched on the runway, it throttled back and reduced speed, coming to a full stop about a hundred yards from the hangar.

The line technician threw another switch, triggering floodlights on the runway, then rushed out to meet it. From the hangar entrance, Don looked back at her and waved.

Sure you'll get on one soon, he shouted. Don't lose faith.

The line technician rolled a set of mobile airstairs up to the plane's passenger entrance as it opened. No attendant came from within, though a figure was apparent through the cockpit glass—the pilot, presumably, though no defining details could be distinguished.

The line technician ushered Don to the stairs. The two men exchanged a brisk handshake, then Don climbed the stairs and entered the plane. The stairs were rolled away, the engine rose again, and soon the plane was rolling back down the runway. Acceleration, liftoff, then the plane's strobes disappeared into the clouds. All of this occurred so swiftly that it was over before Ximena had fully processed what was happening.

The line technician hit the switch to close the hangar doors, then sauntered back over to the waiting area. He peeled off his work gloves and cracked his knuckles.

And so it goes, he said.

How many flights go out a day? Ximena asked.

Variable. We operate under capacity for much of the year. Depends on turnover.

Do you mean how many passengers want to leave?

Want? he scoffed. Want isn't really a factor. Everyone wants something. But we wait until it's our turn. That's how things work here, through spiritual consensus. That's basic civilization.

He looked at his watch.

And now we're really closed for the night. You need to scram.

She was more than happy to comply; this place and this person were both profoundly unpleasant. The line technician saw her to the revolving door, following close behind. Before leaving, she turned back.

Is there someone in town I could speak with?

About what?

Information. General inquiries.

He sighed.

Try the church, maybe. The pastor likes strangers.

WHILE A GRADUATE STUDENT AT UNAM, Ximena had briefly fallen under the mentorship of a professor named Jaime Oropesa. An embittered, hoary loner with a ruinous Vicodin addiction, Oropesa was given to fulminating at length regarding the grave condition of contemporary literature, making great efforts to charge his contemptuous views upon Ximena, advising how she could, and should, modify the content and form of her writing to meet the jaundiced expectations of an international publishing industry. Once she'd established a name for herself and accreted the goodwill and credentials to be eligible for funding opportunities, he'd told her, she'd then be free to pursue her more personal, less commercially viable ideas—what he teasingly called her *idiotez cósmicos*. An easy way to win over an American audience, he advised, was to shamelessly milk the exoticism of their backgrounds—in her case, advancing the work she'd done in transposing Pentateuchal and Augustan allusions into Meso-American mythology. All of the editors worth knowing in New York, he claimed, were either narcissistic Jews obsessed with their own otherness or smug liberals with axes to grind against their parents. Among their sour ranks, a great and powerful thing like her could thrive—but that would require foresight and cunning.

She'd never taken this advice of Oropesa's too seriously, but it had remained with her. Religion to her was largely ornamental. Her family's Catholic observance had been more a function of community and unanimity within diocesan standards than anything like devotion. The occasion to reflect in depth on arcane fixtures or sacred delirium never arose, and she'd never really read religious texts with any seriousness. Her aspiration had always been to write lucidly on the subjects of beauty and malice, and to do so without lapsing into sentimentality; in this pursuit, tradition of any type served only as a referent or an intellectual obstacle. The Church, with its reliance on doctrine and unequivocality, was only a device, a way to meditate on nostalgia, not a thing of any value in itself. And so she felt that relying upon easy symbology, when she herself lacked any Eucharistic zeal, would be the height of cynicism. This was the opposite of the truth she sought.

Perhaps it was this ambivalence, more than any stylistic innovation in her textual interpolations of certain Nahuatl cadences and early Spanish dialects, which had kept her books, published mostly by small Mexican publishers, from ever achieving notoriety. Yet her readership grew, slowly but steadily, even in those supposedly impenetrable American cloisters.

Shortly before Oropesa died, succumbing to a third heart attack while on vacation in Corsica in the early eighties, he'd sent Ximena a brief letter. Its tone was congenial, congratulating her for a recent prize she'd received; his acerbity had mellowed a touch in old age, and when, in subsequent years, she occasionally revisited their correspondence, it was apparent he'd then known his remaining days to be few. In that letter, along with polite praise and well wishes, he'd included admonitions regarding the status she'd achieved.

Never forget the poet's true role. You're not in showbiz. You're not a clown. You're a murderer. Whether a killer of daffodils or gods, that's for you to decide. But when you go in for the kill, make sure it's clean.

Her first sign of the town was the church's bell tower. Seeing it protruding in the distance, she quickened her pace along the road. Still no vehicles passed in either direction. As she came to a pair of parallel brick walls forming a gated entrance into the town, the thought struck her that all this might be an illusion, a false temptation: the town could be abandoned, long dead, or something else entirely. But, again, with no better option apparent, she had little choice but to continue. The road widened to a boulevard lined with simple one- and two-storey buildings, a scene etched with time's passage: potholes in the asphalt, worn concrete, grungy sewer grates.

Anything could be a symbol. Everything a conduit.

The tower loomed several blocks ahead. She hastened down the vacant sidewalk, passing a laundromat, a tobacconist's, a tax preparer's office, offshooting alleys and lanes. All lay dormant. Only when reaching the corner opposite the bell tower did she find any sign of life: a queue of people, mostly white and in sombre dress, climbed the building's stone steps, entering through its arched doors.

Ximena hesitated before proceeding. She hadn't set foot in a church in years. Her family's visits to the cathedral in Xalapa on days of obligations were always an anguish, the incongruent interiors and stained glass that sent her woozing, the solemn liturgies of priests' invoked torments, the frail bodies slumped in pews like previews of their own expiry. Once she was old enough to make her own decisions, she'd avoided such places. Now, as she stood on the corner debating her next move, she realized she wasn't alone. A slender woman with auburn hair wound into a braid stood next to her.

Heading in?

Ximena turned. The eagerness of the woman's smile was disarming.

Is it open to the public? Ximena asked.

Tonight it is. Why don't you come with me?

I'm not sure if this is where I'm meant to be.

Now I'm convinced. You need to come.

Ximena still hesitated.

Please, the woman said. I really think you'll enjoy yourself.

The woman proceeded toward the entrance. Ximena followed, apprehensive but grateful to give in—relying solely on her own momentum was exhausting. Introductions were made as they joined the procession through the vestibule. The woman's name was Clara.

Forty-two and frisky, she said, giving Ximena a wink.

The decor of the church's interior was muted, the walls uniformly off-white and unembellished with any garish iconography, leaving unresolved the question of what denomination might be practised here. The only recognizable signifier was a plaster cross, about eight feet tall, positioned at the chancel over a narrow altar, decorated in an abundance of colourful bouquets.

The pews filled steadily. Clara led Ximena down the centre aisle to a row about halfway from the front. Ximena couldn't determine exactly why this introductory scene felt so odd, so unlike what she knew, until she realized: there was no music, no organist's prelude or choral processional, only the low hum of voices in preparation.

Once seated, Clara craned her neck to look about, auditing the room.

Looking for someone? Ximena asked.

Just keeping an eye out. Certain individuals aren't welcome here.

That sounds somewhat ominous.

Clara looked at her.

Why do you say that?

Before Ximena could respond, the lights dimmed. A hush came over the congregation as a droning sound rose, a synthesizer's held chord, washing from speakers flanking the stage. A man entered from the stage's right and made his way to the lectern. Dressed in a powder-blue suit centred by an opal bolo tie, a tightly sculpted beard outlining his jawline, he met the crowd with an expansive, approving look. From the lectern he picked up a head-set microphone and slid it on; his breath came amplified over the room's speakers.

I feel good tonight, he said. I do.

Cheers came in response. This, Ximena deduced, was the pastor. His booming voice resonated throughout the church, soft in tonality yet carrying urgency. It lulled.

One of those nights when you feel that energy pulsating through you. Rising, like an orchestra warming up. The symphonic richness of being, when you're truly feeling it. It moves you from your inner core. It imbues you with that nourishing spirit. I think you all know what I mean.

Claps, approval.

But I gotta keep myself from being too persuaded by that energy. Can't let it intoxicate me. I tell myself, Pastor Sammy, you gotta keep that humility. Always. Because when you're fired up, and your blood gets pumping, that's when you start making too much noise and you stop *listening*. You feel the Almighty working through you, and that righteous feeling overwhelms you. You get confused. You lose true sight. You get sidetracked by the details and the dialogue and the flashy stuff, and you lose the plot. It happens.

Pastor Sammy began to pace the stage, his hands slicing the air.

Where do we get our true strength from? I don't mean big biceps and all that. I don't mean tough talk. That's not *real* strength. I mean the strength that binds us here as a community and keeps the lights on. What makes us whole? How about let's flip the equation. What are our weaknesses? Gluttony. Indolence. The clouded mind. The lazy and the hazy, as I like to say. Sin. And the root of all this sin is pride. That's what I'm talking about here. It's individual pride that makes us detached from our society. It's the mesmerizing chaos that corrupts us and gets our brains all gooey. Vaingloriousness. That's what leads us to deny the Word.

He lowered his head, as if reprimanding himself for getting carried away.

So what's my job? I'm here to remind you: our communion is a registration of that corruption. We live here, in this place, in this town, and maybe we wonder why we've been left here. Why us? We question the purpose of it. We feel isolated. We might start feeling kind of bitter. Maybe a teeny bit scared? We say to ourselves, none of this is real. This is all just a dream.

But that's just pride talking, friends. Foolish, foolish pride. We gotta align ourselves with that which is true and holy. Bound as a community, we've got to stay dutiful. On the lookout. That's what'll see us through the dark nights. Let me remind you, all that's outside God is an enemy of God. Sure, let's keep our eyes on the sky. But our boots have to stay on the ground. That's how we feed the energy that keeps us united. I'm talking about the obliteration of the self. Each of us alone is nothing. Zip. You, me... we're just blobs of raw energy. But together, we're a people. As the prophet of the Nevi'im said, the wrath of the Lord is the land darkened, and the people shall be as the fuel of the fire. I really can't make this any clearer, can I?

Coming to the front of the stage, he adjusted his headset and rebuttoned his jacket.

Acts of wonder happen around us all the time, if you know how to recognize them. Some of us hear the voice. Some speak with the voice. Some experience, oh, a flash of irrevocable consequence. Others wait forever for that kind of thing and it never comes. But that's just part of this dream we call life. It's a custom-built machine, and it chugs along a little differently for every one of us. But at the heart of it, we're all the same. That's the bargain. That's the covenant. You guys know all this.

Pastor Sammy lowered his eyes.

Phew. But let's not forget the real reason we've gathered here tonight. We're here for a baptism.

With this, another man emerged from the wings, leading a woman by the arm. She wore a long burgundy dress, her black hair loose at her shoulders.

That's Inez, Clara whispered to Ximena. She's so beautiful.

This was true—she was. The two men guided Inez forward, the ceiling bulbs casting her face in a muted gleam. The anticipation in the room notched palpably higher. Inez only stared ahead, past them all, expressionless. Ximena's uneasiness deepened. She felt raw and top-heavy, seasick. But she stayed in her seat, watching with the rest of them.

The baptism sacrament is as old as our faith, Pastor Sammy said. For as long as people have been prowling around, we've been falling. We're impure. The baptism is the way we get saved. It's what makes an old weasel like me into a lion.

The second man took Inez by the hand and guided her to the altar, where she allowed herself to be laid on her back. Her neck's posture released; her eyes closed.

I have to tell you all, Pastor Sammy said, grinning, this is the best part of my job.

From beneath the lectern, he produced a shallow silver bowl and brought it with him behind the altar. The speakers amplified his huffing breath as he leaned over Inez, cupping the bowl in his hands.

Ximena felt the pew beneath her trembling, the accumulative tension of the bodies seated down its length. Next to her, Clara clinched her knees, as if in danger of exploding.

Dearest Inez here, like many of us in our town, exists in a state of perplexity, Pastor Sammy said. But in the presence of the Lord, there's always a light, and always a way. As an emissary of the great and dreadful one, I baptize our daughter here tonight in the name of repentance. But, remember, as is written: He who cometh after me is mightier than I, whose sandals I am not worthy to bear. He shall baptize you with the incarnadine fire of the Holy Spirit. A spiteless world will be yours.

He lowered the bowl to Inez's parted lips and poured its contents into her mouth. Ximena sat up for a better look, but couldn't see exactly what was happening. Inez's arms and legs began to shake. Pastor Sammy kept the bowl in position, emptying it into Inez's mouth. A greyish vapour rose from somewhere below, or within, the altar. Inez's twitches rose into convulsions as the liquid overflowed from her mouth and came flowing down her cheeks. Pastor Sammy forced down the bowl's last trickles, then handed it to the man at his side. Inez's tremors gradually subsided.

Pastor Sammy stepped back, again facing the audience.

The Holy Spirit comes to us through fire and water, he said, but the air and earth determines the nature of our salvation.

He looked down on Inez, now still.

The oil of vitriol oxidizes our sins. Catalysis brings us toward transition. The utility shroud shields us from the fullness of the light.

The second man brought a sheet of black fabric and draped it over Inez, drawing it from her feet up to her shoulders. The ceiling lights dimmed and the droning, synthy soundtrack made a reprise.

We have a choice between the soluble and the indomitable, Pastor Sammy said. Between glory and disaster. Between the wastelands and the kingdom. That's the thing before us. To those who understand, those who truly humble themselves, the way is clear.

A third man came onto the stage. He and the second man both peeled on elbow-high rubber gloves, and together they lifted Inez's smoking body from the altar. Pastor Sammy returned to the front of the chancel, squaring his tie, and cast his eyes upon his congregation.

Go forth in righteousness and security, he said. My family, my flock. Have a wonderful night.

THE ATTENDEES MINGLED OUTSIDE THE CHURCH'S ENTRANCE, the general mood ebullient. As Ximena came down the steps, she felt her knees buckling.

You look a little ravaged, Clara said, coming to her side. Feeling unwell?

Ximena swayed, almost falling backward. A man behind her caught her by an arm, keeping her upright.

Whoa there.

Here, another man said, steadying her by her shoulders.

They helped her to the steps' ledge. Others around them looked on.

I'm fine, she said, sitting. I just need a moment.

Questions were fired her way: her name, what was happening, did she require help.

That woman, Ximena said. On the altar.

Clara and the men crouched before her, pressing in.

Sweetie, Clara cooed, just breathe. This is probably a blood-sugar thing.

All she saw was Inez, choking, then shrouded.

What did they do to her? Ximena said. What was that?

The men looked to one another. One placed a palm on Ximena's cheek.

She's freaked out, he said.

Ximena batted the man's hand away. She stood again, looking past them to the church entrance.

¿Qué coño?

Easy, one of the men said, reaching for her arms.

She shook him away.

Don't touch me.

Her objection came louder than intended. Heads turned.

Sweetie, Clara said. You have to be respectful.

An impelling instinct screamed within her, and Ximena moved to go, but the two men leaned in to suppress any attempt. The gawking crowd closed in tighter. She was helpless against the swarm, this accreted mass siphoning what scant energy she had.

Then, as if a signal had been activated, the gathering parted, making way for the arrival of a stocky man in a long leather coat. Ximena heard someone say: *The sheriff.*

All right all right, he said, wading in. Everyone okay here?

Nothing serious, Buckner, one of the men said. This woman here, she's a little twanged.

This man, this sheriff, waded toward her. His pudgy, pocked frown spoke of one born to exert authority, and comfort in this role.

She's just here?

The question seemed directed at no one in particular. Buckner looked Ximena over.

Let's take her out to the fields, said the other man.

The fields, someone else said.

I'll handle it from here, Buckner said. You folks enjoy your evening.

He slid in to pry her from her captors. Everything in this felt wrong, and again her instinct was to try to escape. But she allowed herself to be taken. As the sheriff led her toward a waiting police cruiser, his hold on her forearm became almost reassuring. It was tactile and real. This authority demanded her submission.

They drove, back on the main road. The streets sat deserted as before, as if the busy scene at the church had occurred somewhere else. Bucker kept his eyes on the road, his belly pressed against the steering wheel. The cruiser smelled of old coffee and baby powder.

Warm tonight, he said. Kinda late in the season for around here. But there's a significant degree of geographical dysfunction we have to contend with. That sort of adversity helps enrich our heritage. Or so they say.

Ximena kept quiet. She knew better than to talk too freely with police.

Now, I've got no business going outside jurisdiction, he said. I'll dump you south of the fields. From there, you're on your own.

And what's in the fields? she asked.

You heard the pastor. All that's outside God's an enemy of God. That means in the physical too.

So it's...banishment.

If you ask me, we're all banished. But no one ever asks me.

Ximena rested her head against the window, still feeling unsteady.

There was a boy in the water, she said.

What's that now?

There was a boy. Drowning. In the reservoir.

Do tell.

I pulled him out, but he ran away.

And where'd he go?

I don't know. He seemed afraid. It looked like he'd been...tortured.

Tortured? I don't think so.

I know what I saw.

Buckner abruptly pulled over, stopping in front of a muffler shop, closed, like everything else. His grip tightened on the wheel.

Look, miss. I'm an officer of the law. Mandated to uphold the status quo. Which means, something goes wrong, it's counted as an error in my own personal ledger. Not an actual ledger, but I mean, it's about accountability. So if something's wrong, I'm the one who has to correct it. And when I say *wrong*, I'm talking about the fabric of society. The law is the embodiment of rightful thinking.

You might want to consider reviewing that mandate.

He turned and pointed at her.

Someone like you, you look at me and think, oh, here's a big man packing a firearm. But the responsibility goes beyond the badge. In a place like this, where there's a lot we don't know and a lot we're not sure we even want to know, someone's got to keep a steady hand on the tiller. My sight is clear. Is *your* sight clear?

No.

I act with the force of untainted will. Do you?

No.

That's right. You *don't*. You might think you have some purpose here, but you're just another defect in the flow like the rest of us.

With this, he shifted the cruiser back into gear and began to drive again. They rolled down this main road for another block, still meeting no traffic, then turned onto a side street, away from the town's centre. Soon they were surrounded by dark forest, the roadsides lined with chain-link fencing, and only more road ahead. Fear rose inside her now—actual fear. She tested the door's handle with a light tug. It didn't move.

Now now, Buckner said.

Look, she said, turning to face him, we may have had a misunderstanding. I'm not—

Buckner slammed on the brakes. Thrown forward against the dashboard, Ximena issued an involuntary sound: *Guh*. She looked ahead to see a figure slicing through the headlights, just barely avoiding contact with the cruiser's hood. Unclothed, sinewy: it was unmistakably him, the young man from the reservoir. He dashed across the road and bounded down into the ditch, scaling the fence and flying into the darkness beyond.

Buckner threw the car into park and leaped out in pursuit, leaving the driver's-side door open. Ximena hesitated only an instant. She slid across the seat and out, rounding the cruiser's rear in the opposite direction the young man had gone. She scurried down and across the ditch, then back up the incline to the fence. The climb took great effort—hooking toes and fingers into the links, stretching her thighs up and over its metal frame—and she landed off-angle coming down. The impact bellowed in her knees, but adrenalin deadened the pain, and she lunged ahead, taking cover among the trees.

Looking back, she saw Buckner back at the car, kicking gravel. He'd failed to nab his prey, and now he'd lost her too. She kept low, fearing he might spot her, hiding there. But he turned and ducked back into the cruiser, pulled a tight turn, and sped back toward town.

DEEPER INTO THE WOODS, she arrived at a marshy pond, quaggy mud at all sides. She followed its edge, treading carefully, her knees still smarting from the miscalculated jump. She soon came upon a trail, leading up a slight grade, that she guessed might take her back along the town's outskirts—once again, she trusted the path presented to her. This was how she'd lived: led by instinct, by circumstance, avoiding the sway of any horde. In doing so, she'd forged her own way, alone.

Desperation had kept her family's home a perennial battleground. In the shadow of Nauhcampatépetl's sleeping volcano, just outside Perote, they fought undousable fires fuelled by scarcity, frustration, uncertainty. Against her father's vituperations, her mother's screeching fits, her brother Gregorio's temper, Ximena had by necessity taught herself to stay silent. To listen. In so doing, she'd decrypted the truth behind their anguish—it was fear, inexpressible and asphyxiating, yet ordinary. With this knowledge, she decided her own fate would be determined through calculated self-extrication.

In 1968, when her friends demonstrated in the streets, Ximena opted to tarry at the turmoil's periphery—present, but separate. She edited a series of interviews with campus radicals for an unofficial student newspaper, a project intended to facilitate expression without annotation, without varnish. Recasting the resistance in the realm of the personal, riddled with all the ambiguities and anxieties of intimate history—this could be a poet's role in the uprising. Her cousin Leticia had been more ardently possessed by the fever of those times, and was on the front lines when the protests organized by the Consejo Nacional de Huelga took full swirl. She and Ximena had argued at length about their divergent approaches to the movement; though Leticia never doubted the sincerity of her cousin's sympathies, she'd accused her of timidity in a situation where only boldness could prevail. Ximena offered no argument, taking notes as her cousin harangued her. Leticia would later be one of many demonstrators to perish during that terrible night in Tlatelolco. To the question of whether this outcome was a tragedy that could have been averted or a necessary sacrifice, Ximena never sought any conclusion. Death, the most reasonable thing of all, often took irrational forms.

The path led her out of the woods and into a clearing, where she found a cleanly trimmed yard surrounding a large brick house with a back patio. Lights glowed behind curtained windows. Farther ahead lay similar neighbouring plots, marked with their own backyard paraphernalia.

As she neared the house, the aroma of a charcoal grill saturated the air, triggering hunger she only now acknowledged. From the patio a man's voice came, low but crisply annunciated: *High on a mountain's highest ridge, where oft the stormy winter gale cuts like a scythe, while through the clouds it sweeps from vale to vale.*

Ximena edged closer. Suddenly, the yard filled with light.

I see you.

She shielded her eyes with a forearm. The figure on the patio was backlit, wafting smoke. She almost scurried back into the trees, but stifled the urge.

I'm just cutting through, she said. Sorry.

Hang on there.

The man came into clearer view: tall, white, in a shirt and loosened tie, a cigarette between his fingers.

Ah. You. Believe I spied you there tonight. The baptism in all its wonder. You're a friend of Clara's?

Not a friend.

Bully for you. That lady's a bit of a rusty snatch. Now you're prowling around in the woods lovely, dark, and deep. I'm almost afraid to ask what brings you here.

Not to be impolite, she said, but I don't think I need to tell you.

Naturally. I ask out of concern for your own well-being. Certain denizens of these parts get jumpy if they think interlopers are sullying their property.

He came closer, extending his cigarette pack. She accepted one and he lit it with a Zippo's snap. On the patio, a glass door slid open and another man appeared.

Down here, Roy, the first man called. We have a trespasser. Go fetch the double barrel.

He crushed his own cigarette on his sneaker's heel.

I'm fucking with you, he said. We're just firing up the coals to stuff our miserable gullets. Let us feed you.

Describing himself as a *luckless thespian by trade and in treachery*, Edward shared the house with his husband, Roy, an engineer, who joined them offering a tray of flatbread and Bleu des Causses. Ximena was reluctant to share information with these men, and looked for an opportunity to make her exit. But the aroma of the food, gigantic sizzling bison burgers, was irresistible, and when they uncapped fat bottles of cold Maibock, she found herself unwinding, if only slightly.

You heard Edward babbling out there? Roy said.

I have to relax my throat, Edward said. Getting over polyps. So I do recitations.

Wordsworth, Ximena said.

Edward's eyes widened with delight.

You've tangled with that quivering fantasist?

In my undergraduate years.

Of course. I can't imagine what sort of psychopath would read the Romantics for enjoyment. This whole thing of inconsolable grief over society's sordid boons and everything, it's all so tacky. Honestly, I barely read anything at all anymore unless it's for a job. I mean, what's the purpose of anything premised in its own subjectivity? Like, everyone insisted that reading that Roberto Bolaño book would recalibrate my life. But here's just a bunch of nobodies doing nothing, then it's over and I'm two weeks closer to death. Okay, now I'm just spewing.

Edward poured the rest of his beer into a long, slender glass. Ximena took a seat on a bench opposite the grill, where Roy worked a spatula. The patio was constructed of a grainy timber, sheltered by a motorized awning, now retracted.

Nice deck, she said.

Roy designed it himself, Edward said.

The entire house is lumber harvested from these very forests, Roy said. Synergy with our environment is the fundament of my craft.

Roy's a genius, Edward said. He's completely reconceptualizing this town.

Hardly on my own, Roy said. But my firm's contracted to undertake some major infrastructure redesigns. *A pedibus usque ad caput.* This place has a very specific configuration, as far as resources and how they're implemented.

I was wondering how you'd get imported beer in here, Ximena said, if access in and out is so limited.

Do you question where every single thing you eat comes from? Edward said.

Ximena didn't press further.

Not too long ago, Roy said, this place was just a landing strip and a half-dozen scattered farmhouses. Now there's a town, with an extensive array of needs and ambitions.

Ambitions, Edward echoed. People are starting to think big.

My job's to translate the underlying ideas into buildable projects. As in, here's an impulse that exists squarely in the imagination of the townspeople. So, we manifest that in a plan, and the materials of creation become actual, spatial things. The struggle's to keep them running at optimal efficiency without limiting conceptual capacity.

Interesting, she said.

Case in point: we just wrapped preliminary installation of high-efficiency clean-emission propane lines from central tanks throughout the grid. Converting the whole shebang from its sooty old fuel system. It's a bold experiment, still subject to tweaking and reinforcement. But that's how the town evolves confluent with the evolution of our imagination. There's an understanding here. Lot of people see this place as a microcosm, as in, everything big out there...

He gestured, indicating his surroundings, everything.

...is small in here. To put it crudely. Whereas me, I see these infrastructural challenges as sort of a system of puzzles. And the key that deciphers that system unlocks all sorts of possibilities. Vast opportunities for growth. Realms that now seem inaccessible will open up to us in the future. You see what I mean?

Maybe. It's sort of hermeneutical. And capitalistic.

Roy smiled widely, turning to Edward.

She's no dummy.

So I see, Edward said.

And the airport's operated by the town? Ximena asked.

The airport is the town. Or, at least, it's what defines it. It's a minor conduit, but vital.

Who do I see about getting on a flight?

Edward and Roy exchanged a look—quick, but Ximena noted it with irritation.

The operations coordinator manages the schedule, Roy said. Her office is back west across town. We can take you there.

I would really appreciate that.

But I'll warn you, she can be a tad prickly. We're headed to the playhouse after we eat. How about you come along, then we'll get you pointed in the right direction.

My production's in previews tonight, Edward said. A domestic tragedy. Think you'll appreciate it, as one who knows her stuff. Hermeneutically.

Ximena finished her beer, and before she'd put the empty bottle aside, Edward was opening her another.

I came in through a wave of light, she said, and then it retreated. It felt almost like some sort of...interference. Or a slip.

Again, Roy and Edward cast knowing looks at one another. And again, Ximena bristled with annoyance. This night had been a non-stop series of irritations—perhaps more like poetry than she'd imagined.

Please don't yank my chain, she said.

No yanking, Roy said. The light...I mean, it's in many ways the crux of the whole thing, isn't it? I see that fuzzy light drifting in and out, and I know the goal's still out there. It gives me purpose and resolve. To always keep innovating. To keep us all on the right track.

This is a strange place.

It is. But believe me, the only trouble you'll face around here is of your own design.

Once you see how things are set in motion, Edward said, your fate's pretty much sealed.

Roy smiled in agreement.

That is, if you believe in such things as fate.

To this, Ximena only sipped her beer.

Well, Roy said, right now, let's get these burgers happening.

No, she didn't believe in fate. Or, at least, she hadn't lived in expectation of its deliverance. Yet she'd also shunned any counter-narrative: contingency, pure possibility, a universe of unbounded weavings. If she'd ever held any stance concerning fate, it had long faded to memory, like her caesarean scar, like her most brutal yearnings.

María Isabel's birth in the autumn of 1975 came during a period of doubt and irresolution. Ximena and Rubén Perez's romance had been swift and spirited—a handsome sculptor who taught at ENAP, his intimate knowledge of the city abetted her self-renovation there; no longer the *bayunco* from the mountains, she steered a bicycle through traffic and argued with prostitutes on street corners. They'd married and moved into a small two-bedroom apartment in Roma Norte, getting by on his meagre teaching income and her occasional earnings from cleaning houses. Her pregnancy passed without complication, and when their household grew from two to three it seemed a natural expansion. Even with all the attendant tasks that came with a newborn, her writing continued apace, and with progress.

But the truth couldn't be denied: being a wife was almost unbearably tedious. Marriage had ushered in total stultification; in coexistence, they'd both become less. Rubén had also soon wearied of it, and of her—it was plain in his every tsk of concession. Though what love they'd shared steadily dimmed, Rubén seemed willing to let matters hover forever: divorce was an ugly word, a vile prospect, never discussed. Stewing over whether her situation was self-orchestrated or merely a thrust of fortune changed nothing. And so she ached.

One rainy night, as María Isabel lay cooing in her crib—she was a contented child, generally tantrum-free—Ximena sat on the living room sofa reading newspapers and trying to tune out Rubén's voice in the other room as he underwent his weekly telephone call with his father, a ritual that always left him distant and surly afterward. When he finally emerged, he lingered in the doorway. When she asked what was the matter, he said he was too tired for a discussion and was headed to bed. She recommended he speak his mind, and get whatever it was off his chest. Please, he'd begged, staring at the floor, not right now.

Seeing him loafing there so dejectedly, so self-pityingly, she'd been overcome with loathing for this man, so precise and intense it could not be suppressed. In a flurry of action, she threw aside the papers and, before Rubén could react, was out the door in her raincoat, leaving both husband and child without a word. At the miscelánea on the corner she bought a bottle of Jack Daniels, then headed to the west side of Jardín Pushkin, empty by night. There she sat on a metal jungle gym, drinking slowly.

Her marriage was over. No hopeful fabrication of the future would alter this. Resistance would only bring misery. But resignation to fate meant honouring a coarse conception of time, and of individual history. That she simply couldn't stomach. Staring tipsily at the walls of faded graffiti tags, the wan city light sieved through hanging cypresses, the hokey bust of the eminent Russian poet lording over the playground, she knew: any true way forward for her would dwell in sovereignty. Only if she accepted this, shedding forbearances, could she achieve any purpose, maybe even joy.

From that understanding, her life would change profoundly. And yet, initially, nothing changed at all. She finished the bottle and returned to the apartment, put María Isabel to bed, soaked herself in their tiny claw-foot tub, then fell asleep next to Rubén without a word between them. It would be almost a year before they initiated divorce proceedings, and soon after that Rubén left Mexico for good. She would raise her daughter alone, and never again invested excess energy in any man or lover. She became herself. She became authentic.

THEY DROVE BACK INTO TOWN in Roy's BMW. They passed more houses, more sprawling lawns, signifiers of easy affluence: driveways of Durangos and Audis, speedboats under tarps, facades crawling with ivy. In her neighbourhood, rich and poor often seemed to exist piled atop one another, oxygen and streets interchanging at overlaying strata, like layers in a sloppy sandwich, and any outflow always seeped downward. But here, everything was level, decompressed.

The car's radio played as they drove, the volume kept low. A man's voice spoke, steady and measured: *Seek the farthest reach of the shore. There you dip your feet in the cool current's froth. Honour the epithelium and the nerves. Swear damnations at tyrant moons. When the moment of catastrophe arrives, you mustn't avert your eyes. Tear ahead and claim your rightful spoils.* Before Ximena could ask what the peculiar broadcast was, Edward sighed and snapped it off.

Hush hush, he said. Let's just bliss out for a while maybe.

Arriving back at the main road, a block north of the church and bell tower, they found the town deserted as before. Ximena hadn't mentioned her confrontation with Buckner to Roy and Edward. She sank down in the back seat, eyes sharp for any signs of police.

Though they called it a playhouse, the building they pulled up to appeared as just another narrow storefront, indistinguishable from others lining the street. Its only marker was a large railroad lantern swinging above the entrance, casting the surrounding sidewalk in a shifting light. The effect was persuasively ominous.

Upon entry they were met by a woman operating a small ticket counter. She knew Roy and Edward, and waved them in. Seeing Ximena, she looked apprehensive.

Our guest, Edward told her. A *poeta* from *Me-hee-co*.

Espléndido, the woman said in clumsy Spanish. *Usted tendrá una experiencia agotadora.*

Ximena followed Roy through the bare-bones lobby and into the theatre. The interior was less of an auditorium and more like a built-out corporate conference space: track lighting on dimmers, commercial carpeting, plastic chairs in a grid. A stage of sorts was set at the front of the room, curtain drawn. Edward explained to Ximena how the program was a collection of short pieces, works in progress—she didn't take this as boding positively for what she was about to see. She and Roy took seats while Edward went to check in behind the scenes. Tension percolated; the turnout was thin, and both men seemed displeased.

Truthfully, sort of a piss-poor cultural market around here, Roy said, his voice hushed. Edward and his gang work hard to deepen the well, but it's a battle.

That's too bad.

Roy leaned in closer, lowering his voice.

You asked if those coloured mists create interference. The short answer is no. The long answer is complicated, and depends on what you mean by quote-unquote interference. You have to begin with the assumption of certain transmutative properties, while at the same recognizing the intrinsic pitfalls of any alchemic change.

Alchemic?

Everyone has their own understanding of what's meant for us here. My belief is that everything attains truth through its symbolic value, vis-à-vis the atmospheric patterns. And, as I often say, in the process of representational transference, genuine, observable trans-formation can begin, even at the level of an individual corrective. Which is to say, the phenomenon of the light is real. Even if the net output is actually nil.

Ximena recalled Pastor Sammy: *Catalysis brings us toward the transition state.*

I'm sure you understand, Roy said. You're an educated person. You get metaphor.

Before she had a chance to reply, the lights went down and the room went silent. A rack of simple work lights ignited as a stage assistant slid back the curtains.

The stage was set as an apartment, divided into two rooms, lit evenly and connected by an archway. At stage right was a living room, furnished with a chaise longue and a single floor lamp. A young woman sat on a rug before a prop fireplace constructed of painted styrofoam, with red and orange tissue paper inside denoting flames. Curled under a long nightdress, she calmly turned the crinkled pages of a hefty hardcover book in her lap while sipping from a mug.

The room at stage left was set as a kitchen, with simulated cupboards and stove. There, a second woman, older than the first and dressed in a pinstriped suit, sat at a table, hunched over an electric typewriter. She typed slowly, concentrating on the page before her. The keystrokes rang in laboured, metallic thunks.

A door to her left opened. A man entered from the stage's wing, carrying a GoodLife Fitness duffle bag and wearing ill-fitting coveralls. At the typewriter's noise, he scowled. But the woman continued typing, outwardly oblivious to his entry. With flourish, he took exaggerated strides to the stage's front and faced the audience.

These old hinges have a squeak, he said.

With this, the woman ceased typing. She rose from the table and headed through the archway into the adjacent living room. The kitchen's lights dimmed behind her, leaving the man in shadow. The younger woman remained before the facsimile fire, absently flipping through her book, and either failed to notice or chose not to acknowledge her visitor's entrance. The woman in the suit circled the chaise longue, testing its cushions with an explorative caress. She sat on its arm, folded her legs, and looked out at the audience.

Every night it's the same tired story, she said. What can we do to break the monotony?

The seated woman then spoke for the first time, still facing the fireplace.

The flames warm my face, she said in a soft, almost childlike, voice. It feels so pleasant as I read my book.

Anything good? the other woman asked her.

It's a story about lost souls, journeying their way across space and time.

And how's that tea you're drinking?

Delightful and bitter.

It should be. I made it for you myself, with eighty milligrams of strychnine. I imagine you'll be stiff before you finish the next chapter.

Now the younger woman turned to face her. The two remained with eyes locked for a prolonged beat, the only sound the simulated crackle of the fake fire. Finally, the woman in the pinstriped suit leaned back, still perched on the arm of the chaise, and again spoke to the audience.

It's an old story, from early days. The elements are basic: beach and sea, land and air, storm and sun. Force and counterforce, proposition and reversal. A place, a territory, access to which many rivals lay claim. But as man's woeful course complicates itself to auto-extirpation, only a limited number of stories remain to tell. Stories of the expulsion of *shedim*, and of the spiteful dead clawing at desiccated soil. Of botched matricides, of deranged seers past their heydays. Other themes suggest themselves: the sadness of clinical instruments at lacking souls, ruthless cartographers lost to obsession, widowers mourning the falsely angelic. But with little time left to squander, any frivolity in the telling of tales must be checked. Rarity has only whittled these apologues, hastening their purpose and steeling their tellers' resolve.

So, with few stories remaining, latent themes arise to be conjured from the gloom. The problem of birthright. The horror of anchorlessness. The allure of revelation's plunder. With such reckoning come lapses. Left untold, like a muck left unskimmed, are those stories of those wayward sons and daughters lost in states of cursedness, uncertain of what has happened, and what happens next.

What truth remains will be rediscovered in old laws, in old patterns. A protagonist swallows her fear. A skyline signifies a dead ambition. A knife is wielded. The triumph of understanding lies just out of reach. Every story is a retelling.

The question before us now is, who are the true heroes of these stories: those who recognize these perpetual patterns and honour them, or those who hope to shatter them and free us of their curse?

She hesitated, perhaps pondering her own question, then continued.

No matter. As Kafka, that dour Ashkenazi, said, from the true opponent a limited courage flows into you. Me, I'm done with old myths. High time to castrate the gatekeepers.

She headed back through the archway. The kitchen lights came up again; behind her, the living room fell dim, leaving the younger woman in shadow. The man in the coveralls was still standing in the kitchen, and greeted her arrival with open arms.

There you are, he said.

The woman moved toward the table and her typewriter, but the man blocked her way. He reached into his bag, producing a large knife, its blade teethed. The woman seemed unalarmed at this.

We both know what I'm meant to do, he said.

If you were a braver man, she said, you'd find another way.

A lengthy pause, with them held in this standoff, followed—long enough, it seemed, the actors might have forgotten their cues. But then the man resumed.

You're right, he said. But in the end, I'm only an intermediary. What's required is a blood sacrifice.

In one smooth motion, he slid the blade into her stomach. He released the handle and left it embedded there, backing away as the woman dropped to her knees in a spreading pool of blood—the effect was convincing. The man then returned to his previous position at the front of the stage.

Squeaky hinges require lubrication, he said to the audience. Upkeep is necessary. And I'm the maintenance man.

As the woman on the floor continued to bleed, the knife's handle protruding from her midsection, he exited through the door from which he'd come.

Fade and curtains. A polite round of applause. The house lights came on. The audience remained seated, expecting a curtain call, a final bow. But none of the actors appeared, and the applause petered out. It was over.

ONE OF XIMENA'S MOST WIDELY TRANSLATED and anthologized longer poems recounted a trip taken in her mid-teens with her father to visit his childhood home in Tepito. The condition of the troubled barrio was then even worse than it would be in later years, and she'd kept close to her father's side as they walked the frenetic streets, the insanity of stalls and toppling vecindades, her father unrelenting in his mission of scouring his old haunts in hopes of tracking cherished old friends—a fruitless venture, it turned out, as most of those spectres had long since abandoned this plane.

The poem lamentingly outlined the barrio's changes over decades, as filtered through her father's dolorous gripes. Its stark lines detailed the auditory indicators of the experience—the chatter of transistor radios, the yaps of old drunks, the growl of moped engines. As was her given mode, it avoided any explicit political contextualization. And so it was praised by her admirers as a document of the city's self-dooming nature, the suffocation of industrialism, the erasure of culture—and condemned by her detractors as too sentimental, too light. She accepted all and none of this, never addressing her interpreters' assumptions, never expounding. In her work she'd always sought to seduce, rather than convince. Sometimes a muddy street was merely what it was. Not every doorway leads to another dimension.

Recalling that old poem, she found it impossible to remember what it was like, the urge to create such a thing. That period, a stretch of about fifteen years from the late seventies on, had been her most successful as far as publications and esteem. The narrative persona she cultivated, as an outsider observing the mob, served her well, and suited the tenor of the day. The radical left from which her contemporaries had sprung found its power in steely virtue; for many, that same virtue would become a weapon. Friends who'd seen casualties fall in the name of toppling the Partido Revolucionario Institucional emerged from that strife imbued with purpose in wildly divergent ways, solidifying their ambitions with the footing of post-colonial theory and the plasma of dreams. They flocked to Indiana and Cambridge; they hobnobbed with the Sandinistas; they attended awards ceremonies at the Folger Shakespeare Library in Washington; they lobbied and opined publicly.

Ximena did none of these things. She'd approached all such considerations only obliquely, operating in the biological, the ahistorical, the sensory—and, some said, in toothless nostalgia. The books she produced in these years earned both scorn and acclaim, her critics doubly deeming her soothsayer and traitor. Much of this was her own doing; in 1993, she'd given an interview to the *Paris Review* in which she called herself a citizen not of Mexico, but of the world. She'd meant this only half-earnestly, but the clumsy declaration would later be one of her greatest public regrets.

After the performance, the small crowd loitered in the playhouse lobby. Ximena stepped aside as Roy made conversation with the woman at the ticket counter. Others looked her way, but she shied from any prolonged contact. This night kept stretching on, and her impatience mounted. She had to reach the operations coordinator as soon as possible—if Roy and Edward could actually facilitate access.

Ximena was debating an exit when she detected a tremor of tension rippling through the room. Two uniformed policemen came through the doorway, their figures made menacing in the railroad lantern's sinister cast. Ximena looked to Roy and found him staring back at her, his expression apprehensive.

With this, the plot against her was laid bare. In disorientation he'd let her instincts go muddy, and had trusted too openly. *The only trouble you'll face around here is of your own design.*

Circumventing the counter, she headed in the direction she'd seen Edward go, into a brief hallway and what constituted a backstage area. Here were more lingerers, actors in wardrobe, and someone called after her. But she was already barging into a tight corridor piled with plywood slats and half-collapsed sets, reaching for a metal door marked EMERGENCY EXIT ONLY ALARM WILL SOUND. She let this warning go unheeded, pushing through, and then she was outside, back on the sidewalk. No alarm sounded.

The previously uninhabited boulevard was now animated with activity. A growing crowd of townspeople clustered under the awning of a storefront, a furniture gallery, all fulgent wood and acrylic.

Ximena hurried past, hoping to avoid the gathering. That unsteady feeling from before had returned, the accreted fatigue and frustration. Again she relegated control to the path ahead, or the idea of one.

But someone stepped in her way, blocking her path. Clara: bug-eyed and frantic. *Forty-two and frisky.*

Well, hello there, she said. Been looking for you. Everyone's looking. For you.

This was not reassuring. Clara came closer, insistent.

I never did ask: where are you coming from, exactly?

Ximena considered this question, the improbability of it. Tonight, she'd regained years, and youth, or something that felt like youth. Vitality, in a way.

Tepito, she said. Cuauhtémoc. Where are you from, Clara?

Clara bypassed this question.

I got a friend of mine to check the transit manifest. You weren't on any recent flights in.

I never said I was.

So you admit to duplicity.

Please get out of my way.

I only want to help you, Clara said, her eyes widening. I can see the anger you're harbouring. You have to believe me, you can be freed from all that craziness. All we're asked to do is lay ourselves on the altar and serve humbly.

Right. I don't think so.

Ximena moved to sidestep her. But Clara blocked her way, turning to the assembly gathered at the storefront.

We have an interloper in our midst, she announced.

This attracted attention.

This woman threatened me, Clara declared, and made direct threats to our community.

Their collective scrutiny was now directed at her. Ximena searched their faces for indications of sympathy, but in aggregate, they all merged as one: irate, vicious—a default setting of American ordinary. Faced with such indignation, she saw any hope of a smooth outcome wiped out.

A voice, familiar and assured, sang out over the din.

Now, now. Let's see what we have here.

The crowd parted as Pastor Sammy came forward, rubbing his hands. His chintzy outfit of blue suit and bolo tie, so ludicrous in the setting of the church, here also effectively stood him apart from, or above, the homogeneous mob. He exuded status.

What's your name, miss?

I don't think I'm going to tell you.

My name's Sam. My friends call me Pastor Sammy. I'm a clergyman. That's a job with a degree of authority around here.

I know. I saw you in action earlier. With Inez.

He gave a look of faint amusement. Bodies pressed up behind Ximena, negating any thought she might have of escape.

How about you tell us what's really going on? Pastor Sammy said. We have sort of a zero-tolerance policy for shenanigans around here.

Right.

Look around, he said. This is a close-knit community, defined by shared values.

A spiritual consensus.

Ximena was quoting the line coordinator. Pastor Sammy smiled.

You bet. It's a noble and holy thing. As our book says, he saves them to the uttermost that come unto God by him, seeing he ever liveth to make intercession for them. But for us to thrive this way, you know, it necessitates vigilance and self-reflection. We only know what we are by knowing *who* we are. And we don't know you.

Maybe let's keep it that way.

Someone in the crowd said: I know a security breach when I see one. Clara pushed in.

She's an interloper, she said. There's no accounting on record.

Pastor Sammy's eyes stayed fixed on Ximena.

That sounds pretty suspicious, he said. It's been a long time since we had anyone new come to town. A real long time. What brings you here?

I was sent here by the gods, she said.

Again: his smarmy smile.

What's that now?

I'm here to judge you.

That smile vanished. Ximena wasn't certain why she'd said this, though it felt right. It was as if she was answering a question she'd only asked of herself.

Judge *me*? Pastor Sammy said, looking around to the others. Seems like someone's got some delusions of grandeur going on. Hate to break it to you, but here, I do the judging. Empowered, of course, by the will of these wonderful people.

This drew exclamations of support from his flock. From among the din, Ximena heard Roy saying: To emplace a corrective. Pastor Sammy gestured to the men behind Ximena. They advanced, pinning her arms behind her. Pastor Sammy hiked up his sleeves and came closer.

The light exposes all, even those who crawl in the shadows. The utility shroud is our filter, protecting us from ourselves.

Clasped in his hands was a black sheet, the shroud they'd placed on Inez. He slipped it over her head. With this, she was blind.

The shroud obfuscates our view of the stars, he said, so true reckoning can be found in the soil.

Send her back out to the fields, someone shouted.

Dump her in the reservoir, someone else said.

Yes, she heard Clara say, drown her like a rat.

She felt Pastor Sammy's hands pressing on her shoulders.

This might get a little rough. But it'll be worth it. Trust me.

What happened next was confusing. Blinded by the shroud, she was aware only of a burst of sound, immediate and piercing. A discarnate wave of force knocked her backward. She was dimly aware of shocked cries and a spray of atomized glass, the noxious fetor of scorched plastic. There was heat. Blackout threatened. Then she was rising, levitating above the havoc. There was reassurance in this extraction, and she submitted to it. The last thing she registered before losing consciousness was Pastor Sammy, screaming *Get me that fire extinguisher goddammit.*

SHE WAS, IT COULD BE SAID, acquainted with wonders. She'd known the strangeness of childbirth, of love's loss, of unshakable seething. She'd seen Mexico City razed by the 1985 earthquake, entire apartment complexes in Cuauhtémoc and Morelos deleted, while her own block was left almost untouched. She'd listened to her upstairs neighbours tearfully describe laying flowers at a shrine to Santa Muerte in the Guerrero highlands, where even the government was afraid to venture, and how their fealty to the spirit protected them from gunfire along the most treacherous stretches of the I-95. In her work she'd interrogated the fluidity of the Jains' *anekāntavāda*, waged defences of the obsidian god Tezcatlipoca, excogitated on the awe of Aeneas upon meeting his father on the river Lethe with the revelation of his lineage's future. She'd had her own writing, verses she'd long forgotten writing, read back to her by blushing Norwegian undergraduates, and blessed their dog-eared editions with her signature. She'd watched money come in and money go out. Mysteries, consonances, nonsensical situations, sprang forth everywhere, in everything.

But just as a third whisky never ignited the same pleasures as the first, with repetition all wonders lost their potency. Everything degraded toward banality. Growing old imposed this loss of urgency. There was less and less reason to expect ecstasy in the irrational. One became lazy and soft, reconciling contradictions—no matter how raw and ghastly their implications—however is necessary, simply to survive.

He paced back and forth, displaying the restlessness of one deeply vexed—or of one working hard at appearing deeply vexed. Pimpled cheeks, JanSport backpack, the slightest trace of beard on his chin, beat-up Nikes: it was evident now how young he actually was. His wounds were hidden under a grass-stained sweatshirt and work pants, but he still looked in rough shape.

Ximena sat on the grass, stretching her legs. Though still shaky, she was regaining awareness of what had occurred, and was occurring now. She tested her elbow to find a worrisome pain there.

They were in a slight gully, enclosed by overgrowth and rough earth, their current proximity to the town's centre and the site of the explosion hard to tell. Crushed Sprite cans and food wrappers lay scattered on the ground, evidence of a shelter, a hideout. A battered Honda scooter stood propped on its kickstand; this, somewhat improbably, was how they'd made their flight. A plastic bag dangled from its handlebars, and from it he produced a ring of Bud Light cans, offering her one. She accepted and introduced herself.

Carson, he said.

As in Carson City.

I'm from Ohio. Findlay. Ever heard of it?

Don't think so.

Not too far from here.

I was under the impression our current scenario was...geographically ambiguous.

Sure, yeah. But no. I mean, this is America. Nothing's too far away.

He resumed pacing, drinking his beer.

Are you in trouble? she asked.

Let's just say I ended up here against my will.

As did I. Or that's the way it seems.

They wanted to quote-unquote baptize me. They said they'd cut out my spine. But I wasn't having it. So they kicked the shit out of me and chucked me in the water.

She recalled Inez's choked cries, and Pastor Sammy's affirmations: *The oil of vitriol oxidizes our sins.*

That's terrible, she said.

Corporal punishment is the by-product of a society's contempt for its citizens.

I'd tend to agree.

And when I say *a* society, I'm talking specifically about this town.

Yes. I gathered that.

He looked away again. This affected non-commitment, working to assert some protective skepticism, reminded her of her ex-husband.

I'm assuming that was your doing back there, she said. With the explosion.

Yup.

I suppose I'll say thank you?

He shrugged.

Little compressed gas, strategically placed. Easy if you know what you're doing. *Kapow*.

Your timing's impeccable. Almost suspiciously so.

It's no coincidence. I knew you'd be needing help.

He stopped pacing, but still avoided looking directly at her.

You'll say you don't believe me, he said. Even though you know it's true.

Try me.

I'm sort of a telepath.

And you are right. I don't believe you.

So you say. Because that's just what you think you're meant to say. But what you know, that's a whole other something else.

Ximena took this in. He was, she believed, telling a version of the truth.

So that's how you found me? You read my mind?

Nah. I can only read my own. But I can do it across time. A few hours ago I read my thoughts and saw how I'd get you away from those fuckers. Just threw you on the back of my ride and *boof*. I knew how it'd go down, because I remember it happening right now. You can do it too. I heard you tell that pick-nose Sammy you're here to judge him. You probably are. And you probably will. Believe me.

And again, she believed him. Her head was clearing; with effort, she rose and assessed her surroundings. To one side of this gully was a road, the lights of the town in the distance. To the opposite side lay a daunting terrain of rutted earth and dense brush. And above, as always: that impossible darkness.

Will it ever be morning? she asked.

Now, that's a question actually worth asking, Carson said. Who knows? Everything's fucked. But we'll pull through, one way or another. My future self tells me so.

So you're saying I should listen to my future self.

Or your past self. Whatever churns your butter.

What I need is to find the operations coordinator.

Ooh. Is she expecting you?

Yes, Ximena lied.

I can get you there. But first, I kind of need your help with something. Out there.

He pointed a thumb in the direction of that uninviting terrain, away from the road.

The fields, she said.

Right. Just a thing to take care of. Then we'll get on that other thing. Trust me. I'm a man of my word. One thousand percent.

He finished his beer, crushed the can, and tossed it aside.

And after that? she asked. What do you do then?

Carson rubbed his nose with the back of his hand, inspected it, then wiped it on his pants.

After that, I'm gonna burn this fucking town to the ground.

They walked on through the murk. Carson led, moving with purpose though the fields bore no landmarks or points of reference, only dense, knee-high grasses, swishing weeds, shallow troughs of muddy water. Several times in succession Ximena skidded out, almost pratfalling backward, and once let out an unintended cry. Carson looked back, annoyed. They continued. The undergrowth thickened. A milky fog rolled across the ground. Losing sight of Carson and his backpack for even a few seconds left her recalibrating her course. In him, she'd found a surer path in which to place her trust, even in the nullity of the fields.

In the foothills of Nauhcampatépetl she could forsake the town and its domination. Often in her younger days she spent entire days alone in the hills' monotony, against the scalding wind and steep climbs, luxuriating in isolation. It was impossible to get truly lost up there—the only way back was simply down, and from there a route home made itself clear. But the feeling of freedom, if only brief, was still true. One afternoon while ambling downhill she'd encountered a group of hikers, white men in plaid wool jackets, following the path of her ascent. Surprised to find a girl alone in the mountains, they'd asked in Spanish if she was lost. No, she'd answered, were they? They asked how far the trail led. Forever, she said. At this, the men laughed. One asked if she was afraid of snakes and scorpions, indicating her simple shoes and bare ankles. She said no, never. Why not? And she'd replied, meeting their stupefied gapes with her best grin: *Porque soy un fantasma.*

Her joy, such as it was, came from the possibility found in such loss. Dislocation, dizziness. The mechanisms that were necessary to not go totally berserk—what old Oropesa called *the divine trinity of mythology, masturbation, and marijuana.* Any thrill of life was in losing one's way, then regaining a path. We know ourselves best in the murk. Then, to make our way out, we search for a lodestar. Or a target.

She caught up to Carson's side. He anticipated her question before she'd had a chance to voice it.

I know what I'm doing, he said. I'm good in the dark. That's where I work.

Are you a cat burglar?

I mean when I'm working in the clubs. Spinning.

What?

DJing.

He cocked his head, miming headphones to ear, twisting knobs.

Oh, she said, and that's a thing?

Fucking rights it's a *thing.* It's my life. The air I breathe. I'm one of the top players in the game, you know. Progressive house, deep trance. Running the globe, on the grind. You've heard of St. Stacco?

I... No.

Paradise Rink? Danseteknic?

Sorry.

So you just wouldn't understand, he sighed. It's a subculture. You're either part of it or you're not.

They marched on. The rolling terrain of the fields had a mesmeric effect, the shoosh and crunch of their footfall creating a droning, sinuous pulse. A few years ago, Ximena's nephew Armando had gifted her a Conair Sound Therapy device, a cheap plastic blobby thing emitting canned sound effects: birds chirping, rainfall, an unhurried heartbeat. *To help you sleep*, Armando had said, though she'd never complained of, nor regularly experienced, insomnia. But now and then, while stoned, she'd play the thing on its white-noise setting and let its easy negation tranquilize her into a state of forgetfulness. The fields were like that.

They told me banishment was the worst punishment, Carson said. They said long after I'd gotten over the physical pain, the pain of exile would stay with me.

And?

Fuck that. You ever get lashed? It kills. Think I give two dicks about community? All the people in this town care about is symbolic virtue. I mean, come on. If you want to look for symbols, they're everywhere. That twig's a symbol. This beer's a symbol. When you want to know what's what, you just know it. Unless you're a total dink.

But a greater meaning comes from how you derive meaning from it, she said. That's how metaphor works. Ideaesthesia. In the mind, a thing becomes more than what it is.

And where does that get us? Let me answer that. Nowhere. And these suckers are gonna see straight up where it gets them.

They came to a slight climb in the terrain, heading toward a ridge ahead.

These people go on about community and opportunity and all that, Carson continued, but look at them sideways, they'll string you up and set your scrotum on fire. You want to know what this place really is? You want to know, really?

Tell me.

A mistake. It's a system glitch. The light washing in and washing out, it's all just like a machine, pushing stuff around, like a convenience belt.

Conveyor belt?

But in every system there's the shit that spills out the side, right. The overflow. The parts of the pig that go to Oscar Meyer. The snout and the butt. That's here. That's them.

The forgotten souls.

Nah. No one forgot anything. It's just part of the whole machine. Everyone knows that, but they can't admit it. Because if they do, they're admitting they have nothing else. But they'll see soon enough. It'll be like this place never existed.

Carson raised his arms, high and wide.

It's all coming *down*.

Ximena recalled Roy: *Everything big out there is small in here.*

I know something that might be of use to you in that regard, she said.

Hit me.

I met this man, an engineer. He was boasting about new fuel lines being installed. Propane, I think he said.

Think I heard something about that. These fuckheads with their maps.

He said the lines are in place but haven't been reinforced yet. So they'd be vulnerable. You know, someone with expertise in incendiary...

Carson stopped.

Sounds like you're abetting a criminal act. Which I'm fine with. But let's make sure we've got our parameters straight here.

Before she could respond, a flashing red light, farther ahead and downhill, caught her attention. He noticed it too. Their previous line of talk was forgotten.

Onward, he said, making his move.

As they headed down the slope, the strangeness of the scene ahead became clearer. The beacon leading them was a pair of ticking rear hazard lights belonging to an SUV, a silver Honda, parked in the brambles. Its driver's-side door was ajar, the interior lights on, but no driver was apparent. As they drew nearer, Ximena read its plate: BEAUTIFUL OHIO BIRTHPLACE OF AVIATION.

Carson rounded its side and looked into the open door.

Egh.

The front was a mess of discarded coffee cups and scraps, the seats and dashboard coated with crumbs and cigarette ash. The keys still dangled from the ignition. In the back, a different type of horror: the seat and cushions were layered with Best Buy flyers, affixed in place by duct tape and coated in purplish fluid.

Weird, Carson said.

The blood was still wet, saturating the base of papers across the entire bench, blending with the illustrated grids of plasma screens and air conditioners into a Pollockian frenzy of colour—less a spray than a soak. Whatever vein had let such blood, it had done so copiously and at length.

The hazard lights ticked away.

Oh, Ximena said, at a loss.

Carson moved to the SUV's hood, looking it over, again working at that air of serious contemplation. Ximena didn't find this reassuring. She was about to warn him against touching anything, the precautions of encountering a crime scene, but any call for sensible action seemed of no use here.

Let's keep going, he said. We're on the right track.

You know, we could drive. The keys are there.

The look he shot her annihilated this suggestion. They continued.

The fog writhed, clinging to the ground in undulating layers. Whenever Ximena turned back, she found the topography behind them unrecognizable. The path they'd followed through the fields was already lost, the SUV's lights faded. They were truly nowhere.

The bliss of loss had carried her through years of living alone in the city. Her daily routines were increasingly a program of non-interaction with the world: visits to the corner store for beer and chips and *La Jornada*, the pugnacious downstairs neighbours and their whining toddlers, occasional missives from her editors and representatives. Menopause. The National Action Party. Her financial situation tightened, then loosened, then became something entirely elusory. María Isabel left for San Antonio while still in her teens, cleaning rooms at a Marriott while taking night classes toward a certificate in Logistics Management at Palo Alto College. Her ambitions were uncurtailable and wide-reaching, and initially things went well, but within the year she was married and living with her schoolteacher husband in suburban Arizona; soon she became a mother herself, with an exasperating daughter of her own. Ximena spoke with María by long distance most Sunday and Thursday evenings, conversations that divagated pointlessly, and often they simply stayed on the line while María prepared her family's dinner, barely speaking at all. This was fine, and enough; Ximena had never felt like a mother in any traditional sense, merely a person who had given birth, only once and what felt like very long ago. Her daughter had emerged as a fully formed person, not merely some appendage or parallel interpretation of her own code, and would thrive or perish on her own terms. This made it easy to let go.

Because this shabby life of hers became one lived through inertia. Because she longed for nothing and no one. Because she'd lived modestly but fully on and through her writing, whatever its fallacies or failures. Because all she needed could be summoned by telephone delivery. Because what was once sharp became dull. *Porque soy un fantasma.* This too was fine, and enough.

Marching through the dark, she almost collided with Carson, who had stopped.

Whoa, she said.

He silenced her with a raised hand, then dropped to a crouch in the tall grass, scoping all directions. Ximena followed his lead, but heard and saw nothing.

What is it?

What we're after. The demon.

Reaching into his sweatshirt, he produced a tan leather sheath with a knife inside.

Need you to draw it out, he said. Get it to show itself. I'll get the drop on it and stab the sucker in the back.

She almost laughed.

I don't think so.

Don't worry. I've already seen how this plays out. It'll be drawn to you. You just need to get its attention. I'll take it from there. This is my fight.

Carson.

Only way we can kill it.

I'm not a killer.

But you are. I know what you're capable of.

In the trust he engendered: a trace of something fishy.

Is that why you rescued me? she asked.

I rescued you because you rescued me, and I'm not a total dick. But that was before. Now we're here.

Ximena breathed deeply and licked her lips.

Trust me, Carson said.

With this, his defensive posture dropped, ever so slightly. His young eyes pleaded. She was unable to say no.

And so: as strangely as everything that had unfolded in this endless night, Carson scampered off into hiding while Ximena reluctantly pressed forward alone. She tried calling: Hey hey hey. She flailed her arms and hopped in place, leaping like a moron to hail this presumed entity, whatever it might be. She looked up into the sky, its unforgiving black. No trace of a sign, no trace of that misty light.

Hey hey hey.

Just as she was considering abandoning her efforts, a sound came from nearby: a distinct scurry in the grass. She held her breath and waited.

The demon came tottering out of the shadows. Middle-aged, white, large-bellied, he wore an unkempt tan suit and gunmetal-grey glasses. A few days' stubble darkened his face. He stopped a few paces from Ximena. His voice came in a register oddly higher than his heft suggested.

According to widely accepted studies, he said, the risk of automobile accident is lower or the same for drivers with a blood alcohol content of zero-point-zero-four percent or less than for drivers with a blood level of zero. For a level of zero-point-fifteen percent, the risk is twenty-five-fold.

Ximena looked around for Carson, but he was nowhere to be seen.

In most states, a law of implied consent applies to all licensed drivers, with those refusing to participate in a blood alcohol test subject to punishment identical to those found guilty.

I don't know what you're saying, she said.

The goal is expedient sentencing. The process must be thorough and resolute.

He advanced on her. But after a single step, he halted, emitting a quiet gurgle. Carson appeared behind him, both hands around the knife's handle, digging the blade into the man's back. For a sustained moment, both men stood bound together. Carson then withdrew the knife with a sharp tug and stumbled back. The man looked down at himself and spun, gasping. Ximena saw blood's darkness expanding through his jacket's cotton, covering him, as if erasing him. He reached wildly, finding the hood of Carson's sweatshirt, and the two of them fell together to the ground.

Ximena moved to intervene, but stopped herself. *This is my fight*, Carson had said. She understood what that meant. She turned away and looked off into the distant fields, waiting for this battle to be over.

Her final book—with its themes of disappearance and forgetting, either a reiteration or a retread of her preceding decade's work, depending on how charitable the view one took of it—was issued just before the millennium's turn, just in time to solidify her categorization as a writer from a passing era; for all time, she would remain a figure of the past. The publication of *Sulphurs of Popocatépetl* ushered in her retreat from public life. She let most correspondence dwindle and notified relevant parties to put any publicity indefinitely on hold. She politely declined invitations for panels, residencies, juries. She made no efforts to be reachable. There was no firm strategy in this; it was simply the way things were working out. Her income had long plateaued, but the place in Roma remained affordable. Her joints wearied with the onset of arthritis, and walking became a chore. When extended satellite options became available on her street, she chose to spend most of her days in front of the television watching Liga MX soccer and *Judge Judy*.

Her life, always quiet, became even quieter. But in this she found no calm. Now that she was old, she realized her lifelong project to sanctify beauty—decontextualized and, in this, somehow incorruptible—had been an inane quest. Only a true fool, blessed with unearned luck, could imagine such a thing could be so important. Flirting with some sort of asceticism, a perverse version of *zhud* amid the city swelter, she'd imagined she might somehow live virtuously. But in renunciation, she'd only permitted herself to remain inert. Instead of setting her free, isolation had crippled her.

Her life, even at its most destitute and overextended, had been one of extravagance. A life as *idiotez cósmicos*.

One February morning, she'd been sipping coffee while watching *CBS This Morning* when a flare of pain had assailed her upper abdomen. She'd never sobbed purely out of physical agony in such a way, not even during María Isabel's delivery. When it hadn't subsided after an hour, she'd called an ambulance, feeling like a dunce as the EMTs wheeled her on a stretcher down the sidewalk for all her neighbours to see.

Until then, her only symptoms had been an occasional throb she mistook for heartburn. But she was told the cancer had already reached a nearly unresectable stage; in mere months, she would be entirely immobilized. Like many, she dreaded a gradual decline more than anything, hoping to instead be snuffed out in a flash, with no time for arduous personal inventory. To lie paralytic and rueful while anticipating death was a scenario she found almost unendurably terrifying.

Yet when it actually came, it was without much fear at all. As her body wound down, the effort of just continuing left no surplus energy for grief. Her regimen of gemcitabine hydrochloride and cisplatin, sided with sizable doses of quazepam, kept her in an untroubled languor. There was no process of self-acquittal. Surrender, it turned out, was painless. Here, at the end, was the transcendence she'd struggled so long to know.

She was kneeling in the grass when Carson dropped next to her, coughing and spitting. His hands shook as he wiped the knife's blade on the ground. She didn't look closely at what he was wiping off.

Let's get another one of those beers maybe, she said.

He dug in his backpack and produced the last two cans. They opened them and drank.

Did it work out? she asked.

Yup. Killed the fucker.

So are we done here?

Maybe give me a second. That bitch took a pretty good swipe out of me.

He rolled over on his back, hands on his abdomen.

You saw it, right? he said. You saw what I saw?

There was a man. I didn't recognize him.

Kind of, like, schlubby?

I suppose you could call it that.

Carson coughed again, a rough wheeze in his lungs.

I've seen where this goes, he said. There's gonna be ramifications.

Meaning what?

Not sure about me, but sooner or later it'll probably come after you. A demon like that always comes back for more. Eventually. Sometimes it skips a generation.

With difficulty, he sat up. He drank his beer, then slid the knife back into its sheath, tucking it into his sweatshirt pocket.

Sure you're okay? she said.

His smile failed to mask his pain.

Fucking rights. Let's go.

RESIDENCIES AT HAKKASAN in Las Vegas, Ministry of Sound, Space Ibiza, Anzu in São Paolo. Main stage at Tomorrowland Antwerp, Stereosonic in Perth, Coachella, Sunburn Goa. *Mixmag* cover shoot. V-MODA sponsorship. It was impossible to tell if Carson's incoherent babble was directed internally or otherwise, and whether the bizarre itinerary he detailed was his own or someone else's. He was not doing well. His face was damp and every few minutes he hacked up something condensed and foamy. By the time he and Ximena emerged from the fields' south ridge, he was barely staying upright. The more she expressed concern, the more he stubbornly insisted he was fine—he was, after all, still a teenager.

Green Valley in Camboriú. Guaba in Cyprus. Self-curated audio-visual experiential artist production designer. *Ack.*

Below lay a furrow of dense marsh, and beyond that, a road. This, Ximena realized, was the way by which she'd entered town; having apparently circumnavigated the town's boundary, they'd now wound up on the opposite side. Past the marsh and up a contiguous incline stood the vinyl-sided building she'd noticed earlier. This, Carson indicated, housed the operations coordinator's office.

Said I'd get you here, and I did. Blam.

You're not coming?

Nah. I have that other thing to work on. Think I better hup to it. I'm in sort of bad shape here.

He peeled open his jacket. His stomach and crotch were a mess of coagulated blood.

Híjole, Carson. I can't leave you like this.

I'll be fine.

So this, she understood, was it for them. He turned to her, unsteady on his feet.

You better, uh. Here.

He reached into his sweatshirt and produced the sheathed knife. As he handed it to her, she thought to refuse, but didn't. *When you want to know what's what,* he'd said, *you just know it.* This, she saw, was what was what. The weight felt good in her hands. Its satisfactions were implicit.

Will I see you again? she said.

You never know. Maybe this is just a premonition. Maybe it hasn't even happened yet.

And we're only just our future selves.

Why not.

He shuddered against his pain.

I have a confession. I lied. I'm not actually some baller DJ. I'm not shit. Only gig I ever got was Mondays at the Yucatán. And I even fucked that one up. I had to pawn my decks last winter to make rent. I never did anything. I never did Ibiza. I never went anywhere.

Don't worry about it.

I lie a lot. It's kind of pathological, I guess. I'm sorry.

That doesn't make you a bad person.

Doesn't make me good. Oh well.

With this, he limped back the way they'd come. Carson had said he'd been brought here against his will, but she never ascertained exactly how, and what he'd done to engender the town's animosity. Why they'd thrown him in the reservoir. *They said they'd cut out my spine.* It was possible he'd lied about all of that too. That shapeshifting demon, the blood and duct tape, his plans of destruction— all of this could be a deception. But as he faded into the trees, she found herself already missing him, even though their time together had been brief.

Against all exhaustion and confusion, Ximena reminded herself of the task now at hand. Pastor Sammy: *You get sidetracked by the details and the dialogue and the flashy stuff, and you lose the plot. It happens.* Indefinite challenges lay ahead. So her only guidepost, once again, was instinct: omens from her future self.

The office was bright and stark, with linoleum floors and unadorned walls, centred by an unmanned service counter. The wooden door behind the counter was closed. As with the hangar, everything here emphasized functionality. A sign hung on a wall: SURVEILLANCE IN EFFECT.

She wasn't alone. A man was seated on one of two benches against this wall, head lowered and hands folded in his lap. Ximena recognized him as the line technician from the airport, his work coveralls now traded for a windbreaker and jeans. His eyes widened at seeing her, and she offered a polite smile. He gave nothing back, turning to the blank wall beside him. She took this as a sign not to engage him.

The situation seemed to suggest she was meant to wait her turn, so she took a seat on the other bench. As soon as she eased back against the wall, staring into the dropped ceiling's grid of fluorescent panels, she sensed fatigue's irrefutable pull. With her energies running low, a shift in her perception was occurring: that precognitive faculty Carson had described kicking in, or something in that department. She was too tired to come to any conclusion, and found herself nodding off.

In this shallow rest she was met with an image, less a dream than a kind of digression. She saw her bedroom's ceiling, a quadrant of late-afternoon sunlight. Bedcovers weighed her down. An electric humidifier toiled. A figure came into focus. It was her granddaughter Alejandra, older now than when Ximena had last seen her: her hair was long, her eyebrows tweezed. Alejandra stood over her beside the bed, but kept a distance, reaching to rest a tentative palm on Ximena's head. In this there was the sensation, however distant and unformed, of connection. Energy ceded from older to younger. Alejandra grimaced, but kept her hand in place. Ximena felt her body's knottedness easing, the accumulated gunk of years being rinsed away. She was divested of obligation. She was lightened. Unburdened.

She opened her eyes to find the line technician gone. Minutes or hours could have passed; no gauge of time was available. A small woman in a pink cardigan sweater now stood behind the counter, sifting through a sizable stack of files, scratching at them with a pen.

Ximena stood and approached the counter. She caught a sound she hadn't before noticed, the source close but unclear: a man's voice, speaking at length. Flat but crisp, like a radio announcer's. It rang as vaguely familiar, but Ximena couldn't place it. *The credit of mercy is weighed in the perspiration of the condemned, the fervour of the misled. Something from another time.* Gobbledygook of some sort. More bad poetry maybe.

Yes, the woman finally said, without diverting attention from her work.

Hello, Ximena said. This is the operations coordinator's office?

I am the operations coordinator, the woman said, and this is my office. So you are safe in making that shrewd deduction.

Ximena knew this tone: that of the beleaguered civil servant, the functionary's protectiveness for her narrow dominion. The trick here would be to allow the operations coordinator to feel empowered in asserting her authority, appeasing through an appeal for mercy.

Sorry to bother you. I know you must be very busy. I'm just wondering about flights out, and how one might get on one.

The operations coordinator looked up.

Yeah, as if *that's* happening.

She spread a folder on the counter, showing detailed worksheets.

This is one ITC statement. *One.* Every single transport that goes out, we process an average twenty-three of these. And by we, I pretty much mean me. Revising the manifest means going back to step one and re-inputting the entire list. Manually. And then double-checking for security protocol. You know who does that?

Sorry. I didn't intend to...

I asked if you know who does that.

I'm going to assume it's you.

Ding. Correct.

You'd think there could be some sort of automated system. To relieve the load on one person.

Well, there isn't. And now it's the last day of the flight phase. That means in...

She consulted her watch.

...twenty-six minutes, the last flight goes out and we shut down for the season. No more flights, no more whiny passengers, no more cargo. No more paperwork.

You must be looking forward to that.

Ximena smiled, her attempt at endearment.

Must I?

This was not going well. She tried to change tack, suggesting as best she could that the season's end was the reason for her urgency in getting a flight, and that although she understood her hope was unreasonable, it was the only one open to her. The operations coordinator, however, was unsympathetic, and resumed examining her pages.

So you're saying what I want is impossible, Ximena said.

Ding ding. Correct again.

Looking past the counter, Ximena saw the source of the strange voice. Atop a waist-high metal file cabinet sat a Sansui stereo receiver and a single speaker. A bulky mahogany box with ornate gold trimmings was connected to the receiver by a mess of cables leading from a hole in its side. Another, fatter cable fed from the box into the wall.

For too long we've stood at the gates, the voice declared from the speaker. *Now access can be ours, but only ours together.*

Ximena now recognized it: it was the voice she'd heard over the radio in Roy's car.

What is that? she asked. That recording.

The operations coordinator followed her gesture, glancing at the audio set-up.

The transmitter broadcasts over a nominal centre frequency on a rotating program. I've been told a particular tropospheric ducting effect propagates the signal far past the expected range. Apparently, it even reaches transceiver stations linked to certain multiple-access cellular clusters. It's been on the same loop for who knows how long. But these are processes that long predate me. I just execute the work order.

So who's listening? What's the...

The words must be transmitted, so I transmit the words. Much to my chagrin.

You can't turn it off?

That box is locked. And no one seems to have the key.

Why not just yank it out of the wall?

She squinted to read Ximena, making no attempt to disguise her contempt.

That you'd even waltz in here asking such things really speaks to the arrogance of people. Not even arrogance. Stupidity.

There's no need for insults.

But the coordinator was clearly irked.

I see this every single day. People look at this town and its operations like a plaything they can fiddle with however they like. As if the entire thing's in service of, what? Some insipid personal realization. The desperate need for validation. The sense of entitlement around here is sickening. Everyone nods along to those pathetic drips at the church and cooks up their own little comfy mythologies, blathering about portals and possibilities. Blatantly disregarding their basic reality.

Which is what?

Finitude. We're in a closed system, more rigid than you could even imagine. And there are processes we have to follow and regulations beyond our understanding. You ask me, that's what that message is saying. It's a warning against indulging delusions. This preciousness of the self. But resistance to the system isn't just futile, it's not even on the menu. The more you deny that, the more you just confirm its necessity. And the more you look like a fool.

I just want to get on that plane and get out of here. Please.

You and everyone else. But it's full. *Acta est fabula.*

Ximena saw she'd reached a dead end, and backed toward the door. The voice went on: *Let nothing hinder your progress. You mustn't avert your eyes. Tear ahead and claim your rightful spoils. A spiteless world will be yours.* As she went for the door, the operations coordinator picked up her pen.

What did you say your name was again?

Back out in the night, Ximena assessed her present options. None were appealing. Ahead, at the end of the office's gravel driveway, was the main road. Farther down, the route to the airstrip terminal. To the north, the town. She could retrace her steps, back toward the reservoir, perhaps. But that way offered only the forest in all its perplexity. She could follow the road away from the town, but where would it lead? Another town, another fearful populace with its own systems of sacrifice. The instincts she'd relied on had led her here, with no way forward.

Never had she been more acutely conscious of her limits.

Catalysis brings us toward the transition state.

At the end of the driveway, she discovered the line technician standing in the middle of the road, vigorously rubbing his foot on the asphalt to scrape something off his sneaker's heel. His windbreaker was unzipped; the T-shirt underneath read I RUN FOR FUN, HEALTH & DONUTS. This time he greeted her with a friendly wave.

Wondered if I'd see you again tonight. She giving you guff?

Meaning the operations coordinator. Ximena nodded.

Don't let her get to you, he said. She's just frustrated. It's a joyless job. But what job isn't, right? Speaking of which.

He flapped a sheet of paper, similar to the one Don had wielded at the airport.

Just pulled my last shift. Got my ticket.

You're on the flight?

Hell yes. Like I said before, we wait our turn. That's civilization. I waited, and I got civilized. Now I'm done with this place.

Me too.

Oh? You got on the manifest?

That's why I'm here.

He took this with a nod.

In that case, we'd better zip back over to the terminal. Time's tight.

They walked south together along the main road. As they reached the turnoff to the terminal, that recognizable mechanical whine rose from afar: an arriving plane in descent. She looked up to see, yes: in the farthest distance, lights winked through the clouds. And among those clouds, traces of that twisting incandescent light.

The line technician looked back in the direction of the town.

Wonder what that's all about, he said.

A herd of townspeople were now passing through the town's gates, loosely headed their way. A pair of police cruisers tailed behind. Leading the charge, Ximena could just make out, was Pastor Sammy—the shepherd steering his flock. Cutting through the mounting noise of the plane, another sound: deep, pealing tones. The bell tower was ringing.

Ximena understood what was happening; her future self knew. She looked back to the operations coordinator's office, and her suspicions were confirmed: the coordinator herself stood in the doorway, watching the advance of the mob she'd summoned.

Gosh, the line technician said. Hope nothing's wrong. Our flight could be delayed.

That won't happen, she said, coming up behind him.

Her hand went to Carson's knife, slipping it from its sheath.

These old hinges have a squeak.

Sorry? he said, his attentions still on the road.

Lubrication is required.

The knife sank into the meat of his back with surprising ease. She twisted it, meeting resistance as its serrations sawed at bone just below his right scapula, then released the handle—just as Carson had shown her, slaying the demon. The line technician heaved forward, flailing to reach for the blade. He looked at her with a strange expression, almost like disappointment, then landed face first on the pavement.

Unsure if she'd yet been spotted by the coming crowd, she took the line technician by the ankles and worked at dragging him off the road. This weight was substantial, the strength required difficult to muster—but, despite her fatigue, she did it. As she slid him onto the shoulder, his face grated against the rough ground, momentarily rousing him, but he only emitted only a meek gasp—*weh*— before passing out again. She managed to manouevre him into the overgrown roadside, hiding him among the sedges and reeds. She searched his pockets, his clothes' fabric already tacky with blood, and dug out the ticket. A quick glance provided no assurance as to its transferability.

The bell tower's chimes ceased, the last peal sustaining. To the east, a squeal and rumble: the plane at the terminal, making its landing.

With both hands she withdrew the knife from where it still protruded. Fresh blood geysered. She tossed the knife into the bushes, then immediately regretted doing so. But she clamped down such compunction, silencing any inner doubt. She knelt and gathered wads of grass and mud, shovelling this over the line technician's body, then sat back, evaluating the mess she'd made.

The line technician would die there, she knew.

She heard Oropesa: *When you go in for the kill, make sure it's clean.* Of these sloppy techniques, her old mentor would surely disapprove.

The townspeople continued their progress toward her.

She rushed into the terminal as a skinny man in coveralls was closing the hangar doors. This, she gathered, was the replacement line technician. Seeing Ximena hurrying over, he hit a switch to halt the doors' motors. Ximena handed him the paper ticket. As he looked it over, she noticed flecks of blood on its underside.

Guess you got here just in time, he said.

First shift on the new job? she said, breathless.

Yup. They got me started before the off-season. All by myself here, not a lot of training. Kinda wigged out, to be honest.

He was clean-shaven and barbered, twitchy, signs of eagerness to prove himself. Whether the operations coordinator had notified him of any interloper headed his way, Ximena couldn't know. It was too late for any such misgivings.

Trust your instincts, she said. You'll be fine.

He seemed pleased by this, and handed her back the ticket. He had a hand-held scanner, like the last technician, but either forgot to use it or didn't bother.

Bon voyage.

The plane was waiting on the tarmac, its engines in full roar. Ushered through by the new line technician, she crossed the runway and climbed the airstairs, her knees still feeling weak. The door was open, but no attendant greeted her. She ducked her head and stepped inside.

The plane's cabin was dim and quiet, its rows mostly unoccupied. As she continued down the aisle, the few passengers already seated—men and women of various ages, all, it appeared, travelling solo—paid her little attention; several were already asleep. Ximena took a window seat toward the rear and attempted to settle in. Her pulse thumped in her temples, competing with the turboprop engine.

Her limited view of outside was of the runway and hangar doors, now sealed. She looked past the terminal, back down the road. Lights converged there, gauzy at this distance. Tinges of mist swirled in the air.

Excuse me. Do you have a tissue or something?

In the subdued light, the woman seated across the aisle was only a slender outline. Ximena was surprised to find she recognized her.

Inez?

Have we met?

Ximena explained: she'd been at the church for the ceremony, the utility shroud, the ritual of obliteration. Inez seemed unbothered at her bringing this up.

I have to say, Ximena said, I was concerned. For your safety.

Oh, that's nothing to fuss about, Inez said. I mean, even Pastor Sammy says it's mostly just pageantry.

A clunk came from the cabin's head as the automatic doors closed and sealed.

I prefer to just think about what lies ahead, Inez said.

And what's that?

I usually get sick on airplanes. So not barfing is kind of my main concern right now. But then we'll be up and away, and everything should be fine after that.

What is it to you? This place.

What is it to me?

Inez sighed.

I'll tell you, when I was young, I was a goat tethered to a pole. I was so wild. But fighting against that leash just makes it tighter and tighter. Now, with the blessings given to me by my community, I really see the bounty in all we've been given. I've learned to just graze where I am. I can love myself unconditionally, even if all I am is just some crazy old goat. And I can apply that positive energy in a purposeful manner as I move ahead to the next phase of my being. Hazy is lazy, as Pastor Sammy says.

She paused.

What was your question again?

This place. The endless night. The mists, the light.

Right. In God's illumination, everything's an opportunity for spiritual reconstitution. That sounds nice, doesn't it?

To be honest, I don't know. It seems we've made up God as a metaphor. And now he's getting us back by making us live inside one.

Oh.

Inez frowned.

Pastor Sammy says it's better to exist in a state of eternal wonder than in a state of eternal doubt. Sorry...you *don't* have a tissue?

Ximena didn't. The plane eased down the airstrip. A graphic ignited above, warning the passengers to fasten their seat belts for takeoff. Ximena turned back to the window. The mob had arrived, dozens en masse, swarming the terminal with the enraged dilation of police lights. But the plane rolled on, gathering speed. Several townspeople rushed the plane, lobbing bottles—the glass clinked across the roof. Ximena thought she spotted Clara among them, though the light was tricky; it could have been anyone.

Just before this scene slipped out of her available view, Ximena made out Pastor Sammy, now dressed head to toe in form-fitting jogging gear, charging onto the runway. With arms raised in appeal, he shouted something after the departing plane. His exhortations were lost amid the engines' noise.

Ximena leaned back in her seat. Across the aisle, Inez stared down at her lap, looking uneasy. For her part, Ximena mostly felt fine, perhaps for the first time that night. That pain in her abdomen was absent; the ache in her knees was finally easing. Troubling questions, however, still chafed. Had she really murdered a man? Or had it all just been symbolic?

Was this the culmination of her narrative? Is this who she really was, in the end?

Had she seen through the shroud?

Maybe this is just a premonition. Maybe it hasn't even happened yet.

She was young again, and old. A memory came, that particular feeling of coming down from the mountains at dusk, finding the crumbling streets of her neighbourhood remade in warped shade—that fierce desire to be lost fading, leaving her grateful for home. There was the dust and concrete she knew, the power lines and pickups, adobe houses painted lime green and baby blue, withered men hunched on cinder blocks outside the carnicería. And her mother's voice, the dissatisfaction that anchored her so: *I just want to sleep until it's time to sleep again.*

The plane circled in a wide arc, passing back over the town. From here she saw it all: the streets, the connective dots and dashes of light, the outlying splotches of lots yet undeveloped. There was, she saw, another source of light, in the town's core: the bell tower billowing dense smoke, its windows burning with a dyspeptic glow.

The main street erupted in white flame. The explosion was deep and resounding, expulsing such a wave of force that the plane shuddered, even at this height—a sound of certainty amid so many illusory forces. Everything solid became fumes. Toward the front of the cabin, one of the other passengers yeeped in alarm.

Carson had done it. *I'm a man of my word. One thousand percent.*

The plane continued its climb. They left the burning town behind, passing over the road and the reservoir, the forest and meadows. Soon this too vanished as they ascended into the troposphere, and all that was obscure became clear.

THE SWAN KING

PETER HAUSEN WAS NINE YEARS OLD when he first encountered the mists. Dubai then was an immense, sparkling nightmare, a place containing all and none of the world. Attended by his father's ever-shifting personnel of lackeys, he was shuttled through limitless malls and concourses, domed tennis courts, wave-simulating pools the size of valleys. Memories of his mother were mostly of drop-offs and departures, until early one morning he watched as Koharu climbed into a limousine under the Mussafah Bridge and drove off into the pre-dawn fog, not to be seen again for years. In day school he met daughters of industrialists and grandsons of false sultans, others similarly bound to this place. He befriended a boy from Beijing others dubbed the Miniature Chairman, and through him Peter discovered the joys of psychoactive drugs, huddling in a chauffeured limousine to crush up the Chairman's inexhaustible supplies of codeine pills, refashioning afternoons into drowsy, unassailable escapes. Once, loafing on his bedroom balcony in a stoned stupor, he saw a formation of American fighter jets scud over the city, roaring from the north as if spat out by an infuriated god. As they vanished into the outskirts' infinity of dunes and highway, Peter laughed with the realization: all of this was just a dream.

And like figures in dreams, the mists initially surfaced as suggestions. They told him: time must be experienced equivocally. They told him: amid all this, you are nothing. They warned: for all crimes, seasons of affliction must follow. Of these admonitions, Peter understood little. Yet he listened, and with time these scolds rang more as pleas. They told him: territories await beyond this one. And they told him: *we grant you admission*. But when the moment came, and the beckoning portal opened, Peter lacked the courage to accept the invitation. Tethered to a knowable world, he could only stare into the mists and imagine what lay beyond.

PETER ARRIVED IN NEW ORLEANS at sundown. He put the car in a lot, paying two days in advance, left his bag at the hotel off Bienville, and immediately headed by foot for the bar on St. Mary where he expected Marc still worked. It had been a nervous drive down the I-59, pummelled by intermittent gales all through Mississippi, and he hoped the walk would help discharge some of the tension.

The city had changed, or his perception of it had. The sidewalks were emptier, the roads wider. Crossing Poydras, he thought he recognized a man puffing a cigar beside an ATM, but it was just another idle ghost. These spectres crawled up out of the grates, loped out from alleys: this city did that. Here he too was just another shadow, occupying no tangible plane. He'd come back to New Orleans hoping to restore honour to the dead, and that was all he'd do.

The bar's sign, as ever, was visible from down the block. At the door he experienced another twinge of nerves, but clamped down any desire to cut out. Inside he found a familiar scene: strings of Christmas lights and vintage Coors clocks, a faction of young guys in one corner arguing football, fIREHOSE on the jukebox. It was still early, and the place was only now filling up. The bartender looked up from her phone and, before he'd said anything, was asking his order. Peter hadn't intended on staying any longer than necessary, and yet he ordered a drink without hesitation, mechanically.

Is Marc around? he asked the bartender.

Her attentions were back on her phone.

Maybe. If not, he'll be in.

Peter's most indelible memory of Marc Beauchesne, Alain's brother, was a backyard party up on Lesseps, about five years ago. An argument had erupted, and though the details were now dim, an image endured: Marc, tequila-wild and gnashing teeth, stripped to the waist and lunging at Peter in fury. What had he done to spark Marc's wrath that time? Any number of perceived violations. When Alain had thrown an arm around his brother, pleading with him to ease up, Marc shoved him away and stormed off, not for the first time vowing Peter's murder. Such a thing, a gathering at such a time in such a way, once common, now felt unimaginable.

The actual last time he'd seen Marc was in Montreal last year, at the interment of Alain's remains. They'd gathered at the plot on Mount Royal's north slope, a dark sloshy day, and befitting a life that had exhibited both magnanimity and disorder, the occasion brought a mixed showing of colleagues and former students, editors and enemies, grey-faced rehab soulmates. Of Alain's family, only Marc had shown—their parents were long dead, and Alain had thoroughly laid any other extended familial ties to waste. Peter and Marc hadn't exchanged words then, only a transaction of stares as others wept and offered well-worn adages. There were many things Peter himself might have said, but he only skulked at the margins, avoiding undue attention. The rain held off until the urn was lowered, then the assembly quickly disbanded.

A fresh issuance of patrons now entered the bar, among them a familiar figure: Wilborn, as ever with his boyish slouch and chasmal, alcoholic eye sockets, slithering to the bar to requisition a row of shots. Mere seasons ago, Peter would have been there with them, determined in such delirium, clinking glasses with a similar mischief of rats.

Wilborn was laughing at—something one of his cronies was yelling into his ear when he noticed Peter's approach.

Wow. It's you.

He downed one of two shots he had lined up, something caramel-hued, then cast an arm around Peter, pulling him in. He was sweaty, smelling of days of concerted drinking.

So weird to see you here again. So weird. I'm amazed.

You shouldn't be.

You're kind of person non grappa around here.

I'm looking for Marc.

Thought you hightailed back up to Canada.

I did. Where is he?

Wilborn granted him a doubtful look, then gestured toward a corner, past the bar. And there Marc was: gym-chiselled frame, posture of a cement truck, his dome sheeny and crucifix dangling. Peter moved to angle himself out of Marc's sightline, still not ready for a confrontation. An inner voice screamed for him to leave, to hurry back to the hotel and the forgiveness of sleep. To abandon this hopeless effort, to let the past die.

But then Wilborn was waving, mouthing something, pointing. Whatever was going to happen was happening.

Marc's expression at seeing Peter indicated disbelief, but also something else: a piqued appetite, a hunger for outrage now to be sated. He motioned for Peter to follow him to the bar's entryway, away from the mounting racket. There they faced off.

When did you get to town?

Drove in just a few hours ago.

And you came right here.

First thing.

Marc nodded, his vein-swollen forehead glistening in stray neon. There was no approval in this nod. Peter fought to come up with anything like repartee.

How's the music going?

A proudly anachronistic Stevie Ray Vaughan guitar disciple, Marc took on his presupposed bluesman calling with the same intensity as he approached his gym schedule: almost monastically, with repetition, avowal, honour. In much the same way, he held actual scripture to heart, having recommitted in his thirties to the Beauchesnes' Roman Catholic heritage. The life he'd made for himself here in Louisiana was the product of rigorous and determined self-definition; against such a spirit, Peter stood no chance. He had no fight in him anyway.

You're really asking me that? Marc said. What are you doing back here?

I felt...there are things that should be said.

So write an email or something.

Peter was quiet. Marc pressed on.

You need to leave. Just leave. Go hawk your poison somewhere else. You're not wanted here.

Look, Peter tried, I understand the feeling that blame must be laid. I do. You and I, we've had our frictions. But maybe there's a better way to—

Shut your mouth, Marc spat, cutting him off. You think you can sashay in here and, what, buy my forgiveness? Think again, my man. You and your father, you want to contaminate the earth, propagating your evil? Well, you reap what you sow. But you bring that on my family? Then it becomes my problem.

It's not like that. Things changed after we left. Alain was doing really well.

So what was it? Just bad luck?

To this, Peter had no answer.

That's shit. It's *shit*. You know that. When are you gonna learn? There's no luck. We suffer and we fail because we turn our backs on Christ. Like Alain did. Because of you.

Peter wanted to object, but felt his mind pulsing against a logjam of strain. Any connection between urge and action had been severed. He could only listen as Marc continued.

We can't evade the scouring sight. There's God's will and God's plan, and that's it. *The heart of man plans his way, but the Lord establishes his steps.* That's Proverbs sixteen-nine. I tell you that because I know you don't understand. You're a trespasser.

This was true—Peter was. This pitiful attempt at reconciliation, at solemnizing Alain's passing, or whatever he was doing here, was a mistake, imagining he could remedy anything through such a gesture. He moved for the door, but Marc blocked his way.

You come to me looking for redemption. You want to be absolved. But it'll never happen, because you shun God. Your effrontery... Only God knows what awaits the wicked. You inflicted your curse upon my brother. For that, your pain will continue and continue. I hope it lasts your entire life.

New Orleans of memory: a plexus of reclining shade and Sazerac-soaked afternoons, an endless well of distraction. Alain and Peter had initially turned up there on a whim, driven only by impulse, just as they'd done everything. Arriving at Marc's doorstep impromptu, much to his annoyance, they'd then remained in the city for more than a year, flitting from hotel to hotel, borne by and bearing disorder. All they desired was always at reach, their nights obscured in lamplight and smoke, effortless and easy—or easy enough.

Such ease, or the sustained appearance of ease, was possible only because Peter was rich. He was rich in a way that negated any need for tracking intangibilities like time, damages, consequences. Diligence and dignity could be feigned by purchase. He could commandeer a VIP lounge, or teleport Alain to his side by limousine, or ride a rented Triumph Triple 675 through the seventh ward boggled on MDMA—he could do such things, living invulnerably and unbound, because he was rich.

But the course of Peter's inheritance was a flow of blood money, streaming from the central abysm of his father. The Hausen name could be found stencilled on thermobaric rockets pummelling Al-Raqqah and whispered by children toiling in Indonesian tin mines. Entire arsenals of destruction, assigned by means of distribution points across four continents, furthered this legacy of wickedness. And Peter, however tenuous and estranged, was its only heir.

For this, despite so much at his disposal, he was marked an outcast. Even in the dim mercies of New Orleans, a city boastful of its iniquity, he walked as one shunned. Wide-bellied tourists in golf shirts hawed into their daiquiris, shielding their wives as Peter passed on the sidewalk. Crackheads and weekending fratboys and garbagemen alike eyed him skeptically. Surely all knew of his corruption; even the ghouls jeered in derision. Marc was right to slam him with holy scorn—whether driven by love or arrogance, Peter had knowingly lured Alain into his abominable sphere, and he would be known, now and forever, by the ruin he'd brought into this world.

An erratic wind had risen, residuum of the afternoon squall. Headed north by taxi, Peter slipped into a doleful stupor, again executing old patterns on automatic. The bleakness of passing streets, the tire lots and Dollar Generals and shotgun houses encircled in slumped wire fences were familiar but stirred no affection.

Dumaine was quiet, with evidence of decline down the block: ruined foundations, boarded windows, desolate yards. Hurricane damage or, just as likely, simple neglect. Lulu's house was recognizable by the chronological array of flags lining its balcony, flapping three-by-five-inch renditions cascading from the Francis Hopkinson thirteen-star variant through to the latter-day 1960 version. Two men met him on the stoop, both in Saints jerseys and nursing forties of High Life. Peter, versed in such protocols, told them he was looking for Lulu. One thumbed his phone, then raised a finger, bidding Peter to hold on. After a few seconds, he waved Peter through.

The house was as remembered, larger inside than its facade suggested, its narrow face hiding a depth of many rooms. It too looked in bad shape. Much of the wallpaper had been stripped and the stained glass of the vestibule doors was cracked, punched in. Peter passed quickly through the front living room, where several women sat on couches, watching television and looking at their phones. The sweetly noxious stink of crack hung in the air.

He found Lulu in the kitchen, seated at the table eating crawfish pie from takeout Styrofoam, her huge face flushed pink.

Evening, Peter.

He kept to the doorway. A skinny man he didn't know stood silent in the corner.

You seem almost disappointed to see me, Peter said.

Lulu wiped her greasy lips with a tear of paper towel.

Hardly. You're a delight. But folks blow, folks return. I wonder. I worry a little.

You needn't.

A half-smoked cigar lay in an ashtray on the table. Lulu pinched its blackened nub and signalled to the skinny man. He came over, snapping a lighter.

Refresh my memory, Lulu said as she puffed her cigar to life. Where you been? My mind's trashed from a lifetime of abusing narcotics.

Just running around. North and south, east and west.

That's my guy. Always a half-hour out of nowhere. Stanislaus...

Meaning the skinny man.

...what's to drink? Help us out.

As the man clinked around in the refrigerator, a yellowed Westinghouse from a bygone era, Peter took a seat opposite Lulu. She wiped away the crumbs of crust and fish littering the table with her forearm, the flesh there dotted with the scars of injection abscesses.

Had any of those cool visions lately? she asked him.

Not in a while.

Visionary sight, you know, the when of it isn't real important. That old magistra Hildegard von Bingen didn't transcribe the *Scivias* until she was in her forties. Took that long to cohere, with all the psilocybin bitching up her medieval mind. Nowadays, you got DARPA and these auroral research stations up in Alaska. That's what causes all the post-traumatic stress disorder and chronic fatigue, you know. No such thing as erectile dysfunction in the eighteenth century.

You know your stuff.

I ain't no intellect. Just receive and relay, receive and relay.

And always cagey about your sources.

Comes from all over. The phases of the moon, the poison of the sky. People washed in from the sea. This kind of stuff I can handle. But don't know the first thing about, like, algorithms.

But when you insist on something...

Then I demand to be heard.

Stanislaus opened two large cans of Budweiser and placed them on the table. Lulu took one and prompted Peter to take the other.

And so, she said. Alain.

Yes.

A beautiful guy. A guy you wanted to talk to. Saw connections between the unconnected things. His eyes were open.

And then he died.

Yes, he did.

Lulu sipped her beer, adding nothing further. Peter knew she'd never deign to comment too directly on matters of grief. The only commodities she respected were those she could manipulate, and the only people she tolerated were those she could control—she was, after all, a drug dealer. To her, everything was money and auras.

All right then, he said, reaching for his wallet.

She sighed.

What, he said, you can't help me out?

You know I can, she said. But this business is all changing. All in the Sierra Madres, and everything's tight at the borders now. Getting across the Gulf, you got Homeland Security, HIDTA, you got narcos. We're in a season of violence. Future's doubtful.

So, no dope.

Now, I didn't say that.

Lulu lifted the flap of her large belly, unearthing a Pokémon fanny pack strapped under her sweatshirt. She unzipped it to dig out a blue plastic baggie.

Be careful. Hot stuff means stay cool. I tell folks, never get emotional when it comes to drugs.

She slid the bag across the table. Peter knew the heroin was probably laced, heavier than anything he'd been used to. He pocketed it anyway, handing her back a few bills. She stuffed the money in her fanny pack without counting it. He stood.

Where you going? Sit with me, finish up. King of Beers. And you can shoot that here. It's not like I judge.

Rather not.

Lulu frowned, her face's chub squeezing with creases.

Peter, Peter. When I first met you, you were six tons of fun. Loved to party. Now you're a real sourpuss. You want to understand those visions, maybe think about getting down off that cross of yours.

That was enough. He needed to move.

This house, he said, looking around. It always feels like it's just about to collapse.

No, sir, Lulu said. This place'll be here well into the next century. Sixth ward won't be around, not like we know it. Floods are coming. Everything not chained down's gonna get washed away. Old haunted house like this, though...she's so flimsy, the tides just seep right on through.

He was staring up into the maelstrom of an impossible sky heaving bands of clouds. Mesas of fissured ice stretched to all points of the compass, slopes of snow milled by katabatic winds. Here, at the bottom of the earth, all was negation, isolation, tumult.

Peter.

He opened his eyes. There was no ocean, no bullying cyclones. Though he was shivering, and indeed in some sort of vessel.

Peter Hausen. You hear me?

His location gradually returned: he was lying in the stern of a mastless sailboat, mounted on cinder blocks in a fenced yard down the street from Lulu's, near Lafitte. He hadn't gotten far; the fentanyl had hit him hard, unmooring him.

I hear you, Peter said, sitting up.

A man stood over him, clad neck to ankles in denim, offering a hand. Peter allowed himself to be pulled to his feet.

Your father needs you, the man said, his voice carrying a Southern drawl.

Wonderful, Peter said, retucking his shirt and adjusting his belt. And you are?

You know who I am.

Peter didn't, though the man's general air was familiar.

How'd he find me?

These things aren't so tough. You know that.

Peter reached into his jacket, feeling for the drugs and apparatus. Months mostly clean had been banished in quickness, back into those opiate hollows; still, he remained a conscientious user, tidy and discreet. How much time he'd erased while on the nod was unclear, but the processes at play, familiar in their trickery, had operated as expected. Though heroin was really Alain's terrain, not his—it had never entirely agreed with him. It demanded too much.

As he stepped out of the boat, his knees gave way and he tumbled into the ragged grass. The man offered an arm, but Peter refused this reach and remained on the ground. There was no frustration in this, just acceptance. He felt all right about it.

I'm not going to Munich.

He's not in Munich. He's in Kenya.

Not going there either.

The man produced a phone and scrolled.

We'll be on a flight in the morning. Commercial, unfortunately. The jet's in San Jose.

I know what Dred's after, Peter said, but it's not available anymore. Not to me. And definitely not to him.

Not my concern. Arrangements are booked.

Whoever the man was, however assured in his distressed Wranglers, he clearly occupied a lower node in DHG's mammoth organizational flow chart. As in all corporate structures, grief in this network flowed accumulatively downward, snowballing, or mudsliding, disseminating through longitudes and sectors and operatives, all in service of Dred's monomaniacal aims. Against this, there would be no reasoning.

Peter compelled himself to rise, finding balance against the earth's persuasion. He sighted an angular figure on the sidewalk, observing: Lulu's Stanislaus, flicking a cigarette. Here was another functionary—Lulu too was known to keep close tabs on all in her circles. Such watchfulness, he knew, was not out of any kindness, but to safeguard her interests.

The man, occupied by his phone, seemed to not notice they were being watched. Let's make a move, he said. I have a suite at the Roosevelt. We'll order up some oysters and hit the airport early when you're in better shape.

But Peter was already headed toward Stanislaus. This wasn't easy; in the fentanyl haze, all sense of space was dislodged. His stereoscopic perception went garbled, uniting the sky's arc with the pavement, and his limbs were mousse. And yet he made it to the sidewalk and took Stanislaus by his sleeve.

You have a ride? Peter asked.

Stanislaus licked his moustache, saying nothing. Peter palmed him a few bills, everything left in his wallet, then the baggie with the remainder of the heroin. This made a dent.

Got my Kawasaki.

The aged Ninja 900 was parked in the laneway behind Lulu's house, padlocked to a dumpster. As Stanislaus wheeled it out, the denim-clad man came charging over and placed a firm hand on Peter's shoulder.

I'm telling you, come with me. Don't be a chump.

Get off, Peter said, batting his hand away.

You know this is pointless. There's nowhere you can go.

Men like this had come after Peter before. For years they'd tracked him, following him into nightclub bathrooms and hailing him from across hotel lobbies, ringing from unlisted numbers before dawn to beseech his signature, his compliance. To their threats, uttered or implied, Peter had always been unmoved. He'd long known the peril of heeding his father's call.

Stanislaus turned the engine over and the Ninja's revs flooded the street, disrupting the block's sleepy simmer. Peter climbed on the back of the bike, taking a quick look back at the denimed man before they peeled away. As they swerved west on Broad Street, ignoring stoplights, Peter felt his spirits lifted—freed, if only temporarily, to sail amid the razed lots and Chevron stations, hoisted from this wretched night and its accusations. There would certainly be awfulness ahead, inevitable and miserable and soon, and already he dreaded the comedown. He was, for all his earthly days, cursed. But right now, he was still high and speeding into the wind.

THE BOY SITS BELTED INTO HIS SEAT in the business-class section, air-borne between Arlanda and Heathrow, his attentions fixed on the panels of a *Spawn* comic book. He is currently the only passenger in the entire section, his father having disappeared to parts elsewhere almost half an hour ago. The boy is attired completely in Reebok, a full track suit and high-top pumps. He chews Juicy Fruit. Though young, he displays the air of a seasoned traveller.

When his father returns to his seat across the aisle, the boy tucks away the comic book and replaces it with a paperback, Emerson's *Representative Men*. The father asks if lunch has been mentioned. The boy says no. The father pokes a button overhead, calling for a flight attendant. Of present concern, causing the father much agita-tion, is the recent deflation of Sweden's housing bubble and resulting bank insolvency, with the proposed bailout and nationalization of Nordbanken and Götabanken impending. This, along with tense ne-gotiations underway with an ambitious Vancouver divorce attorney, has mired him in a state of prolonged sourness.

A flight attendant arrives, pushing a beverage cart. The father requests three mini-bottles of Ketel One and something cold to eat. The boy chooses chocolate milk. The attendant asks the boy if he'd care to visit the pilot's cabin. The boy declines, saying he wouldn't want to cause a disruption.

It'll be fine, the attendant assures. We're at cruising altitude. The pilot's happy to have a guest.

The boy looks up in silence, straw held between lips.

That's not what he means, the father says from across the aisle. *You'd* be disrupting *him*.

With his return to Montreal, Peter closed himself off. He was sup-posed to be packing up the apartment and settling affairs, but had done nothing, even as the realtor had undertaken her itinerary of showings with an almost frighteningly impassioned intensity. The market was robust, she'd taken pains to assure him, and demand in the Lower Plateau was always high, so she expected no difficulty in finding a buyer. Peter had said that sounded fine to him, and there was no need for her to continue forwarding constant updates. She was to proceed as her judgment led her; he preferred to remain uninvolved in the minutiae.

There seemed little to do now except await the fulfillment of his perdition. He popped multivitamins and visited the depanneur down the block for ice cream and Merlot. Dizzy spells assailed him. Sleep came with difficulty. Days sieved into days. The mirror showed a face gone puffy and pink, shedding layers of skin like drywall dust. Nights, he walked aimlessly, scowling at anyone who met his eyes. He fell face first crossing the street near Beaudry station and stumbled home scuffed and bloody. Finding him in the entrance fiddling with his keys, the doorman handed him a handkerchief and advised *maybe take it easy huh*. To this, Peter could only nod and promise: I will.

Peter awoke on the couch to his phone ringing and the bulging veins of Sylvester Stallone filling the TV screen. The call was from Jo-Beth, saying she'd be over in an hour. He attempted to negotiate a way out of this, but she insisted, saying there were matters that needed attending. Hanging up, he jacked the television's volume, rubbing his eyes—it was now late afternoon, another day lost. Stallone had been a defining heroic image in Alain's life since childhood. He'd described in detail to Peter how seeing *Rocky IV* on its theatrical release—a formative trip to the cinema at the side of his first pre-pubescent crush, a scrappy Anglo boy who sadly never reciprocated the amorous vibrations—had been a momentous personal awakening. Alain theorized Stallone's oeuvre, taken as a whole, represented a grand unifying commentary on the evolution of the last forty-odd years of the masculine soul against odds of country, countryman, and birthright.

The apex of this, Alain contended, was *Over the Top*, the movie now playing. Peter was fairly certain he'd seen it with Alain at some point, but, as with all things of late, couldn't string together when or how. It was not, by any measure, a masterpiece. Yet the hokey melodrama about a long-haul trucker earning his son's love through competitive arm wrestling allowed Alain to imagine a world where victories were lasting and meaningful, and good-heartedness could triumph over the devaluation of individuality despite a pitiless socio-political system—all this, of course, rousing memories of Alain's own father's cruelty, that glacial inscrutability that nagged him even after the old man's passing. For Alain, clichés confirmed what he most wanted to be true.

The movie's finale was saccharine, pure fluff, with Stallone and his plucky actor-son cruising down a Nevada highway in a sparkling new semi into the boundless possibility of a new life together. Still, as the closing credits rolled, Peter found himself overcome with grief. To think of young Alain, captivated by this terrible movie, his eager mind so primed and ready for all that was to come—it was like looking back in time to a distinct point of catastrophe.

Should he remember this man, his man, as he'd aspired to be, or as he actually was? Alain's was a polished presentation: a journalism CV spanning decades and continents, a baritone still tingling with an adolescent lisp. Teeth like polished kaolinite, prematurely silver-tinged locks always cleanly barbered. But with his every knowing sniff or pointed witticism, the deranged drug fiend inside slavered to be freed. A variable user since his teenage years, he'd vaulted in and out of functionality with stints in treatment and programs, and like many addicts took tremendous pride in the accomplishment of just keeping it together.

His union with Peter made all things easier. Alain could exert or withdraw as needed, and the freedom of having bills covered would, he thought, inject his work with a nobler purpose. As they jounced from city to city, he passed long stretches immersed in writing and research, meeting deadlines and honing pitches, maintaining a hectic itinerary of travel and meetings, his focus sharp and his keel even. But the day would inevitably arrive when things went volcanic: the demolition of furniture, another butchery of his reputation, and, as happened, a return to heavy drug intake and the smothering of totalizing depression, until he undertook another stab at moderation and they moved on again. They'd thought New Orleans might prove something like an actual home, until it too became overwhelming—*too dark and too willing*, Alain lamented—and they resettled back in Canada. But even here, the cycle resumed.

On a wet Tuesday morning Peter had taxied with Alain to the Gare Centrale, holding back any outburst through their hasty good-byes at the platform. Afterward, Peter headed directly to a crowded bar on St. Laurent where he sat listening through headphones to Mayhem's *De Mysteriis Dom Sathanas*, downing three carafes of bracingly cold muscat, one after the other, fighting the urge to shriek. The weeks slid by, and then, like a springtime hatchling, Alain emerged from treatment clean-shaven and clear-eyed, chatty with avowals of new-found humility and gratitude. Alain would never not be who he was; even in sobriety he wore the chains of his torment. But in the congratulatory view of his checklisting clinicians, his transformation was a victory, and his achievement, his success, was without question. This record would remain untarnished at his death, a mere two months later. The lowering of the cremation urn was meant to symbolize a fidgety spirit now in eternal requiescence, a peace found in death. Again: success.

Despite the protracted havoc Alain had wreaked upon his own body, no one could have predicted the scene as Peter found it that night, returning to the apartment from some now-forgotten occasion, easing the bathroom door open while, in keeping with their household policy of bathroom privacy, calling Alain's name. No one could have expected it: subarachnoid hemorrhage due to a ruptured cerebral aneurysm, cause uncertain. No trauma to the head, no blood, no assailant. It was, as far as any official record held, an anomaly, pure bum luck. And so Alain's story could be interpreted only as a tragedy.

Now Peter was alone, a wastrel, without past or future. When he was younger, the mists' mysterious invitations had offered him a possible way forward. But that was years ago, and any deliverance offered was now long gone. There was nothing for him to do now but bide time. He aimed the remote at the television, pausing as the next entry in this afternoon movie marathon came up: Stallone again, alongside Kurt Russell in 1989's *Tango & Cash*, another relic of Alain's nostalgic enthusiasm. Peter watched until the opening credits came up, then changed the channel.

On a snowy Thursday afternoon at the cafeteria in the Museum Mensch und Natur, the boy and his father sit at a table looking out on the north bank of the Schloßgartenkanal. The boy fiddles with a can of Pepsi; the father drinks black coffee. The father places a battery-powered My First Sony cassette recorder on the table, armed with a blank cassette. He presses the play and record buttons together.

Tell me again, he says to his son, leaning close to the recorder's microphone, what you told me last night.

The boy understands what his father expects from him.

I was in my room, he says, doing my calculus and listening to Mahler. It was about seven o'clock.

And this was two weeks ago. In Dubai.

It was...I think so.

You have to be specific.

But, I, um.

Just continue. You were in your bedroom. Mahler. You were by yourself?

Lailani was downstairs doing laundry. I think maybe I fell asleep for a bit. Then I was thirsty, so I went to the bathroom for a glass of water and I drank it. Then I heard a sound out in the hallway.

What sort of sound?

The boy frowns.

Like *ooooooooo*. But I think it was saying my name at the same time.

Your full name?

No. Just my first name. *Peter. Peter.* I think so.

What did you do then?

I was looking for the sound. I thought I saw something in my closet, in the mirror, and...

I thought you were in the hallway.

Mm.

I told you, you must be specific.

The boy fiddles with the Pepsi can.

Regardless, his father says, you were in your bedroom?

Yes.

And the mirror...

I thought that's where the sound was. I looked in the mirror and I could see myself, but I was far away. And the mirror's edges were cloudy, but there were colours too. Green and red and yellow.

I see.

I saw the mirror was opening and I put my hand into it...

You put your hand in the mirror.

It wasn't really the mirror. It was in the mirror. And then I saw it was behind me.

It?

I turned around and went out to the balcony. I know I'm not supposed to go out there at night. I'm sorry.

That's...that's fine. But the clouds were outside? They were in the air?

Yes.

This is the balcony from your bedroom? Facing west, toward the water.

Yes.

And the clouds came in off the Gulf?

Maybe. It got really bright. I could still hear my name, but the sound was different. It was like a motor or something? And then I put my hands out over the balcony and into the light. It was really weird.

The boy pauses, working through this memory. His father checks to ensure the tape is running, then asks his son if he wants anything else to drink. The boy says no.

What happened then?

I saw this woman in the light. Or through the light. She was lying on a couch and she was talking. Her voice was really soft. I don't think she could see me.

This woman, who was she?

I don't know. She was looking away from me.

She was the one calling to you? I need you to be as clear as you can.

No. The voice was something else. It was like it was telling me to go through.

To where?

Again, the boy pauses.

I don't know. I didn't see.

Yes, you did. You saw. Don't lie, Peter.

The boy lowers his head.

I'm not lying.

Fine. Just tell me what you did next.

I didn't do anything. I went back inside and I think I fell asleep again. Lailani came to get me for dinner and things were back to normal.

Has this happened again?

A few times. But not exactly the same. Not in the mirror.

Where? What did you see?

Different places. More people and things. I'm kind of tired. Can we go home soon?

We came all the way here. You don't want to see the Schönheit-engalerie?

Not really.

The café begins to fill with afternoon visitors, a pack of students on a day tour. The father considers his son, staring at his hands. Then they both turn to the window, watching Nymphenburg Palace wiped away behind a drapery of fresh snow.

Jo-Beth arrived in a huff, her blouse striped with bands of sweat and a canvas sack slung over one shoulder.

Your doorman's a sex offender, she declared, air-kissing Peter at each cheek.

Edmundo? He can be a little overeager, but most people find him charming.

Charming like a flavivirus.

She looked him over, thorough but without eye contact.

You look bad.

Peter said nothing in return, but Jo-Beth didn't look so great herself: harried, jumpy, her usual swagger muted. She and Alain had enjoyed a fervent years-long alliance, friendly in competition while providing anchors of mutual support in pursuits both personal and professional. After he'd helped her find publication with a fashionable American literary press, she'd dedicated her first essay collection to *ma mignonne chauve-souris de la Rive-Sud*. Her position on Peter, meanwhile, had been of overt distrust from their first encounter.

This place is so spiffy and gratuitous, she said as she dumped the sack on the floor and headed past him to prowl the apartment. Sad to hear you're giving it up.

Showings start next week. Or so they tell me.

And where do you go from here?

A good question.

Hearth and home, not really your thing. More his department.

Jo-Beth ran fingers along a wall, almost flirtatious.

But we all know how the lights stayed on. Which, in a way, is something we have to talk about.

We do?

Your generosity has made many things possible. For me. However, it's time to turn off the taps.

For a while now, he wasn't exactly positive how long, Peter had been signing off periodic cheques to Jo-Beth, following Alain's call to help her through what he termed *a difficult patch*. Though *patch* implied temporariness, which hadn't been the case. No discussion had followed of whether this steady issuance was meant as a loan or a gift, and Peter wasn't even certain of how much he'd contributed to the cause. He hadn't cared then, and didn't now.

It made Alain happy to help.

Certainly. But the money never came from him. Did it?

Jo-Beth glissaded toward the kitchen. Peter followed, making weak gestures of hospitality. The fridge offered only grisly takeout containers and gnarls of bagged greens well past edible, so Peter called down to the front desk, sending Edmundo's nephew out for provisions. Again: his life, a succession of indulged whims.

You know who my father is, Peter said.

The mogul. From Beijing, is it?

He's German. My mother's Japanese. Do you know how he derived his wealth?

I want to say disk drives or something.

There's more to it.

I'm sure there is. There does seem to be a great deal of perplexity in your past.

As far as the money...my parents had a pretty hefty divorce settlement. An ungodly amount in trust until I was sixteen. In exchange for, you know, letting him off the hook for any participation in my upbringing. It was a lot of money. But my mother held out and negotiated for stock options instead.

Imagine that was a savvy move.

It was, as far as the outcome. Or income. My mother split and left me to do what I wanted.

That's nice for you.

All I mean is...as I say, helping you out made Alain happy.

Jo-Beth headed back to the living room, continuing her appraisal with the sofa, the carpets, the floors, the coffee table bearing only an expended container of chocolate milk.

Still, Jo-Beth said, the money yokes you with...is it guilt? Or something more?

Yes. Something more.

You could give it all away. Buy pencils for kids in Yemen.

Pencils. I'll look into that.

Or fund an armed militia. I always fantasized about operating my own private order of sōhei monks. Anyway.

Jo-Beth went back to her canvas bag and began unloading its contents onto the floor: envelopes, folders, several spiral-bound notebooks, a stack of books, mostly hardcovers.

From the book files, she said. He left some stuff at my office.

In the last few years, Alain's career had come to a juncture, demanding a change of direction. He'd staled on tossing off magazine profiles and travel features, and the dismal freelance markets were only getting worse. His plans turned to the book he'd longed to write, conceived during his many treks to remote locales, journeys into the Alborz mountains and the Sahelian forests, and the northernmost reaches of Qikiqtaaluk. A meditation, he'd imagined, on the impossibility of losing one's self, of actually being lost, among the man-made forces shaping this contemporary world: the irruption of communications technology, a globalized economy, the insidious surveillance state, the cacophony of it all. The book had been slow to take shape. Beyond copious reportage and travelogue, there was also an inherent autobiographical angle to it, a geographic restlessness reflecting the want for escape of a more inward variety, through drugs, self-insulation, obsession—all those damning and cheap pursuits.

Alain, always more energetic on the research side of things than the organizational, had compiled a sprawling bibliography culling thematic material from an eclectic range of sources, some of which Jo-Beth was now returning. A history of the ascetic Simeon Stylites. Ballantyne's translation of the Sánkhya Aphorisms of Kapila. A brief file on *hikikomori*, Japanese practices of self-exclusion and isolation. Self-published pamphlets by Finnish anarcho-primitivists. From this assortment he plucked a tome in a tattered slipcover, its title in chunky sans serif text: *Sulphurs of Popocatépetl*, by Ximena Nájera.

Late eighties, Jo-Beth said, or thenabouts.

Peter flipped through, not really reading. It was a collection of poetry, the pages musty.

Most of it's too schmaltzy for my tastes, Jo-Beth said, but there's some stuff in there to rev the engines. Vanishing as a sort of state of grace. Alain marked a few passages, maybe something for an epigraph. Oh, and there's this.

From the pile she produced a bulky envelope, postmarked from the NATIONAL SCIENCE FOUNDATION, DIRECTORATE FOR GEOSCIENCES, addressed to Alain. It had already been opened.

His info for Antarctica, she said.

Peter blanked.

He didn't tell you? Alain applied to tag along on an expedition to Antarctica, J-Beth said. This NSF writers program. They accepted him last winter, just before he went to rehab. He had arrangements on a ship out of...the letter says Puerto Madryn.

Argentina?

If you say so. Think he was supposed to leave around the end of the month. This month.

Flipping through the envelope's contents furthered Peter's confusion. Here were project proposals and approvals on government letterhead, scanned waivers bearing Alain's signature, printed jpegs of relief maps, correspondence with climatologists at McMurdo Station. The plans were thorough and by appearances firm.

Jo-Beth noticed Peter's frown.

Something wrong?

No, I just... He never mentioned it to me. I didn't know.

Jo-Beth's smirk betrayed how much she savoured this: holding information Peter did not.

It was hugely important to him, she said. This represented his future. With this book, he wanted to create something that would endure.

Peter was growing annoyed. I *know* that. I just didn't know about—
The buzzer buzzed, freeing him from continuing. Edmundo's nephew had arrived, laden with paper bags. Peter tipped him a twenty and headed to the kitchen, hurrying to work a corkscrew and locate clean glasses. From the other room, Jo-Beth related how she was off to California later that week, to visit some sort of spiritualist retreat in the northeastern Mojave Desert. Her regular explorations of esoteric healing tended to take a multifarious form, a flightiness

that, to Peter, smacked of affectation. This particular trip was being facilitated in aid of an old friend of hers now battling breast cancer in its advanced stages. Jo-Beth gushed about the poignancy of the desert scenery and the revitalizing properties of the *chamber*, whatever that was. Peter, mucking about in the kitchen, missed most of what she said. This apartment, with its coffered ceilings and satin nickel finishes, its extravagant rent and slight apportion of a city view, now recast for evacuation with Alain's extinguished hopes—it was all too much. Too much was laid before him, and nothing could be done with any of it.

Jo-Beth entered the kitchen. Did you hear me?

No.

I said what really matters now is how you mourn. And how you mourn will be defined by how you act upon the information provided to you. How you read the signs.

Lulu: *The phases of the moon, the poison of the sky.*

Peter handed Jo-Beth a glass of wine and forced a smile. I'll cancel the rest of your cheques, he said.

Christmas Eve: the Großer Arber foothills, in the Bohemian Forest. With nightfall, light but steady snowfall sweeps the lower ranges. The stone cottage, central among a half-dozen chalets, is alive with firelight, with socialization, and the congregation of men. They lounge in the cottage's den, chuckling into their cognacs and sampling chocolates, jibing in friendly rivalry. These are men of business, shufflers of capital interests and multinational entities, and they convene here under the premise of well-earned leisure.

One of the men is imparting a story about a battle of wills in which he's been engaged, warring against the lynxes overrunning his property near the quartz mountains in Viechtach.

Damned things are astonishingly stubborn, the man says. Chewing through telephone cables, which of course sabotages communications with the office back in Munich. And I used to think the only foes I had to worry about were the Chinese.

The other men laugh. From the top of the oak staircase adjacent to the room, the boy listens in, drawn by the den's atmosphere, thick with the fire and cigars and liquor, the looseness of men's banter.

My Agnethe is awfully superstitious about such things, the man continues. She says there's no lynx. She believes we have a *wolpertinger*.

You should listen to your wife.

The boy's attentions perk at this interrupting voice, his father's familiar stiff baritone. He edges down a step.

It sounds like your Agnethe comprehends the situation better than you do. You forget who actually rules the forest.

I do admit those wily beasts have me on the ropes.

Another round of chortles. But the boy's father, as always, is serious.

It's because you close your mind to the possibility of the unexplainable. The forest is biting back at you.

I'm sure everyone's heard about Dred's encounters with alternate dimensions, another man says.

The boy slides down another step.

Someone else: I don't believe I have.

Well, yes, Dred says. Years ago in Namibia something happened that altered my life's parabola. I will refrain from specifics. But suffice to say, a breach in the universe's fabric appeared to me. I heard a voice, offering passage to somewhere else. To another realm.

A realm where exactly?

I have yet to find out. At the time, I declined the invitation. There was still far too much work for me to do here. But I remain secure in knowing the opportunity will arise again.

A pause.

You all may scoff, Dred said, but you can't deny my retained earnings. Knowing I have been granted access to a world beyond, while others less worthy have not, has been a key motivator behind my success, perhaps even the prime reason. It guides my affairs with assurance stronger than any directorial board.

How so?

It motivates me to continue crushing my opponents.

Laughter among men. The clinking of glasses.

The boy bites his cheek. A tide of anger rises in him. His father's lie is more than a lie; it's an act of theft. Access to that misty light, and whatever it held, was offered to *him*—and for all he knew, to him alone. He'd confided in his father, hoping for some manner of understanding. But now he knows: the avarice of men will hijack and defile even the purest of mysteries.

AS IF WAKING FROM ANAESTHETIZATION, Peter discovered himself in his regular depanneur, hovering by the Nestlé freezer and watching a pair of wild-haired women argue in French with the proprietor about unredeemed Loto-Québec scratch cards. How long he'd been watching this transpire was hard to say. He wavered, almost knocking over a rack of pretzels. When the Tamil shopkeeper yapped at him for loitering, Peter smiled back and made for the door empty-handed, whatever he'd come here for forgotten.

It was afternoon, following another wet morning. The asphalt of the store's entrance was pasted with clots of trash from an overturned waste bin, next to which a man in a dingy sweatshirt now sat.

Hey. Breezy boy.

Peter knew him, and made an evasive move. But Janko blocked his path, jangling a palmful of change. He looked bad, lapping his lips through a snot-caked beard and stinking of much time outside. His shirt, with its Corrosion of Conformity logo long faded, was speckled with dried blood. His recognition of Peter seemed defective, though he'd last cornered him like this only days before, and several times before that.

Sorry, Janko, Peter said. No change.

Look, man. I'm a bum. I'll tell you. I'll say it. I'm a bum.

Janko.

I wasn't always a bum. I got accepted to Harvard for mechanical engineering. I did seven months on the USS *John C. Stennis*. I was in Fallujah for the counter-insurgency. Operation Phantom Fury. But you don't believe me. You think I'm just a bum.

I believe you.

I flew in an F-14 Tomcat over the Saudi Arabian desert. I drove a Ferrari Testarossa over the Golden Gate Bridge. It's a life full of miracles. And now I'm here. What's that all about?

I don't know.

I spent my entire life thinking about things, Janko said. Now I'm just trying to get my beer on. Can't you have some sympathy?

Peter could, and did. He put his hand on Janko's shoulder.

Come with me.

He took Janko to a microbrew pub down the street. The place was just opening for evening service, and the servers regarded them warily—both Peter and Janko were in decidedly rough shape, albeit in different ways. As they occupied stools at the bar, Peter slid forth his AmEx and ordered two tankards of Dunkelweizen, with the request *garder plus et encore*. A muted TV played CBC News. As soon as their beers arrived, Janko sloshed back half his glass.

You got to understand the ocean as another form of infinity, he said, then you apply principles of combat systems management. What's a Trident II missile anyway? It's a Z-axis. Maybe one coordinate of the X-axis is us, here. Maybe it's Zhangjiakou.

Or somewhere off the map, Peter said.

And the real purpose of psychotropics is to quantify the blood-brain barrier. But the barrier is an axis. You have to understand the optic tectum. The superior colliculus. That's where the deception happens.

A foursome of young men entered the bar, a bookish breed in peacoats and satchels, wiping their glasses. As they took a corner table, one of them briefly locked eyes with Peter. A flash of recognition maybe.

I did tactical consultations at NAVCOMMSTA Diego Garcia from ninety-four to ninety-seven, Janko said. I hijacked NSA algorithms and redrew the map of the Indian Ocean. You don't see those maps on Google. Zero guesses why. Can I get another one of these?

Peter ordered Janko another jug. The men in the corner were definitely staring at him. Their leers indicated not just identification, but something else. Accusations. They had him marked.

You live near here? Janko said, searching his parka. Think I could come over and print out some things? There's these Régie forms that gotta get filed.

Peter watched as the first guy he'd noticed crossed the room and approached the bar.

Peter Hausen.

Do we know one another?

A strained tick passed, then the guy introduced himself as Lyle Bekiempis. He shook Peter's hand as if pumping him for water, inviting him to join their table. Peter looked to Janko, who was now trapping a server in conversation, grumbling something about the impact of highway salt on filtration systems in Côte-des-Neiges. Peter accepted the offer. As soon as he sat among these men, he felt their fascination, their nervous energy crackling.

I'm not going to lie, Lyle said. We know a lot about you.

Another of the men leaned across the table.

You have to tell us about that Deutsch-Hausen compound in Khartoum. Is it true there's a PLA flag painted on the roof?

Or that Aiken DOE plutonium immobilization facility, another said. Are they really accepting contracts from Atomenergoprom?

Is it true your great-grandfather was Bernhard Stempfle?

The men went to their phones, looking things up. Lyle seemed to be actively checking his own nerves, choosing his words with care.

Apologies for the onslaught, he said, it's just such a wild coincidence to find you here, right now. I mean, I knew you lived in Montreal...

On and off.

...but just this morning I was telling these guys about a piece I have in the works. A thing in which your...in which DHG interests are mentioned.

You're a journalist.

Right, Lyle said, I'm getting ahead of myself. Yes. Mostly freelance investigative stuff. Some work for the *Gazette*, more often at large these days. Some of the bigger daily outlets. NPR. Just trying to assure you, I'm not some freak.

Peter believed him. This wasn't the first time he'd been contacted by intrepid aspirants wanting to dig through his father's convoluted tessellation of interests. Rarely did much come of it.

DHG's been low-profile the last couple of years, Lyle said. Then they sell off a majority share of the domestic tech division in January. Around the same time, we start seeing their subsidiaries cropping up again in Aleppo and Tehran. I've talked to sources who toss around wild theories. Here, look.

Lyle pulled out his phone and swiped through screens, landing on a photo he then showed to Peter. Here was an Arabic man wrapped in a wool patu, peering into the sight of a tripod-mounted gun, what looked like a missile launcher. At his side, another man, older and white, observed. A pair of black BMWs sat parked behind them, hoods gleaming; farther in the background rolled mountains of stone and larches. Though the white man's face was buried in a bulky scarf, it was unmistakably Dred, and by his face's creases and the paucity of his grey hair, the photo was recent.

What really fascinates me is your father's reputation, Lyle said, putting away the phone. What I gather is he considers himself on this, like, mystical calling? That to me is the real story, setting aside all the conspiracy whatzit.

Peter couldn't see how, or what, he was expected to add to any of this.

Think you'd be interested in sitting down for an interview? Lyle asked. Maybe you have an office or something we can contact?

Oh. Well.

Lyle handed Peter a card with his contact details.

As I say, I'm really just getting cooking. But I can't help but think running into you here right now represents a serendipitous opportunity.

Peter finished his beer and told Lyle to put the table's next round on his tab. By now evening was falling, bringing the first wave of post-office crowds starting on their cinq à sept. The pranging noise of voices swelled; the bar filled with the aroma of mussels. He had to leave. He settled his bill, picking up another jug for Janko, then slid out through the arriving influx.

As he oozed back onto the street, Lyle's suggestion stayed with him: *a serendipitous opportunity*. But such opportunities, he'd come to learn, always served some mandate—behind the apparent randomness of things toils a fierce and tireless mechanism.

Returning to the apartment was an unendurable prospect, so he wandered east toward Parc LaFontaine. During their first weeks at the apartment they'd indulged in long strolls through the neighbourhood, Alain glad to find relative calm back in his home territory, Peter snorting at the goofy young hippies in their pyjama pants, the spandexed speedwalkers, that tacky de Gaulle statue. Those were nights when some kind of future together still lay ahead, and they knew it, indulging in the purposeful formation of shared memories. Now memories were all there remained of Alain.

The book Jo-Beth had returned, the collection by the Mexican poet, didn't strike Peter as anything remarkable. He'd flipped through the slim volume to find several pages that someone, Alain, had dog-eared, finding a stanza's opening lines underlined in red pen: *The icy windshield of your Plymouth Caravelle/a suitable gateway into the eternal.* As Jo-Beth said, fairly schmaltzy stuff. Nonetheless, reading those lines, led by Alain's insistent hand, he plunged into melancholy.

A suitable gateway into the eternal. The best of their days had hinted at such a promise. But even though this desire had proven in vain, Alain had evidently felt something like this too: the confirmation was here with his doubled pen stroke, trenched deep into the page.

With the weather rotten, the park was mostly empty, only a few umbrella-clutching dogwalkers and teenagers huddled under trees. Peter shuffled along his selected path, attended by the central pond's gush, arriving where Calixa Lavallée bisected the park. He hesitated, weary in his directionlessness. Damning words came to mind: there's nowhere you can go.

He turned south toward Sherbrooke, projecting a circular route back home, when he noticed two men ahead. Coming from a parking lot adjacent to the grey-brick cultural centre, they walked stiffly, side by side, toward him. Both wore baby-blue mock turtlenecks and tight trousers, heads of close-cropped white fuzz. Peter kept on down the sidewalk, and the men adjusted their course to follow. The slap of their plastic flip-flops synchronized with his own pace.

Excuse me.

This voice was strangely high-pitched, the consonants sharply fricative. Peter turned. The men came forward, frowning in the lamplight.

Let us see your phone.

The demand and its delivery were so assertive that Peter reached for his phone out of sheer instinct. But once he had it in hand, he balked.

Is there an emergency?

One of the men, about half a head taller than the other, pointed at the phone.

How's your signal?

My signal?

The shorter man drew nearer, imposing pressure.

We can work together, or we can work against one another, he said in that same shrill voice. Let's try and think in those terms here. Harmony and discord.

Peter eased back a step. The men came closer.

We're not out to yank your chain.

Harmony and discord.

The phone vibrated with an incoming call. The men came still closer. Peter detected a heavy scent of English Leather and cigars. The taller man squinted.

Don't answer that.

Peter did.

The child looks across the divide, bereft for the expiation he has yet to plot.

In contrast to his accosters' squeaks, this voice rang deep, disarmingly clear. Peter found himself unable to respond.

The petulant child effaces the living man. The credit of mercy is weighed in the perspiration of the condemned, the fervour of the misled. The child is you.

Give that here, the shorter man said, reaching.

Peter found himself breaking away, running back the way he'd come, off the path and over the grass. An acoustic guitar's strumming and teenagers' singing led him back to the central encircling path. Looking back as he caught his breath, he saw no sign that the men had pursued him.

The pond ahead glinted with refracted lamplight, the central fountain glowing from within. For a moment he forgot where he was and what was happening. What had led him here. Where had his mind wandered. Something was occurring, or was about to occur, but this feeling of loss was total. All he could certify was the fountain, the pulsing water recast as combustion. It was foolish, he knew, to mistake the delirium of fatigue for anything like divinatory sight, to confuse municipal works with some universal plasma. A fountain's light was no beckoning, a city wasn't a cosmos, and no epiphany was forthcoming. Still, there was *something*.

The mists, the mists.

A blip of motion caught his eye: a helicopter, hurtling over the city, aimed south.

A sound rose behind him, just over his shoulder. Like the parting of jaws, the crepitus of bones, an emetic heave. He stood fast, resisting its claim for as long as he could withstand. Then he turned.

A surge of light came, filtered through an opaque whirl of dust. Forms took shape: trucks and rickshaws, tires spinning in gravel. A pair of motorcycles had collided with a Bisleri transport truck; the riders of the felled bikes, both with faces concealed by kerchiefs, stood arguing with the truck's driver, trading incomprehensible scolds. A queue of traffic bullied forward at all sides, pushing to maintain flow against this stoppage.

Peter turned away from this and back to the counter. He tapped his empty beer can on the Formica and the proprietor fished out another Haywards 5000 from the cooler. Peter drank quickly, before the can warmed in the evening's sauna-like heat. Strong and sweet with glycerin, the high-content beer thrummed his heat-cooked head.

The English Wine and Beer Shop sat among a row of similar stalls along MG Road, overlooking an immense block of lots that, like so much of Gurgaon, sat in a transitional state of what could be construction or demolition, or both simultaneously. Fencing along the roadside stretched into the visible distance, enclosing a meshwork of electrical towers, sharded concrete, exposed arteries of plumbing. Posters plastered along the fence's panels declared DLF INFRASTRUCTURE UPGRADATION WORK IN PROGRESS.

The cyclists righted their bikes, and though no apparent conclusion to the argument had been met, sped off in tandem. Peter looked to the two men next to him at the stall, both drinking beers and smoking cigarettes.

Dangerous, he said.

The men met this with silence. Once again, his attempts at endearing himself to those he encountered here in India, on the streets or in the shops, the hired drivers and shopkeepers and rickshaw operators, went nowhere.

Leaving his beer unfinished, he handed the proprietor a five-hundred-rupee note and flagged down a bicycle rickshaw. His direction to the operator to head back to the complex in DLF Phase II was received with a noncommittal nod. Peter climbed aboard and the rickshaw rolled south, the young man pedalling through the crush of cars and transport trucks, tight enough that the rickshaw's bumper grazed the side of a Mahindra three-wheeler. In his weeks here, Peter had tried to adapt to these nerve-racking situations, hoping that he, an outsider, might decipher the system by infiltration. But his efforts had mostly been in vain. Such was the devious nature of systems: that in the attempt to understand, one could get lost inside them.

The rickshaw navigated the roundabout, riding its perimeter until the curve spat them out onto Faridabad Road. Here were more announcements for development projects on the rise, more merchant outposts heaped with refuse, more itinerant contingents on mopeds and on foot. Monsoon rains of the previous month had eroded the ditches and embankments, with makeshift barriers of spray-painted planks set in place against hazards of shifting earth. The rickshaw clambered along, cutting past a lot where he'd watched students' afternoon cricket matches; wild dogs now gathered there on the pitch, picking over a spill of trash.

The gates at the apartment complex were still open. The security guard on duty, drowning in his ill-fitting uniform, observed their arrival without reaction. Peter climbed out of the rickshaw and handed his rider a hundred rupees. This too was accepted with only a nod.

At the building's entrance he was met by a sign indicating the elevator was again out of order. Drained by the heat and a beery afternoon, Peter whined inwardly as he began up the concrete stairwell. Gurgaon's rapid growth was still grievously underserved by its electrical grid, and power outages were frequent, even in this building, considered a luxury dwelling by the municipality's standards. These summer months were punishing, the city a furnace, the heat inescapable. It wore one down. By the time Peter reached the sixth floor his legs were trembling. And just as he entered the hallway, a subsonic *voosh* emanated from the building's core: the power had returned.

The wave of cool air hitting him upon entering the apartment affirmed that the AC was again functional. Listed as a two-bedroom suite, the place was spacious as a hangar, echoing with vitrified tile floors and cement ceilings, glazed windows looking onto the concrete quadrangle below. The rent was laughable by standards of Manhattan or even Montreal, though the attendant frustrations of utilities and minor pests were many.

A half-bottle of Blue Riband Gin sat open on the kitchen counter, next to a chopped cucumber and a tabbed can of soda water. A thump came from outside, then a vibrating plunk he recognized as the balcony's steel railing. Peter toed off his shoes, listening, then headed outside.

Alain was sweeping the balcony's concrete with a wiry broom and dustpan, his back to the door. A tumbler of gin and an ashtray were set atop the railing. Looking closer, Peter saw the blackish sediment collected in the dustpan was actually dozens of dead geckos, their bug-eyed corpses dried to chaff. Alain turned and found him watching.

It's like the goddamn geckocalypse here, he said.

Peter told him he was going to run a bath. Alain only gestured absently, brushing up more desiccated bodies.

The tap trickled lukewarm water into the bathtub as Peter squeezed out the last dribbles of lavender aromatherapy wash. Watching the lucent goo eddy into suds, he felt very tired, befuddedly tired. He peeled off his clothes, reeking with the day's accumulation of sweat and dust, and checked the mirror. His face looked ravaged, wrenched, as if in alarm—he looked like he'd been electrocuted.

Alain knocked at the bathroom door. Peter told him to hang on, just a minute. A minute, this was what he needed. Just to think, to cool down, to try and get himself straight. Harmony and discord. Just a minute, here, to try to understand things for what they were.

WHAT DOES INDIA OF THE FUTURE LOOK LIKE TO YOU? The woman on the screen beamed invitingly, gesturing to the camera with a questioning tilt. From her cupped palms a crystal of animated light fizzed to life, digital filters blowing out her brown skin to a taupe-ish hue; she held the light, regarding it with something like affection, then with a graceful parting of hands freed it to fill the screen with its radiance. The spell cast introduced a swerving journey through animated mock-ups of developments along GK-II, E-Block in New Delhi, shimmering structures of molten curves inhabited by eyeless, genderless, deracialized humanoid blobs. The offer was presented: to join them, to live among them, to accept their embrace.

What did the future look like? Peter had no idea. Delhi of the present was baffling enough: a city in transition, an economy of spikes and plummets, crises of air quality and congestion, frequent protests in the streets, and, most of all, the sheer volume of it all—this is what had enticed Alain to India. Changes were afoot, he reasoned, essential clashes. While America frothed and rotted, out of India came energy, turmoil. Alain had volleyed hasty pitches to his editorial contacts, and in days had lined up enough work leads to justify booking two AC1 IndRail passes and transferring three months' advance rent for the apartment in Gurgaon.

For Peter, the trip kindled images of his mother. Five years after leaving the UAE for good, Koharu had adjured him to Goa, where they joined her then-beau Jasminder at his beachside villa in Candolim. A month of strangeness followed: scores of oiled, intoxicated strangers attended by tray-laden servants; a cow festooned in saris unloading a heap of dung; the persistent dread of a hurricane that never arrived. At fourteen years old, he knew his mother more as a force than as a person. Reincarnated through her divorce settlement, she let her hair fly loose and tossed a Frisbee with boisterous Irish partyers, snapping at Peter for his shyness. Repelled, he sank as far as he possibly could into reading Thucydides, into his Bolt Thrower and Sepultura and Anthrax CDs. Koharu was then, and would remain, a frustrating mystery.

But nothing of Goa resembled Delhi's intensity. July's heat pummelled from the moment they touched tarmac at Indira Gandhi; the toilsome jet lag refused to loosen its grip, and even with the mandated immunization shots, they both suffered incapacitating digestive aggravations. Alain, to his remorse, shat his pants the second week there. But he persevered—there was work to be done, and so he had to adapt.

The restaurant booth Peter occupied overlooked the outdoor galleria in DLF Phase IV. Even amid the city's harrying forces, respite like this wasn't too difficult to find. Ceiling fans spun and a phalanx of waiters stood ready to refresh his gin and tonic, as he idled through Ingmar Bergman's autobiography, *The Magic Lantern*. Such relief was its own form of gluttony—the self-distinction of affluence, a mode of indolence known to very few. This was his own way of adapting.

The TV's real estate pleas flowed to a news bulletin, the parliamentary coverage, and cricket scores. Peter turned to the window, watching the stream of auto-rickshaws packing the plaza entrance below. Now Alain emerged from one, a Slazenger tennis visor shading his face, assisting a small Indian woman in a flowing sari as she stepped out. Peter didn't recognize the woman, but even from this distance it was clear Alain took great care in leading her into the building. Minutes later, Alain came bounding over to the booth. Clearly energized, he dragged a chair over for the woman, who maintained a demure distance. Waiters surrounded the table, meeting Peter's call for more gin and Alain's request of beer. The woman ordered tea. Once settled in, Alain introduced her as Aradhya Goel.

We met through Yashwant at the *Times*, Alain explained without being asked. I was looking into some of these latest court rulings, the street protests...

Right, Peter said.

...and Yash said there was no way I could write with any authority about what's going on with women in India without meeting Aradhya. We met for a walk at the Lodi Garden and ended up talking all morning. I'm spent. Need that beer.

This was a thing Alain invoked often and with gusto: the need to speak, to write, with authority. For him, there was no higher achievement than to confidently *know*, and to opine backed with actual clout. In his work he'd espoused the value of street-level realities, even as he lived in a rotation of executive class cabins and day-long brunches and plush sake lounges. An idea would apprehend him like a fever—at least until it inevitably vaporized, taking with it elusive ideals of authority and its virtues. He would hate himself for this, until the cycle began again.

Aradhya still had yet to speak beyond a murmured hello. Peter asked her if she was also a journalist.

No, no, she said. I work as a data analyst with CitiBank.

She'd only recently graduated from DTU, Aradhya explained. She lived with her grandmother in Dwarka but was familiar with this district, as she'd had to commute to Gurgaon for her co-op placement. Living in Delhi, she said, meant being accustomed to long transit rides. One learned to be patient.

That's why Peter and I fit right in, Alain said. Our undying patience.

This was a joke, but it went unacknowledged. Their drinks arrived. Aradhya touched her cup to her lips without swallowing. Her reserved air suggested not timidity, but self-control.

Aradhya's embroiled... Do I say *embroiled*? She's involved, let's say, in a case that's headed to the high court. It's this huge, stratified...

Alain turned to Aradhya, giving her a sort of cue. She put down her cup.

I was assaulted by a group of men, she said. They followed me from my office and attacked me in the metro station. They raped me, one by one. I was able to identify several of them by name, but the authorities have not been sympathetic.

To put it lightly, Alain said.

Pushing back against the system makes you an object of scorn, Aradhya said.

I can only imagine, Peter said.

There's a whole mess of issues in it, Alain said. The inefficacy of the courts. The misogynistic culture. These businessmen, their cronyism. The corruption runs deep. The entitlement.

And you're writing about this? Peter asked Alain.

Timeline pending. The case is slow to get to trial.

Peter only nodded. But Alain read him clearly.

This is really going to be significant. And you don't see any international correspondents at the High Court.

No doubt. I've just never known you to take on this kind of story.

Well, now I am.

The TV showed an air quality report, the familiar footage of traffic bedlam and the soup of smog over the roadways.

Sure you don't want something stiffer? Peter said to Aradhya. Cold gin in this heat hits the spot.

Aradhya shook her head with a detectable grimace. Her hands went to her midsection. A subtle move, but with it, Peter finally clued in: she was pregnant.

Well then, he said, waving for the bartender's attention. I'm having another.

Alain often bemoaned his memory's fading, how the further he was from his own past, the more he relied on some imagined retroactive childhood idyll rather than the horrible way things had actually been. This he saw as the essential human tragedy, affecting everything he knew and did. Peter couldn't relate—his own earliest days defied any such pining, marked not by despair but by confusion. So when Alain grew weepy for the past, Peter did his best to provide consolation, but this was a melancholy he never really understood.

In some ways, Alain was like Koharu: always yearning, always disappointed. Many nights in his teenage years Peter had sat with his mother in her flat near Sloane Square, holding her hands at the kitchen table. Her bitterness was largely justified: her engagement to Jasminder was eventually thwarted by his infidelity and compulsive gambling, while her sadistically manipulative parents made her terrified of returning home to Fukuoka. The divorce settlement, while ostensibly in her favour, had only temporarily quelled her rage. Money had given her a comfortable life in a hideously expensive area of London, a life of opulence without constraints, and yet her existence would always be saddled to a diabolical man she loathed more than anything. When she became wound up, consumed by anger inexpressible and without outlet, there was only so much solace Peter could provide. So he sat with her as she wept, repeating her name like a cradle song—just the two of them, in a beautiful apartment full of beautiful things.

That evening they sat on the apartment's balcony, both stripped to undershirts, drinking as always. Alain scrolled on his laptop while Peter read Bergman: *I talked to Märta about the Nature of Love, explaining that I didn't believe in eternal love, human love was egoism, and Strindberg had said that in* The Pelican. Every few minutes Alain read something aloud off his screen.

Have you heard this term, the *creamy layer*?

I thought you were writing about judicial corruption.

This is part of that.

But all this, caste commissions and civil liberties cases...these disparities go back centuries. Aren't you a little out of your depth?

How so?

We're tourists here.

Only according to our visas. *I'm* working.

But a guy from the West, jumping in to rescue the defenceless Indian woman? I'm not saying that's what's happening. But that's how it'll seem.

Seem to who?

I don't know. Whoever you're writing for. Whoever you hope to...get to.

A pause. Alain stared at his screen.

I just mean, Peter said, at some level, you're only transposing your own issues.

Really. Why don't you explain these issues to me?

Peter wanted to say: Your self-loathing, your unchecked impulses, your guilt. But instead he said, There's just a lot you and I don't know anything about. That's all I'm saying.

And that's why I'm talking to people. I'm just trying to shed light against darkness.

Peter flipped a page in his book. Okay, then. Sorry to be snide.

But Alain wouldn't let it go. I'm serious. I want to serve the cause of justice. That's my goal. Maybe I do it in a kind of sloppy way. Maybe I fuck it up and fail completely. But at least I make the attempt.

Peter got up and headed inside. They'd again left the screens open, and the living room lamps were mobbed with houseflies. The bugs, the water, the traffic—an endless, teeming squirm. Alain envisioned some cosmic justice that might transcend ethnocentric divides, here and wherever. But justice depended on people, and people were undependable. People were unjust.

He called to Alain, saying he was going to the shop for more gin. Alain only grunted in return.

Another sweltry evening met Peter, the air ruthless in its absence of flow. Approaching Faridabad Road, he was met with the now-familiar sight of wild boars pillaging a garbage bin on the roadside, the horde tearing through Lay's bags and Thums Up cans and wads of decomposing food, their greasy hides glistening with raw, bloody scratches. He kept his distance and hurried across the road through a break in traffic.

The liquor shop in the plaza across the street kept inconsistent hours. To his relief, its keeper was there, parked on a stool behind the counter. A group of men in suits stood at the counter, drinking cans of Kingfisher and dabbing their faces with handkerchiefs. Peter ordered a bottle of Blue Riband plus a can of his own.

Hot night, he said to the shopkeeper.

The man folded his arms over his wide belly, a T-shirt reading DKNY JEANS EST. 1989, tinted-lens glasses almost sliding off his nose. He set the gin and beer in a bag on the counter, along with a spill of change. Peter pocketed the change, then opened the beer and drank.

You drink like your father, the shopkeeper said.

Peter was uncertain whether he'd heard what he'd heard. The man offered nothing else, turning to serve fresh beers to the suited men. Peter downed half his can, then tucked the gin under his arm and left.

The boars had continued farther down the roadside to raid another row of garbage cans. From that direction came a trio of silver-haired women in silk saris, led by panting Spitzes tugging at their leashes. It was unsettling to see domesticated, shampooed pets among the apartments, where wild hounds still roved and scavenged among boars and monkeys. Arriving at the complex's eastern entrance at the same time as Peter, the women offered no greetings, and he did the same. In Delhi he was always on alert, ever aware that he might be committing breaches of decorum, especially around unaccompanied women. Deep-seated assumptions were at work here, and how he was regarded—Asian, discernibly gay—was impossible to know. He held back, making room for the women to proceed, but they paused at the elevator, blocking his way. They traded hurried words among themselves, then made for the stairwell, almost colliding with him. He mumbled an apology and pinned himself against the wall to let them pass. The dogs' huffs and the clop of the women's soles echoed up the stairwell, gradually tapering out.

The elevator arrived. The car was tiny, its button panel warning MAX CAPACITY 4. A ceiling-mounted vent groaned yet provided no ventilation. As the doors jerked shut and the car began its ascent, Peter picked his sweat-saturated shirt from his chest and wiped his forehead with his sleeve.

You drink like your father. The implications of this were beyond him.

A sharp mechanical noise resounded from somewhere above, and the car abruptly halted. The lights went out. The vents went silent.

Peter remained still, staked like a flagpole, anticipating a prompt restart and renewed traction. Such outages rarely lasted beyond a few minutes, though there had been instances of entire days in blackout earlier this month. Peter examined the cramped space.

The only source of light came from above via the sliver of the misaligned doors' seal, confirming the car had stalled between floors. He punched buttons on the panel, hoping for some emergency signal or switch. Nothing happened.

The air's deadness pressed on him. He tried to remain calm, conscious of letting seconds tick by.

But helplessness won, and he found himself pounding the flimsy metal interior with his fists. He cried out—*Hello, hello*—surprising himself with the enflamed timbre of these calls. They went unmet, and he backed down.

In the silence, a different kind of pressure began to assert itself. A suggestive hum rose, like vacuum tubes warming up, powering some unseen operation. The elevator's inner walls began to liquesce, giving way to new planes of shadow. A familiar destabilizing feeling crept in. To his right, he felt a wash of frigid air—not the concerted drive of air conditioning, but an actual thermal shift. The floor beneath him listed to one side as the dimensions of the elevator shaft peeled away. The hum widened into a disembodied groan, creaking and hacking—something he'd heard before. An opening was there. Miles of ocean expanded at all bearings, black waves peppered with studs of white, a jagged horizon just visible. Below him, the freighter deck heeled at an impossible list. Voices shouted, men giving commands, but these were drowned out by the wind. Their course pushed southward, bound for the end of the world. He swallowed hard, bracing for what was coming.

In mid-August they flew north to Srinagar. Alain had another story he hoped to follow, something regarding the complex network of poppyhusk smuggling across the Line of Control at Kaman, but the contact in the municipal government he'd intended to bribe for an interview waffled, then quit returning calls. With tickets purchased, they went anyway, lining up a houseboat rental on Dal Lake. The only other passengers on the tiny ATR plane were a platoon of soldiers in transport to Kashmir. The jovial comportment of these young men, all in ill-fitting fatigues and armed, betrayed nothing resembling fear. Peter's attentions were caught by one skinny soldier with a hand grenade dangling from his belt; his acne-cratered face remained fixed in undeviating focus as he played Sudoku on his phone for the flight's duration.

At the airport in Jammu, drivers mobbed the arrivals gate for fares, pressed back by security guards flagrantly brandishing rifles. The houseboat operator, a hefty man named Pavak, in an Adidas track suit, found Alain and Peter, pushing his way through to shepherd them to his waiting van. Pavak didn't question their arrangement as two seemingly unmarried men travelling together; tourism in Srinagar had suffered in recent times, with travel advisories still posting warnings of *sporadic terrorist activity and violent demonstrations*, so any visitors were met with an exuberant welcome. Pavak sped through the old city's close streets, laying on the horn, nearly mowing down a team of men directing a cartload of flowers. Preempting Peter and Alain's questions, he swore there was no military action in Srinagar, no present threats to security, no reason for their vacation to be anything but tranquil. Ignore the news, Pavak said. The curfews and separatist protests, the increased militarization—everything was fine.

Dal Lake itself was otherworldly: the water a glossy tray of pale blue, the dappled rows of houseboats, the snowy peaks of the surrounding Zabarwans. As they puttered across in the motorized dinghy manned by one of Pavak's two minions, Alain placed his hand on Peter's shoulder.

There's a branch of Islam, the Ahmadis, who say Srinagar's where the grave of Jesus lies, he said to Peter over the boat's engine. You can see the appeal, as far as resting places go. Sunny, breezy.

Like Florida, Peter said.

That night in the houseboat they had sex without hurry, without discussion. Afterward, they spread out on the sheets in the dark, letting their bodies be cooled by a window's draft. The boat's cedar frame creaked. A large ash-coloured spider patrolled the rafters above. Alain was talking about his recurring feeling of non-existence, the helpless feeling of each minute slipping from any grasp, a possibility that was both terrifying and seductive.

I've burned through so much of my past, I can't bear to even consider the future. The unknown no one knows.

I know, Peter said. The future's clear to me.

So tell me.

We stay in India until fall. For the entirety of September it rains non-stop and we basically lose our minds. You file an article on the Indian judiciary in three parts, and even though it takes some tough turns with editors, it runs in the new year. We spend a few weeks letting loose in New York, staying at this obscenely expensive hotel in the East Village. We go for dinner in Harlem with that guy Frederick, the guy with the documentary film company. Afterward we go back to his apartment and he suggests we smoke some heroin. We both accept this as no big deal, and we have a wonderful goofy night, and from then you're back on it. It's like you never even stopped. Back in Montreal you dive into work, including a story about a sexual assault case up in Manawan that's just merciless. It attracts some heat, which at first you take with pride, but then it starts to stress you out. The winter is hard. We get depressed and antsy. Things are tense. We push each other away like we never have before. You discernibly change. I see it in your face, in your posture. It's in me too. Everything's slower and harder. I'm mostly able to lay off the drugs, but you're in it deeper and deeper, in a more fatalistic way than before, and it's harder than ever to see a way out. For the first time, we wonder about the viability of our future together. One day in January you tell me you've made arrangements to go away and clean up. Not that place in Montana, a place closer by, in Montérégie. You leave the next day. Except for a couple of stunted phone conversations, we don't speak for two months. When you come back, it's like you're fifteen years younger, but I'm the same old me. You've had what you call an *anagogic reckoning*. You say, in earnest, how you feel *blessed*. Blessed in this life. You mean this in complete sincerity. It's a hokey sentiment. But it actually sounds kind of nice, coming from you.

Hm. And you know this...

Because my future self tells me so.

And then what?

Peter wished he could project further, but his access only went so far. The intuition could only be borrowed.

Then we live hornily ever after, he said.

Upon their return from Kashmir to the apartment in Gurgaon, their mood downshifted into a sedated torpor. Their unity began to show seams. They were both sleeping poorly, knowingly backing into themselves, though neither would admit this aloud. Alain continued his work with a pointed dedication, clocking hours crossing the city for interviews, pacing through video-conferenced arguments with his stateside editors. The city held them in its oppressive tactility, with rainy season coming, smog subduing all sun. The apartment's atmosphere shrank and grew pyretic. Alain repeatedly mentioned returning to Kashmir to take up the investigation he'd never had a chance to begin, describing an ambitious trek into disputed territory via the Karakoram Pass. But these plans went nowhere.

Many nights in those onerous weeks Peter sat on the balcony, staring out at the bleak cement courtyard below, his stomach wracked and his eyes scratchy, plagued with what felt like the foreknowledge of impending disaster. He'd lost the trace on his future self—things weren't meant to be this way. Everything was misaligned. Nothing was secure.

Bergman wrote: *It is hard to say whether great myths are unremittingly magical because they are myths or whether the magic is an illusion, created by us consumers; but at that particular instant there was no doubt.* Here he was describing Greta Garbo, already at career's end at thirty-six and, for Bergman, wasted and sorrowful, her former beauty a shrill discord, her mouth a *pale slit surrounded by traverse wrinkles*. Alain saw a similar figure in Sylvester Stallone: a quintessential figure of masculine pathos, of faded splendour. So when the latest entry in one of Stallone's action franchises opened at the PVR Cinemas at the Sahara Mall on MG Road, Alain deemed it imperative they attend.

The exultation Alain expected, however, was not be found. He fidgeted throughout the movie's duration, rubbing his face and sighing at the hackneyed contrivances, and was out of his seat and making for the exit before the credits ran. They moved with the crowd from the cinema back out into the muggy night. The road was wild with floodlights and neon logos, queues of rickshaws, officers corralling waves of shoppers. They hurried through this congestion, targeting the TGI Friday's across the road, a place they'd come to frequent for cheap Heineken on tap and revved air conditioning. Tonight it was bright and rowdy with a stew of families and post-cinema students squished into booths, smelling of bleach and a fryer, regulated by over-anxious servers—*Welcome to Three-Buck Thursdays!*

Old Sly's looking like a wet pile of protein these days, Peter said after they took a table.

Alain gave no acknowledgement. He was elsewhere, livened only when a server arrived with their tray of beers.

Aradhya's doing an interview with the *Guardian* tomorrow, he said. It'll be big for the case, as far as public sentiment. But her worries are closer to home.

Meaning what?

Angry mobs outside her building. She had to hire a private bodyguard. The police are like, do as you do. Blasé.

When's the court date?

Postponed. Again. As it stands now, early next year.

So what happens next?

Alain shrugged, a move expressing ambivalence on this question and the whole matter, but also the restaurant, this night, everything. Despite Alain's mopey mood, Peter remained confident in his indefatigability. The agonies of his youth—sadistic parents, an early speech impediment that magnetized the savagery of Catholic school bullies, the necessary self-cloistering of growing up gay in rural Quebec—had forced a choice between misery or resilience, submission or self-actualization. Shucking such hindrances was how he'd survived mostly intact when all others failed him. Even at his gloomiest, hints of that self-generated light were always there. He was a tough person.

Back outside, the night hit them like a heave of stale breath. The intersection at MG Road and Dakshin Marg swirled with humans, animated billboards, clattering filmi music. By reflex Peter reached for Alain's hand, then caught himself—they'd been warned against such open displays. As they stepped aside from the flow to consider their next move, Peter's phone vibrated. The incoming number was a string of digits from a 254 international code, which he knew to be Kenya. While he answered it, Alain wandered toward a bank of pay phones, saying something Peter missed in the noise.

Peter Hausen, a man's voice demanded.

Peter answered in the affirmative, struggling to hear as a spasm of alarm rose from the stream of pedestrian traffic. Cupping the phone, Peter found himself pulled by the throng, craning to see the source of the agitation: a Hindustan Ambassador had rolled onto the semi-paved sidewalk, its hood now compacted against a street sign's pole. As Peter drew closer he saw the driver was still behind the wheel, his bloodied face and shocked expression apparent through the cracked glass. But the crowd's attention was directed at something to the car's rear, downed in its path.

The call's connection was weak. Most of what the voice on the line said was lost in the clamour. Something about a request *for the discussion of a transfer of power*.

Peter turned against the pressing tide. Alain was still by the pay phones, a receiver to his ear, nodding along to whatever he was hearing. The crowd roiled as three men barged through. Dangling between them was the lifeless form of a small woman, long hair hiding her face. The crowd again shifted. Phones, held aloft, stole pictures.

This isn't a conversation that can be avoided, the voice said.

They'd come for him again, the proctors of his abhorrent past. Years may have hurtled by, cities into cities, a continuous segue of gleeful decadence. But the network would forever have him ensnared in its sensors, and no matter what the future held, no matter what fantasies Peter and Alain might indulge in, its reach would never be escaped. It was everywhere, always there, dragging everything into submission. It was in him.

An ambulance van pulled up over the sidewalk, dispersing the swarm. Peter hung up his phone and squeezed to one side, into a glass-enclosed alcove near the mall's entrance. He again looked back to the bank of pay phones, but Alain had disappeared. Exactly how much time had passed since leaving the restaurant, he was unable to ascertain. Many things seemed to be occurring simultaneously. He sent a text: *whered you go???* The message indicated delivery, but no receipt.

As he paced in circles gripping his phone, three young men blocked the alcove's entrance.

Hello hello, they leered.

Peter asked if they'd seen his friend, though even as he said it he knew this question to be foolish. His desperation only elicited more laughter. Two of the three moved upon him, taking him by the forearms. Peter batted away their gropes, but they held him tighter as the other raised a phone to prep a picture. More laughter. Peter stared past, into the distance: the lights of the Grand Mall pulsed in panels of emerald and orange, advertisements for SBJ, Noritake, Tata Indicom. The ambulances' sirens renewed their alarm. The phone's flash stuttered, then blasted with a release of light.

Trapped in the elevator, Peter listened, waiting for the power to be restored. No portal had opened, no freighter deck below him had heaved against the icy sea. Whatever presence might have been there had retreated, back into the hoistway's bowels.

In India, Alain had pursued absolution where none could be found, expecting affirmation where there was only silence. All Peter had found was confusion—confusion that forced useless recollections, a set of neglected obligations that couldn't be bypassed. They gotten no further ahead and no further away. Delhi was, after all, just another city.

Long ago the mists had shown him the frayed edges of this world. He'd rebuffed their invitation, and everything since had been a stream of nonsense. Excess. Frivolousness. Deception. It was all just management of thirst, with no security against the fuckery of time. Reliance on sequentiality, a belief in an order to things, had been his delusion. And he knew this would be his undoing.

But even as the elevator's doors finally parted in a scathe of light, even as the men hauled him by his sweat-slick arms up to the third floor, even as he found himself shirking their gestures of concern and feigning nonchalance as he climbed to his feet and staggered toward the stairs, the gin bottle still tucked in his belt—even then, and for a long time after, the thought persisted: that there was still something he might do to make things right.

THE FIGHTER JETS HAD COME AT DAWN every morning this week, tearing north from Edwards AFB and across the valley as far as Hunter Mountain before veering back south. With each pass, Hulda had told Peter upon his arrival, the force of these manouevres rattled the walls and petrified her cats. But it wasn't their deafening roar that caused the greatest disturbance for the compound, she said, but rather the fighters' onboard communications; when conducting low-altitude operations, the F-15E Strike Eagle and others in its class utilized wide-range radio communications on 315.9 MHz, which created interference in the operation of the oscillation chamber, even at such a distance.

When we're dealing with matters of spiritual life and death, Hulda had said, our progress can't be impeded by meddlesome deviations in the electromagnetic spectrum.

Forty-one degrees and sunny in Panamint Valley today, the air inert and dry in the convection of its immense basin. The view from Peter's assigned trailer faced west to the Argus range, where mottled greenish-orange slopes merged with low-lying clouds. In these mornings long shadows stretched across the gravel yard and up to the Seekers' Refuge; this entire ridge had, according to Magne, been cleared by borax miners more than a century ago as a transport route for their mule teams, en route to the railroad in Mojave. Now the ridge was occupied by the water filtration sheds that made settlement possible here in a tough clime, along with a solar grid working in tandem with the generator. Peter now watched the shadows slowly withdraw as he sat finishing his second cup of coffee, wondering what he should do with the rest of the morning. Things here moved at a sluggish pace.

Across the yard, Magne and Marlon were pouring concrete for the extension slab. It was apparently proving a difficult task, with much debate between the two over a screed board technique and the messy result of their efforts. Keep it level keep it level, Marlon urged, to which Magne shouted back, Move that rake move it. From this distance, Peter could see the entire base was off-level, but said nothing.

With the pour complete, Magne stepped back, wiping his brow with his sleeve and muttering to himself in his sibilant Norwegian growl. Marlon lit a clove cigarette, turning his back on the burgeoning slab, looking peeved. Magne called to Peter, waving him over. Despite his disinclination to venture out from the shade, Peter rose from the trailer steps and headed across the yard.

We need you to judge, Marlon said. Does this look correct to you?

Magne raised his hands, as if pawing something invisible to avoid being swept away by his own annoyance.

With all due respect, he said, it's not about it being correct. It's about rightful coherence with the larger structure. I'm the one who'll have to live with it.

Peter considered the slab, the beginnings of a framework for the chamber expansion. To him, it was just a rectangle of wet concrete, butted up against another, older rectangle.

It might look a little wonky, he said.

This was the answer Magne wanted. He huffed with deliberation. Marlon bit his cigarette.

Wonky? That a technical term?

Peter started back toward his trailer. He could sense Marlon glaring at him as he went, but felt nothing of it.

No one answered at first when he knocked at Jo-Beth's trailer. But as he was leaving, Frannie appeared, wearing a khaki bodysuit.

Think she's still rising, Frannie said. She was up late.

Peter thanked her and started away, but Frannie insisted he join her for breakfast. It was an appealing offer; he hadn't eaten since his arrival the previous day. He'd been introduced around and given an overview of the layout, but much was still a blur. The modified Airstream where Jo-Beth and Frannie were lodged was identical to Peter's and the others in the compound, one currently occupied by Marlon and the other by a young couple from Tempe. Magne and Hulda Myklebust, the property's owners, resided in the permanent bungalow at the top of the circular drive, marked by an oval sign: PANAMINT VALLEY SEEKERS' REFUGE + OSCILLATION CHAMBER TESTING GROUNDS. This description of it being a testing grounds, Peter had been informed, was meant to underscore the entire project's status a perpetual work in progress, with extractable data always in flux.

Peter sat at the foldaway dining table as Frannie chopped grapefruit. Her skin-tight outfit revealed sunken flesh, a suggestion of atrophy—her cancer had reached a late stage and, according to Jo-Beth, had spread from her breast tissue to her lymph nodes. Frannie's skepticism toward conventional medical practice, along with a set of complicated and enduring Obamacare-related gripes, had brought her here in pursuit of the chamber and its purported rejuvenating properties. Her optimism was dauntless.

Citrus maxima, she said, placing a tray of grapefruit wedges before him. Natural source of putrescine, a compound related to biological decay. Paradoxically, it also aids in DNA synthesis and regrowth.

Interesting, Peter said, biting into a wedge.

Paradoxes are everywhere. I came to Death Valley to find life. Now, that's cuckoo.

A mechanical clonk from the other end of the trailer announced a water valve shutting off. Jo-Beth appeared, wearing only a towel.

Morning, she said, her hair dripping as she reached past him for the fruit tray. Let me guess. It's hot out.

How'd you sleep? Frannie asked.

Weirdly. I was up late smoking purple kush and counting the stars. I think I bent my brain.

Frannie snickered. Jo-Beth headed outside. After a moment, Peter followed, watching as she shed the towel and lay back on a picnic table next to the trailer, exposing her naked body to the sun. He averted his eyes, looking across the compound toward the oscillation chamber. A domed structure fashioned in clay and cement, it sat on the parched terrain like a satisfied sleeping monster. He asked Jo-Beth if she'd been inside yet.

Sure have. It's quite a thing. There's a session scheduled for this afternoon. You'll be pulverized. In a good way.

Peter flicked grapefruit residue from his fingers. He felt testy, full of vague unease—the sort of nerves he used to feel before school examinations. It wasn't the anxiety of unpreparedness; rather, it was the fear that all such preparation was in vain, and that unwanted convolutions were forthcoming.

You drove up from L.A.? she said, spreading her arms and legs into a lazy savasana.

Yeah. My rental's parked down the road.

This was true, but he had zero recollection of the drive or its origin. There was a baggage carousel at LAX bleating alerts, traffic on the 395, the endless swaths of desert, little else.

I'm feeling a little off my game, he said.

Jo-Beth sat up. His last recollection of her was as looking somewhat careworn. But the body now displayed was tanned and toned, her biceps rippling with muscle, her large breasts standing pert like those of a woman half her age.

If there's one thing I know about you, Peter, it's that you've never been too restricted by reality. Always the foolish prince, doomed to waywardness.

Frannie joined them, bringing the tray of grapefruit. At Jo-Beth's brazen nudity, she sighed.

Seriously, JB? We don't know the people around here. We don't want to tick folks off.

Jo-Beth stretched her arms, drinking in the sun.

I coughed up decent cash to bake my biology out here. I'm doing as I please.

Leah and Carvell, the couple from Tempe, emerged from the trailer across the path. They waved and he waved back; she in a bikini top and cut-offs, he in tennis shorts and shirtless, they made an extremely good-looking pair. Peter had yet to interact much with them, but Jo-Beth had described them as *amiable ditzes*. Cupping coffee mugs, they sat at their own picnic table and looked at their phones. Service out here was spotty at best.

And how do you find the desert? Frannie asked Peter, pouring out tea.

Oh, you know, Peter said. The heat's a little gruelling. But we adapt.

We do, Frannie smiled.

Peter's been *everywhere*, Jo-Beth said. He's like a galaxy unto himself.

Frannie was interested. Oh? Do tell.

Jo-Beth bared her teeth, as if stifling a response. Play-acting or not, it was irksome, and Peter bristled.

Always the foolish prince, doomed to waywardness. There was no way Jo-Beth should or could have known this, but among his father's nastier nicknames he would often dub Peter *der Märchenkönig*, after Ludwig II of Bavaria, the swan king of the Rhine. The insinuation being that Peter was an airhead, a dreamer, rather than a hero of prudence and wisdom. It was true: his reign had been one staked in nothingness. Shipped from country to country, connectionless, he'd learned elasticity, to dematerialize, to bleep on no radars. He was no monarch, requisitioning ostentatious grottos and Versailles replicas. He was barely a person.

I've been around, he said to the women, but I've never been here.

That afternoon, they entered the oscillation chamber.

Barefoot and minimally attired, they stripped off any metallic or ferromagnetic materials as instructed, then moved in single file into the entrance vestibule. Once all the participants were inside— Jo-Beth and Frannie, Leah and Carvell, then Marlon, with Peter bringing up the rear—Magne sealed the red oak door behind them, deadening all external sound. A heavy insulating curtain covered the archway leading into the main chamber. Before leading them in, Magne again explained how, once powered on, the oscillators' effects would be instantaneous, though the feelings and manifestations elicited might be slow in coming.

The process of noetic divination is an intimate, individual thing, he said as he drew back the curtain.

The chamber's interior was dim, the only window a narrow skylight. The floor and rounded walls were fashioned with uneven, rough-hewn clay, the unbroken contours shaped like a sort of squashed, esophageal tunnel. Poles stood at either end, long probing antennae poking out of a curved, layered body fashioned of a copper alloy. Magne had earlier explained how each was an adaptation of a continuous wave Tesla coil and a split-ring resonator. Working as a contained system, the device emitted ultra-wideband electromagnetic frequencies that interplayed with the intermittent fields—the valley, the earth, the very physical matter of those entering—to generate plasma in the form of a coronal discharge and negative air ionization. The unique design of the chamber would in turn harness the valley's anomalous geomagnetism and grant the visitant full exposure to these waves. The outcome would be an acute resonance with the biomagnetic structure of the human body, encouraging rejuvenation from the base cellular level.

Peter understood none of this. Moving with the group into the chamber, he eyed the closer of the two poles warily, nervous about accidentally touching it and causing damage—either to it or to himself.

Magne kept to one side, making room for the others to circulate unhindered. No one spoke; the sharpest sounds were measured breath and the shuffle of feet. Unsure of what he should actually be doing, Peter tried to follow the others' cues. Jo-Beth paced the chamber's length in slow lengths, hands splayed before her, concentrating on her footsteps' metre. Leah and Carvell sat cross-legged on the floor facing one another, intent in some unspoken mutual exchange. Frannie situated herself in the centre of the dome, standing as firmly as her wasted frame allowed, her face raised to the skylight. Pale, trembling, she looked as if ready to vaporize—by all accounts, her lengthy battle with her illness had been hard-fought, adopting many forms and making many demands. Bathing in the imperceptible rays of the device's oscillations, she was fully present in whatever was or was not happening. Whatever transformations she was experiencing were her own. Peter envied her.

Later, the Myklebusts hosted dinner in the garden behind their bungalow, with shade provided by an elaborate rockery of cacti and desert succulents. Trays loaded with cabbage slaw and a pungent venison stew were served, and drinks were plentiful and cold. Once all the visitors were seated and served, Magne sat at the head of the table, raising a foaming glass of dark beer.

To the land, he toasted.

All clinked glasses. Seated at the table's end, Peter drank from a tumbler of Hulda's extremely tart homemade Chardonnay. Already his head was spongy with heat and sleeplessness—and, perhaps, any residual effects of the oscillators.

That your Corolla parked down the road? Marlon asked him, chewing on a sprig of tarragon.

It's a rental.

Ah, Marlon said, as if this meant something. Might ask you for a solid later.

Peter didn't like the sound of this. But his attention was then drawn to Magne, who was imparting something to Leah and Carvell, drawing the others in.

In the latter days of the Plassfolk, Magne was saying, many of its adherents were confuted as fools and white supremacists. Opportunists masked as seekers. But when Hulda and I initially encountered them, years back, everything was still in the spirit of pure discovery.

Earlier, Jo-Beth had shared with Peter the few details she had regarding Magne and Hulda's history pre-California. Back in Norway, they'd been aligned with the Plassfolk, a fringe religious group based on the coast of the Barents Sea. The organization's core principles seemed to have involved belief in a messianic return of ancient alien visitors, an agrarian Luddite-ish skepticism toward technology, anti-Semitic conspiracy, various strains of new age esotericism, or elements of all of these.

But you parted ways? Frannie asked.

Magne licked suds from his moustache.

One of our founders sent a threatening letter to members of the Norwegian Stortinget, intimating the Oslo Metro would spontaneously disintegrate on the eve of that year's syttende mai Constitutional holiday. Of course, it was only a silly stunt. But it put us on the authorities' radar, with debilitating effects on our ability to operate. It also showed how some of our ranks had turned from the hopeful essence of our core principles toward radical and dangerous delusions.

Many in the group saw friction as the only force worth understanding, Hulda said. Magne and myself, our interests come wrapped in a less abrasive fabric. Our work is to be students of the universe.

Magne smiled at his wife. Peter imagined they'd given a version of this account many times before.

We now understand the Plassfolk's passions to be just one manifestation among many of interdimensional visitations, Magne said. These visitations are occurring around us all the time, constantly. The evidence is everywhere. Subtle and sibylline, yes. But discoverable.

Discover how, Carvell asked.

You're already doing it. EMF attunement. Experimentation.

But keep in mind, Hulda said, that's only one facet of a greater project. The onus of discovery rests on the individual. Data, it can be gathered endlessly. The narrative one weaves out of it, however, is highly subjective.

I don't follow, Leah said. I thought the chamber was supposed to do something.

Oh, it certainly does, and it will. But it doesn't end there. There's the challenge of conversion and utilization of the repurposed plasmic energy. Especially when you go submerging yourselves back into the distresses of daily life. Balancing our supernal evolution with more prosaic demands, that's the perennial challenge.

You mean, like, money and shit, Carvell said.

Among other distractions. The heinous constructs of modern society.

I'm sure Peter knows something about that, Jo-Beth interjected.

All at the table looked to her, then to him. Peter was caught mid-chew.

I know how you wrestle with those things, she said. Corruption. Ethics. Plunder and profit.

Peter was unsure of what to say.

I imagine everyone does to some degree, he said.

But come now. You have to admit, your case is much more extreme. Your father's dealings and everything. You said yourself how your family name yokes you with guilt.

I believe *you* said that.

Jo-Beth turned to the table.

Peter's rich. Disturbingly rich.

Peter put down his fork. He was sure he heard Marlon mutter something to himself. Whatever Jo-Beth was doing, he willed her to stop. She didn't.

If your past brings you such disconcertion, you should be willing to confront it. Like Hulda says, the onus of discovery and all that.

It's not what we acquire, it's what we *are*, Carvell said.

Jo-Beth laughed once, sharply: *Ha*.

My father had this thing, Leah said, he said a man isn't truly a man until he owns a Corvette from the same year he was born. Then again, he was a hypomanic depressive and became a born-again evangelical in his fifties. So, you know. Who's to say.

Mistaking possession for knowledge is the surest route to a spiritual death, Magne said.

And yet we all had to pay real money to be here, Peter said. Pretty handsomely, actually.

To this, the table fell silent. Magne's face flushed. It was Frannie who finally broke the tension, turning to Leah.

Why a Corvette?

Don't know, Leah said. I really should have asked him. But he jumped off the Sunshine Skyway Bridge two years ago.

By night the desert lay quiet, devoid of snarl or squeal. A blue-black sky stroked with starlight lorded over the valley. Doubtless, this was a thing to behold, yet as he looked out over the sloping stretch below, the vast valley of grit and rubbled outcroppings, Peter felt nothing.

He headed back across the compound. Lights glowed behind the trailers' curtains where the visitors had retired for the night. Looking up to the bungalow, Peter made out Magne seated under a porchlight, waving him over. Reluctantly, Peter complied. Leaning back on one of two wicker recliners, Magne wore a pair of bulky headphones, a glass of something amber in hand. One of the Mykelbusts' many cats slept in his lap.

Everything okay? he said, removing the headphones and pausing the Discman to which they were attached.

It's quiet.

Until the coyotes get going. Ornery little spastics.

Magne cast Peter an assessing look, then pointed to the other chair.

Sit down, he said. Wild Turkey's your best friend in the desert at night.

Peter obliged, taking a seat on a bench next to the recliner. Magne produced the bottle from beside the chair, topped up his own glass, then handed it over. Without a glass of his own, Peter sipped from the bottle.

What are you listening to? Peter asked.

Just some old CDs. Jamiroquai, Moby. You a music lover?

As much as anyone. I tend to go for heavier stuff.

Heavier.

Morbid Angel. Lamb of God. Killswitch Engage.

Ah. You're a rocker.

Peter nodded and drank again. We might have needlessly butted heads earlier, he said. I really don't want to seem ungracious for your hospitality. And the entire...experience.

I appreciate that. We understand these processes can sometimes prompt an inflammatory effect.

I did want to ask...or, let me pose a question.

Fire away.

You said something earlier, about dangerous delusions.

Oh. Yes.

But do you think it's more dangerous to be deluded about reality, as in concrete, verifiable reality, or, I'll say, less material states of reality, which may or may not even exist?

What a question.

Let me try and rephrase.

No, I think I understand what you're driving at. You wonder how navigating the metagalactic vale helps you get through the day. How to reconcile the abstruse with the insurmountable.

In a sense. Sure.

I'll say this. The universe is mighty, and humanity—we're bridled by our smallness. The only way we fathom such complexities is by imposing some sort of order. Ergo, mankind's lust for self-mythologization. To sit astride our gods.

Dred, indomitable: *It guides my affairs with assurance stronger than any directorial board.*

Every seeker brings their own story, Magne continued, and each is convinced theirs is unique. Yet, whittled down to their essence, there are only so many stories to tell. A haunted man stares out at the ocean. A stranger arrives in town. A girl flees a predator. Your story may feel like it belongs to you, but its contours were carved out long ago.

Peter hesitated. The desert's silence felt almost synthetic, antiseptic. Quiet beyond quiet.

My man died, he said, because of me. Since then, I've been only halfway here. Or anywhere. I'm carrying a curse. Maybe I always was, before this. I don't know.

And what brought about this curse?

I received a calling, when I was younger. But I resisted.

A calling. As in, a prophetic visitation?

No. More like...

Peter worked to choose his words, finding none adequate.

...a curtain was pulled back.

Magne leaned in.

And what was revealed?

A way to somewhere, Peter said. Another place.

Somewhere extraplanetary?

I don't think so. It was always hazy. I saw figures, people.

Were they extremely elongated in stature, and costumed in elaborate robes, as if members of some sort of legislature?

Uh. No.

Did they speak in a series of clicks and cheeps? Were they of an androgynous form, and seemed to cherish specific gemstones?

No. Just people.

And you say you resisted their offering.

I don't think I understood what was happening at the time. I still don't.

Magne leaned back. He extended his cup, and Peter topped it up.

This is all extremely fascinating, Magne said. What I recommend is you run it by Hulda. She'll have a much clearer view of what you're undergoing than I ever could. She has insights.

Magne smiled and lifted his glass.

I salute you and your yearning, Peter. There *is* another world, and it calls to us. Here's to finding it soon.

Later Peter lay on the narrow bunk in his trailer, covers tossed aside. The feeling of dread persisted, foiling sleep. There was no logic in what he was doing or what was being done to, or for, him—he found even describing his situation impossible. This, more than anything, had been his life's plight: paralyzing bewilderment.

The mists had last appeared to him when he was sixteen, while at the Gstaad International School in Berne. The fatigue of exam season was in its full oppression, the students addled with depression and nerves. Trudging back to his dormitory to face another night of commitment to Chapter 21—"Transmission Mechanisms of Monetary Policy"—he'd located an alcove behind a discreet hedgerow where he could light the single Muratti he'd been saving. Sheltered there, hunched in his uniform jacket and pinned-up trousers, he felt, if only temporarily, something like freedom.

Halfway through his smoke, he'd sensed a change occurring. The footpaths and bushes, the snowy backdrop of the Alps' peaks, all began to dematerialize. A subsonic rumble rose. Then, as before, turbulent fields of varying colour bloomed and opened before him, and whatever lay within was again presented to him, offering access to other places, other realities. By then, however, Peter had seen this before, so he only puffed his cigarette and watched this phenomena occur. More pressing matters weighed on him: term deadlines, hormonal leaps, the crawling awareness of his own insignificance amid the school's cutthroat social structure. By the time the Muratti was smoked down to its filter, the ghostly vapours had dissipated and he'd resumed the walk back to his room, his thoughts already returning to Keynes and the consumption expenditure function. And so that last summon had gone unacknowledged, just like all the others before.

Only now were the full consequences of his failure being made clear. He'd been too young and too headstrong, too unglued in years since, to recognize the possibility in what he'd been offered. His denial had consequences: even if unwittingly, he'd enabled Dred to usurp the mists' call as his own justification for an inexorable career of destruction. And so ruin had been introduced into the world.

Yet Dred was merely a man, fallible and frail—to credit him as anything more was to believe in the indomitability of power, to believe in human voracity as something transcendent. Sustaining Dred's grand lie depended most of all on the complicity of the quivering flock of lackeys and adherents at his feet. Only they upheld his power.

He may have commandeered Peter's visions, but that didn't give him ownership. *Mistaking possession for knowledge*, as Magne said.

Perhaps his story was indeed written long ago, his fate long decided. And yet the mists had told him: time must be experienced equivocally. Maybe this really was all just a dream. If so, it might not be too late to alter things. The end could be a beginning—like the mists, ungoverned by time's unrelenting flow.

Outside, the coyotes began to howl.

In the morning, he accepted Hulda's offer of a hike to the edge of the salt flats. They headed down the trail with few words exchanged, reaching their destination in about half an hour. At a bouldered ridge among a sprawl of creosote, they sat to drink the Thermos of tea Hulda had brought along. The scene before them was raw and alien: splotches of ash-grey soil and reddish salt deposits across the playa, the sun blading the horizon's range. Keeping her face shaded under a floppy nylon sun hat, Hulda scooped sunscreen from a jar to rub on her thin, freckled arms; it smelled strongly of cucumber.

I'm amazed you can operate out here, Peter said for lack of any other conversation. I'd have thought there'd be…restrictions on the land or something?

Most of it's UNESCO Biosphere Reserve, Hulde said. We're in the buffer zone. The oscillators neutralize most telecommunications technologies. So we go undetected.

Undetected by whom?

By the powers that be.

More questions came to mind, but he refrained from asking. Much about Hulda was mysterious. She moved and spoke slowly, with poise, her mellow Norwegian inflections coloured with a sapid Californian yawn. Overall, she radiated an aura of assuredness, of sagacious ease—though how much of this was innate and how much was calculated, Peter couldn't say.

Magne told me about your conversation, and a bit about your circumstances. I believe I understand the root of your problem, and I think I can help you. But the question is whether you're willing to take the leap required to truly understand.

I suppose I'll say yes, he said. I mean, I'm here.

She pushed back her hat's brim, looking out on the flats.

Do you often feel wracked by the feeling that actual events in your past might not be as you've perceived them to be?

I do.

Do you often lose track of the apparent sequence of things?

Constantly. Always.

You've been visited by entities with mysterious purposes.

An image came to him: white-haired men in mock turtlenecks, pressing upon him in Parc La Fontaine, imposing demands. We're not out to yank your chain.

I have.

And in the light of such instability, you long for order. For some evidence to finally confirm your suspicions.

My suspicions?

That there really is a message contained in what you've seen. A true purpose. And that it's meant to be yours. The structure of our minds may be limited, but it's also highly mutable. Apparitions like the ones you describe operate as a mechanism by which we comprehend the unfathomable, within the otherwise overwhelming possibility of deep time. It's the plight of the visionary, and one of many repercussions of unmediated contact with the astral realm.

Mm.

You have to understand, our allies from parallel dimensional tracts are limited in their abilities to communicate with us. Their missives often seem impenetrable at first blush.

Our allies are who again?

The Zaurians, from the K Quasar. Evidence shows us that the Zaurians, or their emissaries probing the earthbound strata, employ cryptographic methods similar to the Arabic ciphers of al-Durayhim. Though obviously with much greater complexity. But even when deciphered, they tend to be highly allusive and ambiguous. This is how the Lord appeared to Eliphaz in those theophanic encounters. The Zaurian conception of time itself can seem, filtered through our sequence-driven cognitive processes, rather unstable.

There has been considerable instability.

That's because you see. The influence of Zaurian telepathy unshackles your mind. What feels to you like anxiety is actually your heightened awareness of temporal divagation and the celestial anatomy. But through exposure to specific frequencies, we can alter our cognitive capabilities in gainful ways. Realignment of one's cellular structure is just the first stage.

In the chamber.

Yes. With continued effort, we find ways of tapping into rich baryonic matter, and in so doing we develop methods of deciphering the information received. It's a process, requiring diligence and perseverance, and it can often be frustrating. But gradually those confounding signals will cease to baffle us.

She brought her hands together, a sort of pleading move.

Peter. I'd love for you to consider making your stay here a more long-term thing. Seekers like you are the reason we do what we do. That said, we remain perpetually under-resourced. We'd love to work with you in exploring ways we might help each other to, you know, make the refuge more sustainable and efficacious in the long run.

You're looking for an investor.

I'd say...*collaborator*. I confess, I did a little reading up. On you. Someone with such curiosity and purpose, along with the practical resources you wield, could really be an invaluable member of our slapdash family out here.

Peter took this in, looking back down the valley, the sun now in its full fury. It was going to be another hot day.

I see.

This curse you've mentioned, Hulda said. This is troubling. It seems to me the only way to lift a curse is to return to its source. Face it headlong and snuff it out.

Snuff it out.

Yes.

But then what?

Then you can find peace.

A flutter of brownish-grey birds, thrashers or wrens maybe, came tearing up over the hill, as if fleeing an enemy. And, yes: seconds later, an unearthly noise came rising from the south valley. Hulda seemed untroubled by this. She dumped the remaining dribbles of her Thermos onto the ground, then stood.

Nothing really ends, Peter. We only move through dimensional phases, clinging to recognizable patterns. Endings and beginnings, preambles and epilogues...they're only just parentheses.

As if to punctuate this thought, an F-15 sliced the sky, low enough for Peter to make out the missiles mounted on its fuselage. It crossed the span above and was out of sight in seconds. In the wake of this assault, there seemed nothing else to say. Hulda started back up the hill. After a moment, Peter did too.

Marlon was waiting on his trailer's front steps, beaming a generous grin. This was odd; bug-eyed and growly, Marlon had so far been less than amiable. Peter attempted a smile back and in the spirit of civility, offered coffee—all the trailer's cupboards held was Maxwell House, but he could put on the kettle. Marlon kept to the doorway.

Just wondering again about that Toyota of yours.

Right. Like I said, it's a rental. And I'm the only driver on the contract.

Thinking maybe you could give a lift? Just down to Ridgecrest. I gotta see this hombre about my truck.

That's more than two hours away.

Hour fifteen, max, Marlon said. Come on. It's a nice drive. Otherwise I'm stranded. I can slide you something for the gas once we get there.

This was something Peter really didn't want to think about. But he gave Marlon a maybe; right now, he had things to do. Back inside the trailer, he closed all curtains and sat on his bunk, massaging his sun-broiled forehead with apis mellifica cream provided by Frannie. Weather forecasts called for more hot and dry days, tomorrow and for the foreseeable future.

The oscillators were activated. Peter stood solo in the centre of the chamber, wearing only his briefs, in what he gauged to be the same position Frannie had assumed. This time he actively felt for any effects, allowing himself to be guided by the prelusive instructions he'd been given—open, as led, to any change in awareness of sublunary or celestial anatomy. Zaurian telepathy, atmospheric revolt, anything at all. The real challenge was to remind himself of what was actually happening, and where he actually was.

He eased his head back, stretching his trachea and releasing his shoulders.

It could be decades ago, the far-flung future. He was homeless, beholden to nowhere, neither a titleholder nor a lessee.

He was crossing the Sea of Hoces from Cape Horn, southbound through catastrophic gales, his lungs burning against the vortex's whip.

Alain: *I'm just trying to shed light against darkness.*

The circular skylight above presented a constricted sky, unnervingly blue: a pupil-less, sclera-less eye, or the mouth of a well seen from the bottom. In the dim light, the unvarnished clay of the chamber's interior was like bone, the rough contours like a skull. Something on the ceiling toward the rear section caught his attention. A blemish, a couple of feet above his reach. He tried to ignore this and retune himself to his efforts, but his curiosity demanded a look. He crossed the chamber and stood on tiptoe, balancing against the wall. Yes, there were letters there, scrawled in what appeared to be pencil. He craned his neck, fighting to discern this message.

In shaky block letters: EAT SHIT.

They drove south along Route 190 as the sun sank behind Telescope Peak. Marlon had explained how if he didn't get to the repairs lot in Ridgecrest that night, someone named Nick would take off for Sacramento with his truck, and then all sorts of headaches would ensue. Peter paid little attention to this explanation.

He was only giving Marlon a ride because he'd failed to come up with an excuse not to.

But once they got on the highway, he found himself actually enjoying the drive. The rental was brand new; it was like driving a furnished condominium. Marlon seemed anxious and withdrawn. The radio offered unobjectionable rock: Stone Temple Pilots, Cheap Trick. The highway cut through broad ranges of flatlands, traps of low brush and mountains to both horizons. Signs along the roadside announced territory zoned off by the China Lake naval station, but other than a few stray buildings, no evidence appeared of military operations, or anything else at all.

People disappear in these deserts all the time, Marlon said, looking out on the passing landscape.

Neither of them had spoken in a while. Peter looked over.

They get tricked by the GPS. But that shit don't work out here. Just sends them right them up the butt of the beast. Where they *die*. You got to find your way by the stars. Only way. That's the natural world.

Night had fallen by the time they reached the town limits. Marlon directed Peter to turn off at a 76 station onto a barren back street populated by rows of commercial sheds and taped-up storefronts. They proceeded until met with a decisive dead end barred by a guardrail, an undeveloped lot beyond.

Marlon looked at his phone.

Go back.

Peter turned the car around and they headed back the way they'd come, crossing to the road's opposite extension. The scene here was even less promising. Marlon had Peter pull over at the entrance of a gravel lot, housing about a half-dozen cars and pickups of various makes, surrounded by a chain-link fence. The gates were bound by a large padlock, and the office kiosk at the lot's far boundary looked empty.

Gotta get Nick, Marlon said.

He hopped out, working his phone. Peter left the engine running. The plan was to get Marlon to his truck, then they would part ways.

Whether or not Marlon would then return to the seekers' refuge had not been discussed. How an apparent transient like Marlon afforded the Myklebusts' exorbitant nightly rate was a mystery.

Peter's own next move was also uncertain. He could head back to the seekers' refuge—he'd paid in advance for a week's stay. But what really awaited him there, he couldn't say. Of the immediate future, he saw nothing. He rolled down the window and waited.

There's nowhere you can go.

A man, who he took to be Nick, appeared on the other side of the fence. He was big, his head razored, wearing a hoodie and baggy cargo shorts. Without a greeting, he produced a key ring hooked to his belt and undid the padlock. The chain fell away and the gates parted. Marlon came back around to the driver's side.

Go on, Marlon said to Peter, and waved him through.

Peter eased the Corolla into the lot as guided, even though, as far as he understood things, his role was done. He braked a few yards from the entrance, watching Marlon and Nick in the rear-view. They lit cigarettes, talking closely, their faces cast demonic in the smoke and tail lights.

Another memory: men, huddled like this, discussing pressing circumstances of navigation, somewhere within those tempests of ice. Researchers, sailors, bracing themselves on a steel platform as of chunks of riven berg slam against the freighter's hull. The question, as always: was this a memory, or a premonition.

Marlon returned to the car's side, gesturing for Peter to get out.

What's the story? Peter asked.

Just hop out for a sec. Help us out here.

Peter tried to read his face, but Marlon turned away, cagily puffing his cigarette. Peter turned off the ignition and pocketed the keys before getting out.

Thith ith from Hert-th? Nick said, lisping.

Decal's on the bumper, Peter said. Look, I have to get back...

Why don't you give uth the keyth, Nick said.

Peter looked to Marlon. Marlon looked at the ground.

Keyth, Nick said again.

Peter reached for the Corolla's door, but Nick slammed it shut. He came chest first, pressing Peter against the car, breathing into his face. Staring into Nick's maw, Peter saw a full deck of spotless false teeth, spaced perfectly uniformly, like piano keys.

Do yourthelf a favour, Nick said. Thtand down.

Peter was transfixed by his teeth. The lot, the torpid town, Marlon, the Antarctic wilds—all gone. Even in the sparing light, those teeth were everything.

Marlon pressed a hand on Peter's shoulder.

Wallet, keys. Come on. What you gonna do?

Peter tried to shake Marlon away, a weak attempt at freeing himself. This gesture of resistance was pointless. Nick brought up his knee and pressed it into Peter's crotch.

Thith is me being nithe, he lisped. Don't make me get nathty.

Peter felt his midsection go cold. He handed over the keys.

Wallet, Nick said.

In the glove compartment.

The what?

The glove compartment. The thing in the dash, the drawer.

Nick stepped back and spat over his forearm. In this, he seemed to be making a decision. He slapped Peter across the face—a solid blow, and Peter felt something shift inside his cheek. Then Marlon lunged in with a shove to the sternum, sending Peter spilling back onto the gravel.

The two men climbed into the car, Nick at the wheel and Marlon in the passenger's side. Peter regained his footing and started forward, but abandoned any such move. Nick threw the car in reverse, almost mowing Peter down as he executed a tight arc to aim for the exit. He leaned out the window, shaking his head.

Glove compartment. Fuck you.

They sped out through the gates and away.

Years had been lost, but things were becoming clearer. Endings, beginnings: *they're only just parentheses*. And all of this, after all, was only just a dream.

He sat on the curb near the 76 station, watching cars roll in and out, mostly taxis. His face burned. A police cruiser marked KERN COUNTY SHERIFF pulled into the station, the cluck of its radio cutting through the night's silence. The white cops inside glanced in Peter's direction; he stared back, daring any disapprobation. How they saw him, who knew. Alain once joked, *Police see a guy like you as their oncologist, not a carjacker*. But here he was a rogue entity, a potential hostile. If questioned, he'd have no answers to give. The authorities might attend his complaint, file his report of the car's theft, but ultimately there was nothing any county clerk could do—the justice he was looking for was outside their jurisdiction. The officers cast Peter apprehensive looks, then drove on.

The solidity of things was again in question. Hulda's diagnosis had been delivered with conviction: *What feels like anxiety is actually your heightened awareness of temporal divagation*. But as everything was stripped away, even that temporal awareness, a purpose was becoming clearer.

He'd been left with no money, no ID, but still had his phone. The signal was stronger here than in the valley. He scrolled through contacts, looking for a number he was sure he'd programmed there. The call he had to make would be difficult yet necessary. And with it would come the first advances toward realignment, toward rectifying his cursed life—toward *trying to shed light against darkness*.

It wasn't enough for him to grieve. He was done with that. Now he had to atone.

AS PER ARRANGEMENTS, A DRIVER MET PETER at the arrivals gate and whisked him to the InterContinental. It had been more than a decade since he'd last been to Nairobi, but downtown in mid-afternoon was as he'd remembered: humid and overcast, a wash of pushy traffic and drab, boxy complexes. DHG had since shuttered its offices on Halle Selassie Avenue, but the city still felt to him like an extension of the company's all-amassing reach. Callous industry, the toil of enterprise, was present in everything.

After checking in, he headed to the pool terrace, where he'd arranged to meet Agnes. At the deck's far end men in suits, middle manager types, were milling about; a placard announced WELCOME EAST AFRICA DIASPORA BUSINESS COUNCIL ANNUAL SUMMIT. Servers offered trays laden with chocolate and spritzers; a hired guitarist sat on a stool, strumming a flamenco-ish version of something familiar, a Don Henley song.

Peter found a shaded table and at his command a waiter brought a dry, plastic-sealed pastry and a bottle of Tusker beer. Opposite him on the terrace a teenage white girl in a bikini sat on a lounger, engrossed in the hefty Thomas Piketty hardcover perched on her legs. Peter watched her with curiosity, imagining what circumstances had brought her here, but she paid him no mind.

When Agnes arrived, it was with a smile that spoke of competing impressions: gladness surely, but also at least some degree of pity. He rose and they embraced. Agnes was thin, nervy in his hold. He couldn't imagine how he appeared to her.

I was surprised to receive your call, she said. I've lost track of everywhere you've been.

I have too.

He asked about her family, the mother he'd once briefly met, and to whose care he knew Agnes's life was now mainly devoted. Stricken by pneumonia among a long list of recurring ailments, her mother now lay in a costly private health facility in Ngara and was likely not long for this world.

I want to say she's had a happy life, Agnes said.

She didn't expand on the thought. She ordered coffee, and they talked for a while about the political situation in Kenya, to which he admitted knowing little. Agnes waved it off.

Parties rise, parties dwindle. Old allegiances resurface under new names. The same issues again and again. Corruption and cronyism at all levels. It has nothing to do with humanity, or even ideology. Only gamesmanship. We have a debt crisis, a security crisis. Protesters all this week at the Jeevanjee Gardens. But we're told repeatedly, this is an era of unprecedented progress. Innovation. Yet nothing changes.

Hard not to be cynical, I suppose.

Agnes looked past him, across the pool. She seemed far away, tired.

Cynicism is for the entitled.

The teenage girl had set aside her book and was coating her thighs with a bottled spray. A pair of men, summit attendees, observed this from under an awning, snickering to one another.

I need you to bring me to him, he said.

What for? You can't expect a teary reunion.

Atonement.

She gave him a long look.

There's nothing there, Peter.

That may be true. We'll see.

You haven't changed at all, she said with a sigh. You remain exactly what you are.

Which is?

A foolish prince.

At this, Peter winced. *Foolish prince*: his title, enduring across time and territory.

But you know, Agnes said, you and I are just subjects, bound to the same kingdom.

As the sailboat skimmed across the channel from Manda Island, Peter felt himself again tugged adrift in time. The first time he'd seen the Indian Ocean was during a trip to the Seychelles with Koharu when he was eighteen, before his ill-fated first and only semester at NYU. It was a trip conceived in liberation, prompted his mother's then-recent split from Jasminder, and they'd freely uncorked magnums of champagne on the coral beaches, toasting tortoises. But amid the lagoons and orchids and medusagyne, Peter felt crushed by the radical immersion, all this swooping space. The granite islands and ocean breezes, the sprawling openness: it had been too much. The wonder of it made him sick.

Now, squinting into cool sea spray as the boat traced the beach south toward Shela, he could hardly imagine being so overwhelmed. Any reverence he'd once held for the mighty ocean—for anything at all—was long gone. What wonder remained was of an altogether different breed: conditional, amorphous, corroded.

As was spoken by Janko, the battle-weary bum: *You got to understand the ocean as another form of infinity.*

They reached the opposite shore and the boatman let out the sail, easing them up to the dock. Men rushed forward to meet them, money was exchanged, then Peter was following their procession up the beach and into the close, coiling pathways that led to the house.

Epochs had risen and fallen on Lamu, from its days as a stronghold for warring traders to its current role as backpacker haven and sporadic target for Somali *mujahideen*. It was easy to indulge some idea of timelessness here—Lamu as a haven for ghosts or seraphs, beyond history. But this was swiftly dispelled on arrival. The inbound charter plane had been crammed with Irish women in designer track suits and backpack-laden NGO workers plugging itineraries into their phones. Armed soldiers patrolled the Manda airstrip even as the jumpy men attending the docks insisted, *You go home and post the good reviews.*

Humans were forever slumping onto shores like these, thirsting for the sublime and the charms of the holy, bathing in the residue of centuries. It was therapeutic—consoling the anxieties of meaninglessness with a morning at the mosque, a glimpse of a crumbling monument, a fortnight off the grid. Alain had lived this way, and Peter, semi-unknowingly, had too. Hunger for magical experience, and what it might confirm, injected them both with energy. But it was an insatiable hunger. And though geography could be conquered, time was the unyielding adversary, beyond commerce or logistics, beyond bullies and villains. Time was the uniting thing.

Dred had purchased the complex on south Lamu following his first visit to the Swahili Coast about fifteen years ago during another extended spell of laying low during prolonged disputes with the Central Tax Office in Bonn. Within hours of his arrival on the island, he'd found himself possessed by the spirit of Bwana Mkuu, the Sultan of Pate—or so he'd once claimed to Peter, back when they were in semi-regular communication. In his egocentric cosmology, of course he'd self-bestow such birthright, lording over the oceanic slave trade, his dynasty ordained by the winds. Of course.

Aside from the hefty motorized gates shielding it from the outer pathways, the two-storey villa was like any of the island's upscale cottages or tourist residences: glassy limestone, zidaka niches, caliginous floodlights seeping through neem trees. Peter was met at the front steps by an attendant offering a platter of fruit and a pot of tea. He accepted a wedge of melon, then went inside.

He hurriedly checked the halls, the bedrooms, the neatly tended baraza courtyard, finding the place unoccupied. Little here had changed, though the place bore subtle traces of neglect: creases of water damage, a rust-streaked sink, mildew in the air. The shelves were mostly bare, the few flourishes just cheap Maasai carvings and Africa kitsch, a poster of a zebra wearing a monocle and top hat above blocky text reading KENYA: MODERN SAFARI ADVENTURING! Peter stared at this for a full, unbroken minute. When he turned, he found his attendant at the end of the hall, observing dutifully, a question in his eyes. Peter sent the man away, stating a preference to be left alone. Of course, he couldn't truly be alone here: cameras were mounted in every corner and hired security patrolled the grounds, trailing cigar smoke. It was safe to assume they were armed.

He checked his phone. During the trip from Nairobi, he'd missed a call, an unknown number. He considered ringing back, but was too sapped to summon the energy, and instead headed to one of the second-floor bedrooms. Without bothering to undress, he shoved aside the bulky fly net enveloping the bed and crawled onto the thin foam mattress. It was astonishingly uncomfortable. And yet, against expectations, he was soon asleep.

When he awoke, the house was dark—power was forever erratic here, the generator output fickle at best. Downstairs, he found the back terrace had been prepared with citronella candles and a jug of filtered water wrapped in cheesecloth, but in keeping with his directive, he was alone. He downed water while looking down on the yard, the ashlike sand and huddled acacias illumined by linked floodlights. A guard stood posted at the far end, facing the house. Peter didn't bother to wave.

He'd been dreaming of Alain again, another version of the same dream he'd had many times before. They were swimming together, along with dozens of anonymous others, through a huge, maybe limitless, glassed-in pool. This strange structure was partitioned into a complex system of multiple descending levels, like locks in a canal. With each successive stage, the current increased, driven by some titanic mechanism, suctioning the swimmers forward, downward. Through his vertiginous dream perception, Peter lost sight of Alain among the countless heads bobbing atop the choppy waters. Heaved over and over against the relentless waves, the swimmers multiplied and merged, until they all became fused together as one terrible, massed coagulum.

As before, Peter woke from this dream not in terror but in a kind of desolation. What was most troubling about the dream wasn't its substance; such primal anxieties were familiar and decodable. What was troubling was its persistence, its tireless loop of loss. His dreams were now almost unfailingly about Alain. Perhaps they always would be.

His phone buzzed, again an unknown number. He let it go unanswered, and a beat later an alert came of a new voice-mail message. His arrival, he assumed from this, had been noted. There was no avoiding what lay ahead.

He listened to the rustle of cordias and acacias, portending a coming storm. And underneath, there it was: the ocean, its whispering shoosh steady in the background.

He headed to the beachside restaurant for the arranged time. The man was already there, waiting at a corner table. At Peter's approach, he set aside the book he was reading, but offered no gesture of welcome. Wearing a crisp-looking denim shirt and jeans, he was flushed, damp, overheated. A phone lay on the table and a leather valise rested at his side.

I ordered clams, the man said with the pronounced American lilt Peter had heard in his message, something Southern. You must be hungry.

Peter was—he'd barely eaten in the last few days. The man raised two fingers to the server behind the counter, a request that seemed to be understood. The man turned back and checked his phone, scrolling. This goddamn country, he said, shaking his head at whatever he was reading.

You're not a fan.

Hell no. Not with all this Sharia law fundamentalist garbage. Decapitations in Mogadishu and all that. The police flap around like pigeons. Everyone's jittery about moving any money here. Every time you try and get something going, it gets stifled by these bozos.

Pretty sure guys like you will be just fine.

Guys like me. What, you know all about guys like me?

You seem familiar. Or maybe it's just your type.

My type. Okay. The man gave his phone another look, then set it aside and wiped his nose with a serviette.

What's this? Peter said, meaning the book.

The man spun it around to show the cover, then tapped a second byline below the author's name.

This person was hired to work on Mr. Hausen's book. Some L.A. hack.

Peter blinked.

A book. You're kidding me.

The man shrugged.

Actually, we're considering voiding the contract. Mr. Hausen's sensing this character might be somewhat of a flake.

The book's cover image was of a young blond woman, styled as a mid-century starlet à la Veronica Lake, though her prominent sleeve tattoos and the photo's tawdry digital effects offset any chasteness of the homage.

Keep that, if you need some mindless reading material, the man said. But that's a whole other thing. Not what concerns us.

He wiped his nose again. Peter decided it was better to not ask questions. All would surely be revealed.

As you're probably aware, the man said, I've been tracking your various goings-on for the last...let's say, a while.

I'm touched.

Just doing my job. The request was to keep tabs. When I say tabs, I'm saying tabs on you. Mr. Hausen has flowed a considerable amount of financial support to you and your mother over the years.

He has. Of course, he's legally obliged to support her.

He's a meticulous person, professionally and personally. It's in his interests to stay on top of where such support goes, and how it's put to use.

Tell Dred and his sniveling attorneys it's none of their fucking business what my mother does with her money. It's *her* money.

That's so not my department. I deal with logistics. And logistically, changes are, as you know, afoot in DHG's corporate structure. Major shifts are underway. That's why I'm coming to you. Mr. Hausen is preparing to bring you into the fold.

Peter hadn't expected this. Though, in a way, it wasn't entirely a shock.

Really.

He always intended for you to come on board, the man said. Why do you think his legal team agreed to that stupid-ass divorce settlement? It was about maintaining a link with you until it came time to initiate the next phase. That time is now.

My father knows I don't go for that stuff. Palling around with warlords and megalomaniacs in Cupertino or wherever. You're way down the wrong track.

Actually, we expected you to hop on years ago. But you've clearly made a few missteps. That's all good though. Some people need extra time.

He reached into a valise and produced a letter-sized folder, bound in an elastic, and slid it across the table. I was asked to throw together a high-level dossier, to give you a lay of the land. Working toward a transfer of power.

Peter peeled off the elastic and spread the folder open. It contained about a hundred pages of printouts and summaries and tables from a disparate range of sources, with the heraldic DHG logo displayed prominently. None of this was immediately enlightening. But as he flipped through, Peter paused on a stapled collection of field maps showing Iraq and contiguous territories, scanned from some other source and marked up by hand. Though the copy was degraded and the annotations were indecipherable, the emphasis appeared to be shipping routes zigzagging the Persian Gulf, with points of integrality at the Strait of Hormuz denoted and circled in red ink. Whatever it signified, Peter found it disquieting.

Their server arrived with two plates of fried clams. The man dug in, and Peter followed his lead. The fish was mercilessly overcooked, the crumbling batter luminous with grease; driven by his intense appetite, he didn't mind. As they ate, Peter recalled a conversation he'd once had—something about DHG and its illicit interests—but with whom or when, he had trouble pinpointing. Yet another memory divorced from context, like an artifact plucked from under a ruined city.

So it's true. He's back in the gun-running racket. Or he never got out.

Don't be so hasty in your assumptions, the man said, his attention on his plate.

I'm just saying, if he wants meticulous…well, let's be meticulous. Where is Dred? Is he here, or isn't he?

Don't sweat that. Read the dossier. Acquaint yourself.

I will. But if we're doing this, then let's do this. Let's set up a meeting.

A meeting.

The man coughed loudly, dabbing his mouth with his sleeve, his eyes tearing. My body wasn't made to skip around the world like this, he said. My immune system goes haywire. What I need's a vacation.

Lots of people take their vacations right here.

The man snorted. Here. This place is bee-you-*busted*. These Somali burcad badeed pissants recruiting along the coast, the AMISOM mopes running around like chickens. The whole point of situating here was so we could lie low. But the risk of exposure's like anywhere. Maybe worse. Everything's devolving into chaos.

Maybe it always was chaos, and you just didn't notice.

The man looked at him.

Eat your clams.

The wind rose as Peter walked back along the beach, the dossier and book tucked under his arm. Aggravated clouds haunted the horizon, foretelling storms for tomorrow morning. He passed a pair of men lugging a stack of timber planks bound in ropes down the shore. One acknowledged him with a nod, but Peter averted his eyes and hurried along.

In one of his journalistic dispatches from the Alborz mountains of northern Iran, Alain had written: *Surely I was and would remain an outsider among these men, merely a spectator venturing into terres inconnues. But even knowing this, I was never denied from experiencing a reassuring sense of genuine belonging.* This was how Alain had situated his work, and by extension his entire being: despite geopolitical demarcations, despite barriers of culture or regulation, he dove in always with expectations of transcendence. All journeys were personal, and all significant. In each venture, he'd hoped for the epiphany, the encounter with the ineffable, that might bring him closer to communality with his fellow man. And he'd been disappointed every time.

Unlike Alain, the only eminence Dred recognized was his own. It fed his callous ambitions; it reassured him of his absolute supremacy. Unchecked, his father would continue, less a person than a gravitational field, a colossus, all-encompassing. A force that, also unlike Alain, seemed poised to thrive forever—unless some equal and opposing force cut him down. *A transfer of power.*

As Peter reached the pathway leading back up to the house, his phone vibrated with an incoming message. *7pm tmrw. Expect pickup.*

Here was his true mandate after all: to wait, to endure until the moment of catalysis. For a long time he'd been lost, yes—but he'd been patient. Now, tomorrow, he would right many wrongs. Tomorrow his curse would be lifted.

A BRISK SPRING MORNING, and the boy sits on the shore of Lake Lucerne, on the outskirts of Weggis. The lake before him is immersed in fog. He wears tennis shorts and a windbreaker; tucked in his jacket pocket is a spiral-bound notebook and half a nusstorte. A wedge of swans skims across the water, targeting a pier to the north. The boy turns to a fresh page in his notebook, marked with a graphite pencil, and begins to write.

Today I am thirteen. Tomorrow I will fly back to Dubai. Everything there is false. The people are ignorant and materialistic.

A buzzing sound rises from the lake's southern stretch. A speedboat appears out of the fog, its hull trowelling through the water's surface. The boy watches as the speedboat executes a wide arc across the lake's centre, then returns to his writing.

Here are two things I know. One: I know there is a way to see things other than how they seem. Two: I know there is something I am missing and it is important. But when I concentrate I start to think about other things and I lose track. I think about interdimensional light for example and my thoughts get very disorganized. It is possible I am too stupid to see things properly. Father says I have a brain like a trash compactor.

The speedboat arrives at the pier and its passengers hastily debark: a grey-haired patriarch and presumably a wife and two daughters, all in emergency-orange life jackets—a family. The boy does not know them. He watches as they toss backpacks onto the pier, preparing for a landward excursion. The daughters, blond and comely, shout at one another, their voices echoing across the lake.

One day everything will be gone, the boy writes. *Mountains and schools, the Sheikh Zayed Mosque. Times Square. William Rehnquist. Saddam Hussein. Lars Ulrich. Every single person on earth. The global economy will be gone. The rainforests will be gone. The sharks and koalas will be extinct. You name it. But I will still be here. I will be here even when everything is gone. That's the only thing I know for certain.*

At the pier, the mother and daughters head up the dock. The father tails behind, lugging a nylon sack over one shoulder, and inadvertently notices the boy watching from afar. The father smiles and offers a wave of salutation, then beckoning, inviting him to join them. The boy only waves back with his pencil, then returns to his notebook.

Maybe if I work hard enough I will see things properly. I will see into the future. I will see into every future.

He rereads this, frowning. He starts to scribble out this last line, then reconsiders. He closes the notebook and reaches upward to stretch his stiff arms. Ahead, an emergent sun deletes the residuum of fog.

Undeterred by the morning drizzle, the regular flow of townspeople packed into the market square. Commerce unfolded: merchant stalls offering toppling heaps of passion fruit and loquat and buckets of dry goods, women in hijabs topping up supply sacks, European tourists ogling textiles. Peter sat on a set of steps at the square's periphery, sipping tea procured for a few shillings. Lamu town's hawkers typically refrained from undue aggression, and today his presence here went mostly unnoticed. Having slept in fitful starts, his gut felt rotten, his joints stiff. The market, for all its abundance, offered nothing he needed: he would gladly shell out for every mango or trinket here, he thought, if he could trade it for a single vial of alprazolam.

A man came to the steps, leading a donkey. He lashed its bridle to a post, then sat beside Peter. Together, they watched the bustling square. The donkey's fecal reek was intense, and Peter was considering making a move when the man spoke.

The rain. Going to get heavy.

Yeah?

Thunder and lightning later.

Peter believed him; the air was alive with atmospheric tension.

I'm going to kill my father today, he said.

The man turned and gave Peter a quizzical look.

That's crazy, man! He erupted in laughter.

Peter could only laugh along.

I know. I know.

Kill your *father*? You don't want to do that.

I don't want to. But I have to.

The man shook his head with exaggerated disbelief. Crazy. You go and do that, then what are you?

Don't know. Guess I'm a bad son.

With this, the man laughed again.

Doesn't matter anyway, Peter said. Soon I'll be out on the Antarctic Peninsula, at the end of the world. That's where my story's headed.

The man slapped his thighs and stood. He yanked the rope to rouse the half-conscious donkey, then patted Peter on the shoulder.

Good luck, he said as he started away. Stay crazy!

Peter was drying off from a lukewarm, elbow-deep bath when the knock came, half an hour ahead of the arranged time. At the door were two men, both wearing tent-sized cotton shirts spotted with rain over beefy physiques. They waited as he dressed and readied himself, then convoyed him to the compound gates. There they handed him off to another pair of men, hired guides, to escort him further. Peter questioned none of this; this was what he'd wanted.

The sky was depthless, the rain's full barrage close. His guides moved fast, and Peter had to force an occasional jog to keep up. They led him uphill along a narrow pathway of tramped dirt, imposing stone walls on both sides. His eyes were slow to adjust, and he lost any orientation as they headed farther into the twisting alleyways.

They continued for what seemed half an hour, aimed inland, though he had no meter of time or direction. His guides were quiet, never relaxing their pace. Finally they emerged onto a dirt path lined with dense trees, arriving at a stone edifice and an unmarked wooden door. One of the men rapped on the wood, and a moment later another man, short and broad in a floral-patterned shirt, answered. He ushered Peter in, leaving the guides outside.

This door led into what appeared to be a storage room, packed with shelves of boxes and plastic containers, putrid with fish. Peter shook rain from his hair and jacket as the man in the floral shirt led him into a dim, carpetless hallway. A radio played from somewhere, an impassioned male voice speaking in Swahili. Heading down the hallway, they passed several carved wood doors, all closed, until they reached the base of a steep staircase. The man stopped.

Up, he said, pointing.

Again, Peter did as instructed. He climbed to a second-floor landing, finding only a single door, locked. An identical scene met him on the third. By the time he'd arrived at the fourth and top floor, he was short of breath and beginning to sweat. Here an archway led into an open dining room filled with oak tables and benches, windows on all sides. A large lobster tank by the entrance sat empty; a bar sparkled with bottles and glassware. There was no indication of any staff, or observance of his arrival. The unseen radio played a sequence of synthesized chimes marking the hour. Peter moved cautiously into the room, rounding the bar.

And there he was, seated next to a window, picking at a tray of olives. Seeing Peter, he stood.

You.

Dred opened his arms for an embrace. Peter, though taken aback by this gesture, went to him. They stood there locked in contact for a full second before Dred released him and returned to the table.

We have a chef, he said. I promise you this will be remarkable.

Peter took a seat. Of course his father had aged. He wore his years heavily, in his hollowing cheeks, the whitening tufts of thinning hair, his neck beset with some sort of rash. Yet his voice remained crisp as ever, no slowness weighing his words.

I'm reminded of the last time you were here. That must have been ten years ago.

Give or take.

We went sailing out into the Ras Kitau bay. A terrific day, if memory serves. It was clear you also saw what I find so inspiriting about this place.

My recollection's a bit different. You got hammered on that cheap rum and berated those women from Oxfam.

Dred angled his head back, as if smelling something disagreeable. No, no. That didn't happen. But speaking of which, let's wet your whistle.

As if willed into being, a waitperson arrived via a pair of swinging doors located behind the bar, delivering a platter of smoked mackerel sided by macadamias, dates, and an odd chalky cheese, along with a chilled bottle of Kenyan Sauvignon Blanc. Glasses were poured. Dred raised his.

To fortuitous reunions.

They clinked glasses and drank, though Peter could hardly taste the wine. Their attendant produced a long, slender knife with which to portion out the mackerel, serving plates to them both. Peter gave a gesture of thanks, watching as she placed the knife back on the tray next to the fish's glistening remains.

The knife, it was clear, was an important component of this situation. Symbolic.

I wouldn't say fortuitous, Peter said. Your guy's been calling me.

Anders?

He never gave his name.

Don't let him browbeat you. He's merely a chargé d'affaires.

You surround yourself in all this silly cloak-and-dagger shit. Seems kind of unnecessary.

Dred picked at the tray with his fork. Carelessness gets you on lists. Drones fly over this beach all the time, you know. I've come to learn no precautionary measure is a wasted effort. The one time you let things become lax is the one time things go awry. A lesson my brother Landric, your uncle, never internalized. He died of lifestyle-related causes.

As you've told me. Many times.

In many respects, you remind me of him. The silliness, the drugs. That self-damning nature that causes so much anguish. If steered correctly, your compulsions might prove a source of power. Let's eat.

They did. Peter found himself eating quickly, mechanically seeking fuel.

One thing I truly appreciate about Kenyans, Dred said, is how they're both ruggedly practical yet unabashed in their superstitions. I frequently deal with these kinds of men at the Nairobi Securities Exchange, and they don't kid around when it comes to witchcraft. Juju and business go hand in hand. They've been able to seamlessly integrate magical belief with capitalism. Or almost seamlessly. Catastrophes are inevitable. The way these men reckon with disaster is fascinating.

Seems to be plenty of corruption at the top. But I guess that's also where the magic comes in.

How so?

To justify the ends.

I try and take the long view. History is my most trusted counsel.

Sounds like something said by a person whose best days are behind him.

Dred chewed on a date. A suggestion of a laugh. Perhaps. Which, I suppose, brings us to the reason for being here.

He refreshed their glasses and leaned back, a pause for effect.

I don't know how much you understand about my work and what we do. It's evolved into an extremely atomized form. I rely on the expertise of my staff, from the top in Munich to those running things on the ground level worldwide. But at the executive level, a vacuum has emerged. A few of my top personnel have made their true loyalties known, much to my distaste. I also have further concerns regarding my physical health. My physicians have advised me to adjust how my energies are exerted. They find things. Atherosclerosis. Which runs in the family, by the way. I suppose you should probably know that, for your own well-being.

Dred shifted in his chair. Such admission, any intimations of his own fallibility, clearly pained him.

In my view, Dred continued, the conception of any inviolate familial bond has always been discordant with reality. My own parents were vile creatures. But with years, one slides into sentimentality. You start to reflect on those hackneyed old notions. Family, legacy. I was never really able to work harmoniously side by side with my brother. The prospect of now doing so with my son, even one so shiftless, pleases me tremendously.

Peter looked past Dred to the window. The expected downpour had come. In the rain-streaked glass: a reflection of their improbable faceoff, two men with little family resemblance, if any.

However, Dred said, if we're going to proceed, we need to have some mutual understanding of what's at stake.

He again edged forward in his seat. This restlessness was uncharacteristic of the man Peter remembered. The frustration with one's own physicality—it was an old person's frustration.

Ever since you were a child, you had that certain acuity. Like me, you saw there was more at stake than just this ordinary sphere. You and I, we saw that. We were shown. Like Ramakrishna and his cranes.

Peter smiled. Your favourite story.

Rama knew the path to truth's light meanders, carved out by the interference of men. You have to understand, the particulars of my work, the politics, the technology... I fell into all of this almost unwittingly. What matters to me is my perdurable impact on this world. And worlds we've yet to negotiate.

Immortality, Peter said.

Once you've stared into those mists, you can't help but be altered. You recognize the immateriality of all things. And this knowledge brings the freedom to pursue a greater calling. This has made me a wealthy man and, more importantly, a powerful man. But much more crucially, it's made me free. My hope is to share the bounty of that freedom with you. All I ask is that you agree with me.

Agree?

That what you and I share, what we've seen, is significant.

You and I. You, and me. What we saw.

Yes.

This, Peter saw, was it. Dred possessed so much of this world, yet still wanted more. He wanted to possess all worlds, even those already granted to others.

Peter stood, glass in hand, and went to the window, leaving Dred at the table. The rain was coming steadily now, sweeping the shore, the channel below.

I was wondering if you'd ask about him.

What's that? Who?

About Alain. He died, you know. Last spring. It was very sudden and rather devastating. For me.

Come. Sit down. We'll get ourselves another bottle.

Coming all the way here…I wondered what you might have to say about that. What asinine euphemism you'd fall back on to avoid saying anything. But you haven't even mentioned him.

Dred pushed back his chair. Wood clonked on wood.

And what would you have me say, Peter? Should I encourage you to wallow in senseless bereavement? I understand the pain of loss. But we're talking about your…*boyfriend*. Not family.

Peter turned from the window and faced his father.

Fuck family.

Pardon me.

Fuck family. Bounty of freedom. Fuck all that. And fuck your lies. No. I won't go along with it, and I won't agree. Not to any of it.

Now Dred rose from the table. Anger quivered on his lips. I'd hoped you'd gained some semblance of clear-sightedness after your years of dalliances, he said. But it seems you're still just an idiot. The Fairy Tale King. Still utterly useless.

With this, Dred headed to the bar and the doors beyond.

Left alone, Peter returned to the table and set down his glass. At some point the radio's chatter had ceased. The waitperson also appeared to have vanished.

He took the knife from the platter. Its grip felt solid, even in his trembling hands. A range of unclassifiable impulses charged through his mind. As he stood there, he glimpsed his reflection again in the panoptic windows, and was dismayed at what he saw:

a foolish person, sun-fried, unhinged. Vulnerability in all its inelegance—never had he felt so ridiculous, and so alone.

The kitchen was bright and cramped, packed with stainless-steel ranges and sinks and dishware on racks. The rumble of a toiling dishwasher dominated. The attendant who had served them was here, speaking with a man in chef's whites; as Peter entered, they glanced his way but raised no objections to his presence. Peter headed past them to the back of the room and a large glass-doored refrigerator. There he found Dred, on his knees and rummaging through a lower shelf's stock of wine bottles. Peter considered the person before him. With his ass in the air and faced buried in the refrigerator, he cut an absurd figure, an old man desperate in decline. But this was only his bodily form, which would soon expire. The totality of the symbolic void would thrive in other forms.

With a bottle retrieved, Dred climbed stiffly back to his feet. Only then did he notice Peter standing there, bearing the knife. Dred seemed almost amused by this. Peter drew closer.

We both know what I'm meant to do, he said.

Dred placed the bottle on the counter beside him and stepped closer. If you were a braver man, he said, you'd find another way.

This was true. The forces conspiring to shape Peter's past and days to come, the whims of birthright and execration and corporate reshuffling, had all interwoven to lead him here, to this absurd moment—as that voice calling from beyond had forewarned: *The petulant child effaces the living man*. He had the knife in hand, and nothing but opportunity. Yet any such act would be a senseless gesture. No curse would be lifted. His father would find his own damnation, with or without him. Once again, Peter had been a fool to imagine he wielded any power. He was, now and still, merely a trespasser, even in his own life. Peter dropped the knife. Its blade clinked on the ceramic floor.

You're right, he said. I think I'll leave.

And before his father could say anything else, he did.

Back in the town's alleys, he moved through the labyrinth of crumbling embankments and arches, looking for anything familiar among the indistinguishable corridors and circuits. Darkness and rain addled his perception; twice in succession he misjudged the grade ahead and almost went tumbling.

The muezzin's evening call, distorted and echoing, rang out.

He came to an unlatched wooden gate. Pushing through, he found another tight passage of rough, uneven coral. The walls tapered until he was sliding through almost sideways. He looked for any guidepost among the unmarked doorways, the vacant third-floor balconies, the conduits branching to either side, but nothing here was of help.

The already scarce light diminished further. He kept going.

He heard: *Ooooooooo*.

An influx of warm air grazed his face and outstretched hands. He was advancing, losing any firmness of earth below. The barriers were dropping.

The mists, as ever, slithered in as a wave of pressure and varicoloured light. The alley quaked in brightness. He heard a man's voice, flat and affectless, from some invisible source: *No more obstructions. Look for the moment when the clouds gather.*

He was the malingerer king, sleepwalking through the remote arcades and grottoes of Schloss Neuschwanstein, eternally unfinished in lazily conceived *Burgenromantik* grandeur. He was helicoptering over Dubai in midday, swooping along the E11 and over the Palm Jumeirah's artificial archipelago. He was slumped in the back seat of an SUV parked along the Congress Parkway in Chicago's west side, Olivia Newton-John on the radio, purchasing drugs from a preadolescent girl in an oversized Bulls jacket. He was on a ridge off the Antarctic Peninsula, facing the ocean's variable push, listening to the subterranean convulsions of an ice shelf's splintering from miles away.

Louder: *Ooooooooo*.

Out of the wash of light, a figure appeared: a woman, with a bathrobe tied tight at her waist. Not young, not old, black hair, eyes telling of sleepless nights. Patchy grass crunched under her ankle-socked feet as she stepped toward him. She stood in an unkempt garden of aloe and agave plants, what appeared to be the backyard of a small suburban home, one of several identical houses down a row. The yard was messy with construction supplies and loose piles of lumber. It was early, a warm desert morning, the sun just rising. From close by, a dog barked.

By all signs the woman was astonished to see him. Yet she also appeared unsurprised, as if he'd been expected. One of her hands fiddled with an unlit cigarette; the other was a fist. She extended this hand and opened her palm to him. In it lay a brass key.

Her eyes met his, pleading. And even though she remained silent, Peter understood: she'd been holding on to this key for a long time, without knowing what or who it was for. He would relieve her of its custody. It was for him, at least for now.

As Peter placed the key in his pocket, the woman stepped away, and the scene of yard and suburb began to dematerialize. The brightness of the desert gave way, fading back into the spectral haze, returning him to the alley's stony darkness.

As had been underlined in red pen: *a suitable gateway into the eternal.*

He finally broke away from the narrow alleys to the town's outskirts. Trees abounded here, with a semblance of a trail snaking up a brush-dotted ridge. Reaching its crest, he discovered the beach below, and the island's southern shore.

A figure was hunched at the water's edge, working at an unspecific shape at his feet. Peter started down the slope, then halted as this figure stood and began dragging the object away from the waves and uphill. Peter didn't recognize the man—white and paunchy, bedraggled in trousers and a wrinkled dress shirt, a loping drunkenness to his movements. But some instinct warned Peter it would be best to remain out of sight, and he slid into the cover of trees. Even over the rush of waves, the man's laboured breath was audible; it took him several fits and starts to reach the top of the ridge. There, he slid his burden into a mess of brush, then backed away, reeling with effort.

Peter held his breath. What had been hauled from the water, he now saw, was unmistakably a body. The man remained bent over, winded and hacking.

As he watched, Peter unconsciously shifted his feet, stepping on a fallen branch. The splintering sound severed the quiet; the man's attention snapped in his direction. Peter shrank further back into hiding, but the wall of trunks behind him formed a non-negotiable impasse. His only options were to confront the man or break away and back down the ridge.

He took flight, but misjudged the slope. His feet betrayed him and he fell onto his ass, skidding on sand. For a second, he remained lying there, demobilized. Then, sensing his follower's approach, he rolled off the path to hide in the low-lying brush.

A beat later, the drunken man came, huffing like an animal. He charged past Peter, continuing downhill and into the trees. Peter waited a solid three-count, then slid out from the brush. His pursuer appeared to be gone.

He crept back up the way he'd come, to the body. Dropping to a crouch, working to stay quiet, he pried away the branches. Here was another stranger: young, wearing an NBA jersey, a bandana slung around his neck. Wet from head to toe, his eyes were closed and blood flowed from his throat. But his lips trembled—he was still alive, if only barely.

Peter hugged the man's torso and hauled him upward in a clumsy version of a fireman's lift, managing to secure the limp weight on his shoulders. He took a preparative breath, then lurched back the way he'd come, keeping a lookout for the other man's return.

The strain, the weight, the warm blood seeping down the back of his shirt—it was almost too much. But he kept on over the slope and rough terrain, and made it back to the alley, heading once more into the intricacies of the passages. He chose a course he guessed might lead northward back to the villa, but almost immediately again lost his way, instead finding another confounding forking of paths, then another. Listening for any signal or passing villager, he tried calling out—*Hello*—but it was a feeble try, and led to nothing. His grip on the wounded man grew increasingly shaky until, trudging into yet another pathway, his legs finally gave way. He dropped to his knees, landing hard. The body spilled from his hold and fell onto the wet ground.

There they remained. He bent closer to the man's face, looking for a whiff of life. Only flecks of spittle, a sweaty human stink. No sound. The rain kept on.

There was no way he could make it any further like this. Peter willed away the ache in his kneecaps and assessed the present scene. Ahead, an unhitched donkey cart sat chained to a post. Once the decision was made, it took only seconds to haul the young man over and heave him into the empty cart among piles of folded burlap. Peter considered saying something to him before leaving him there, but didn't. Any reassurances he might offer would be empty.

Yes—it was easy to bask in timelessness here, to imagine a sense of permanence. But this was just a dreamer's wish—a trespasser in prohibited territory can never rest. To drift forever was a condition of Peter's curse.

He moved quickly, navigating the path before him while trying to retain how he might later retrace his steps. It was impossible, the way too obscure, his perception too faulty. But then he arrived at a juncture that rang as familiar, and as he followed the incline uphill, the villa's gates appeared. He was met at the entrance by the beefy security guards, now in matching plastic rain jackets. Seeing him, they stubbed out their cigars and came forward.

Easy, one said, reaching.

There's been a crime, Peter said, semi-breathless, dripping. We need...police.

He knew how preposterous this sounded. The man's hand fell heavy on Peter's shoulder. No, no. Come.

Peter again tried to explain: about the fallen man, of the need for action. The men weren't interested. When he started toward the villa's gates, they blocked his way.

No, the man said again. Come.

There was no countering their command. They'd received a call, they told him. Before Peter fully understood what was happening, he was being led away from the villa and back down toward the beach. The men spoke to one another quietly in Swahili, nothing to him. At the water an aluminum speedboat waited, its engine idling. Peter saw his single bag had already been loaded.

A charter plane was en route to fetch him at the Manda airstrip, the men told him. He'd be on his way back to Nairobi within the hour.

Under his attendants' watchful administration, he climbed aboard and took a seat at the stern. The boatman eyed Peter and pointed at his chest. Peter looked down; his shirt, soaked through, was a mess of rain-smeared blood. He nodded back, then turned away: north, toward the old town, then south to the archipelago's reach. All lay dark, the island in repose.

Only once the boat jerked away from the shore, headed northeast across the channel through sheets of rain, did Peter reach inside his pocket—the brass key was still there. He held it tight.

He'd come to Lamu seeking blood, and had found it. But no curse had been lifted, and nothing had been gained. He would remain, as before and always, a wayward prince.

THE REALTOR'S CALL CAME EARLY. Peter was still in bed, half-awake, and before he fully understood what was happening the realtor was tearing into a confessional as to the reasons for her *sorta frantic vibe lately*, explaining she'd been suffering a kind of metaphysical crisis—*shouldn't couldn't wouldn't get into the grisly details*. However, she was—she vowed this repeatedly and emphatically—back in counselling and pledged to not let her obligations to her clients suffer in any way. Peter said he had complete confidence in her ability to bounce back; she needn't rush or fret on his account. The realtor heaved a sigh that spoke of genuine gratitude, her voice cracking with a heartfelt promise to not betray his faith. Showings were being booked for that week, and they should have zero problem meeting above asking. Peter wished her well.

The apartment was a crypt. In the spotlight fixtures, in the custom walnut console table, in the lacquer countertops and accent cushions, in the wall-mounted tweeters and the fan coil unit and heat pump—in it all were painful remnants of expired time. Yes, it was time to go.

With summer came that unblenched, intensive glee that seized Montreal every year: the terrasses overloaded with sunburned drinkers sopped in gaudy indulgence, creeping Miatas blasting forth subsonics, incoming herds of tourists in muscle shirts and bared midriffs. Come autumn's encroachment, such short-lived euphoria would be annulled, and soon the ossifying miseries of another Quebec winter would once again sink in. But in the meantime, all and everyone was absorbed in the season's fleeting swoon.

Peter taxied to a bakery in Outremont to meet Lyle Bekiempis. He arrived early, so he ordered coffee and sat at a window table with his headphones on, listening to the new Kvelertak album. In the corner park across the street, a duo of dachshunds puttered about as their dead-eyed owner observed from a bench, puffing on a vape pen. The music's dense wall of triumphant guitars and guttural Norwegian howls provided a fitting soundtrack to the dogs' aimless scurrying, the heat, his own uneasiness. When Lyle arrived, he too seemed on edge, his manner evasive.

Really sorry, he said before he'd even sat down, but I can't stay long. He eyeballed the DHG dossier, already on the table.

I've looked it through, Peter said. The first chunk's mainly basic information on corporate structure and internal memos, who's who in the branches and chains. Thought that could be helpful.

Sure, Lyle said. Why not.

The juicier stuff's toward the end.

Whether any of these documents, the lists and charts and memoranda, bore any real substance was difficult to say. In this dossier lay only an opening of avenues, rather than any damning evidence, but it was something. The transaction records outlining DHG arms sales to Triple Canopy's efforts against pirates in the Gulf of Aden were not, on their own, revelatory. But if certain accusations lodged against DHG were true—that such sales were made to provide cover for further shipments to Salafi factions in Syria and Iraq—then here was connectable evidence of activities that could safely be considered extralegal. While tenuous, the lines could be drawn.

As he led Lyle through the documents, Peter saw no trace of the fervour he'd shown in their first encounter. He almost seemed bored by the whole thing.

They couldn't have gotten this to you on a hard drive or something?

Paper's easier, Peter said. Paper can be burned.

And they gave this to you to offer you a job?

It was possible, Peter could admit, the entire scenario was a ruse, or constituted some sort of demented test. His father and his operatives were capable of anything.

There's something else, Peter said.

He told Lyle of that night on Lamu, and what happened with the body. Since returning he'd made calls to the Interpol Operations

Centre in Ottawa, eventually speaking with a disarmingly affable agent who probed for specifics on location and time, the individuals and their alleged level of involvement, the precise nature of the crime witnessed. As he related what details he had, Peter felt his own understanding of what had happened slipping from his grasp. There had been a body, and a man; little else made sense. His recall of that wheezing figure was dimmer by the day, and his own role in the scenario was admittedly suspicious. The agent affirmed corroboration with Kenyan authorities would be the next course of action, but the conversation ended with many considerations left unresolved. Peter was advised to stay reachable. When he asked what that meant, the agent chuckled and said, *Oh you know*.

So what's the story? Lyle said. Someone knew something and got iced?

Right now, your guess is good as mine.

Lyle rubbed his nose. Tell me what my next move is here, Peter.

I'm not sure. But I know how this plays out. You ask questions, maybe against your better judgment. And you get some answers. There will be inconsistencies and complications. A lot will seem impossible, or simply pointless. It will be exhausting. But there will come a time when all the factors converge at just the right moment, at the right rate of flow, and all will be made clear. And when that happens, those who've done wrong will get their comeuppance. Justice will prevail. This happens through you and what you do. You shed light against darkness.

I have to ask how you're so certain about this.

Because my future self tells me so.

Lyle's phone vibrated. He checked it, and his already downcast demeanour sank even further.

Apologies if I seem distracted, he said. It's been a... It's a bad day. My daughter's been having some issues. I want to say usual sixteen-year-old problems. But they're not really usual, and they don't seem to be getting better.

Peter was surprised that Lyle, by appearances so young, had a teenage daughter.

Sorry to hear that.

Right now, I don't even know what to think. The right response, I just don't have it. You visualize a better way, but when you just can't see it... I'm not used to this kind of powerlessness. The frustration. And it never lets up. You know what I mean?

Peter did. Lyle excused himself, saying he had to get over to his ex's place in Saint-Henri. Could he take the dossier with him? Peter said yes, by all means; he was done with it. Lyle affirmed his interest in moving the story forward, though he admitted to some misgivings about what he could actually accomplish on his own. He was merely a journalist, producing investigative pieces in a tough time across the industry. But he had access to others who wielded deeper resources and sway, so he'd do some asking around, get wheels in motion. If there was a story in all this, it could be something significant. All he asked was that Peter hang on for the time being, and be patient. That, Peter knew, he could do.

When Jo-Beth found out Peter was back in town, she demanded he attend an informal party at her apartment. It was her thirty-fifth birthday, and she decreed recognition of this milestone to be of utmost consequence. His initial reaction was to decline, but he caved to her dogged insistence. So, as expected, he found himself in a room of strangers, most speaking in French, and after some courteous introductions he located an unobtrusive position in the kitchen and made his outpost there, propped against the sink. Speakers wafted ABBA and Basement Jaxx. The entire scene exuded untroubled bonhomie and peaceable drunkenness. Peter, unsurprisingly, felt remote from the occasion and its attendees. Two stiff gin and tonics made him sleepy; a third made the room quaver. The politesse of small talk heightened his discomposure. And yet, for some reason, he stuck around.

Later in the evening, when the party had thinned to its most dedicated, Jo-Beth zeroed in on him, joined by another woman he didn't know.

I was just telling Viv about your interdimensional vicissitudes, Jo-Beth said, sloshing a glass of bourbon. The phenomena that wracks you so.

Incredible, Viv said.

Before he could offer any rejoinder, Jo-Beth squeezed in closer. I'll tell you, she said, this guy is pretty remarkable. He's not just the exemplar of coolness you see here. There's a whole other side to Peter unlike anything you could imagine.

I believe it, Viv said, moving in at the other side.

I'm a real people person, Peter said.

Jo-Beth flashed a mock-lascivious grin. There had been no mention of California, the oscillation chamber, whether Frannie had achieved anything like the healing transformation she'd gone there for. It truly was like it had never even happened. He wanted to bring it up, but Jo-Beth was buoyantly drunk, and Peter decided against spoiling her mood.

I told you, she said to Viv, about the time Peter and I had a threesome with this poor lad on New Year's Eve in Joshua Tree, about three years ago.

That never happened, he said.

Oh, it probably did. Or it will. You tell me. You're the one who, you know, haunts the astral planes.

More women Peter didn't know had joined them in the kitchen.

Maybe you can settle an argument for us, one said. Do they celebrate Halloween in Japan?

How would I know?

You're Japanese! Jo-Beth said.

Only half.

But the good half, right?

Peter had no answer to any of this, and the women had already launched into a somewhat spurious back-and-forth about Obon ghost festivals and the Westernization of the Buddhist Pāli Canon. Peter, happy to be left out of this, watched Jo-Beth as she moved along, floating throughout the party as unhindered and undiminishable as always. Right now, at least for this instant, she was the exact version of herself she hoped to be. *There does seem to be a great deal of perplexity in your past*, she'd told him, and it was true. Yet more than just the past had the power to perplex.

A while later, as he made his way to the door, he found Viv sprawled in the foyer, face first in a pile of boots. Peter stepped over her, asking if she needed help.

Just having a bad month, she said into a mound of wet leather. Everything's down the drain.

I could call you a taxi.

That'd be nice. Maybe just let me sit here for a sec first. I smoked some G13 with a dab of ketamine and it kind of liquidated me. Need to get it together a bit before I can do anything. If you know what I mean.

Peter knew what she meant. He took a seat on the floor next to her. Viv turned over onto her back, staring at the ceiling.

It's just so hard to know when to heave-ho, she said. Know what I mean? It's hard to know when things are *over*.

Yeah, he said, it really is.

They sat like this, among the shoes and boots.

Since I was young, I've had visions. Of other places and times. After a while you lose sight of what's where and what's when. What's a memory and what's just your mind hunting for connections. Is a flock of cranes against a storm cloud a sign, or just a puff of wind? How much is preordained and how much is bum luck? Probably best to not know. And yet, there's still this...need. To know.

Gnarly, Viv said. Well, when you know, you know. The knowledge becomes yours. And that's how you become immortal.

A pause, then Viv broke into a spasm of stoned giggles, repeating the word again: Immortal. Peter offered a laugh in return, but it was only a gesture of concession, nothing more. He was too tired.

He dreamed again of Alain, of surging water, and of incontrovertible monolithic structures. Once more they were separated and spun into the maelstrom, rushing downward to unknowable ends. The dream unfolded as before, except this time it concluded not with many bodies congealing together into one consolidated glut, but with their dispersal throughout an ever-expanding pool, smeared like nebulae, until there was only the flow—not even the water itself but its force, its separating power. And whereas in previous dreams the panic occurred in brutal aggregation, this time the fear came with the loss of any connection at all.

In his work Alain had tried to tackle this idea of transcendence through absence—as Jo-Beth put it, of *vanishing as a state of grace*. Maybe there was a point at which knowledge became weightless, at which enquiry became a useless way of gaining understanding. Maybe it was useless to formulate meaning from nonsense delivered via unverifiable channels. Maybe humanity was best found in non-existence. But this notion, true or not, was of little help to those desperate to be found, looking for a way through the haze.

Sometimes he wondered if Alain had even existed. Or if he still had yet to meet him.

Janko: *I spent my entire life thinking about things. Now I'm just trying to get through the day.*

Mysteries persisted. There was the brass key, entrusted to him across an impossible divide. Maybe he'd find out what it was for, maybe he wouldn't. The significance of any key was only in its potential to unlock a door. And behind a door, countless other doors. He'd hold on to it nonetheless. It was his turn. Again: patience.

What were the mists? A life in perpetual pursuit of results, driven by vengeance or blinded by naïveté—easier to live that way than to accept there might be no answer to root out. An addict seeks self-obliteration. A fanatic's plot goes askew. People go missing, then are forgotten. One season of languor rolls into another. A call goes unanswered.

Peter stood at the sink, looking out the window at the street below, where a Prius was fighting to squeeze into a parking spot that was not actually a spot. He crossed the kitchen, opened the refrigerator to examine its empty racks, then closed it. He did the same with the dishwasher, the garbage disposal. Everything moved fluidly, cleanly, with ease.

A stack of unopened mail sat by the door, bank statements and Hydro-Québec bills, magazine subscription renewal notices, campaign flyers in advance of upcoming provincial elections. Also: insurance paperwork from Hertz in Los Angeles, related to stolen-vehicle claims. It fell upon him to broom this all away. Among this stack, he discovered an envelope he hadn't noticed, postmarked from India. When he opened it, a three-by-five photograph slipped out. Here was an infant in blankets, brown-skinned and big-eyed, mid-laugh. The accompanying letter was addressed to Alain, two stapled and folded pages.

Greetings to you on a balmy Saturday afternoon here in Greater Kailash. The first sections of Aradhya's letter dealt mainly with developments in her case, the details of which were lost on Peter. She made it clear, however, how her situation had changed. Public opinion had dramatically shifted, due largely to her work with Alain and other journalists she'd rallied. Whereas in the earlier days, she'd endured reproves and shamings in the press, now support was voiced. It had the makings, as she put it, of a pivotal moment. Aradhya's son had been born shortly before the case had gone to trial, further delaying proceedings but lending her story another dimension—to some, of tragedy.

In its concluding paragraphs, the letter took a turn.

My days now are full of conflicted emotions. The anger I harbour against those who wronged me, and my determination to have them be punished, has only intensified. Often while nursing Vihaan, I think, what have I done? Why introduce another life into this callous world? Why subject yet another unknowing soul to such brutality? Or, an even more frightening prospect, have I birthed yet another horrible man who will grow to bring about such malice?

Ultimately, none of this dampens my hopefulness. I remember those conversations you and I enjoyed during our long walks in Delhi, when you described your own parents' prolonged cruelty. You confessed how, denied of their love, you'd longed for any form of confirmation of your greater worth, wishing for some promise of transcendence. You said on several occasions how you surprised even yourself in the determination one could muster, yearning for such confirmation, or such escape.

In my most despairing moments, I recognize this type of hope as what stirs grandiose ambitions in desperate men, leading to dehumanization, oppression, violence. Yet there is also the hope that such aspirations might also rouse consequential acts of benevolence, and of justice. The man my son will become lies mostly beyond my control. But I must stand by my decision to carry to term this poor bastard child, the product of my humiliation. If he grows up to be yet another scoundrel, this is an outcome I will have to live with. There are few reasons for us to remain hopeful in this difficult world. However, at the risk of sounding naive, I firmly believe we must, and I must. Otherwise, those men who forced themselves upon me in that station that night claim more than my body.

In your last message, you told me you'd checked yourself into an addiction treatment facility. All of us have our own spectres to contend with, whether chemical or societal, or—to employ a term I know makes us both cringe—spiritual. I hope you find success in subduing the forces that haunt you. You have helped set in motion changes in my life and the lives of others for which I will be forever grateful. As requested, I will keep you updated as we resume hearings in October, and I look forward to seeing you again.

The letter concluded with the simple sign-off *AG*. Peter read it again, then stacked it with the rest of the mail for recycling.

Endings and beginnings, preambles and epilogues—they were, really, only parentheses.

On his way out through the lobby, he dropped the front door keys on the security desk without a word. Roused from his mid-morning daze, Edmundo the doorman coughed and sat up in his seat. Before he could react, Peter was already gone.

A short taxi ride took him to the dealership near Boulevard Pie-IX. The showroom was only just opening, and the eager young salesman on duty was clearly surprised to find a customer so early.

When Peter said he had his eye on the 1982 Corvette Coupe advertised on their website, the salesman seemed delightedly stunned. As he led Peter across the lot, he began detailing in tentative English the vintage car's components, both original factory and modified: the leather interiors, the 350 V8 engine, the lightweight body, the original dark-claret body paint. Peter allowed him to complete his pitch, though it was unnecessary; when the question was put to him, he simply asked where to sign. The young salesman excitedly began running down financing options and credit check procedures, but Peter explained there was no need, as he'd be paying the full balance now on his Platinum AmEx. This was of course unorthodox, and the salesman had to consult his manager. But the call was made, and it happened: the card was swiped, the paperwork was completed, and the keys were handed over.

As Peter sat behind the wheel, running his hands over the leather and getting a feel for the stick, the salesman leaned in the window, smiling. The swift exchange had clearly left him giddy.

I like the way you do things, he said.

Peter drove the car off the lot, his head feeling light. But as he merged into the boulevard's clog, this exhilaration was already seceding to a wave of dread. Traffic was heavy, a long day's drive lay ahead, and what awaited at the end was unclear. But at least there was a destination: it was almost seventeen hundred miles to the port in Savannah, then fifteen days by freighter to Puerto Madryn.

INVISIBLE PUBLISHING produces fine Canadian literature for those who enjoy such things. As an independent, not-for-profit publisher, our work includes building communities that sustain and encourage engaging, literary, and current writing.

Invisible Publishing has been in operation for over a decade. We released our first fiction titles in the spring of 2007, and our catalogue has come to include works of graphic fiction and nonfiction, pop culture biographies, experimental poetry, and prose.

We are committed to publishing diverse voices and experiences. In acknowledging historical and systemic barriers, and the limits of our existing catalogue, we strongly encourage writers from LGBTQ2SIA+ communities, Indigenous writers, and writers of colour to submit their work.

Invisible Publishing is also home to the Bibliophonic series of music books and the Throwback series of CanLit reissues.

If you'd like to know more, please get in touch: info@invisiblepublishing.com